MW00830918

UNDENIABLE
Love

KELLY ELLIOTT

Undeniable Love
Book Two in the Journey of Love Series
Copyright © 2015 by Kelly Elliott
Published by K. Elliott Enterprises Inc.
Visit my website at www.kellyelliottauthor.com

Cover Designer:
Angie Fields with I Love It Design Studio

Cover Photographer:
Shannon Cain

Editing:
Nichole Strauss with Perfectly Publishable

Design and Formatting:
Christine Borgford with Perfectly Publishable

All rights reserved.
ISBN# 978-0-9903210-9-5

No part of this book may be reproduced or transmitted in any form or by any means, electronic or mechanical, including photocopying, recording, or by any information storage and retrieval system without the written permission of the author, except for the use of brief quotations in a book review.

This book is a work of fiction. Names, characters, places, and incidents either are products of the author's imagination or are used fictitiously. Any resemblance to actual persons, living or dead, events, or locales is entirely coincidental.

BOOKS BY
Kelly Elliott

WANTED SERIES
Wanted
Saved
Faithful
Believe
Cherished
A Forever Love
The Wanted Short Stories

THE BROKEN SERIES
Broken
Broken Dreams
Broken Promises

JOURNEY OF LOVE SERIES
Unconditional Love
Undeniable Love
Unforgettable Love ~ Coming June 2015

LOVE WANTED IN TEXAS SERIES
Without You
Saving You
Holding You ~ Coming April 2015

STANDALONES
The Journey Home

Prologue

TRISTAN

I HAD BEEN SITTING ON the beach for the last hour just staring out at the black ocean. I tipped the bottle back and drank the last of my beer.

"Well hell. Looks like I have to go back," I said as I got up and brushed the sand off my pants. I turned and looked back at the house. My brother, Lark and his new wife, Azurdee had left two hours ago for their honeymoon and I couldn't take watching Ryn another second.

I sucked in a deep breath of salty air and slowly let it out. My phone went off and I pulled it out of my pocket. I let out a deep breath when I saw it was Liberty.

> Liberty: *Just letting you know I'm thinking about you. If you want me to join you I'll come down. Just text me back and I'll be there.*

> Me: *I think I just need some time to think, Liberty. We need this time apart.*

> Liberty: *I didn't mean to push you. I'm always pushing you, I know. I just really wanted to see your parents and would have loved to have seen the wedding but I understand you have your reasons for going alone. Things haven't been so great with us lately. I'll work on that. Promise.*

Me: We'll talk when I get back to Austin.

Liberty: Okay. I love you, Tristan.

Drawing in a breath and releasing it, I shook my head. I've never told Liberty I loved her. I wasn't sure anymore how I felt about her. We had been on again and off again so many times I was beginning to lose count. Currently, we were off. All she had been doing was pushing an engagement ever since she found out Lark and Azurdee were getting married. When I thought of my future, I didn't see Liberty. I only saw . . . Ryn. And that scared the piss out of me.

I turned my phone to silent and shoved it in my pocket. I started heading back to the house and began putting on my game face. The one I'd been wearing for the last ten months. The one where everyone thought I was happy, but deep down inside I was the unhappiest I'd ever been in my life.

I walked up the stairs to the deck and the first person I saw was Ryn. She was leaning against the railing with her head back and her eyes closed. There was no one else out here.

She looked tired. I smiled when I thought about what I had overheard earlier when Mom and Azurdee's best friend, Jessie, were talking. Ryn had taken a two-week vacation and was renting a house on the beach just two houses down from here. I already began planning ways to 'run into her' while we were both here.

She hadn't talked to me in over ten months. No matter how many times I called and left her messages begging her to call me, she never would.

Her cell phone rang and she quickly answered it. I walked around to the other side of the deck and sat down to where she couldn't see me.

"Hey, Dodge. Are you on your way? Yes. I thought I could, but I can't. I need you."

Dodge? Who the fuck is Dodge?

Laughing at something he must have said, Ryn continued to speak. "Well, considering I still need my RFB, I'd say yes . . . it's been a sucky last three days."

I peeked around the corner and saw her smiling. She reached her hand up and began playing with her nipple.

What the fuck?

"That sounds like heaven. Yes. I'm going to need it a lot. I don't know, you'd think after all this time you'd have been able to fuck him out of my head and heart. Maybe you're not as good as you think you are?"

My mouth dropped open and I quickly turned back and stared out in the night sky.

She laughed again and said, "I'm still at the wedding. Yes. It was hard to see him. I don't know. Maybe, I've thought about that. Yes. I realize I only use you for sex to forget about Tristan, but maybe I'm falling for you and just want your company. You ever think of that?"

My heart started beating faster and I wanted to pound this asshole's head in.

Taking in a deep breath as if she was savoring the moment, she slowly blew it out. "Okay. I'll see you then. Oh trust me. I'll be waiting and I will most certainly be ready for you. Yes naked. Hey, Dodge? Hurry please. I need to be fucked in a bad way. Bye."

After Ryn said goodbye, there was a minute of silence before I swore I heard her crying. I slowly stood. She was looking out toward the ocean. Her shoulders were moving up and down and when I saw her wipe away her tears, my knees about buckled out from underneath me.

I started making my way toward her. I didn't want to walk up on her crying, so I cleared my throat and asked, "May I join you?"

She quickly wiped her tears away and looked the other way. "It's your house," she whispered. "How have you been, Ryn?" She turned and looked at me. If looks could kill, I'd be laying on the floor right now. "You've ignored me for three days and *now* you ask how I've been?"

With a nonchalant attitude, I said, "I wasn't sure you wanted to talk to me." She let out a small laugh.

"Usually people attempt to talk to a person before they make that assumption."

"Well, considering I've been calling you for months, and you ignore my calls—" She took a step back and shook her head.

A look of hurt moved across Ryn's face as she slowly said,

"You're seeing . . . another . . . girl."

"It's not like that. We are kind of off and on. I mean . . . I'm not seeing her right now." She rolled her eyes before looking into mine.

"Do you have any idea how much you hurt me?"

My heart felt like it was physically hurting as I swallowed and said, "I just thought . . . I wasn't planning on—" I looked away and then back into her eyes. "I thought you just wanted to have fun, Ryn. Then you started acting different and I started having these feelings and . . . I was confused."

Anger replaced the hurt in her eyes. "The only thing that confused you is why you brought the wrong girl to meet mom and dad."

She turned and began walking into the house. I wanted to call out for her, but I couldn't. My heart felt like it was squeezing in my chest as I stood there and listened to her retreating footsteps.

I turned and stared out at the dark ocean again. That's what my heart felt like. A deep sea of . . . darkness.

CHAPTER
One

TRISTAN

HE SUN SHINING IN THROUGH the window caused me to let out a low grumble. I knew the moment I opened my eyes I'd feel the hangover. Yesterday was my younger brother, Lark's wedding to his spunky and beautiful new bride, Azurdee. I still couldn't believe Azurdee had won over my brother and tamed his wild ways. For a while there I was pretty sure he was more against a committed relationship than I was. I heard my phone vibrate on the side table. Reaching over, I grabbed it.

> *Lark: Why the hell do you want to know about Dodge?*

Sitting up, I let out a frustrated moan as I ran my hand down my face. Last night I watched as Ryn said goodbye to my parents and walked out the door with this Dodge guy. A built, blond-haired, blue-eyed asshole who had his arm wrapped around her waist and held her like she was his.

Motherfucker.

> *Me: Ryn mentioned him last night. He showed up and he is with her now. I remembered you mentioning a Dodge guy once when you and Azurdee were split up.*

> *Lark: He manages Red 7. According to Azurdee, he is Ryns RFB.*

RFB? Ryn had said that last night to Dodge. *What the fuck is a RFB?*

Lark: Before you ask it means Rebound Fuck Buddy.

My mouth dropped open as I stared at the text. "You've got to be shitting me," I whispered.

Lark: Azurdee said Ryn is pretty much exclusive to the guy. They're dating, but not really dating. Guess Dodge is into Ryn and she doesn't feel the same.

Interesting.

Me: Thanks, Bro. I think I'm going to be staying another week . . . or two. I've got the time.

Lark: Ah shit. Don't start any trouble down there. Have fun.

Me: I'm gonna try not to. Later.

Setting the phone on the bed, I headed into the bathroom. I took one look at myself in the mirror and frowned. I looked like shit. Tired and hungover was not going to work if I wanted to try and run into Ryn today.

Glancing back into the bedroom, I looked at the clock on the side table. Seven on the dot. Ryn would be heading out for a run any time now if I knew her.

I quickly splashed water on my face, brushed my teeth and changed into a pair of jogging shorts, a white T-shirt, and running shoes. One quick look at myself in the mirror and I was headed down to the beach.

Glancing up and down the beach, I was almost positive Ryn would run this way. Looking toward the beach house she was renting for the next two weeks, I smiled when I saw her heading down the steps to the beach. She did a few funky ass yoga moves and then took off running, in the opposite direction of me.

Shit.

I pushed my ear buds in and started running. My full on run was quickly catching up to Ryn's jog. I smiled as I took a good look at her ass. She had the nicest ass of any girl I ever dated. I loved Ryn's body. She had curves and wasn't afraid to eat me under the table when it came to a large buffalo chicken pizza from Double Dave's. Liberty, my ex-girlfriend, was boney as hell and I swear the only things she ate were carrots and cheese sticks.

Ryn's long wavy brown hair was pulled back into a sloppy ponytail. Ryn never cared too much about being prim and proper. She could dress up and look like a million bucks easy, but she only did it when she had to. Otherwise, she was in her favorite pair of comfy pants, as she called them, and a T-shirt.

Running by Ryn, I passed her up and acted like I didn't know who she was. Out of the corner of my eye, I saw her glance up at me. I kept running at my speed. She had headphones on as well; the only difference was I was positive she had music coming out of hers and I didn't. I needed to be able to hear her call out my name. If she called out my name.

I could feel her eyes on my back. I slowed down just a notch so she could catch up to me. "Tristan?" I heard her call out. Acting as if I couldn't hear her, I kept on running.

"Tristan!"

Smiling, I kept up my pace. This was turning out to be a successful run. My plan to run into Ryn on accident while we were both here was starting out with a bang. Inhaling a deep breath of crisp ocean air, I kept up my steady pace. The cool morning air actually made it a great morning for a run. Finally, I felt her coming up next to me. Keeping my eyes straight ahead, I attempted to appear as if I was in the zone. Grabbing my arm she yelled again, "Tristan, goddamn it, stop running!"

I stopped on a dime, causing Ryn to run a few feet ahead of me. Glancing at her, I pulled my ear buds out. "Ryn?"

She leaned over and put her hands on her knees as she dragged in a few breaths. "Jesus, now I realize . . . I'm only . . . a light weight jogger."

I knew damn well I was running faster than Ryn was able to run. Looking at her like I was confused, I asked, "What are you talking about, Ryn? I thought you'd be heading back to Austin?"

She shook her head. "Nope . . . staying here for two weeks."

Pulling my head back to act as if I was surprised, I grinned. "Really? So am I."

Suddenly stiffening her posture, she practically shouted, "Wait. What? You're staying here?" She started pointing to the sand. "For two weeks?"

Glancing down at the sand, I rubbed my chin. "Well, not in this very spot, but here in South Padre. Yeah."

Ryn swallowed hard. "I see. Did you have this planned?" She raised an eyebrow at me.

"Yeah, I was playing it by ear, one to two weeks, maybe three. I have the time to take, and I have to burn it before the end of the year or I lose it."

Ryn stood and stared at me. I couldn't tell if she was happy or pissed. "You look like you didn't sleep much last night. Rough night, Ryn?"

Ryn's eyes widened and she went to talk but shut her mouth and looked back toward the house she was renting. We hadn't run that far and now I was wishing we would have. Looking, I saw Dodge standing on the back deck.

Fucker.

"Boyfriend?"

Ryn snapped her head and looked at me. "Excuse me?"

Gesturing with my hand, I pointed and asked, "The guy, is he your boyfriend?"

Ryn's eyes searched my face as if she was trying to read my reaction to seeing some douche bag asshole, who I was pretty sure fucked her senseless last night, standing on her deck.

"Um . . . no . . . he's um . . . well . . . he's . . ." Turning to look at Dodge, she began chewing on her lip before looking at me.

"A fuck buddy?"

Her eyes narrowed as her hands went to her lips. "What?"

I lifted my shoulders in a shrug. "I don't know, Ryn, you seemed to be stumbling on your words so I just guessed." Smirking, I winked at her.

"Are you still seeing Liberty?"

My smile faded a bit. "No. We're over."

Lifting an eyebrow, I could tell she was holding back a smile. "How come? You get bored with her and pick up another girl on the side?"

Ouch. That hurt.

"No, she wanted something with me that I didn't want with her."

Clearing her throat, she whispered, "And what did she

want?"

"Marriage."

Ryn's eyes widened in shock as she took a step back. "Oh. Well um . . . I guess I'll see you around, Tristan."

My heart instantly felt as if someone had put a vice around it and squeezed the hell out of it. I wanted to take her up in my arms and kiss her. Show her why the fuck buddy couldn't wipe me from her mind.

I barely nodded my head. "Yeah, I'll see ya around." Turning, I went to start running again.

"Tristan!"

I stopped and turned to her, "Yeah, baby?"

Her eyes closed briefly before she opened them and looked into mine. My knees wobbled when I saw the hurt in those beautiful blue eyes. "Why did you bring me to your parents' for Christmas? Why didn't you just bring Liberty if she was the one you wanted to be with?"

That . . . I was *not* expecting.

CHAPTER Two

*M*Y HEART DROPPED THE SECOND he called me baby. Tristan only called me baby when we were making love, or when he was lost in a passionate moment.

"Ryn, it's kind of—complicated."

I shook my head. "I don't think it is, Tristan. You brought me to your parents' for Christmas, yet you sat on the porch and told another woman you missed her and couldn't wait to see her."

His eyes narrowed. "That's not what I said to her."

Letting out a sarcastic laugh, I said, "Pretty much, Tristan. You were fucking another girl when you were with me. Forgive me for thinking we were in an exclusive relationship."

Tristan pushed his hand through his hair and I fought to hold pack the tugging motion in my core. I loved when he did that. There was something extraordinarily hot about it.

"Ryn, I thought you and I were just having fun, and then something happened."

Smirking, I asked, "Liberty couldn't get time off of work to visit good old mom and dad, so you took the runner up?"

"No! It wasn't anything like that at all. I couldn't decide between the two of you."

He did not just say that. Motherfucker.

"No, wait . . . that's not what I meant. I mean it is, but it isn't. I wasn't dating Liberty when I was with you at Christmas.

It's always been an off and on relationship with her." Dropping his head back he let out a frustrated breath before looking at me. "I got confused, Ryn. I started feeling things . . . I mean . . . I had feelings for you that I've never had for any other woman before."

Oh my. That was not what I was expecting. My stomach flipped a little, but I was sure as hell not going to let this prick know that. "I see, so these feelings caused you to call your other part-time girlfriend. Makes total sense. You're such a prick."

I started walking away from him. His hand grabbed my arm and I let out a gasp from the instant tingles that spread through it. "Ryn . . . can you please just stop?"

I stopped walking and stood there. "I have nothing to say to you, Tristan."

"You wouldn't take my calls. I tried to call you for months. Do you know how pissed I was when you were dancing with that dick . . ."

Spinning around, I placed my hands on his massive, hard as a rock chest and pushed him as hard as I could. He stumbled backwards but was able to keep from falling.

I wasn't sure if I was pissed or if the hurt was all re-surfacing. "Fuck you, Tristan! You fucking called another woman and told her how much you missed her for Christ sake! You ignored me. It was if I was no longer there. No talking to me, no kissing me, you didn't even look at me!" I quickly wiped a tear away.

Tristan's face looked pained as he took a step closer to me. "No!" Shaking my head, I whispered, "No. You don't get to try and make up for that now." Turning, I quickly made my way back to the beach house I was renting. And to Dodge, the only man who could make me forget about Tristan Williams, at least for a little while.

Walking up the stairs to the deck, I heard Dodge on the phone. "I can't make it back tonight, but I'll leave first thing in the morning."

My heart started pounding. He's leaving?

Dodge smiled as I walked up to him and slammed my body into his. He wrapped his arm around me and I instantly felt better. Dodge kissed the top of my head and I had a brief moment of feeling guilty. I had a feeling Dodge wanted more from our relationship than I did. To me, it was just about sex. Although I had to admit I was beginning to feel something more for, Dodge. I wasn't sure if I was afraid to let him in or unable too.

"I'll call you back later, Lefty. Yeah, the deliveries for this afternoon have all been paid and taken care of. Just sign the paperwork and put it in the coolers."

Tightening his grip on me, he pulled me closer to his body. I felt his hard dick pressed against my body and smiled. Dodge had a way of giving me attention, even while he worked.

"I'll be back tomorrow night. Right. Later." Pulling his cell phone away, he hit End. I glanced up to his face, stuck my lower lip out and pouted.

"You have to go?"

Dodge let out a chuckle. "I do, but not until tomorrow. We have all of today together."

I had to admit, the idea of spending the entire day with Dodge had my stomach dipping with excitement. Not the same excitement I felt ten minutes ago when I saw Tristan running by, but it was still excitement.

"What do you want to do today?" I asked as I pulled back and looked into his breathtaking blue eyes. His dark-blond hair had that messy look to it. Like he just ran his hands through his wet hair and let it dry.

Raising an eyebrow, Dodge gave me the sexiest smile. The pulling in my lower core told me he wanted to start off the day on a happy note. "I did drive all this way to fuck you. I haven't fucked you anywhere downstairs yet."

Oh yes. Now he was talking my language.

I slipped my hand behind his neck and pulled his soft plump lips to mine and whispered against them, "The kitchen?"

Before I knew it, Dodge was swooping me up and carrying me back into the house. I laughed as I turned my head and looked back toward the ocean. I must have sensed him standing there. My laughter faded away as I saw Tristan watching Dodge carry me away.

Closing my eyes, I turned and gripped Dodge harder as he headed to the kitchen. Slowly sliding me down his body, Dodge pressed his lips to mine as he kissed me tenderly. My hands went to his hair as I grabbed a fist full of it and tugged. Dodge let out a low rumbled growl as his hand moved under my T-shirt and pushed my sports bra up. The moment he twisted my nipple, I moaned into his mouth. I needed this. I needed raw passion. For some reason, last night Dodge needed love making. I had wanted to be fucked senseless to drown out Tristan's voice and the piercing look of his hazel eyes.

"Ryn, baby, you feel so good," Dodge whispered against my lips. Squeezing my eyes shut, I did what I always did with Dodge—I blocked everything out. I stopped thinking, feeling, and just let myself go.

"Dodge, take me now. Please," I begged.

Dodge dropped to the floor and quickly took off my running shoes and socks. His strong hands slowly moved up my legs as he began pulling my jogging shorts and thong off all at once. I watched him as I slowly smiled. Lifting my legs out of my clothes, my body shook with anticipation of Dodge burying his dick deep inside me. Pushing my legs apart, he slipped two fingers inside me as I dropped my head back.

"Fuck, you're wet, baby," Dodge hissed through his teeth. Standing up, he unzipped his pants and pushed them down. His dick sprung free and I licked my lips as I prepared for what he was going to give me. Rolling a condom on, Dodge lifted me up and pushed me against the island.

Dodge's eyes lit up as he looked into mine. "Ryn," he whispered as he pushed into me. Gripping a hold of his shoulders, I held on as Dodge pushed in hard and pulled out painfully slow.

Yes. Yes this is exactly what I needed.

CHAPTER
Three

TRISTAN

I'D NEVER WANTED TO KILL someone like I wanted to kill the bastard carrying Ryn into the house. I knew what they were up to the moment I saw her start laughing when he picked her up. Quickly jogging toward the house Ryn was renting, I looked around before walking around to the right side. I had no idea where in the house they would be, so I made my way to what looked like the kitchen window.

Fuck! I needed a boost up. I quickly looked around and saw a stepladder up against the side of the house. Grabbing it, I brought it back to the window, opened it up and climbed up the three steps. I slowly peeked through the window and about fell off the fucking ladder with what I saw.

"Motherfucker," I whispered. Gripping onto the windowsill, I attempted to pull my eyes away. Dodge had Ryn up against the island, fucking the shit out of her. Closing my eyes, I started to step down.

"May I help you with something?"

The unknown female voice scared the hell out of me and I missed the last step. Stumbling, I fell back and landed on my ass in the sand.

"Oh my goodness, are you okay?" she asked.

Looking up, a beautiful blonde stood over me, holding her hand out to help me up. I noticed her blue eyes immediately.

Jumping up, I shook my head. "Um . . . I'm fine. I ah . . . I was trying to see if my friend was home."

There was an older gentleman, who was dressed in a jumpsuit that must have been covered in at least fifty different colors of paint, who stood behind the blonde and narrowed his eyes at me. "You didn't think of using the doorbell?"

My mouth dropped open slightly.

"The truth, son, before I call the cops."

My mouth opened and the words fell from my lips. "My ex-girlfriend is staying here and I'm staying two houses down and I was trying to see what she was doing and when I saw, I didn't like what I saw, so I was getting down and then you showed up and scared the piss out of me."

The blonde laughed. "At least he's honest, Daddy."

The older gentleman chuckled. "Son, trust me, if she doesn't want you, it's best to move on."

I stood there and nodded my head. My heart hurt like it had never hurt before . . . and that confused the hell out of me even more.

"That means move along, son. Now."

"Oh! Right, moving along. Y'all have a nice day." Glancing to the blonde, she smiled and winked. Lifting her hand, she waved.

"Hope to see you around, Tom."

I stopped and said, "Oh my name isn't Tom." Then it hit me. *Peeping Tom.* I laughed, gave her a quick wave, and got the hell out of there.

Walking into the house, I let out a frustrated moan as I sat down on the sofa. Scrubbing my hands down my face, I fell back against the cushions. My heart was pounding as my mind tried to erase the image of Ryn and Dodge together. Attempting to control my breathing, I looked up and saw a vase sitting on the credenza. Quickly standing, I headed across the room and picked up the vase. This was my fault. I pushed Ryn into Dodge's arms. Turning, I threw the vase against the wall and yelled out, "Fuck!"

My cell started ringing the moment the vase crashed against the wall. Reaching into my pocket, I pulled it out to see it was Liberty. I was not in the mood to deal with Liberty right now.

Rolling my eyes, I sent her to voicemail.

Walking into the kitchen, I pulled open the refrigerator. "Is it too early to drink?" I mumbled under my breath.

I grabbed a bottled-water and shut the door. There were a few things left over from Lark and Azurdee's wedding, but no real food. I made a note to hit the grocery store later today when my stomach growled.

My phone beeped, alerting me to a voice mail. I swiped my phone to open it and stared at the message. I hit Play and listened to Liberty beg me to call her back. Hitting delete, I headed upstairs to change.

After taking a shower, I changed into a pair of Wrangler Jeans, my favorite boots, a Dallas Cowboys T-shirt, and Dallas baseball cap. Reaching for my truck keys, I headed out the door. The salty air hit me and I couldn't help but take a deep breath. Shutting the door, I hit Liberty's number. I hadn't wanted to deal with Liberty during this trip, but it looked like I needed to. If I didn't, she'd be calling me every day.

"Tristan, darling. I've been worried," Liberty whispered from the other end of the phone.

"Why?" I asked as I pulled out of the garage and headed into town.

Letting out a nervous giggle, Liberty said, "I don't know. I didn't hear from you last night or this morning and I just got worried. I love hearing your voice."

Sitting at a red light, I closed my eyes briefly then snapped them back open. Every time they closed I saw Dodge . . . fucking Ryn.

"Liberty, I didn't want to have to do this over the phone, but since I'm not planning on coming back for two more weeks—"

"Two weeks?" Liberty shrieked.

Pulling the phone away from my ear, I shook my head. "Yeah, Liberty. I had the entire month off, but was planning to come back early. I changed my mind and decided to stay down here for a few weeks. I needed some time to myself. To think."

I heard a door open and then shut. I imagined Liberty was getting up from her desk and either going to the breakroom or outside. She worked for the State of Texas as some personal secretary to some hotshot in the capital. "Honey, what are you thinking about? Us? Have you thought any more about what I said?"

Aw shit. Here we go.

"Liberty, I think I made it pretty clear when I packed up all my shit from your place and left. I'm not wanting to get married. I have no desire to get married. Marriage and me . . . we don't mix."

"Tristan, it's time to grow up. We've been together for over a year now off and on. I'm tired of this scene. You either make a promise to me right now, or we are over."

My mouth dropped open. *Is she for real?* We aren't even together right now!

Pulling into Clayton's, I put the truck in park and sat there listening to Liberty give me an ultimatum.

"So what's it going to be, Tristan? I want an answer right now."

Dragging in a deep breath, I quickly pushed it out. "Liberty, I'm sorry. I care about you, but I don't love you. I don't see the two of us having a future together. I'm sorry."

Silence.

"Liberty?"

Silence.

"Hello?"

Clearing her throat, Liberty asked, "Is there someone else?"

Was there someone else? Hell, I didn't know. If there was, she was currently being fucked by another guy who she considered her fuck buddy. Although, by the way I'd seen him looking at her and holding her close to him, he considered himself more than just a fuck buddy.

"I'm going to take your silence as a yes."

Pushing my hand through my hair, I let out a frustrated breath. "Right now, no, there is no one, Liberty."

She sucked in a breath of air. "So what . . . you're breaking up with me for no reason?"

Jesus H. Christ. Has she always been this fucking dense?

"Liberty! I don't love you. I don't see a future with us. I thought maybe . . . at one point I might have seen what we had going further, but I just don't see that now. I'm sorry. I just can't keep living a lie."

"A lie? So you mean to tell me the last year has all been a lie?"

More like a means to escape.

"No. I care about you . . . I just don't . . ." Closing my eyes, I whispered, "Fuck, Liberty; don't make me say it again."

Hearing her sniffle, my heart dropped. *Shit. Shit. Shit.*

Liberty whispered, "Is it because I'm not into the things you like to do . . . in the bedroom?"

Yes. No. Maybe.

"That plays some part in it, Liberty."

I heard her take in a deep breath. Another door opened and closed. "Tristan, I'll admit all of your sexual toys scared me. But I'd be willing to try some of them, if that would make you happy. I'll let you tie me up . . . hell, you can even fuck me in the ass if you want. I know you want that; you've told me so when you were drunk."

My dick jumped and I cursed my betraying body. Liberty was right; I liked to play in the bedroom. *A lot.* Liberty was as vanilla as they came. Me on top, her on the bottom, and if she was feeling frisky she would ride me, but that was a once a month treat for her . . . and me.

Ryn, on the other hand, liked to be a bit daring. I had never brought her to my condo in downtown Austin. She'd only been to my house in Round Rock. My condo had my playroom; I had shown it to Liberty once. I thought she was going to pass the fuck out when I asked if I could tie her up and fuck her.

"Liberty, sweetheart, I'm not going to ask you to change for me. You are who you are, and I am who I am. We gave it a try and it just didn't work."

Liberty sniffled once more before clearing her throat. "Fine. I hope you're happy with the tramps you pick up to fuck in your little playroom. You're going to see how good you had it with me. I love you, Tristan. I'd have done anything for you."

I needed to be direct with her. I owed her at least that. "Liberty, I have to be honest with you. I um . . . I have feelings for someone else. It's someone I dated before, but I pushed her away because I was confused about my feelings for her, and I just can't keep pretending everything is okay with us. I can't do that to you or me."

I waited for her to say something.

"Fuck you, Tristan. Asshole."

Then the line went dead. Pulling the phone away from my ear, I looked at it. "That didn't go as I planned."

Walking into Clayton's, I looked around. The smell of bacon filled the air and caused me to lick my lips and moan internally. I was starving. A young girl, maybe three years younger than me, looked my body up and down as she smiled. "Hey there. Breakfast?"

Nodding my head, she motioned for me to follow her to a table. She handed me a menu and asked, "You alone?"

Now I really looked at her. Yep, she was at least three years younger, maybe more. Her eyes danced with the possibilities. Two years ago, I would be asking her what time she got off and taking her back to my place, if we made it that far. Winking, I gave her the smile I knew melted their panties. "Yes, ma'am, I am indeed alone this morning."

Tilting her head she said, "That's a shame, guy like you shouldn't be left alone."

"Hey there."

I looked up and the waitress turned her head. I smiled bigger when I saw the girl from this morning standing at my table.

Chuckling, I said, "Hey, paint girl."

Throwing her head back she laughed. It was a nice laugh. She glanced over to the waitress. "Hey, Lisa."

Frowning, the waitress said, "Hey, Sierra."

"Um . . . would you like to join me, Sierra?" I asked as I peeked over to the very pissed off waitress named Lisa.

Pulling out the chair opposite me, Sierra sat down. She looked at me and smiled, "I'd love too, Tom."

Lisa cleared her throat and asked, "Coffee?"

Letting out a chuckle, I nodded my head and looked at the waitress. "No cream or sugar, just black."

Raising an eyebrow, Sierra smiled. "Ahh . . . a man after my own heart. It's rare to find someone who likes their coffee straight up. I'll take the same, Lisa."

I leaned back in my chair. "Sierra? Like as in the mountains? That's a beautiful name. Did your parents conceive you in the mountains or something?" Raising my eyebrow, I smiled as I said,

"I believe the name also means dark."

Sierra smiled bigger. I liked her smile. It was real. Nothing fake about it at all. Her eyes sparkled as she searched my face, landing her baby blues back to my green eyes.

"You're seriously going to judge me when you were caught peeping at your ex getting screwed by what I'm guessing was the new guy?"

Ouch. Straight shooter. Pinching my eyebrows together, I asked, "How did you know they were screwing?"

She gave me a polite chuckle. "Please. I was painting that side of the house when she began calling out his name. It didn't take long to figure out why you had that look on your face when you were stepping off the ladder."

Bile moved up into the base of my throat. The idea of Ryn falling apart with that fucker buried inside her pissed me off. Swallowing hard, I looked down at the menu.

"Recent breakup?" Sierra asked as she smiled at Lisa and took her coffee. Placing mine in front of me, Lisa winked at me.

Glancing back at Sierra, I barely said, "What?"

"You and Ryn? Have y'all recently broken up?"

Setting my menu down, I placed my arms on the table and looked at Sierra. Indignantly, I asked, "How in the hell do *you* know her name?"

Something moved over Sierra's eyes. She placed her arms on the table and stared me down. "It's *my* house. *I* rent it out; therefore, *I* know who is there at all times. Just because I'm covered in paint doesn't mean a damn thing. My daddy paints houses for a living and I'm helping him paint *my* beach house that I rent out when *I'm* not here in South Padre."

I dropped back in my chair and was about to apologize when Lisa walked up and was ready to take our order. "What will it be, Sierra?"

Sierra sat back, never taking her eyes off of me. "Two eggs, over easy, side of sourdough bread, bacon, and a small stack of pancakes with blueberries on top."

A small smile played across my lips. Lisa turned to me. "What would you like, Tom?"

Flashing a smile that would knock any guy out of his shoes, Sierra let out a giggle when Lisa called me Tom.

"I think I'll have exactly the same as Sierra."

Handing her my menu, she took it and turned on her heels, stomping away. Clearly annoyed that Sierra and I were in a flirting stare.

"We broke up ten months ago."

Choking on her coffee, she quickly set it down. "Ten months? Ten. Months? You're still pining over her after ten months? Shit . . . is she that good in bed?"

Hmm . . . a girl who speaks my language. "You immediately think it's because of the sex?"

Raising her eyebrow, Sierra lifted the side of her mouth and made a face. "Please, I'm thirty years old, Tom. I've been around the block a time or two."

Now it was my turn to lift my eyebrows and give her a look. "No fucking way you're thirty. You look about twenty-two. Twenty-five max."

Wiggling her eyebrows up and down she took another sip of her coffee and then whispered, "Flattery will get you everywhere. Especially if you tell me you're a kinky lover. I may have to take you right here on the table—after I eat my pancakes of course."

I threw my head back and laughed. I liked this girl. She was feisty and not afraid to speak her mind. That seemed to be rare in women these days. "What are you doing tonight?"

She took in a deep breath and blew it out. "Let's see. I think my date is picking me up at seven tonight, and we're heading to grab a bite to eat. Then we're heading over to Max's Roadhouse for some serious dirty dancing that will bring us to the brink of wanting to take each other right there on the dance floor, but we won't."

"You won't?" I asked.

Shaking her head, she smiled faintly. "Nope. We won't because he is pining over his girlfriend he broke up with ten months ago and I'm trying to move past learning my husband of six years cheated on me. With my best friend. In my house. In my bed, while my damn dog watched."

"Fuck."

Nodding her head, she whispered, "Yeah—fuck."

Lisa brought our breakfast and Sierra and I spent the next

hour talking. Sierra was a labor and delivery nurse in Austin. That made me smile for some reason. She just bought her own house, a small two-bedroom house in Hyde Park that she swears she had to sell her soul to the devil to be able to buy. I found myself smiling more during our conversation over breakfast than I had in the last ten months. Sierra was easy to talk to, had a wonderful sense of humor, and I could easily see us being friends. I'd never been just friends with a girl before, so this was new territory I was willing to explore.

"So, you're a mechanical engineer, huh? You like taking shit apart and fixing it?"

Smiling, I nodded my head. "Yes, ma'am, I do."

Leaning back, she placed her hands over her stomach. "I'm stuffed." Tilting her head she smiled at me again. I was quickly learning to like this girl. She was fun and had a positive attitude. What a fucker of a husband not to see what an incredible woman he had. "I have a proposition for you."

Looking surprised, I said, "I'm listening."

"Ryn told me she wasn't dating anyone. The guy she's with is clearly into her more than she is him."

"You're observant."

Smiling, Sierra tossed her head to the side and half-heartedly lifted her shoulder. "My job maybe? Or the fact that Daddy used to be involved in the Italian mafia and I learned a lot . . . too much really, when I was younger."

Shit. Sierra just keeps getting more and more interesting.

Gesturing with my head, I said, "Go on."

She popped up in her seat, nodding her head. "Oh right. So, my guess is, this guy . . . shit, what was his name?"

"Dodge," I growled between my teeth.

Laughing, Sierra said, "Right. Dodge. I'm guessing he is just a friend who serves as a fuck buddy in a sense. I can see the idea of him drives you crazy. *Very* crazy. If Ryn still needs a fuck buddy after ten months, that tells me she is still hung up on you. Now, you said you're both here a good two weeks or so. I think what you need is to somehow show Ryn what she's missing. Show Ryn she doesn't need Homerun after all."

"Dodge. His name is Dodge."

Grinning like a fool, Sierra chuckled. "Trust me. By the sound of that orgasm, his name is *Homerun*. Now, I need a few things taken care of at my place. Namely, my lawnmower needs to be fixed and a new garage door opener needs to be installed like ASAP. I'll be your Dodge. Your pretend fuck buddy for the next—" She looked down at her cell phone. "For the next week. Our goal . . . make Ryn see what she really wants, and that's not Dodge."

Lifting, my mouth into a smile, I asked, "Are you sure you don't want to put sex on the table with this agreement?"

Laughing she shook her head. "I'm nobody's fuck buddy, Tristan."

I was stunned into silence. *Who is this girl?* I looked up at the ceiling. Sierra leaned forward and looked up as well. "What are you looking at?"

I shook my head. "I'm not sure, but I think heaven just sent me an angel."

Peeking over at her, she laughed and held out her hand. "Do we have a deal?"

Glancing over Sierra's shoulder, I saw Ryn walking in with Dodge. His arm was thrown over her shoulder. My stomach instantly felt sick at the sight of the two of them together. As my mind traveled back to this morning, the anger began to bubble up. I made the decision right there that I liked Sierra's plan. Quickly grabbing Sierra's hand, I pulled her halfway across the table. Placing my hand behind her neck, I pressed her lips to mine. It took a bit of prodding, but she finally opened her mouth to me. The sweet taste of blueberries lingered on her tongue and I moaned. When I pulled away, I took a quick peek toward the door. Ryn stood stunned as she watched me kiss Sierra. Kissing her quickly on the lips again, I whispered, "Deal."

Leaning back, I relaxed in my chair as Sierra sat back. "Holy shit. I like how you seal your deals."

Looking into her eyes, I gave her a smile that I could tell affected her. "You should see me in bed, sweetheart. I really know how to seal that deal."

Her mouth parted open slightly. "I don't doubt that one bit. I bet you're a good lover."

"I'm better than good." I stood and took out my wallet. Throwing a few twenties onto the table, I took Sierra's hand and brought it up to my lips. "It's show time, sweetheart."

Sierra's eyes widened. "What? Ryn's here? Is that why?"

Nodding my head, I pulled her to me. "Where did you go to college?"

"Um . . . University of Texas."

Nodding, I pulled her closer to me. "By the way, my name is Tristan. Let me take the lead."

She giggled nervously. "Pesh, you're gonna have to because I wasn't prepared to slip into role. Besides, that kiss and your name left me slightly turned on."

Looking at her, I chuckled. "Really?"

She looked straight ahead, nodded, and whispered, "It's show time."

CHAPTER
Four

"OH . . . MY . . . GOSH," I WHISPERED.

"What's wrong, Ryn?" Dodge asked.

I stood staring at Tristan, kissing—Sierra. The girl I was renting the beach house from. Holy shitballs.

I couldn't utter a word. All I could do was stare at them. Shit. They were walking this way. I felt myself lean in closer to Dodge.

"Tristan," I whispered.

Dodge looked up and held me tighter.

"Hey, Ryn. Long time no see," Sierra said in that bubbly-ass way she had about her. Okay, that was mean. I really liked Sierra when I first met her in Austin at the Starbucks down from my house. When I found out she had a place down here, I asked if I could rent it out. She had just separated from her asshole husband and said the extra income would help out a lot. Sierra told me she would be down here painting the house with her father while I was here.

I was expecting to see her the next few days. What I wasn't expecting to see were her lips pressed to Tristan's . . . or them walking out arm in arm—together.

Anger filled my veins, or was it jealousy? I really liked Sierra. Even pictured us hanging out together in Austin. She was a runner. She loved going to movies. She had an amazing personality. She was dumped by the man she loved. Ugh. So. Many. Things.

In. Common. Tristan messed up my possible friendship with one damn kiss.

So. Angry.

Inhaling deeply through my nose, I got ready to put on a fake smile and try to keep my hands to my sides and not claw her eyes out for kissing my man. Glancing at Tristan, I shot him a dirty look.

Asshole.

Gathering my wits about me, I realized I had no right to be feeling this way. Dodge had fucked me not more than two hours ago and here I was mad because I saw Tristan kissing another woman. At least I knew for sure he was not with Liberty. Sure didn't take him long to move on.

Dick.

"Hey there . . . um . . . Sierra." Looking at Sierra, I smiled sweetly. Then I turned to Tristan, who was looking directly at Dodge. Reaching his hand out, I held my breath.

"Tristan Williams."

Dodge shook Tristan's hand. "Dodge Walker."

I couldn't help but notice the veins in Tristan's neck jump out as he clenched his jaw together. He was pissed. I knew him well enough to know that happens when he is mad and attempting to hold it in. For some reason, knowing that Tristan was pissed about Dodge made my stomach flip.

"You two know each other?" I asked, looking between Tristan and Sierra.

Tristan smiled that damn panty-melting smile of his. "Yeah. Sierra was a couple years ahead of me at UT."

Sierra raised her eyebrows and smiled. Then she turned and looked at Dodge. Her mouth parted open slightly before she quickly shut it. Dodge had that kind of effect on women, but I didn't think he held a candle to Tristan by any means. Tristan was slightly taller but their builds were the same. They were both breathtakingly handsome. If you put them side-by-side and told any woman to pick, they wouldn't be able to. But Tristan's smile won out every single time. As did his laugh. Tristan's smile and eyes, when he made love to me, were like nothing I'd ever seen before. Especially during the time we spent at his parents' last Christmas. That's when everything between us changed.

Sex between Tristan and I was never *ever* bad. Or boring. But that one night was all it took to tip the balance of our relationship.

TRISTAN HAD TAKEN ME FOR a drive in the Jeep to get away from everyone. His father had asked to speak with both Lark and Tristan. Tristan left his father's office and was clearly shaken. Taking my hand, he said, "Let's go for a drive."

We came upon a trail. "Where does that go?" I asked as I glanced at Tristan.

Stopping the Jeep, he smiled. "One of our hunting cabins. Want to see it?"

Shrugging my shoulders, I shivered.

"Shit, Ryn, baby, are you cold?"

"A little, but it's really okay. We can keep going."

Seconds later I was in Tristan's arms as he carried me down the path. Using his key, he opened the door and set me down inside.

Picking up wood from the rack that sat next to the fireplace, Tristan began building a fire. After he got it good and going, he reached over and pulled the quilt off of the bed and placed it on the floor.

Motioning for me to sit down, I made my way over and sat in front of the fire. The warmth hit my face and immediately began warming up my body.

"Mmm . . . that feels so much better."

Glancing over to Tristan, I couldn't help but notice he was staring at me. He had been doing that a lot the last two days. Clearing his throat, he looked at the fire. "Are you having fun here, Ryn?"

Grinning, I nodded my head and said, "Oh, yes. I adore Azurdee. She is so sweet. Your mother really is so nice."

Nodding his head, he continued to stare into the fire. "Yeah, Mom's great. Lark picked out a good one I think with Azurdee. She seems to have settled his wild ways."

Letting out a laugh, I said, "They are cute together. He seems to really love her."

Tristan's head snapped over to me. I choose not to acknowledge his action as I focused on the fire.

"Are you warming up?" Tristan asked as he moved the back of his hand down the side of my face. The sweet gesture caused me to lean into his hand.

"Almost," I whispered.

Tristan stood and quickly lifted me up into a standing position. "What's wrong?" I asked as my eyes searched his face. I wasn't sure how to read the look in his eyes. Slowly shaking his head, he reached for my shirt and began to lift it over my head. Closing my eyes, I inhaled the smell of the burning wood. It felt as if my heart was on fire as Tristan reached behind my back and skillfully had my bra undone in less than two seconds. Dropping both my shirt and bra to the floor, he moved to my jeans. It wasn't long before I stood before him, in front of the romantic fire, completely naked. Tristan's eyes moved across my body as if he was memorizing every inch of me. I'd never had a man look at me like he couldn't get enough. Placing my hand on my stomach, I attempted to calm the butterflies.

Taking my hands, he led me to the bed. "Lay down, Ryn."

Moving onto the bed, I was flat in record time. Watching Tristan undress was like watching a Broadway show. So, so good, and you just didn't want it to end. Rubbing my legs together, I counted down the seconds until he would be inside me.

Reaching back into his jeans, he pulled out a condom. Smiling, he crawled onto the bed. Rolling the condom on, he made his way between my legs. He had most of his whole body weight on me as he cupped my face and stared into my eyes. I could see the light from the fire dancing off his eyes.

Tristan had never moved so slowly. He began kissing along my neck as he whispered how beautiful I was.

"I've never seen anyone as beautiful as you, Ryn."

My heart soared and I slowly began to let down the wall I had built up to protect myself. I was starting to picture a future with this man.

Whispering his name was all I could manage to do. He had my stomach in ultimate flutter mode.

"Tristan."

Slowly pushing inside of me, we both let out a moan. This

28

had been the first time in our relationship that we had truly had slow, passionate, meaningful sex. Tristan was making love to me. In the most romantic way imaginable.

As the buildup began, Tristan began to move faster. Gripping onto his arms, I felt my orgasm about to explode. Arching my back, I softly called out his name. Once my orgasm was over, Tristan moved closer to me, dropping his face into my neck as he moved his lips to my ear. I could feel him growing bigger inside of me. He was about to come.

"I'm falling in love with you, baby."

One deep thrust and Tristan let out a soft moan as he whispered, "Ryn . . ."

Oh my. I whispered my feelings back to him. "Tristan, I'm falling in love with you."

Wrapping my arms around him, Tristan held me for the longest time before he pulled out. Rolling over, he stared up at the ceiling with a confused look on his face. I wasn't sure what to do. Tristan finally turned and kissed me. The kiss was long and passionate. It almost felt as if he was saying good-bye. Whispering my name against my lips, he got up and got dressed.

Those whispered words changed our relationship. Unfortunately, it was changed in a different way for each of us.

I'm falling in love with you, baby.

From that moment on, he acted as if I no longer existed.

DODGE SQUEEZED ME, PULLING ME out of my memory.

Clearing my throat, I said, "I see. Well, it looks like you both knew each other fairly well, and still do."

Oh shit. I sound like I'm jealous. Wait . . . I am jealous. No I'm not. Get it together, Ryn. Get. It. Together.

Tristan smirked, while Sierra's face looked sad. Closing my eyes, I shook my head. "I'm sorry, that sounded bitchy."

Sierra smiled warmly. "I ran into Tristan. We had breakfast together and . . ." Sierra looked up at Tristan. "Some old sparks might have flared up. We're just having fun, isn't that right?"

Looking down at her, Tristan winked. "Right." Looking at

Dodge and me, Tristan nodded his head. "I've got to get going."

Attempting to not show Tristan kissing Sierra had rocked my world, I smiled. Or attempted to anyway. I was afraid it came across as more of a toothy grin. Stepping out of the way, Tristan and Sierra walked out of the restaurant. Looking over my shoulder I watched them as we waited to be seated. Tristan placed his hand on the side of Sierra's face. My heart dropped at the tender notion. Leaning down, he brushed his lips against hers as he smiled. Sierra grinned back and they both went their separate ways.

"Ryn?"

Tristan and Sierra? Shaking my head, I fought to hold back my tears. I wasn't sure if I was in shock that Tristan and Sierra knew each other, or if it was because I'd seen them kiss each other in the last five minutes.

Feeling Dodge place his hand on the small of my back, I jumped. "Ryn, baby, are you all right?"

"Yeah. Um . . . yep, I'm totally fine." I faced Dodge and gave him a big grin. "I'm starved. I worked up a pretty big appetite between last night and this morning."

"My girl calls and I come running, willing and eager to please her."

My smile faded briefly. Oh God. Is that what this is? Ten months later and I'm still using Dodge to hide my feelings for Tristan. Giving a weak smile to Dodge, I followed the waitress to our table. The entire time we ate breakfast I tried to keep their kiss from replaying over in my mind. Dodge talked about going out dancing tonight. Nodding, I agreed it sounded like fun.

"Shall we go hit up some stores?"

I loved how Dodge was willing to do whatever I wanted. If I told him I wanted to go to a quilt show, he'd go, no questions asked. And he would smile and act like he was having the time of his life.

Strolling along a small street lined with mostly beach bum stores, Dodge held my hand. We walked in silence for a bit before Dodge guided us to an ice cream store. After getting one scoop of my favorite ice cream, Rocky Road, Dodge and I sat down on a bench. I ate my ice cream as I people watched.

Clearing his throat, Dodge began to talk. "Ryn, I need to ask you something."

Turning to face him, I scrunched up my nose. "Sure! Dodge, you can ask me anything, anytime. You know that."

Giving me a weak smile, he asked, "Where do you see our relationship going?"

Fuck. Me. That was the one thing he couldn't ask. No. He shouldn't ask it. We don't have a relationship. Do we?

"Um . . . do you see this as a relationship?" I asked as I kept licking my ice cream, turning my eyes away from him.

He let out a gruff laugh. "Well, maybe. I mean it could be, if you let it, Ryn. I don't see anyone else. You don't see anyone else. I enjoy being with you and when I say being with you, I don't just mean fucking you so you can attempt to push another guy from your heart."

Snapping my head, I glared at him. "Do you think that's what I use you for?"

Tilting his head, he looked at me like I'd just grown another head. "Seriously? You're asking me that, Ryn? You call, I come running. You see him in Starbucks, you call me and I come fuck you. You see him at a UT football game and then call me. I spend the next twenty-four hours having sex with you until you can't even walk. You see him at a wedding. You call and I drive six hours to be with you."

I felt sick to my stomach. Dodge and I had a really fucked up . . . relationship.

"Have you ever called me to come to you when you haven't seen Tristan?"

I closed my eyes and thought about it. Had I? Yes! Of course I had. I got up and walked over to a trash bin and tossed my ice cream out. I was pissed. Pissed that I had been pretending that there was nothing wrong with this arrangement I had with Dodge. Pissed that Dodge thought he saw this as a potential relationship, and pissed that I was beginning to feel like a tramp because I didn't see this going any further than what it was. Turning, I marched back over to Dodge. "The RV show. I didn't see Tristan. I went and all I could think about was you. I called and you showed up. If my memory serves me right, it was your idea to sneak into a RV and have sex, which by the way ranks up there with the hottest public sex yet."

Dodge smiled.

I continued to talk as I attempted to drown out the fact that I had mostly just used Dodge for sex. Sex to forget about Tristan. Sex to just forget everything. "Then there was the home and garden show two weeks later. I called and asked if you wanted to go with me. I hadn't seen Tristan then. Fourth of July, I invited you to my house because I wanted you there, Dodge. I wanted to be with you."

Of course, I left out the part about Tristan and I going camping over July fourth. We did nothing but stay in the tent and make love the entire weekend. It was our first trip together.

Dodge stood. "You have to know I care about you, Ryn. I want something more."

Oh dear God. I stood before one of the hottest guys I'd ever met, besides Tristan, and he was uttering the words every normal blue-blooded woman wanted to hear.

I want something more.

My heart hurt for Dodge. He wanted something more. I wanted Tristan.

CHAPTER
Five

TRISTAN

ULLING INTO SIERRA'S FATHER'S DRIVEWAY, I stared blankly at the house. *What in the fuck am I doing?* Leaning my head back against my headrest, I tried to rationalize what in the hell I was doing by pretending to be going out with Sierra to make Ryn jealous.

Closing my eyes, the image of Dodge fucking Ryn this morning invaded my mind. Snapping my head forward and opening my eyes I inhaled a deep breath. "Why the fuck not," I said as I pushed my truck door open and got out.

I was about to walk up the steps that lead to the little blue house when the door opened. Sierra came bouncing out.

Holy. Shit.

She was dressed in a silver cocktail dress that hugged her body in all the right ways. Her blonde hair had been pulled up and piled on top of her head. Swallowing hard, my eyes traveled down her long tan legs and I moaned out loud when I saw her silver high heels.

"I'm going to guess I look good since you're eye fucking the hell out of me right now, Tristan."

Looking back up at her face, I shook my head. "What the fuck was wrong with your husband?"

She smiled and I had to catch my breath. Sierra was full of life and her husband was a fool.

"You just scored more points. It's a good thing we aren't really fuck buddies . . . I'd have to give you head tonight."

My mouth dropped open as she walked by me and winked. I was so stunned I couldn't even move.

"Hello? Tristan? Let's go . . . chop chop. I'm in the mood to do some dirty dancing. I haven't rubbed up against a guy in years."

Slowly turning around, I made my way over to her door. I opened it and held her hand while she climbed into the truck the best she could in the short tight dress. I leaned in closer to her and smiled. "Do you talk to every guy like this?"

Giving me a bigger grin, she shook her head. "Nope. It's just with you I know it's safe. You won't act on any of it. We're just having fun."

Raising my eyebrow, I tilted to my head as I asked, "How do you know I won't act? A beautiful woman like yourself comes walking out dressed in a barely there dress, killer legs that I'm sure would wrap around my body nicely, and she talks about sucking my dick." Sierra licked her lips as her eyes glanced down to my lips before looking back into my eyes. "Sierra, my dick jumped at the idea of your lips around my cock."

Sierra's mouth parted open slightly. "Why, Tom, you like to talk dirty?"

Giving her a seductive smile, I said, "I like to play dirty as well."

Laughing, Sierra tossed her head back. For one brief moment, I wanted to run my tongue along her neck. Looking back at me, Sierra shook her head. "I'm not going to lie to you, Tristan. I'd love to see what you would be like in bed, but I have a feeling we'd be better off as friends."

Nodding, I leaned in and brought my lips close to hers. "I have a feeling you're right, Sierra. But I'm still a man and you still made my dick jump seeing you in that dress."

Grinning, she whispered, "Thank you, Tristan. I needed to hear that."

Kissing her gently, yet quickly, on the lips, I whispered back, "I know. Let's go have some fun."

AN HOUR LATER, SIERRA AND I were on the dance floor at Max's Roadhouse. She was an amazing dancer and the more I got to know her, the more I wanted to pound her ex-husband's head into the wall.

"I need a drink!" Sierra shouted over the music. Nodding my head, I turned and walked toward the bar. Someone grabbed my arm and pulled me to a stop. I quickly turned to see it was Sierra.

"What's wrong?"

Her eyes looked panicked. "Kiss me! Now!"

I pulled my head back and looked at her. "What?"

"Kiss me! Now, Tristan!"

I leaned in closer. "Have you been drinking and I haven't noticed?"

Rolling her eyes, she laced her arms around my neck and pulled me to her.

"It's show time," she shouted as she pressed her lips to mine. It took a few seconds for it to kick in.

Ryn.

I wrapped my arms around Sierra and pulled her closer to me. I had to admit, she was a damn good kisser. Her hands went up to my hair and she tugged slightly, eliciting a moan from me.

Pulling back slightly, Sierra whispered against my lips. "Ryn is here."

"I figured that much out," I said.

Iggy Azelea's "Beg for It" began playing. Something in Sierra's eyes changed and she instantly started grinding up against me.

"Is she looking?" I asked. A huge part of me knew what Sierra and I were doing was wrong. I didn't like deceiving Ryn, but I also wanted her back. I wanted her away from Dodge.

Smiling, she nodded her head as she placed her finger in her mouth and sucked on it. I grabbed Sierra and began moving my hands all over her. I wanted to see Ryn's face, but I didn't want her to know I knew she was here.

Sierra turned around and pushed her ass up against my dick

as she put her hand behind my neck. Placing my hands on her hips, we were practically having sex on the dance floor. Moving my hand up her arm, I grabbed her hand and pushed her out while she spun around. Pulling her to me, she wrapped her leg around me as I moved my hand up her leg.

"Tell me how far to go, Sierra," I said.

Taking a quick peek over to Ryn, Sierra said, "She can't stop watching. Slip you hand up my dress a little."

Swallowing hard, I did what she told me to and was met with bare lips. Closing my eyes, I cursed under my breath. "Shit! You're not wearing panties, Sierra? What the fuck? You told me to touch you!"

She gave me a naughty smile and winked before I quickly removed my hand.

"I said, slip your hand up my dress a *little*." For some reason, I felt like I had done something wrong. What the fuck is wrong with me? I just felt the bare lips of a pussy. Any man in his right mind would want to bury his cock there.

The song ended and Sierra walked into my arms and smiled. "She can't pull her eyes off of us."

Grabbing Sierra's hand, I pulled her from the dance floor. She allowed me to take her down the hall toward the restrooms. I stopped and pushed her against the wall. "I just fucking touched your bare pussy, Sierra."

"I didn't think you were going to go for the homerun, Tom."

Rolling my eyes and letting out a sigh, I leaned my forehead against Sierra's. "Sierra, I'm so sorry."

"It's okay, Tristan. It's been so long since any guy has touched me, I'm pretty sure I have cobwebs growing down there."

Pulling my head back, I looked at her. Her smile wasn't reaching her eyes. "How long?"

Looking down at the floor, Sierra began chewing on her lower lip. Glancing back up at me she had tears in her eyes. "About eight months before I caught him in bed with Kim, my best friend. Not even so much as a kiss. I thought he was just stressed at work. Every time I attempted to touch him, he would pull away and say it wasn't fair to me that he couldn't give me his full attention. After four months, I stopped trying. Not being touched like that by someone you think loves you, it does shit to your head."

Placing my hand on the side of her face; my heart hurt for her. I could see the pain in her eyes. "He's an asshole, Sierra."

Sierra placed her hand over mine. Nodding, she whispered, "I know, but it still hurts."

"Let me do something for you."

Narrowing her eyes, Sierra looked at me. "You're not fucking me, Tom. Sorry."

Laughing, I shook my head. People were walking by us as they made their way to the restrooms. Placing my knee between her legs, I pressed against her pussy. Sierra let out a gasp. Moving my lips to ear I asked, "When was the last time a guy gave you an orgasm?"

Grabbing onto my arms, Sierra squeezed them as she began grinding against my knee. "Almost . . . a . . . year."

Biting on her ear lobe, I began moving my knee as Sierra began riding it. She leaned her head back against the wall and bit down hard on her lip. I didn't know how she would react to what I was about to do, so I just did it. Removing my knee quickly, I slipped my hand up her dress and pushed my fingers into her wet pussy. Sucking in a breath of air, Sierra let out a moan and fell apart. Her moans mixed with the loud beat of the music as people continued to walk by, paying no attention to the fact that I was finger fucking a girl against the wall.

When her pussy finally stopped pulsing, I pulled my fingers out. Sierra was still grabbing onto my arms. Moving my lips back to her ear, I whispered, "Better?"

Nodding her head, Sierra's chest was moving up and down as she attempted to get her breathing under control. A year ago I would have probably gone ahead and fucked Sierra hard and fast against the wall. I wouldn't lie to myself and say I wasn't attracted to her, but I really liked her has a friend. Sleeping with her might ruin that.

Bringing her head forward, Sierra looked into my eyes. "I'm still not fucking you. Or giving you head."

Laughing, I pulled her dress down more and took a step back. This is what I liked about Sierra. She had a way about her that kept everything lighthearted. "Damn it, I was so looking forward to you giving me head, too."

Giving me a smirk, Sierra turned and began heading back out to the club. We both came to a stop when we saw Ryn standing there. Her breathing was deep and heavy as she held her hands to her sides, fists balled up. She looked at Sierra and then me. Clearly she was pissed.

"Ryn! Are you here with your boyfriend?" Sierra asked.

I sucked in a breath at the words as Ryn's eyes snapped over to me. "He's *not* my boyfriend."

I attempted to hold back the delight I felt at hearing Ryn stress the fact that Dodge wasn't her boyfriend.

"Oh. I just assumed since . . . well I mean. I couldn't help but hearing y'all getting it on hot and heavy this morning. Yikes. I had to take a break from painting if you know what I mean."

I quickly looked at Sierra, as did Ryn. Holy shit. She just put it right out there.

"Um. Ah. I don't—" Ryn looked at me as I looked away. The thought of Ryn with Dodge turned my stomach.

Ryn quickly stood taller and looked from me to Sierra. "Looks like you and Tristan were getting it on pretty hot and heavy your-selves."

Sierra laughed. "Just having a bit of fun, that's all. Didn't mean anything. Hey, we have a table on the other side of the club, why don't you and your boy . . . I mean . . . your friend join us."

I squeezed Sierra's hand and looked at her as she contin-ued to smile at Ryn. *What in the hell was she doing?* I didn't want to sit there and watch Ryn hang all over Dodge.

Ryn quickly looked over her shoulder. I followed her gaze and saw Dodge standing at the bar. Turning back to us, Ryn smiled. "Thank you, but I don't think that would be a good idea." Ryn looked at me and hurt filled her eyes.

Letting out the breath I was holding, I looked at Sierra. "I'm not really in the mood for dancing any more, Sierra. I think I'm going to call it a night." Sierra nodded her head. Glancing to-ward Ryn, I said, "Enjoy your evening, Ryn."

Ryn opened her mouth like she wanted to say something. I was silently willing her to ask me to dance. Or maybe step out-side and talk. Anything to keep me there. Instead, she nodded her head, turned and walked over to Dodge. She placed her hand on his lower back as he leaned down and quickly kissed her on the lips.

Fuck this.

I quickly started toward the exit. I felt Sierra right behind me. The moment the door opened, I sucked in a breath. It felt as if I couldn't breathe. "Fuck. Fuck. Fuck," I said as I placed my hands on my knees.

"Why are we leaving, Tristan?"

I looked up at Sierra. "She fucking saw me getting you off!"

"Good. She needed to see it."

Standing up straight, I pushed my hand through my hair. "I don't know, Sierra. Maybe she really has moved on. Maybe I just need to . . ."

Sierra lifted her hand up and made a funny face. "Don't you dare say it, Tristan. Stop right there. Ryn practically admitted that Dodge was her play toy. She was angry when she saw us together. I can see it in her eyes, Tristan. She still loves you."

Shaking my head, I began walking toward the truck. "No. She doesn't. She doesn't love me, Sierra."

Grabbing my arm, Sierra pulled me to a stop. "Are you for real right now, Tristan? Did you not see the same girl I saw? The one who was so upset she was trembling? The one who looked like she was about to get sick when I mentioned her boyfriend? Yes, she very much still loves you and you . . ." Sierra stopped talking. Her mouth hung open as she looked into my eyes. "Oh my God. You got spooked. Didn't you?"

I looked away and down to the ground as I kicked a rock.

"Tristan, you broke up with Ryn because you got spooked by your feelings, didn't you?"

Swallowing hard, I lifted my head and dropped it back as I looked up at the perfectly clear night sky. The stars looked amazing, shinning against the black night. Sierra instantly picking up my reason for pulling away from Ryn didn't surprise me. She was insightful to say the least.

Sierra took my hand and gave me a slight pull. I dropped my head forward and looked into Sierra's baby-blue eyes. "It was last Christmas and we had been driving on my parents' ranch. We stopped at one of my father's hunting cabins and before I knew it, I was making love to Ryn and something I'd never felt before swept over me. I told her I was falling in love with her."

Sierra smiled. "What happened?"

I let out a gruff laugh. "My admission scared the fuck out of me, and right before that, my dad started talking about my feelings toward Ryn and some stupid fucking bottle. He called it the journey of love bottle. Some fucking family tradition you do with the person you're wanting to spend the rest of your life with." Pushing my hand through my hair, I let out a breath. "I had been seeing another girl off and on. Her name was Liberty. I hadn't talked to her for some time, but I called her and told her I missed her. Ryn overheard the phone call and headed back to Austin in the middle of the night. Of course, it didn't help I barely spoke two words to her after I let my emotions take over and told her I was falling in love with her."

Sierra's hand came up and covered her mouth. "What a dick move."

Closing my eyes, I nodded. "Yeah. I know."

Turning on her heels, Sierra headed to my truck. "Take me back to your place, Tristan."

Walking behind her, I asked, "My place?"

Sierra stopped at the passenger side door of my truck. Looking up into my eyes, she nodded. "We have some serious talking to do, my friend."

CHAPTER
Six

Ryn

T HE MOMENT I SAW SIERRA and Tristan dancing, I felt sick. I couldn't pull my eyes away. Dodge shouted he was going to get us drinks as I nodded and watched Tristan pull Sierra from the dance floor.

"I'm going to head to the restroom. Be right back!" I shouted to Dodge who nodded his head.

I quickly made my way through the crowd. I couldn't believe how packed it was. By the time I finally made it across the dance floor I started down the hallway. I stopped dead in my tracks as I watched Tristan and Sierra.

I couldn't move. I wanted desperately to turn and walk away but I couldn't. I stood there the entire time watching as Tristan worked Sierra up into what was clearly an orgasm. Sierra said something to Tristan and then quickly turned and started walking. The moment Sierra and Tristan saw me, they stopped dead in their tracks. I politely declined Sierra's invite to join her and Tristan. When Tristan said he was ready to leave, I silently said a prayer of thanks. I knew I wouldn't have been able to stay and watch him and Sierra together. I already felt like I wanted to get sick.

"Ryn? Are you even listening to me?" Dodge shouted over the music.

Looking at him I smiled. "It's the music. It's really loud." He smiled and nodded his head. "Want to leave?"

"I think so," I said as I nodded my head. After seeing Tristan and Sierra together, I was no longer in the mood for dancing. Grabbing my purse, I slipped out of the booth and began making my way out of the club and to Dodge's truck. Dodge took my hand in his as we walked silently through the parking lot.

The image of Tristan's hand up Sierra's dress filled my mind. As I stepped into Dodge's truck, I grabbed his hand. Smiling I said, "I want you."

Leaning into the truck, Dodge kissed me softly. "Your wish is my command."

Dodge jogged around the truck, got in and headed back to the house I was renting. We weren't even through the door and we practically had our clothes off. "I want it slow, Dodge. I want to feel you inside me all night," I whispered as I slipped my panties off and made my way to the master bedroom.

Dodge didn't disappoint. He took his time as he made love to me. Each touch I prayed would push Tristan further from my heart. If only it had worked. When we finally called out each other's names, Dodge rolled off me and pulled me next to him.

"Sleep, sweet Ryn."

Closing my eyes, I felt my tears fall. I was doing exactly what Dodge said I was doing—using him as a means to push Tristan away. I needed to decide once and for all what I was going to do. Was I moving on with Dodge or would I allow Tristan to keep a hold of my heart?

RUNNING ALONG THE BEACH, I found myself looking for Tristan. Dodge had left to head back to Austin. He was going to try and make it back down in a few days and I felt like a fool when I practically begged him to come back. I thought back to what he had said to me before he left.

"Ryn, we need to talk when I come back. I need to know if this is going somewhere."

Ugh. Why can't Dodge just keep it like it is? Why do we have to take it further?

"Hey, Ryn!"

Her voice stopped me dead in my tracks. *Sierra.*

Turning, I attempted to smile. A surge of jealousy ripped through my body. That should have been me against the wall with Tristan's fingers inside of me.

"Oh hey, Sierra," I panted between breaths. I hadn't realized how hard I had been running.

"I'll be finished up by this afternoon with the painting and then I'll be out of your hair."

I nodded my head as I took in a few deep breaths through my nose. "Sounds good, Sierra."

She tilted her head and stared at me. "Hey, listen I'm sorry about mentioning you and Dodge being together yesterday morning."

My heart dropped. I wanted to ask her if Tristan had said anything about it. Had the comment bothered him? Was he unaffected by it or did it piss him off knowing I was being fucked by Dodge?

Smiling politely, I said, "S'okay. I just didn't know how Tristan would feel about it, because you know we dated not too long ago."

Sierra narrowed her eyes at me. "Do you still have feelings for Tristan, Ryn? I mean, there is nothing at all serious going on between us."

Now it was my turn to narrow my eyes at her. "Really? Because last night it sure looked like he was being pretty serious with that orgasm you obviously had."

Oh God. I sounded like I was gearing up for a catfight.

Sierra gave me a weak smile. "I'm gonna go ahead and head back to the house and finish up the painting. Enjoy your run, Ryn."

Turning, Sierra took off running toward her house. Dropping my head back, I let out a long frustrated moan. "Shit!" I said as I began jogging. I had really liked Sierra and it wasn't her fault she and Tristan had a past. It's not like Tristan was taken, not that that would stop him anyway.

I wasn't sure how long I ran for before I stopped and sat. Staring out over the waves, I thought back to the day I decided I would never again let anyone make me feel like I was nothing.

STARING STRAIGHT AHEAD, I STOOD there and listened to Tristan talking to another woman. Tears began streaming down my face as every moment we had spent together the last two weeks vanished in an instant.

"I've missed you too, Liberty. Yeah, it's been okay. I'm ready to get back home. When can I see you?"

Every gentle touch of his fingers on my body now meant nothing. Whispered words in my ear . . . nothing.

WIPING THE TEARS FROM MY eyes, I stood. I hated myself for the way I was feeling. As much as I wanted to tell Dodge that I would be his everything, my heart was putting up one hell of a fight for Tristan. Closing my eyes, I could still feel his breath against my skin.

I'm falling in love with you, Ryn.

My head was telling me it was all a lie, but my heart couldn't erase the look in his eyes when he made love to me that night. Wrapping my arms around myself, I tried to make sense of it all. One minute Tristan professed his love and the next, he made plans to meet up with another woman. Was he scared of his feelings? Did he regret the whispered words?

My phone buzzed in my pocket and I jumped. Shaking my head, I pushed all thoughts of Tristan away.

The name flashing across the screen made me smile.

Joyce. Tristan and Lark's mother.

"Hello," I said, attempting to sound chipper.

"Kathryn darling, how is the beach?"

Smiling, I began walking back toward the beach house. I had just seen Joyce a few days ago at Lark's wedding. Azurdee and I had grown really close in the last ten months. I was happy she and Lark had found their happily ever after.

"The beach is wonderful. How are you and Peter?"

Peter was Tristan and Lark's father. He was spit and fire like his sons. His passion in life, besides his wife, was the hunting ranch he owned.

Letting out a gruff laugh, Joyce said, "He's out on the four-wheeler. I've asked him not to ride that thing, but he won't listen. He is stubborn and has to do things his way or it's the high-way."

Huh, must have passed that down to his son.

"You know boys and their toys," I said with a giggle.

"Kathryn, I want you to come visit us. We haven't seen you in so long."

Laughing hard, I shook my head. "Joyce! I just saw you at the wedding."

"We were too busy to visit. MaryLou wants you to finish that quilt you started a few months back with her. You don't want to break the poor old lady's heart, do you?"

I stopped walking as my mouth dropped open. "Joyce Williams, you are not laying a guilt trip on me right now?"

"Oh, but I do believe I am."

Rolling my eyes, I looked down the beach as I pulled the phone away from my ear. I sucked in a deep breath and blew it out. I had fallen in love with Tristan's parents last Christmas. We had kept in touch and I was one hundred percent positive, Tristan knew nothing about my growing friendship with his moth-er and father.

I had gone to visit them four months back and spent a week with them. I had learned to quilt, castrate cows, shoot a 30 ot 6 with more of an accurate shot than Peter had ever seen, and gut a hog. The last one, gutting a hog, I wasn't too thrilled about and threw up at least three times during the whole process. My heart was torn. If I was going to walk away and forget Tristan forever, that meant walking away from Joyce and Peter.

"Kathryn? Are you still there?"

Attempting to control my tears, I replied, "When should I come down?"

Joyce made a silly sound and yelled out, "Kathryn is coming for a visit!" Giggling, I shook my head. I had no idea who she had just told, but it made me smile. Joyce and Peter were the only people who called me Kathryn since the day I left Florida to move to Texas. The only other people who called me by my full name were my parents and my best friend, Mindy, from high school.

"What about the week before Christmas?"

"Um, I don't know, Joyce."

"He won't be here, Kathryn. I promise you."

Closing my eyes, I pulled my phone away and let the sob escape.

Damn you, Tristan Williams. I hate you.

Taking control over my emotions, I barely got out the words. "Sounds like a plan."

"Wonderful. I'll let MaryLou know. Talk to you soon, darling."

"Bye, Joyce," I whispered as I dropped the phone to my side. I'd go one last time. I was going to have to explain to Joyce why this would be my last visit. It would be hard as hell, but I needed to move on.

Pulling my phone up, I searched for his number. Hitting his name, I smiled when he answered.

"Miss me already?"

Dodge. Even his voice calmed my nerves. Maybe my dependency on Dodge was more than just sex. He had a way of making me feel at ease and wanted. Was I just too afraid to let go of the past that I couldn't see what was in my future?

"Checking to see if you had changed your mind and turned around yet?"

Dodge laughed and I could tell he had his windows rolled down. "Hey babe, the club is calling. Can I call you back?"

My smile faded. "Sure. I'll talk to you later."

"Bye, Ryn."

"Later."

Walking back to the beach house, I wondered how many times I would run into Tristan and Sierra. I was hoping none. I didn't think I would be able to take seeing them together like I had last night.

Shaking my head, I began to run. I pushed Tristan from my mind and began thinking about work.

CHAPTER
Seven

TRISTAN

$\mathcal{S}$ TANDING ON THE DECK OF my family's beach house, I closed my eyes and just let the salt air hit my face. I was worn out from last night. Sierra had insisted on coming back to my place and we sat for almost three hours talking . . . about feelings. I'd rather push pins through my eyes.

"Hey."

Turning, I smiled when I saw Sierra standing there with Starbucks coffee in her hands. "I'm going to head on over to my place and help Dad finish up painting. You doing okay?"

Reaching for the coffee, I nodded. "I didn't sleep much last night." Raising an eyebrow, Sierra nodded her head. "Okay, Sierra, just spit it out."

She slowly took a sip of coffee and then walked up next to me. She faced the water as I leaned against the railing, my back facing the beach. "I ran into Ryn this morning and let me tell you, I think she was still pretty pissed about what happened between us last night."

Blowing on my coffee, I asked, "Really?"

"Yeah. Tristan, I'm pretty sure Ryn has some strong feelings for you. I think her boy toy has gone back to Austin. If you want to make a move, now is the time to do it."

Swallowing hard, I turned and looked down the beach. "What if she can't forgive me, Sierra?"

Placing her hand on my arm, she gave it a squeeze. Turning, I looked down into her blue eyes. They were filled with compassion. "If she loves you, she'll forgive you for the dick-ass move you made on her."

Laughing, I placed my hand on the side of Sierra's face. "I wonder what would have happened if we had really met back in college?"

Smiling, Sierra wiggled her eyebrows up and down. "I'm guessing we would have had crazy, hot, sex every day. Maybe even dabbled in a threesome, which by the way has always been a fantasy of mine. You would have taught me some kinky shit and I probably would have opened up a naughty lingerie store and catered to bored housewives who wanted to spice up their marriages."

Standing there staring at Sierra, I had to process everything she had just said. "Who are you? Where did you come from? You're like the girl of my dreams."

Taking a step closer, Sierra reached up on her toes as she placed her hand on my chest. Instinctively, I lowered my lips closer to hers. When her hand began to move down my chest, to my stomach, we both smiled. "Do you think it would be worth risking our blossoming friendship to see how we would be in bed together?" Her hand landed on the hard bulge in my pants.

"Jesus, Sierra. Do you know how fucking seductive you are, or is this just you being you?" I asked as I licked my lips.

Biting on her lip, she shook her head. "I think I should go before we make a mistake I know we will both regret."

My dick was so hard in my pants; I reached down and pushed her hand against my hard cock. "I'm thinking I don't care at this point."

"Tristan . . ." I dropped my coffee cup and grabbed both sides of Sierra's face. Smashing my lips to hers, I kissed her. I couldn't believe how much my body wanted Sierra, but my heart was fighting it like a son-of-a-bitch.

Sierra wrapped her arms around me as I moved my hands down and picked her up. Wrapping her legs around me, I carried her into the house. Something snapped in both of us. The way our tongues moved together was like we were crazed. Teeth hitting against each other as I walked over to the sofa.

Dropping down, I never took my lips off hers. Sierra moaned as she began pushing off her shorts. Our kiss broke for less than ten seconds as we both ripped our shirts up and over our heads. One quick look at her breasts, I moaned and whispered, "Fuck."

Pressing her lips back to mine, Sierra crawled on top of me. She began grinding her pussy against my hard dick as she pulled her lips from mine. "Oh God, what are we doing? This is . . . wrong . . . so wrong."

Pushing her bra up, her tits dropped down. I quickly pulled one into my mouth and began sucking on it.

"Oh God. Tristan, I'm going to come if you keep doing that." Her body had been neglected for so long. The way Sierra reacted to my touch was amazing. Her body was begging to be fucked.

"Sierra, I want to fuck your body and give it the attention it deserves."

Lifting up so I could pull my pants down, Sierra watched as my dick sprung free. "Ahh . . ." was all she said as she took my dick in her hand. I jerked and grabbed her hair, pulling her head back and exposing her neck to me.

"What do you want, Sierra?"

Closing her eyes, she whispered, "To forget."

Turning, I saw my wallet on the end table. Reaching for it, I opened it and took out a condom. "Sierra, look at me."

Her eyes sprung open and tears began to build. "You are not my fuck buddy, Sierra. I'm giving you what is long overdue."

"Tristan," pulling her head closer to me, we rested our foreheads together, "make me forget him, please. Make me feel desirable again."

Picking Sierra up, I moved her off of me as I slid the condom on. Motioning for her to sit back on me, she quickly moved over me. She positioned her pussy right at my tip. Looking into my eyes, she said, "I haven't been with anyone but my ex-husband in over ten years."

Smiling, I said, "Then I've got a lot of teaching in this fuck session, don't I?"

She quickly sank down on me and let out a whimper. "Holy fuck, you're huge."

"And that would be the correct thing to say to a man you

just pushed your pussy down on."

She began moving as she placed her hands on my chest. "Feels so good. So. Much. Better. Than. A. Vibrator."

Laughing, I placed my hands on her hips. "Ride me, Sierra. Let it go and fuck the hell out of me."

And that she did. I had never had a girl let go like she did. I wondered what kind of sex life she had with her ex. Probably vanilla. The way she was grabbing her tits had me fighting like hell to hold off.

"Sierra, you're getting close. I can feel you're body trembling."

She looked into my eyes and said, "Oh God, Tristan!" She began moving faster as her orgasm ripped through her body. She called my name out over and over as she rode me until the last ripple of her orgasm vanished.

I wasn't done with her yet. I intended on showing her what a real man would do with her body if she was his.

Lifting her up, I set her on the sofa and stood. "Stand behind the sofa, Sierra. I'm fucking you from behind."

"I've never . . . I mean . . ."

Damn it. That asshole husband of hers neglected her in every possible way.

Pulling her up, I walked her around to the back of the sofa. "Lean against the sofa and spread your legs open."

I dropped to the ground and before she could protest, I buried my face in her pussy.

"Mother of all . . . oh God yes!" All it took was a couple of sucks on her clit and she was screaming out my name again. In the middle of her orgasm, I stood up and spun her around, pushing her over the sofa. Spreading her legs apart, I buried my dick deep inside her. Sierra hissed through her teeth, "Fuck!"

Grabbing her hips, I began to fuck her hard and fast. She began calling out my name and a few other words I couldn't make out. The way her body responded to mine was unreal. I was sure it was because she had not had sex in so long, and had never had a good fucking before.

Pulling out, I told her to turn around. Lifting her up, I sank her back down on my dick. I turned and walked up against the door to the garage and pushed her against it. Looking into my eyes, Sierra hissed out, "Yes. Oh God yes!"

I began to move in and out of Sierra. Her pussy was so fuck-ing tight and it had taken everything in me not to come the mo-ment my dick sank deep into her. "Sierra, come again for me."

Sierra began thrashing her head back and forth. "Can't. I've never . . ."

I pulled almost all the way out and pushed back in hard. Screaming out, Sierra began moving along with me and it didn't take long for her to cry out in pleasure again. I'd fucked plenty of girls, but this was different. Sierra needed to know what it was like to have a man desire her body. What it was like to let go and enjoy sex to the fullest. Seeing her let herself go and knowing I was helping her to move on and gain some self-esteem was amazing.

"Yeah, I can feel you pulling my cock in further."

Her eyes lit up as she bit down on her lip. "Tristan, God I'm coming so damn hard."

Smiling, I gave her my all until I couldn't hold it back. "I'm gonna come, Sierra." I whispered as I called out her name and poured my cum into the condom.

Sierra dropped her head back against the door as we both took a few moments to get our breath back. Sierra whispered, "I feel you jumping inside me still." Giving me a drop dead gor-geous smile, she purred, "That was amazing."

Chuckling, I lifted her up and pulled out of her. "Yeah, it was. Are you tired?" I asked as I picked her up and carried her over to the sofa.

Sierra stretched out on the sofa as she took slow, deep breaths to calm down her breathing. "Yes. I've never done any-thing like that before. I can't seem to . . . to catch my breath." Pulling the condom off, I walked into the kitchen and tossed it in the garbage.

Walking back into the living room, Sierra was smiling at me. "What?" I asked.

"I've never met someone so confident in himself."

Lifting my eyebrow, I tilted my head. "Once I know what I want, I go for it."

"I'll say."

Walking over to the sofa, I motioned for her to move over. I crawled in behind her and pulled her to my body.

Taking in a deep breath, Sierra blew her air out slowly. "You know I don't need you to coddle me, Tristan."

"I know, Sierra. I want to hold you, if that's okay."

Her body relaxed a bit as we laid there for a good ten minutes with neither of us talking. I didn't feel like we had done anything wrong. It was obvious we both wanted each other. I hadn't known Sierra all that long, but I liked her company. Her friendship. If we hadn't done this now, it would have probably gotten in the way of our friendship.

"Tristan, this doesn't change anything between us. I mean, the sexual tension was for sure there, but our friendship feels like the more dominant feeling."

Pulling her in closer, I took in a deep breath as I inhaled her smell. "I've grown to really enjoy your company and if we hadn't done it now, we would have sooner or later, Sierra."

"You weren't lying when you said you were good in bed. Holy shit, I've never been so thoroughly fucked. And how in the hell do you manage to give a girl three . . . no wait, I'm pretty sure I tipped four, orgasms?"

Laughing, I eased up on my hold of her. "I can't imagine what you'd be like making love to someone you truly loved, Tristan."

The image of Ryn and me in the hunters cabin popped into my head. Closing my eyes, for the first time in my life, I fought to hold back my tears.

Smiling, I kissed the back of her head. "Do you want me to make love to you, Sierra?"

Turning in my arms, she looked at me for a good twenty seconds or so. Shaking her head she whispered, "No. The next time you make love to a woman, Tristan, it should be with the woman you love with all your heart."

Swallowing hard, I nodded. Leaning down, I brushed my lips against Sierra's. Her hand moved up and through my hair where she tugged on it slightly. "I need to go and help my father finish up painting."

"Are you leaving after that?" I asked as I searched her eyes. The hurt was gone, but I couldn't tell what replaced it. Was she really okay with all of this?

Smiling, she nodded. "Yeah. Thank you, Tristan. Thank you for everything."

There was a glow about Sierra's face as she thanked me. In a way, Sierra taught me something about myself as well. I was bound and determined to make up for the mistake I made ten months ago. "Thank you, Sierra."

Sierra moved and stood. She began pulling her bra over her magnificent tits. I watched as she got dressed. I was surprised my attraction for her hadn't changed. One thing I knew for sure, the sexual tension between us was definitely sedated.

Reaching over, I grabbed my shorts and pulled them back on. Sierra handed me my T-shirt and I slipped it over my head. She began walking over to her purse, but I reached for her hand and pulled her back to me.

"Friends?"

Giving me a big ole grin, she nodded her head. "Yes, friends for sure. I already programmed my cell and work number in your phone and put BFF next to my name."

Laughing, I shook my head as I followed her to the front door. Before opening the door, she turned and looked at me. "I am faced with two serious problems now though."

My smile faded. "What?"

She took in a deep breath and quickly exhaled. "My vibrator will *never* be able to compete with those orgasms. And, I'm pretty sure my next boyfriend's performance in bed will be measured up to the amazing fucking I just got."

Laughing, I pulled her into my chest and hugged her. "Go paint, crazy girl."

Stepping back, Sierra threw me a wink and held up her hand as she walked out and yelled over her shoulder, "Later, Tom!"

CHAPTER
Eight

*R*UNNING BACK ALONG THE BEACH, I realized I was near Tristan's family's beach house. Glancing over, I saw Tristan and Sierra on the deck.

Placing my hand on my stomach, I felt sick as I watched Tristan take Sierra into the house. Was he taking her in to make love to her? How serious was their relationship? Sierra had said they were just having fun. *That* didn't look like having fun. Pulling my eyes from the house, I ran as fast as I could two houses down. Sierra's dad was painting the back of the house that faced out over the Gulf of Mexico. Lifting his hand, he shouted a hello.

I couldn't find my voice. I lifted my hand and smiled weakly before slipping in through the back sliding glass door. Walking into the kitchen, I grabbed the counter and began trying to get my breathing under control. That was twice I'd seen Tristan and Sierra in an intimate moment.

I was slowly beginning to dislike Sierra. Closing my eyes, Dodge fucking me against the very counter I held on to caused me to open my eyes and take a few steps back.

Placing my hands up over my mouth, I slowly shook my head. I dropped my hands. "What is wrong with me?" I shouted. Here I had been letting Dodge fuck me the last few days and I was upset that Tristan was with someone else. I pushed my fingers against my temples and began massaging them.

"Shit! Shit! Shit! I hate you, Tristan Williams!" Dropping to the floor, I pulled my legs into my chest. Resting my chin on my knees, I let my tears fall as I whispered, "I hate you, Tristan."

I QUICKLY SAT UP AND looked around. The doorbell had rung and woke me from a dead sleep. Hearing it ring again, I jumped up and headed over to it. Peeking through the peephole I saw Sierra.

Shit.

Closing my eyes, I took a deep breath and slowly let it out as I plastered a fake smile on my face. Opening the door quickly, I scared Sierra by practically shouting, "Hey, Sierra!"

Smiling, she looked me up and down. "Are you okay?"

Making a face like I had no idea why she would ask me that, I replied, "Yeah. I'm doing . . . great. How are you? Been a good day?"

I rolled my eyes inward. *Jesus what's wrong with me?*

Sierra tilted her head and paused for a moment. Something about her was different, but I couldn't put my finger on it. "The painting is all done so you can enjoy the rest of your vacation in total privacy."

My mouth opened slightly. "Oh, does that mean you're leaving? I mean, um, are you headed back to Austin or . . ."

Sierra smiled sweetly. "I'm headed back to Austin. I only took a few days off to work on this and visit with my father. Maybe when you get back we can grab dinner and catch a movie?"

Is she for real? She's fucking my ex-boyfriend and she wants to go to a movie?

Attempting to smile, I nodded. "Yeah. Sure, maybe we could."

Sierra looked into my eyes and I was instantly taken by the tenderness in her blue eyes. "I hope you enjoy the rest of your vacation, Ryn."

Smiling weakly, I nodded my head and watched as Sierra turned to walk away. "Sierra?"

Stopping, she turned and looked at me. "I . . . um . . . I know I have no right asking this and it is not any of my business, but are you and Tristan . . . um . . . dating?"

Something flashed across her face quickly before she smiled and shook her head. "No, Ryn. He's just a friend, that's all."

Chewing on my bottom lip, I decided to just ask about what I saw instead of letting it eat me alive. "I saw the two of you earlier, kissing, and Tristan carried you into the house."

Sierra walked up to me and took my hands in hers. "I think we were just trying to see if there was anything at all there."

I fought to hold my tears back. My voice cracked as I went to ask her what they found out. I hated how weak my voice sounded. "Was there?"

Lifting the corner of her mouth, she said, "No, honey. Tristan and I are just meant to be friends."

I instantly felt my body relax. I knew this was so unfair of me, especially knowing that Sierra had heard Dodge and I having sex. "I can't imagine what you think of me, Sierra. Here I'm asking about Tristan's love life and I've been . . . I've been with Dodge and . . ."

Squeezing my hand, Sierra looked into my eyes. "Talk to him, Ryn. I know he hates how things ended with the two of you. Talk. To. Him."

Nodding my head slowly, I said, "I'll think about it."

Sierra's smile faded some as she nodded her head. Giving me a wink, she turned and headed to her car.

Shutting the door, I leaned against it. My heart ached knowing that Tristan and Sierra slept together. It wasn't fair of me to feel angry but I did. Closing my eyes, I knew the real reason I was upset. I was jealous of Sierra and the relationship she had with Tristan. I needed to get out for a while. Walking to the kitchen to grab my keys and phone, I decided I would not think about Dodge or Tristan. I needed to clear my head. As much as I adored Dodge, I knew I didn't want the same thing he wanted.

Checking my phone, I saw I had two text messages. Opening them up, one was from a client who couldn't seem to understand I was on vacation, and the other was from Dodge.

> Dodge: *Missing you, baby. I'm not sure I'm going to be able to get back down there. Sorry. Things are crazy here at the club.*

Hitting reply, I typed out my response.

> Me: *No worries, Dodge. I think I need some time alone to think things through. Take care of the club. I'll call you when I get back.*

Dodge responded immediately.

> Dodge: *I hope that means you're thinking about us and our relationship.*

Ugh. There he goes using the words *us* and *relationship*. I backed out of my text messages and dropped my phone into my purse. I'd deal with Dodge when I got back to Austin. Right now, I needed some shopping therapy.

SOUTH PADRE HAD SOME PRETTY awesome shops that were tucked away on the side streets. Sierra had told me to check them out. Stepping into Sisters Interior, I smiled. Oh, yea. This was my kind of store. Sierra just moved up a little bit more onto my good side with this place.

Walking around the store, I couldn't wipe the smile off my face. I loved buying things for my house back in Austin. It was my place and I could do whatever I wanted with it. No overbearing mother to try and control how I decorated it. I cringed thinking back to the day I set up my dorm room. She did it exactly how she wanted. The moment she walked out the door, I spent the rest of the day re-arranging it to how I wanted it.

I let out a small gasp when I saw a mirror hanging on the wall. It was beautiful. The mirror was framed in a brushed-silver finish, but the inside frame had the most unusual pastel pattern design. I walked up and admired it. Turning, I looked for an employee. A young girl with dark-red hair began walking up to me.

"May I help you?"

Grinning like a fool, I pointed to the mirror. "How much is this mirror?"

"It's eleven hundred dollars."

I was pretty sure my eyes about popped out of my head. "Come again?"

The sales lady giggled. "I know, it's a bit of sticker shock. But it's one of kind and the artist lives here in South Padre."

Turning back to the mirror, I debated if I wanted to spend that kind of money.

No. I didn't. Not for a damn mirror. I began gnawing on my lower lip as I thought about it. I wasn't sure why I was even entertaining the thought. There was no way I would ever pay that much for a stupid mirror. No matter how beautiful it was.

"Let me put you out of the internal struggle. That gentleman over there has already stated he wanted to buy it."

Turning and looking over my shoulder, I saw him. "Motherfucker," I whispered as my eyes landed on Tristan.

"Um . . ."

Looking back at the young saleslady, I covered my mouth. "I'm so sorry; I didn't mean to say that."

Chuckling, she held up her hands. "No problem, but I'm going to guess you know him? Or you really wanted that mirror."

Laughing, I said, "Both." Reaching up, I took the mirror off the wall. The saleslady's eyes grew bigger. "Go with me on this."

Not even giving her time to answer me, I began walking up to the register with the mirror as the poor girl walking briskly behind me said, "Um, ma'am. Ma'am, you can't have it."

"Oh my goodness. I can't believe I found the perfect mirror. I'm just so overjoyed."

Tristan turned and looked at me. He smiled at first, until he saw the mirror in my hands. The older gentleman who had been helping Tristan stood there stunned.

Men. I swear.

"My mother is going to love this." Looking at the lady behind the counter, I turned my smile to a somber look. "She's so sick and this will just make her feel so much better." Acting as if I was going to start crying, I said, "We're not even sure she will make it through . . . the holidays." I dropped my head and acted as if I was crying.

The young sales lady placed her hand on my shoulder. "Oh my goodness, I'm so sorry."

Peeking up, I stole a look at Tristan. His mouth was gaped open and he looked shocked as hell. Wiping away my fake tears, I smiled at the girl behind the counter.

"Thank you so much. Anywho, I'll take the mirror and send

her a picture. She'll be so happy. Especially knowing it was made by a local artist here in her beloved South Padre.

"Oh. My. God."

I looked at Tristan. "Tristan? What are you doing here?"

Narrowing his eyes at me, he looked at the mirror. "Buying a mirror."

The gentleman helping Tristan cleared his throat. "Ma'am, I'm afraid that mirror . . ."

I interrupted him. "Is perfect!" Looking at the girl standing there, I lifted my shoulders and smiled bigger. "Isn't it? Momma is going to be so happy." I attempted to hold back my fake sob. "Here's my credit card."

Handing her my credit card, she just stared at me. I jerked my hand toward her again, as if she hadn't noticed me holding my card out to her.

"Ryn, your damn mother isn't sick. You can't even stand your mother. When was the last time you talked to her?"

Ignore him, Ryn.

"You don't have to wrap it up, sweetheart. I'll take it just like that." The poor girl at the counter snapped her eyes to the gentleman who was helping Tristan.

"And, you're mother has never even been to fucking South Padre!"

Pulling my head back, I gasped. "Oh my, is it necessary to use such language?"

Placing my hand up to the side of my mouth, I leaned closer to the girl. "He doesn't like me very much and does anything he can to give me trouble. Can we speed this up a bit please?"

Pointing to the girl, Tristan shouted, "No! That is my mirror. I saw it first, and Bill here was just about to ring me up."

I placed my hands on my hips. "I don't see your name written on it. If it had been sold there should have been a sold sticker on it. As far as I'm concerned it was hanging on the wall, ready to be bought by someone who has far better taste than you."

"Ryn, watch it."

"You don't scare me. Man whore!"

Stepping around the counter, the gentleman put his hand up to me. "Ma'am, the gentleman is right. I'm in the middle of his transaction. The mirror is not for sale."

Turning, I looked down at Bill's nametag. Shit. He was the manager.

Lifting my shoulders, I looked back at Tristan. "Fine. Hang it somewhere you'll be able to see all the bitches you bring home to screw."

Hurt flashed across Tristan's eyes, but I didn't care. Turning on my heels, I headed to the door.

Ugh. I *hate* him. He even gets the stupid mirror I wanted but didn't really want because it was too expensive. I just wanted to keep Tristan from buying it. *Ohmygod. How pathetic am I?*

Walking up to my car, I was about to get in when someone grabbed my arm. Tingles immediately moved down my arm.

Tristan.

Turning me around, he pushed me against my car. "Are you fucking kidding me? What in the hell was all that about?"

The image of Tristan and Sierra at the nightclub flooded my mind. My eyes filled with tears and I hated myself for letting him upset me again. "Let me go."

"No. What was with all the man whore shit back there, Ryn?"

Swallowing hard, I asked, "Did you fuck her?"

He pulled his head back and looked at me. "Who?"

My lower lip trembled. "Sierra. I saw you together this morning, on your deck."

Tristan dropped his grip from my arm. Closing his eyes, he whispered, "Sierra and I are just friends."

My heart was beating so loudly in my chest I was sure Tristan heard it. I wasn't sure why I had to know, but I did. Taking control of my emotions, I said, "That's not what I asked you."

Opening his eyes, he whispered, "Yes."

I couldn't stop the tear if I wanted to. Tristan reached up and wiped it away. "It didn't mean anything, Ryn."

Slowly nodding my head, I whispered, "It never does where you're concerned."

Tristan looked like I just slapped him in the face. "Enjoy the mirror, Tristan." Turning, I opened the door to my car and got in. Starting my car, I quickly began backing up without looking at Tristan. The moment I was far enough away, I pulled over and let out a frustrated scream.

How can you hate someone you love so much?

CHAPTER
Nine

TRISTAN

$\mathcal{I}$T HAD BEEN TWO DAYS since I saw Ryn. Sierra had sent me a text message asking if Ryn and I had talked yet. My response was the same as it was yesterday when she asked. No.

Stepping through the door of Dirty Al's, I headed to the bar. The bartender flashed me a toothy smile. "What will it be, handsome?"

"Bud Light, please."

I sat at the bar for a few minutes before the hair on my arms stood up. I quickly looked around and saw Ryn. She was sitting at a table with some asshole guy who was sitting way too close. She was laughing as she finished up what looked like a margarita. Turning back to the bartender, I asked, "Excuse me, the brunette over there. How long as she been here?"

The bartender glanced over to Ryn. "About four hours. That douche has been feeding her shots in between the margaritas. I've been keeping my eye on her. Do you know her, because I was getting ready to call her a cab. No way I'm letting her leave with him."

Nodding my head, I looked back at Ryn. "Yeah, I know her. We used to date. I'll take care of getting her home."

"Awesome. Do you want to settle up her tab as well?"

Reaching into my wallet, I pulled out some money and tossed it on the bar. Standing, I headed over toward Ryn. Stopping at the table, I cleared my throat. Ryn looked up and smiled that beautiful smile of hers. "Tristan. If you came here to buy a mirror, I'm sorry, we are fresh out."

The dick sitting next to her laughed. Glancing at him, I said, "Beat it, buddy."

He stopped laughing and stood. "Excuse me, asshole? I was with her first, so you can just go take a flying hike."

Grabbing him by the shirt, I gave him one good push, causing him to stumble back and fall to the ground. Ryn jumped up and let out a scream. "Tristan! He was just talking to me."

Grabbing her hand, I pulled her to me. "Bullshit, Ryn. He wanted to do a lot more than talk."

Leading her out the door, she protested the entire way. "Tristan Williams, you let go of me right now. I'm not that drunk. I knew what he wanted and I wasn't going there. I was about to ask the bartender to call me a cab."

"Where's your car, Ryn?"

She stopped walking and jerked her hand from mine. "I took a cab here. I wanted to get drunk and I knew I wouldn't be driving."

Walking up to her, I looked down into her eyes. She looked so sad and I knew I was the reason why. "I'm taking you home, Ryn."

Swallowing hard, she nodded her head. "Okay."

Helping Ryn into my truck, we drove along in silence. Every time I glanced over to her, she was staring out the window as she fidgeted with her purse strap.

Fifteen minutes later we were walking into Ryn's place. One quick look around, I noticed the place was a lot smaller than my family's beach house.

"Kitchen?" I asked. Ryn pointed to her left and I walked away. The moment I saw the kitchen island I felt sick. Pushing any thoughts of Ryn and Dodge out of my mind, I headed over to the coffee maker.

Ryn called out, "I'm going to get out of these clothes."

My dick jumped and I had to bite the inside of my cheek to keep myself from doing what I wanted to do.

Filling up the glass container, I poured it into the coffee maker. Four cups should be plenty. Hearing a loud crash, I turned and ran toward the sound.

Ryn was sitting at the bottom of the stairs holding her ankle. "Ryn! What happened?"

Running to her, I dropped to my knees. Ryn's ankle was swelling already. Looking up, my heart dropped and I wanted to hit something. Ryn was crying. "I think . . . I broke it."

Lifting her up, I carried her to the couch. Ryn's cries echoed through my brain as I gently placed her down. "Baby, let me go get some ice."

Slowly nodding her head, she whispered, "Okay." I turned and headed into the kitchen. Finding a hand towel, I took some ice cubes out of the freezer and wrapped the towel around them. I quickly unplugged the coffee pot and headed back to the living room. Setting the ice down on her ankle, Ryn whimpered. "Oh God. Tristan, it hurts so bad."

"Shit, Ryn. I think we need to go to the ER."

Leaning her head back, she moaned. "Double damn it! I never was a good drunk!"

Stifling my laughter, I reached down and scooped her up into my arms and headed back out to my truck. "Tristan, it hurts so bad." Ryn buried her face into my shoulder and cried. I hated that she was in pain. I'd give anything to take it away.

Opening the passenger side door, I gently placed her down in the seat of my truck. "Baby, please don't cry. Please, please, don't cry."

"Hurts so bad." Ryn whimpered. Leaning down, I kissed her forehead then wiped her tears away.

"I'm going to fix it, baby."

Grabbing onto my shirt, Ryn looked into my eyes. "Tristan, please don't leave me."

Swallowing hard, I whispered, "Never, Ryn. Never."

THE NURSE WAS PUSHING RYN out of the hospital in a wheelchair as I pushed off my truck and walked over to them. "She's more than ready to leave. I'm afraid she is a bit loopy from the pain pills and the alcohol that was in her system. She can't be left alone tonight."

Nodding my head, I leaned down and picked up Ryn. She wrapped her arms around my neck and whispered against my chest. "It hurts, Tristan. I'm such a baby."

Laughing, I said, "No, baby. You have a grade-two sprained ankle and a zero pain tolerance."

Ryn started crying. "I know. I'm never drinking again!"

The nurse opened the door to my truck and waited as I put Ryn in. I buckled her in and looked into her eyes. "I'm so sorry, baby."

Ryn stared at me with a dazed look. "Why are you sorry, Tristan? You weren't the one who got drunk."

Hunching my shoulders, I said, "I'm pretty sure I'm the reason you got drunk though."

Glancing back up, Ryn was staring at me. Tears began to fill her eyes as she started chewing on her bottom lip. "Yeah. Yeah you were."

The nurse behind me giggled.

The ache in my chest grew more as I stared into her eyes. "I promise to make it up to you, baby." Giving Ryn a small smile, I kissed her quickly on the lips, stepped away and shut the door.

"You understood all the discharge instructions?"

I nodded. "Yes, ma'am. I'll make sure she follows through with all of it."

Giving me a wink, she said, "Good luck. We all got an earful about you from Ryn."

Rolling my eyes, I turned and headed to the driver's side of my truck. My heart was breaking for Ryn, but at the same time, I was overjoyed that I would get to take care of her for a few days and there was nothing she could do about it. If there was one thing I knew about Ryn, she didn't do well with pain. Any kind of pain.

I HAD HARDLY SLEPT AT all last night. After getting back to my house, I carried Ryn to the master bedroom that was downstairs. I stripped her of her clothes and put one of my T-shirts on her. Tucking her in, I made my way back to the living room to sleep on one of the sofas.

I heard something fall in the kitchen. Then I heard, "Shit," coming from Ryn, and quickly sat up. Reaching for my shirt, I slipped it over my head and walked toward the kitchen. Ryn was attempting to make breakfast. When she turned and saw me, I had to suck in a breath. Tears were rolling down her face.

I quickly walked up to her and placed my hands on the sides of her face. "Ryn, did you hurt yourself?"

She slowly shook her head. "No."

"What's wrong?" I asked as I wiped her tears away.

"I'm starving, I have a terrible hangover and . . . and . . . I don't know where you put my pain medicine."

Reaching down, I lifted her up into my arms. Ryn wrapped her arms around me and buried her face. "I feel like such a baby."

"No, you've had a lot happen in the last twelve hours, sweetheart." Sitting her down, I covered her up with the blanket I used last night. "Let me go get your pain meds and some ice."

Walking into the master bedroom, I grabbed the pills that I had set on the side table last night. Ryn must have forgotten I told her they were there. When I walked back into the living room, Ryn had the blanket up to her nose, inhaling its smell. Smiling, I felt a bit of hope that Ryn had missed me as much as I missed her. I found myself smelling her shirt last night as I held it and watched her sleep.

I started walking back into the living room. "I had them next to the bed."

Ryn quickly dropped the blanket and looked at me. Her smile about dropped me to the floor. Reaching out she took the pills from me. "Let me go get you some water."

Turning, I attempted to calm my heartbeat and get my breathing settled. Knowing that Ryn was in pain was tearing me apart. I'd give anything to take her pain away. *Anything.*

Grabbing a towel, I opened the freezer and took out some ice. Wrapping it in the towel, I took a bottled water out of the refrigerator. I assessed what food I had. Biscuits, jelly, some fruit.

Shit. I needed to get her some real food. Setting the towel and water down, I rubbed my hands up and down my face. Reaching for the phone, I hit speed dial one as I grabbed the towel and water and walked back toward the living room.

The pain on Ryn's face made my heart hurt. Handing her the bottled water, I sat on the coffee table.

"Hi, I'd like to place a to go order for delivery. Yes. Two egg, bacon, cheese, and potato breakfast tacos. Can you make sure the bacon is in strips and not cut up? Great."

Ryn looked at me and smiled. Giving her my panty-melting smile back, I winked. Her mouth opened slightly and she quickly licked her lips before looking away.

"Then we'll take two carne asada tacos, a Dr. Pepper and a root beer. Oh, and make sure you send green sauce with that please."

After giving the girl over the phone my address, I hung up and set the phone next to me. "I have some peaches. Do you want me to cut one up for you?"

Ryn began chewing on her lower lip. "Tristan, you don't have to be doing this."

Pulling my head back in surprise, I looked at her. "Doing what?"

Her eyes looked away from me. "Taking care of me. I'm sure I'll be fine in a few days. I'm just glad I didn't break my ankle."

Smiling, I reached for her hand. It wasn't lost on me how her whole body shuddered. "Ryn, I want to take care of you." Grinning, I squeezed her hand. She gave me a shy grin back. We sat there and stared at each other until the sound of her cell phone snapped us out of the trance.

"Where's my purse?"

Standing, I walked over to the dining room table and grabbed her purse. Handing it back to her, she quickly dug around and pulled out her phone.

Clearing her throat she said, "Hello?"

I motioned that I was going to take a shower and then turned and headed to the stairs.

Halfway up, I heard her say, "Hey, Dodge, no everything is fine. I'm sorry I didn't get back in touch yesterday."

Knowing she was talking to that fucker had me balling up my fists. I'd like to pound his face into the ground. I slowly made my way up the stairs but stopped at the top. Ryn had lowered her voice some.

"Honestly, I'm perfectly fine. I just need some time like I said.

I have a lot to . . . think about it. Yes. No! No, I don't think you should try and come back down here. I may actually leave earlier."

I smiled hearing her tell him not to come back down, but then that smile quickly vanished when she said she might be leaving early. Fuck. How can I convince her to stay and how do I convince her to stay here with me?

"Take care of the club, Dodge. I'll be fine. I've got some work I need to catch up on so I'm going to take advantage of the peace and quiet and catch up on some emails and things."

I started to turn to head to my room. Ryn laughed, but still kept her voice down. "No, I'm going to just enjoy sitting on the deck, maybe go for a run."

A run? How in the hell does she think she is going to run with a . . .

Then it hit me. She wasn't telling him she was hurt. Grinning from ear to ear, I made my way to the shower. Operation: Win Ryn Back had officially begun.

CHAPTER
Ten

*W*HEN DODGE MENTIONED HEADING BACK to South Padre, I had to control myself. I about yelled out *no* in my panicked state. I definitely didn't want him knowing I sprained my ankle. He would have dropped everything to come back down and that was the last thing I wanted. Not when I was sitting in the middle of Tristan's living room and he was giving me one hundred percent of his attention.

Dodge was on the other end of the phone talking to someone at his club. "Just leave the delivery at the back door; I'll take care of it."

Closing my eyes, I did the one thing I wasn't totally sure I should be doing. "Dodge, we'll talk when I get back to Austin. Right now I just need some time to clear my head."

"Ryn, baby, you know I care about you. If you want to take this relationship further, I'm totally in all the way."

Letting out a breath, I whispered, "I know. I'm just not sure where I see *us* going."

Silence. "Ryn, I'm falling for you. You have to see that."

Dropping my head back against the sofa, I shook it slowly. Fuck me. Why do I have the wrong guy wanting to make a future together? "I do. I just don't want to rush into something because I'm trying to forget someone else. I like being with you, Dodge, it's fun and there are no expectations. Can we just keep it like that at least until after the holidays?" Hearing his frustration over the phone, he whispered, "Yeah, baby. I'll talk to you when you get back."

"Okay, talk to you soon."

Hanging up I felt a bit of pressure removed. Dodge was just supposed to be my rebound fuck buddy. Then it changed to just my fuck buddy. I liked it that way. I had no expectations of him having to romance me. We were just having fun. I had to admit I enjoyed his company, but he didn't make me feel alive like Tristan did. His touch didn't cause my stomach to drop. His smile didn't melt my insides completely.

Turning, I glanced toward the stairs. Tristan could be unbelievably sweet when he wanted to. I'd never let him know I heard him talking to me last night when he came in to check on me. Tristan whispered how he wished he could take the pain away and I almost called out to him when he began to leave.

Looking straight ahead, I admitted to myself what I had been so desperately trying to push away.

I was still in love with Tristan and I didn't want to get over him.

Ugh. I wanted him so damn much. It was all I dreamt about.

Even after him admitting he had slept with Sierra, I still wanted him. I was beginning to think I would forever want Tristan Williams. Not only did I want him in my bed, but I also wanted him in my heart.

What in the hell is that smell?

Looking around, I lifted my shirt I had slipped back on this morning. Pulling my head back quickly, I gagged.

"Ohmygod . . . I stink like a bar!" I needed to take a shower. I not only smelled like a bar, but I never took a shower after I went for my run yesterday morning.

Instantly feeling yucky, I went to stand. The pain medicine they had me on was strong and I felt dizzy. Attempting to move, I made it nowhere.

Shit. *Did the hospital give me crutches?*

Then the doorbell rang. I remembered the tacos Tristan had ordered and my stomach growled. Running down the stairs in nothing but sleeping pants, Tristan called out, "Don't move, Ryn! I've got it."

Standing there with my mouth hanging open, I reached up

to make sure I wasn't drooling. Tristan stood at the door dressed in nothing but a pair of cotton pants that hung on his hips, so low I was sure one small move and I'd see his ass. His back muscles flexed as he moved and I let out a soft moan.

Holy crap. I had forgotten how freaking amazing his body was. He had just the right amount of muscles. Shutting the door, Tristan began talking about the food as he walked toward me.

His abs. Oh lord almighty, his six-pack abs were moving in my direction. Licking my lips, I wanted to lick every inch of his body.

Get it together Kathryn Webster. Get. It. Together.

Stopping in front of me, Tristan looked at me. "What's wrong?"

His hair was wet and his emerald eyes pierced my baby blues. It should be a sin to be this good looking. I forgot how to talk.

"Ryn?"

My mouth fell open and I attempted to talk. The pressure between my hips was beginning to push the pain in my ankle way, far away. Or it was the pain meds I took. Either way, I was feeling like I was floating on a cloud of pure delight.

"Mmm . . ."

My stomach growled. "Damn, baby, sit back down and I'll get your tacos ready for you."

He called me baby. Something about Tristan calling me baby had my heart slamming against my chest and my stomach taking a deep dive south. I wonder if it would be too much to ask him if I could get a side of hot sex with those tacos?

"I need you." Tristan's head snapped up and looked at me. "Um, I mean I need a shower. I need to take a shower," I mumbled as I attempted to pull my eyes from Tristan's body.

Tristan looked at me like I was crazy as he asked, "Right now?"

Nodding my head, I said, "Yep. Right. Now."

Tristan set the bag of tacos down and then walked into the kitchen. Grabbing the crutches, he brought them back out to me.

"Ohh . . . that's right. I forgot I had used those earlier."

Tristan gave me a smile that melted my heart. "Those pain meds kicking in, Ryn?"

Grinning back, I whispered, "I'd say."

Handing me the crutches, I slowly made my way back to the master bathroom as Tristan followed. Once I got in there, the room started spinning. Tristan was by my side in less than a second.

His arms twisted around me and I instantly felt like I was in heaven. "Shit. Those pain meds really have you loopy, baby."

Turning, I took in a deep breath. Tristan smelled so damn good. There were so many things I had forgotten I loved about him. His smile. Okay, that I didn't forget. His touch, the smell of his body after he took a shower. The way my body hummed when Tristan laughed.

Ugh. I hate him.

Leaning closer, I decided I could take one more smell. Then I'd go back to hating him.

"Ryn, are you going to be able to do this? I should wrap up your ankle so the bandage doesn't get wet."

Looking down at my ankle and then to the shower, I shrugged. "How hard could it be?"

Tristan guided me to the small chair that was pushed into the vanity. "Here, wait here while I go get a trash bag."

Spinning on his heels, he left the bathroom and I sat there for a few minutes. Wow. *How many pain pills did I take?* I was going to have to ask Tristan if I was supposed to take one or two. I'm pretty sure I took one. *Maybe I took two? Wait. Did I take three?*

Shaking my head, I chuckled. "No, I wouldn't be stupid enough to take three. Would I?"

After having a brief conversation with myself out loud, I reached down and pulled the shirt off my head and tossed it to the floor. My bra went next. It was then I noticed I had only been in my panties.

Huh. How did I not notice that before? Wiggling my ass back and forth, I managed to slip them off and down my legs.

Whoa. There goes the room spinning again.

I stood and stared at the large walk-in shower. I was about to walk toward it when I remembered I was waiting for Tristan and a plastic bag. I also remembered I just stripped myself down to no clothes.

"Fuck," I whispered as I reached down for my panties and

shirt. My ankle was throbbing as I hopped around and sat back down on the chair. Carefully lifting my left leg, I slipped my panties on.

Shit. Shit. Shit. I heard Tristan walking through the bedroom. My heart raced when I realized he was going to walk in and see me sitting here, almost naked. Looking up right when he walked through the door, I saw his face. He slowly licked his lips as his eyes traveled over my body. When his mouth opened some, I was almost positive I heard him moan. Or whimper. Whimpering would be better. Yeah, I like whimpering. Serves his ass right. Get a good look at what you walked away from.

"Um . . ."

"I forgot you needed to wrap my ankle, I was just going to jump in," I said as I tried not to look at him.

"Ryn, how many pills did you take?"

Looking back at him, I touched the base of my neck as I tried to think of how many pills I took. "I don't remember."

He closed his eyes and moved closer to me. "Shit. I should have remembered to tell you to only take one. Then with the morphine they gave you last night, you're probably feeling pretty good right now, huh?"

An idea popped into my head. I knew what I was about to do was wrong on so many levels, but I had the perfect excuse. I was high on drugs. *Kind of.*

Smiling my most seductive smile, I bit down on my lower lip. "I guess you could say I'm feeling pretty good."

Tristan's eyes widened before he looked away and dropped to his knees. He gently lifted my ankle and began wrapping the plastic bag around it. Tying it on good, he leaned back onto his heels and smiled. "No water should get in. I've got it on pretty damn good."

I went to stand and really did feel dizzy. Tristan reached out for me. "I don't think I can stand in there alone, Tristan."

"Ahh . . ." I couldn't tell if the idea of being in the shower with me made him happy or scared the hell out of him.

My lower lip trembled as I asked, "Please? Everything is spinning and I feel so funny."

"Um . . . yeah, no."

My heart dropped the moment he said no. Nodding, I

whispered, "Okay, I'll make it work." Slipping my panties off the best I could, I reached for a crutch. I let out a small scream when Tristan reached down and lifted me up. He began walking me into the shower and I fought like hell not to smile.

"I didn't mean no, I wouldn't help you. I meant . . . I don't know what I meant, Ryn. Let's just get you cleaned up."

It wasn't lost on me that Tristan had kept his sleeping pants on. A part of me was glad he did. I wasn't sure what I would've done if I had seen his dick.

Oh. My. God. What is wrong with me? Get it together, Ryn.

Getting the water to the perfect temperature, Tristan moved me into the water. He had lifted my ankle and set it on the bench seat. "Does that hurt?"

Slowly shaking my head, I whispered, "No."

I reached for the soap and washcloth, but Tristan took it from me. Before I could stop him, he had the washcloth moving over my body. My heart was slowly breaking all over again when reality hit me. He was only taking care of me because I sprained my ankle. He felt responsible for taking care of me. Maybe I should have had Dodge come down.

Closing my eyes, I tried to just enjoy the few moments I had with Tristan. He slowly moved the washcloth over my body, cleaning me so tenderly as if another part of my body would break if he went too fast. Tristan squatted down as he cleaned both my legs. Glancing up, his eyes caught mine. Since my left ankle was sitting on top of the bench I was spread open to him. Tristan ran the washcloth up my right leg and I felt my body shudder as he grew closer to the area of my body that pulsed with desire.

Swallowing hard, Tristan began to clean between my legs. Biting down on my lip, I fought like hell to not let out a moan.

Then he withdrew the washcloth and I internally screamed out no. He stood and rinsed the washcloth off before he grabbed the removable showerhead and began rinsing me off. When the warm water hit between my legs, I sucked in a breath.

"Sorry," Tristan whispered as he quickly pulled it away. I shook my head and wanted to beg him to not stop. Hell, I wanted him to take me right there in the shower. Fuck the sprained ankle, I'd be able to push through the pain to feel Tristan buried inside of me.

Turning the water off, Tristan turned to me. "Let me get a towel and dry you off."

Jumping out of the shower, he stripped out of his pants and wrapped a towel around himself so fast I didn't even get to see a thing. I wanted to stomp my foot on the ground.

Then he reached in and took my foot down and helped me out of the shower. He dried off every inch of my body and then took the plastic bag off my foot. "Sit down, baby. I'll grab you some clothes."

Nodding my head, I sat down. As soon as he left the room, I let the tears fall. Maybe Tristan had found something with Sierra. Or maybe I had pushed him away for too long and he . . . he wasn't interested anymore.

I thought back to the other day on the beach when I ran into him. He seemed like he wanted me back, but maybe I was reading everything wrong. So many emotions ran through my head and I couldn't make sense of any of it. Wrapping my arms around my body, I attempted to stop my shivering.

Why did I have to be in love with Tristan still? Why?

I hadn't heard Tristan walk back into the bathroom. When he appeared in front of me and placed both hands on the sides of my face, I began to cry harder. I wanted this. I wanted Tristan to place his hands on my face and look at me like I was his entire world . . . not Dodge. I knew it in my heart, so why was my head fighting so hard with my heart?

"Ryn, baby what's wrong? Did you hurt yourself?"

His thumbs moved across my face to wipe the tears away. Closing my eyes, I took in the heat that was left in the path he made.

I couldn't stop crying. I felt like a fool sitting here getting upset over a man who pushed me away from him when things got to be too serious. Opening my eyes, I couldn't help but notice the pain in Tristan's eyes.

Slowly nodding my head, I whispered, "I'm sorry."

Tristan's hand moved down to my neck as he pushed his hand through my hair and pulled me a bit closer to him. "Baby, don't be sorry that you're in pain. I wish like hell I could take it away."

I wanted more than anything to tell him to kiss me and tell

me that he loved me. That would be the only way he could take this pain away.

"You can't," I barely said as our eyes locked. Tristan leaned in as my heartbeat picked up to a ridiculous rate. He stopped just short of my lips.

Inhaling a breath, I waited.

"But know if I could, I would."

Pulling back abruptly, he stood. "Let's get you dressed and back into bed."

Holding out a pair of boxer shorts and a T-shirt for me, I smiled and took them. Tristan helped me with the boxer shorts. Pulling his T-shirt over my head, I was overcome with his scent. Slowly standing, I reached for the crutch, but before I could grab it, Tristan reached down and picked me up. I snuggled my face into his chest. I wanted to tell him he didn't have to carry me, but I also wanted to be wrapped up in his arms.

Walking back into the living room, he set me on the sofa. Smiling, he gave me a wink and said, "First you have to eat. You can't be taking those pills on an empty stomach, Ryn."

Tristan and I ate our tacos in silence. The meds were for sure kicking in and I felt like I was fighting to keep my eyes open. I decided to shut them for just a few seconds.

I felt the motion of moving. Opening my eyes, I saw I was in Tristan's arms again. "Tristan, I'm so tired."

Tristan laid me down on the giant king-size bed. Pulling the covers over me, he leaned down and kissed my forehead. "Sleep, baby."

"Mmm . . . night, Tristan."

Hearing him chuckle he whispered, "It's only ten in the morning." Smiling, I lifted my hand to touch his face, but sleep took over my body.

I dreamed of a cabin in the woods and Tristan making love to me as he whispered how much he loved me.

CHAPTER
Eleven

TRISTAN

RYN HAD BEEN STAYING AT my place ever since she sprained her ankle. I was trying like hell to keep my hands to myself, but each day was getting harder and harder. There were a few times I thought for sure she wanted me to kiss her, but I wasn't going to take advantage of her being hurt to make a move on her. I wanted to show her I could take care of her and be with her without it being about sex.

Knowing Ryn was probably going stir crazy inside, I had arranged for us to eat dinner on the beach tonight.

Walking into the living room, I smiled. "You ready to head down to the beach?"

Smiling, Ryn nodded her head. "Are you sure you don't mind me staying here? I feel bad for taking up all of your vacation."

Shaking my head, I laughed. "Nonsense. It's been nice having you here."

Ryn's eyes lit up and I felt a sense of hope. I just needed to be patient. She hadn't talked to Dodge in over three days. At least, not that I knew of anyway. Reaching down, I picked her up.

"Tristan, you do realize I can walk."

Chuckling, I held her tighter. "Maybe I like having you in my arms."

Ryn looked at me with a weak smile before looking away.

For a brief moment, I saw something flash across her eyes. The time we were spending together was slowly bringing us closer.

We walked up to the blanket I had put out a few minutes earlier. Setting Ryn down on the blanket, she looked at me with a surprised look on her face. "What is this?"

Giving her a look like she had just wounded me, I said, "Dinner, what does it look like?"

Shaking her head, she said, "Something I can't picture Tristan Williams doing."

Placing my hand over my heart, I dropped to my knees. "You wound me, Kathryn."

Her smile instantly faded. I wasn't sure if it was from me calling her by her full name or if something else bothered her. Pushing it away, I opened the basket that contained our dinner.

Ryn leaned over to peek into the basket. The moment I pulled out the Subway sandwich, she started laughing. "Subway, huh? Wow you put some serious effort into this dinner."

Flashing a smile in her direction, I gave her wink. "Hey, it's a BMT and if my memory serves me right, that is your favorite sandwich from Subway."

Ryn's smile dropped as she nodded her head. "Yeah, it is."

After we ate, we talked for a bit about Ryn's company.

"How is your business doing?" I asked.

Grinning from ear to ear she said, "It's doing amazing. I've hired on two sourcing managers so I have a lot more time to take on other things, like gain more business."

Lifting my mouth into a smile, I looked into her eyes. "I'm proud of you, Ryn. I hope you're proud of yourself."

"I am. I've worked really hard to make this company successful."

Looking away, she shrugged. "Guess I wanted to prove to my parents I could do it."

Ryn hardly talked about her parents. Really she never talked about her past. The most I knew was that she went to college in Florida and moved to Austin the day after she graduated. She hardly ever talked to her parents, which seemed weird to me. Both Lark and I were close to our mother and father. I couldn't image my life without them in it.

Once the sun went down, we laid back and stared up at

the endless stars. I wanted desperately to tell her how sorry I was for what happened last Christmas, but something kept holding me back. I hated that I let my fear of giving myself to Ryn one hundred percent get in the way.

I wasn't sure if my lifestyle would be what Ryn wanted. My dream was to take over my father's ranch someday. Then, of course, there were my sexual hobbies. I never took Ryn to my condo in Austin. A part of me was scared to death that the moment I opened the door to my playroom, Ryn would turn and never look back. Liberty on the other hand, I knew she wouldn't get into my playroom. A part of me knew by bringing her there, I was hoping it would push her away. Unfortunately, it hadn't worked. If anything, Liberty tried harder to show me how amazing vanilla sex was.

No thanks.

I closed my eyes and thought back to the first time I ever saw a playroom filled with sex toys. It was a BDSM fan's dream come true.

STANDING AT THE BAR OF a new club in downtown Austin, I looked around at everyone. One of my college buddies, Nick, had said we had to check the place out. I couldn't help but notice the brunette that couldn't stop eye fucking me. Smiling, I nodded my head. She quickly made her way over to me and sat down next to me.

Reaching her hand out, she said, "Michelle. You are?"

Taking her hand, I kissed the back of it. "Anyone you want me to be."

Laughing, she gave me a wink. Her shoulder length hair fell in her eyes before she pushed it back behind her ears. "I knew my gut instinct about you was spot on." Looking out on the dance floor at Nick she gestured to him. "He single?"

Ahh hell. If this girl wanted a threesome, she was going to have to move along.

"Yeah. Why?"

Looking over her shoulder she motioned for another girl. They both looked to be around twenty-eight or twenty-nine. Turning back to me, she leaned in closer. "My friend Ash is interested in him. Tell me your name sweetheart."

Grinning, I said, "Tristan."

The other girl, Ash, walked up and ran her hand up my thigh and smiled. "Your friend's name?"

Moving my eyes over her body, I said, "Nick."

Ash and Michelle exchanged looks before Michelle moved closer to me and moved Ash's hand out of the way and placed her hand closer up toward my dick. Biting her lip, she grazed over my hardening dick. "Do you and Nick want to have some fun, Tristan?"

The way she said my name caused me to moan. I'd fucked plenty of girls while in high school and college, but something about these two had me thinking we were going to have more than just fun. This would be an experience I was more than ready to try.

"I'm game and I'm pretty damn positive Nick is down as well."

My eyes moved up and down Michelle's body. She was beautiful. Her body was wrapped in a tight black dress that barely covered her ass. Her long slender legs were finished off by red fuck-me shoes. Turning to Ash, she was almost a duplicate of Michelle, except she had short blonde hair.

Thirty minutes later, we were walking into a condo in one of the more expensive high-rise buildings downtown. Michelle turned on a few lights and pointed to the bar. "Make us some cosmopolitans, Tristan. Ash and I are going to go change into something more, suitable for the evening. I suggest the two of you start losing some of that clothing."

Turning, I looked at Nick who smiled and nodded his head. Looking back at Michelle, I wanted to ask what their plans were, but I closed my mouth and waited for them to leave.

Heading to the bar, I looked at Nick. "Dude, if they want some kind of foursome, I'm saying no right fucking now."

Nick held up his hands. "I'm right there with you. I'd be fucking scarred for life if I had to lay my eyes on your dick."

After making the drinks, Ash came out first. My mouth dropped to the floor as I watched her walk over to Nick. She was dressed in a red see through nighty and red high heel shoes.

"Nick baby. Are you ready for me?"

Nick stood there stunned. Like me, he had had his fair share of girls, but Ash and Michelle . . . these were not girls.

Nodding his head, Nick followed Ash as she led him down a hallway, but not before grabbing two drinks.

I watched as they disappeared around the corner. Turning around, I about dropped my drink. Michelle stood before me a baby-blue corset, black high heels and in her hand was a tie.

"You want me to put that on?" I asked as I smiled.

Shaking her head she smiled. "No, baby. I want you tie me up and fuck me in the ass."

"Holy fuck," I whispered. Walking up to me, Michelle took the drink from my hand and drank from it. Letting some of the liquid run down her chin she gave me a smile I would never forget.

"Tristan, I'm about to teach you things you've only dreamed about. Your world is about to be rocked, honey."

Taking my hand, she led me down another hallway opposite of the one Ash and Nick went down. Reaching the end of the hallway, she turned the doorknob and pushed open the door. Pulling me inside, I stopped and took a look around. The walls of the room were painted almost the same color as her blue corset. There was a giant king-size bed in one corner with bars along the back headboard. Looking to my left there was a giant chair that looked like a chaise lounge. Walking over to it, I ran my hand along the leather. "We'll start here, baby. I sure as hell hope you have stamina, if not, I'm going to teach you."

"TRISTAN? HEY, ARE YOU SLEEPING over there or what?"

Opening my eyes, I quickly sat up and looked at Ryn. She was staring at me with a concerned look on her face.

Could Ryn ever accept that part of my world? I'd only been twenty-three when I was introduced into another level of sexual satisfaction. A level I liked and wasn't sure I could give up for anyone. Would she find out and leave me for Dodge, or would she stay and let me teach the many different ways I could satisfy her? And satisfy her I could. Michelle had taken to me and we were together for over six months. I wouldn't say we dated. When she was in the mood for something a little more challenging she would call me. She also introduced me to the other side of the club that was more for those people who enjoyed a spicier sex life. Anytime I wanted to use my playroom, I just went to Midnight Rodeo and found a willing partner. And there were plenty. I sometimes would hook up with the same girl, sometimes I went for someone new. I gave up the club scene when I started dating Ryn. I picked it back up about six months ago when Liberty and I were more of an on again and off again couple.

"Tristan, where are you? Shit, you're like a million miles away."

Shaking my head, I stood up. "Sorry, I got to thinking about shit and one thing led to another."

Smiling, she winked. "Are you thinking about that stupid job of yours that you hate so much?"

Seeing this as an easy out to what I was really thinking about, I nodded my head. "Yeah."

Helping Ryn up, we gathered up the blanket and slipped it into the basket. I handed the basket to Ryn and picked her up. She giggled and said again, "You know I can walk if you would start letting me use the crutches. What am I going to do when we go back to Austin and you're not there to wait on me hand and foot?"

Winking, I said, "You'll just have to stay at my place."

Ryn ignored my comment and looked up as I walked back up to the house. "I'd give anything to look up and see this every single night," Ryn whispered.

"Do you not like living in Austin?"

She shook her head. "Not really. I tell Azurdee all the time how envious of her I am. I've actually thought about moving out toward the hill country. I need more space. It helps me think and clear my head."

I couldn't pull my eyes from her. I watched her as she stared up at the star-filled night sky. I gently set her down on the deck as I took the basket from her. Hope began to fill my heart. Ryn would probably love living at the ranch.

Taking in a deep breath, I was about to say something when Ryn began talking. "I guess we should head in. I'm kind of tired."

Nodding my head, I helped her back into the house and to her crutches.

Another missed moment that I let slip by. Again.

CHAPTER
Twelve

SITTING ON THE DECK OUTSIDE, I typed away on my computer. I had to admit when I first sprained my ankle I wanted to just cry. My whole vacation was ruined. But Tristan had made it even more fun. His sense of humor was beyond amazing. His cooking was to die for. If only he would touch me, or kiss me, or show some sort of interest in something other than being a gentleman and taking care of my every need.

My cell phone rang and I reached down for it.

Dodge.

I was pretty sure Tristan was out running, so I answered it.

"Hello?"

"Hey there, darling. How are you doing?"

Smiling, I said, "I'm doing good. How are you?"

"I'm better now that you've turned your cell phone back on and I'm hearing your voice."

I instantly felt guilty. I loved hanging out with Dodge. He was fun, carefree, and never made me feel like I owed him something. Well, at least until two weeks ago when he made me feel that way. Now he wanted more out of our relationship. I wasn't sure I wanted more with Dodge. I've always thought of him as my friend, well really, my fuck buddy friend who, for a while, was able to make me forget about Tristan—the man I so desperately wanted, but couldn't have.

"I know, I'll be glad to get back home. I miss my place."

"So, I'm thinking Christmas Eve. Dinner at my place?"

Closing my eyes, I let out a sigh. I didn't want to deal with this right now. I needed more time to think. "Um . . . well . . . I'm headed out of town the week before Christmas so I'm not sure I'll be back by Christmas Eve, Dodge."

"Oh, okay. No problem. What about New Years Eve then?"

Laughing, I looked out over the beach to the ocean. "Maybe."

"Ryn, I'm trying to be patient and let you decide what you want to do with our relationship. Shit. I guess I'm just missing you."

Smiling, I whispered, "I know, Dodge, I miss you too, I'm just not sure . . ."

Hearing something behind me, I turned to see Tristan standing on the deck. He was holding a coffee mug and his face showed he had just heard what I said.

"Hey, um, maybe we can chat later?"

"Yeah, sure. Let me know when you're coming home okay?"

Nodding my head, I said, "Yep. Will do. Bye."

Hitting End, I smiled. "Hey, I thought you were out running?"

Tristan looked away from me. "Why would you think that?"

Staring down at my hands before looking back to Tristan, I said, "Um . . . I guess I just thought you would be."

Tristan looked back at me. I sucked in a breath of air. Was that . . . hurt in his eyes? "So, I guess you're going to need to go back to Sierra's place and pack? I'm sure you're ready to get home."

"Tristan, is something the matter? You seem angry."

Setting the coffee cup down onto the table harder than I think he meant to, he stared into my eyes. "Nah, everything is fine. I just figured you were anxious to get home to Dodge, or at least it sounded like you were."

Shit. I hadn't wanted Tristan to hear me talking to Dodge. We had made so much progress the last week and a half. I was hoping this would carryover once we got to Austin.

"I'll get changed and bring you back to Sierra's place so you can get ready to leave."

Feeling like my whole world just stopped, I slowly nodded.

Tristan walked up to me and I looked at him. He looked as

if he wanted to say something to me. Closing his eyes, he whispered, "I'll be ready in ten minutes."

Barely talking above a whisper, I said, "I need to get my things together and I'll be ready to head over there."

Tristan turned on his heels and made his way past the pool and back into the house. My heart actually felt like it was breaking. Again.

The drive back over to Sierra's house was dead silent. Tristan had come over earlier to check on the house and my car. I felt guilty that I hadn't been staying at a place I was paying for. I didn't care though; I was thrilled at the idea of being alone with Tristan. It was part of the reason I had turned off my phone. There were so many times Tristan looked like he wanted to kiss me, or say something. He just couldn't do it. I wasn't sure if I was glad or happy. My days of hating him slowly disappeared with each time he picked me up and carried me in his arms, or he made me the most amazing home-cooked meal and served it to me in bed. He would then get under the covers with me and we would watch movies. It had been a perfect week and a half together.

Ugh. Why does my heart have to be so set on this stupid man sitting next to me?

Tristan pulled up and parked in Sierra's driveway. Helping me out of the truck, we made our way up to the house. Looking over my shoulder at Tristan, I couldn't help but notice he looked like he was feeling sick. As he pushed his hand through his hair, I wanted to ask him what was wrong.

I was managing to get around much better now with the crutches. Tristan walked up and dropped my bag onto the leather couch then looked into the kitchen. He shook his head as if he was trying to erase something from his memory. My eyes dropped to his hands, they were balled into fists. He was staring at the kitchen island and my conversation with Sierra resurfaced.

Oh. My. God. He knows.

"Did Sierra tell you?"

Pulling his head back, Tristan asked, "Tell me what?"

Swallowing hard, I turned back and looked at the kitchen island. He knows Dodge took me against the kitchen island. I saw it in his eyes. Looking back at him, I felt the need to explain everything about Dodge. How I had only used him for sex and that our relationship was nothing more than just that. Sex.

"Tristan . . . I'm so . . ."

Tristan held up his hand and attempted to smile. "Hey, whatever happens with you and Dodge is your business."

My eyes filled with tears. "Did you mean it?"

Tristan stared at me with a confused look. "Did I mean what?"

I let the tear fall and I could see what that single tear did to Tristan. He sucked in a breath of air and took one step closer to me. "You just answered my question by not knowing what I was asking."

"Ryn, what in the fuck are you talking about? You're talking in circles."

Smiling weakly, I said, "Thank you for taking care of me. I loved spending time with you again."

Tristan's eyes lit up and he moved closer to me. "I enjoyed it too, Ryn." My cell phone rang but I ignored it.

Taking another step closer to me, Tristan lifted his hand and placed it on the side of my face. Leaning my head into his hand, Tristan smiled. I wanted nothing more than for him to pull me into his arms and kiss the crap out of me.

Leaning in closer, Tristan's lips hovered just above mine. My cell began ringing again and for some reason thinking it might be the office, I reached into my back pocket and swiped to answer it without looking.

"This is Ryn Webster."

My eyes moved across Tristan's face before they landed on his lips. *Kiss me damn it!*

Tristan reached up and was about to take the cell phone from my ear.

"Hey babe, are you packing up?"

Dodge.

Taking a step away from Tristan, I spoke into the phone. "Hey. Yeah, I um, I'm getting ready to start packing now."

In that moment I could see it on Tristan's face. He knew it was Dodge.

Oh God. Why did I answer the phone? Why didn't I just let him take my phone and hang up?

"When you get back, dinner's on me if you get in early enough."

"That sounds like a plan. Okay, I'll let you know when I'm leaving and . . ."

Tristan turned and began heading to the front door. Panicking, I began to try and walk after him.

"Dodge, can I call you back in a few minutes?"

Tristan picked up his pace and made it to the front door. Pulling it open, I called out after him. "Tristan? Tristan, please wait!"

I stared at the door as I listened to him start up his truck and pull out of the driveway.

Dropping the cell phone from my hand, I wrapped my arms around myself to control my sobs.

"Why did I answer the phone? Oh God . . . why?"

CHAPTER
Thirteen

$\mathcal{S}$ HUTTING THE DOOR BEHIND ME, I walked away quickly. I knew Ryn couldn't move fast enough to catch me before I got to my truck.

Opening the door, I jumped in, started my truck and backed out of the driveway. I didn't bother to look back. It was clear to me that Ryn had moved on. Sierra was wrong; Dodge wasn't Ryn's fuck buddy. He was more.

I wanted to get back to the house, pack my shit, head back to Austin and put the last two weeks behind me.

WALKING INTO STARBUCKS, I SMILED when I saw her. Standing there talking away to some poor older woman was Sierra. The older lady would nod every now and then to be polite, but I could tell she just wanted Sierra to stop talking to her. Ordering my coffee, I made my way over to the table.

It was as if Sierra could tell I was there before she saw me. Looking over her shoulder, Sierra smiled when she saw me. Turning back to the older lady she said, "Excuse me, my fuck buddy is here. Gotta run."

The older woman's mouth dropped open and she said, "Oh my goodness," as she watched Sierra walk up to me. Kissing me on the cheek, Sierra asked as she wiggled her eyebrows up and down, "So? Did y'all make up and end up having hot sex?"

Feeling my stomach drop, I looked away.

"Well? I'm waiting to hear all the juicy details."

My expression was emotionless as I turned back to her. "Sorry, darlin.' There are no juicy details to share."

Sierra narrowed her eyes at me. "Tristan! You promised you were going to talk to her. You had her living in your house! What in the hell!"

Looking around, I grabbed Sierra and pulled her to the side of the room. "Jesus, Sierra, keep your voice down."

Placing her hand on her hips, she rolled her eyes. "What happened?"

The barista called out Sierra's name and then mine. Getting our coffee, we headed outside to sit. Letting out a deep breath, I started talking. "I wanted to show her I could take care of her, without sex and all that other shit. There were a few times I thought there was something brewing between us, but one of us would pull away."

Blowing on her coffee, Sierra shook her head. "Okay, so y'all didn't get it on, but how did you leave things? Did you make plans to take her to dinner or anything?"

Looking away, I mumbled, "Not really."

Leaning closer to me, Sierra said, "Excuse me? I didn't understand what you said."

Remembering how I left Ryn was making me feel sick to my stomach.

"Oh. My. Gosh. You didn't. You acted like a dick again, didn't you? Pushed her away when things got to heated huh, Tristan?"

Giving Sierra a dirty look, I shook my head. "No. Not really. Well, kind of."

Taking a drink of her coffee, Sierra gave me a look. "What does that mean? Kind of?"

"I tried a few times to talk to her, but I just couldn't."

"Pussy," Sierra said as she sat back in her chair. The guy next to us turned and gave Sierra a look.

"I tried, I was about to kiss her the last day we were together. I brought her back to your place so she could pack up and her damn cell phone rang. She answered it and when she realized it was Dodge, she took a step away from me and kept talking to him while I fucking stood there like an idiot."

Sierra made a face and whispered, "Ouch."

Taking a sip of my coffee, I nodded my head. "Yeah. Ouch."

Leaning forward, Sierra placed her elbows on the table. "Maybe she was just being polite."

I shook my head and looked away. "Nope. Heard her talking to him before I brought her back to your place. She said she missed him. My guess was they were making plans to get together when she got back."

Blowing out a breath of air, Sierra asked, "Why didn't you offer to follow her home, Tristan? You know. Make sure she made it home okay with her sprained ankle and all."

Shit. I hadn't thought of that.

I fell back in the chair. "Sierra, guys don't think like girls."

Chuckling, Sierra said, "No shit. Life would be so much better if you did."

Giving her a smirk, I asked, "How have you been?"

A look of sadness spread across her face as her eyes looked down. "My ex is taking me to court. He's claiming I used money that belonged to him to buy my house."

"What? Did you?"

Snapping her head up, she glared at me. "No! Why would you ask me that?"

"Guys don't think like women."

"Ugh. I hate him so much, Tristan. He is just trying to make my life miserable. He had the nerve to call and ask me if I've been dating. If not, maybe I'd like to . . . to . . ."

"To what? What did he want you to do?"

Shaking her head and smiling like she couldn't believe what she was saying, she whispered, "He wanted me to come over and puff his peter."

Pulling my head back in shock, my mouth dropped open. "What?"

Lifting her eyebrows. "Puff his peter, you know."

Slowly shaking my head, I looked at her. "What?"

Dropping her shoulders and letting out a frustrated moan she said, "Suck his dick, Tristan. He wanted me to come over and suck his dick. Peter puffing. You know, give him a blow job, deep throat his ass."

Holding up my hands, I started laughing as I looked around. The gentleman next to us got up and walked away. "Jesus, Sierra. Why do you talk so damn loud?" I asked as I continued to laugh.

"I'm glad to see this is giving you a good laugh."

I was almost doubled over from laughing so hard. "Sorry . . . can't . . . stop . . . laughing!"

Sierra rolled her eyes as she lifted her coffee and took another drink.

When I finally got my laughter under control, I asked, "What did you say when he asked you this?"

"I told him to go get his lover to do it. Then I hung up on him."

Nodding my head, I said, "Good. You shouldn't even be talking to him. Next time he calls, just send him to voice mail."

"Okay, dad."

Chuckling, I took in the light chatter of everyone sitting around us. There was something about a coffee shop that just seemed to put me at ease.

Taking a drink of my coffee, I casually looked around at everyone. Looking back over Sierra's shoulder, I saw Ryn and Dodge walking up. Motherfucker.

Looking down quickly I acted like I hadn't seen them. "So what are your plans for the holidays?"

"Oh gosh, I don't even want to think about the holidays."

"Why?" I asked, genuinely wanting to know.

Drooping her shoulders, she said, "I used to love the holidays. We would always go to my ex's family's. It was fun and I loved my mother-in-law. This will be my first Christmas in a long time I won't see them."

Tears formed in her eyes and I almost reached across the table to take her hand, but saw Ryn and Dodge walking up to our table.

"Fancy seeing y'all here," Ryn said. Glancing up at her, I could tell she was pissed. She had no right to be pissed. She was standing next to her boy toy.

Sierra jumped up. "Ohmygosh! Ryn! Tristan told me you sprained your ankle. How are you feeling?"

Ryn gave Sierra a weak smile and then looked at me.

"Appears y'all share a lot with each other."

Sierra looked at Ryn with a surprised expression. "What does that mean?"

Ryn's eyes showed she immediately regretted what she had said. I couldn't help but notice Dodge staring at Sierra.

Ryn smiled. "Nothing. Sorry, pain meds are still making me loopy and kind of grumpy."

Sierra smiled and looked at Dodge. It wasn't lost on me the way her eyes moved up and down Dodge's body before she quickly looked back up at his face. Flashing that smile of hers, Sierra stuck out her hand. "I don't think we've really been introduced. I'm Sierra Jackson."

Dodge took Sierra's hand. "Dodge Walker."

Lifting her eyebrow and tilting her head, Sierra said, "You don't look like a Dodge. Nickname?"

Letting out a laugh, Dodge said, "Yeah. My first name is Aaron."

Biting on her lip, Sierra looked him up and down as I rolled my eyes and looked away. Catching a glimpse of Ryn, I noticed she was staring at me.

"I like that. Suits you well."

Turning back to the two fuck buddies, one a real one and the other a terrible fake, I cleared my throat. Sierra was pulled from her temporary trance and turned back to Ryn. "Would you like to catch a movie sometime? If I thought this one would hit up a chick flick with me I'd ask him, but I highly doubt that will happen."

Ryn's eyes bounced from me to Sierra. I knew she was trying to gage the relationship and having a hard time doing it.

Standing, I reached for my coffee. Hoping to let Ryn know there was nothing going on between me and Sierra, I looked at Sierra and said, "I need to leave and what you need, Sierra, is to get laid and soon."

Spinning around, Sierra reached over and slapped the hell out of my arm. "Shut up, Tristan." Turning back to Ryn and Dodge, Sierra said, "I've got to run to. Have to be to work in a few minutes and I'm going to be late. I hope we can get together soon, Ryn."

Smiling weakly, Ryn nodded and said, "Yeah. Sure." Then

she looked at me. I lifted my hand and said, "Have a good day, Ryn . . . Dodge."

Dodge gave me a head pop and said, "Um . . . yeah, you too."

Walking away, I felt the jealousy and anger building. Didn't take Ryn long to hook back up with Dodge. I was beginning to think there was a hell of a lot more going on than just fuck sessions between the two of them.

Getting in my BMW, I slammed the door shut and dropped my head back against the seat and whispered, "Fuck."

I jumped when someone knocked on my window. Opening my eyes and lifting my head, I looked to see Ryn standing outside my car. My heart started beating loudly and for one second I was scared to death to roll down the window. My hand felt like it was covered in lead as I reached over and hit the button to roll the window down.

"Hey, what's up?" I causally asked.

"You left and didn't give me a chance to thank you for everything."

Giving my best smile, I tried to talk but nothing came out. Clearing my throat, I said, "Nah, you thanked me enough over the week, Ryn. It was my pleasure."

Her eyes looked sad. "You didn't give me a chance to explain why I answered my cell."

Swallowing hard, my eyes darted over to where Dodge was standing, waiting for Ryn. Slowly looking back at Ryn, I asked, "Does it matter anymore?"

"I think it might," Ryn said barely above a whisper.

Shaking my head, I looked away. "I saw the conflict in your eyes, Ryn. In that moment it was as if you had to pick—kiss me, or talk to your precious Dodge."

Glancing back, my eyes caught hers. "I still see the conflict in your eyes, but the problem is, you picked him, Ryn."

Starting the car, I put it in drive and pulled away.

CHAPTER
Fourteen

$\mathcal{S}$ TARING AT TRISTAN'S BMW AS he drove away, I fought to hold back my tears. Closing my eyes, I wrapped my arms around myself. It wasn't cold outside, but my body shook.

"Ryn? Are you okay?"

Dodges voice was filled with concern. I had asked him to coffee this morning to tell him I didn't see our relationship going any further.

Shaking my head, I whispered, "No, Dodge. I'm not okay."

"Let's head inside and order some coffee, Ryn."

Dodge placed his hand on the small of my back as he led me toward the door to Starbucks. My mind was racing as I took Tristan's words in.

He thought I had picked Dodge. I knew those days we spent together we were getting closer. I could see it in Tristan's eyes how many times he wanted to kiss me. Why we were both pulling away from each other, I didn't know.

Dodge ordered both of our coffees as I mindlessly moved to a table.

I sat and stared out the window. I did know why I was pulling away from Tristan. I was scared to death to open myself back up to him. Was he interested in me because he didn't have Liberty or Sierra around? Was I second best?

Closing my eyes, I thought to that moment when Tristan was

going to kiss me and I answered my cell. The hurt in his eyes about dropped me to the floor. Then not even five minutes ago, I saw the same hurt in his eyes.

You picked him, Ryn.

Setting both coffees onto the table, Dodge pulled out a chair. Looking up, I tried to smile but I knew Dodge would know it was a ruse.

"Talk to me, Ryn."

Taking in a deep breath, I slowly blew it out. I knew I couldn't keep doing what I had been doing the last ten months. I was using Dodge as a means to push Tristan from my head . . . and my heart. It wasn't working and what I needed was time alone to clear my head and think.

It was time for me to, for once in my adult life, not have a man confusing the hell out of me.

"Dodge, I wish I could sit here and tell you that I saw us moving forward but . . . I . . . I just can't."

Dodge looked down and then quickly back up into my eyes. He slowly nodded his head as he smiled weakly. "I guess I always knew we were just having fun."

"I want to be completely honest with you, Dodge. I still love, Tristan."

Dodge tilted his head and stared into my eyes. "I know that, Ryn. Believe me, I know how you feel about Tristan."

My heart hurt for what I was doing to Dodge. Shaking my head, I said, "Dodge, did you see how Sierra looked at you today?"

Jerking his head back, Dodge laughed. "What?"

"Sierra, the way her eyes lit up when she looked at you. I see women all the time look at you just like she did. I'm holding you back and it's not fair."

Reaching across the table, Dodge took my hand in his. "I don't want any other women, I want you. I'm falling in love with you, Ryn."

I tried to dig deep down inside to say what I was about to say. "Dodge, I wish I could give you what you wanted, but I need to clear my head and figure out some things. I care about you so much and you've been such an amazing friend . . . but . . ."

Letting go of my hand, Dodge whispered, "But you don't love me like you love, Tristan."

My voice cracking, I whispered, "Dodge."

Dodge stood and gazed down at me. He nodded his head and gave me that grin that I loved so much. "I'm not going to push you into anything or make you feel like you have to decide now. I'll be here, Ryn. I'm not sure for how long, but for now . . . I'm here."

I stood and moved into Dodge's arms. "Thank you for giving me the space and time I need, Dodge."

Pulling me closer to him, Dodge whispered against my forehead, "I'll talk to you soon, baby."

Dropping his arms he took two steps back. Winking, he turned and began to walk away.

Placing my hand over my mouth, I began to cry. I wasn't sure why, but it felt as if I lost something I wasn't ready to lose.

WALKING INTO MY HOUSE, I heard my home phone ringing. No one ever called me on my home phone. Running to it, I picked it up and hit the answer button. My ankle throbbed from the motion. It had only been a month since I sprained it and it wasn't healing all that well.

"Hello?"

"Kathryn?"

My heart stopped beating as I heard my mother's voice on the other end of the phone. "Mom?"

"I would have called your cell phone, but I must have misplaced it. How have you been?"

"Um . . . I've been good. How have you and Dad been?"

"We've been good. So have you had your fill of Texas yet? Are you coming home?"

Dropping my purse on the table, I rolled my eyes. "No, Mom, I'm not going to be coming back to Florida. I told you this."

"Kathryn, this has gotten old. Your father and I have been patient with you while you've gone off and found yourself. Now it's time to come back home."

Letting out a sigh, I leaned against the counter. Here was

the overbearing mother I left Florida to get away from.

"Next week is Thanksgiving, book a flight and we'll spend a few days looking for a place for you."

Irritation flared within me as I listened to my mother try to run my life. Again. Not this time. Hell would freeze over before I ever let my mother run my life.

"Mom, I'm a grown woman and you can't tell me how to live my life or where to live it. I'm happy here in Austin. My business is growing and . . ."

"Oh, Kathryn, you have such a bright future here. I've already made plans for a friend of mine to join us for Thanksgiving dinner. I think you would be interested in hearing what she does for a living. I think a new career is exactly what you need, darling. Oh, I almost forgot. Kathryn, guess who I ran into? Your old high school boyfriend, Ward. He asked about you, darling, and I told him you would probably be home for Thanksgiving."

Oh. My. God. Was I hearing this right? My mother was insane.

"Mom, I need you to listen to me and listen closely. First, I'm not coming home for Thanksgiving. As a matter of fact, I have no intention of *ever* coming back to Florida. Second, I don't give a rat's ass about Ward, Mom. And third, when you learn to accept the fact that I am happy with my life and where I have chosen to live that life, and who I want to spend it with . . . then maybe we can talk. Until then, we have nothing else to say."

"What has happened to you, Kathryn? Your father and I just want to see you. Is it so much to ask for you to come home and see your parents?"

Sucking in a breath of air, my mother went to talk again but I cut her off. "Mom, I'd love to have you and dad here. Think about coming and visiting me here in Austin. I have a meeting, Mom, I have to go. Tell Dad I said hi and I miss him."

Hitting End, I tossed the phone on the counter and stood there for a few moments. Shaking my head, I decided to not let my mother get under my skin today.

Reaching in my purse for my cell phone, I pulled it out. Scanning my phonebook, I saw Sierra's number. For one brief moment, I wanted to call her and see if she wanted to go to dinner and hit a club. I knew the only reason I wanted to see her was to find out about her and Tristan. Mainly Tristan.

Shaking my head, I kept scanning until I found Marie's number. I'd met Marie at a conference in Chicago last year and we hit it off fabulously. A night out was just what I needed.

Heading to my closet, I pulled out my latest little black dress and looked it over. Smiling, I hit Marie's name and began making plans to let loose for the evening.

CHAPTER
Fifteen

TRISTAN

ULLING UP TO THE FRONT of Midnight Rodeo, I quickly got out of my BMW and smiled at the valet driver. Tossing him my keys, he nodded his head. "Enjoy your evening, Mr. Williams."

"I intend to," I said with a wink and a smile. Making my way into the club, the bass moved through my body and instantly had my dick coming to life. Heading over to the bar, I motioned for Renee and she gave me a quick head pop. I came in this place enough for them to know what my usual was. Taking a quick look around while I waited for my beer, I spotted Michelle. Shaking my head, I smiled. That woman would never get tired of this scene. She was talking to a guy who couldn't have been more than twenty-two years old. I gave him two minutes tops before he was following her out the door.

"Here ya go, Tristan! It's been awhile," Renee shouted over the music.

Nodding my head, I yelled back, "Been busy."

Winking, she gave me a thumbs-up. "It's on the house. Enjoy yourself and stay safe."

"Thanks, Renee."

Renee was a thirty-three year old single mother. Her five-year-old daughter was adorable. The only reason I'd ever met her was because I ended up with Renee one night when I couldn't find anyone I wanted on the other side of the club. I sat at the bar and talked to her all night. Before I knew it, I was in her bed fucking the hell out of her. Renee's ex decided to bring their daughter home early that morning before I ended up leaving.

Glancing back over to Michelle, I couldn't help but notice the poor kid she had successfully wrapped around her finger. Taking him by the hand, she led him out of the club. Shaking my head, I looked at my watch. "She's still got it."

Taking a drink of my beer, I scanned the dance floor. The other side of the club was just an extension of the main club. Most people knew you only made your way over there if you were interested in hooking up for a night of good hard fun. Some though, just went over because they were able to dance and have a bit more hands on fun. It wasn't a sex club and anyone caught having sex was thrown out immediately.

After not really seeing anyone of interest, I began making my way over to the other side. Kesha's "Sleazy" was playing and there was some hot and heavy dancing going on.

A brunette walked up to me smiling. "Dance with me, handsome?"

Grabbing her hand, I made my way to the dance floor. What I needed was a mindless fucking. Someone to bury my cock in and forget all the other shit going on in my life.

Once we started dancing, I had a feeling I'd found my fun for the night. Turning, she pushed her ass into my dick and began rocking against me. She grabbed my hands and pulled them up to her tits as I grabbed them and moaned against her neck. "You want to be fucked, honey?"

Turning to me, she ran her tongue along her top teeth. "You like to play?"

Grinning from ear to ear, I nodded my head. "Fuck yeah, I do."

"My place or yours?"

I hadn't brought anyone back to my house since last Christmas. I wasn't sure why, it just didn't feel right. "Your place."

Wrapping her arms around my neck, she said, "I want to dance some more, you cool with that?"

I started to answer her when something caught my eye. Looking to my right, I saw Ryn dancing with a guy. His hands were moving up and down her body as she grinded up against him. *What in the fuck is she doing here?* There was another girl on the other side of the guy. I wasn't sure if Ryn knew her or not. I'd never seen her or the guy Ryn was dancing with before on this side of the club.

I couldn't pull my eyes from Ryn. My palms began to sweat as anger flowed through my blood. I wondered if Ryn had any idea what this side of the club was even used for. The brunette turned and followed my stare. "Don't bother with that group babe, they're only here for the music. I already approached them. I was in the mood for a ménage a trois, and they clearly were not." She started laughing as she shook her head and turned back to me. "You know what, handsome, I'm so damn horny; let's bust out of this place."

Looking back down at her, I shook my head. "Changed my mind, honey. Sorry."

Walking away from the brunette, I made my way over to Ryn. Stopping at them, the guy looked at me. "Sorry, dude, they were mine first."

Ryn turned and stopped dancing the moment she saw me. "Tristan, what are you doing here?" Looking around, Ryn must have noticed how everyone was dancing. She took a few steps away from the asshole she was dancing with.

"What the fuck are you doing here, Ryn?"

Anger moved over her face. "I'm dancing, asshole."

Grabbing her hand, I pulled her closer to me. "Ryn, this side of the club is for people who want to hook-up for sex, and not just any kind of sex. Most are into fetish shit."

Ryn's mouth gapped open in surprise. Thank God. By her response she had no clue.

Hitting the other girl, Ryn shouted, "Marie! We need to go back to the other side of the club!"

Marie jetted out her lower lip, but nodded her head, turned and began heading back to the other side. I was still holding onto Ryn's arm as I moved her through the group of people. Once we got through the mob, she yanked her arm from me. "I think we can manage from here, thanks."

Ryn went to turn and leave before she stopped and looked back at me. Her eyes widened and she went to say something, but closed her mouth quickly. Looking away for a few seconds she turned back and captured my eyes. "What were you doing over there, Tristan?"

Fuck.

"Looking for my friend, he headed over to that side a few minutes ago, I was checking on him."

Tilting her head, Ryn looked my body up and down. I was pretty sure she wasn't aware that she was biting down on her lip, causing it to turn white from how hard she was putting pressure on it.

Giving her the smile that I knew made her weak in the knees, I winked. Her mouth parted open slightly, and for one brief moment, I wanted to take Ryn back to my condo and show her how I could make her feel pleasure she'd only dreamed of. Then, I remembered the look of horror that was on her face not more than a minute ago.

"Are you here with Sierra?" Ryn asked.

Jerking my head back, I just stared at her. I wasn't expecting that. Was Ryn jealous of Sierra? Narrowing my eyes, I said, "No. Should I be?"

"Oh . . . um . . . well I guess I just assumed."

Leaning closer to her, I moved my lips to her ear. "You assume too much, Ryn."

Pulling back, I smiled, turned and headed toward the exit. I needed to get the fuck out of this club. Ryn looked amazing in the black dress she was wearing. I wanted to rip it from her body and take her right there on the spot. I did want to chuckle though when I saw she was wearing flip-flops. I'm sure because of her ankle, she couldn't wear heals yet.

Once the cool air hit my face, I dragged in a deep breath. Closing my eyes, I dropped my head back. "Son-of-a-bitch," I whispered.

"Leaving already, sir?"

Snapping my head forward, I was looking at the valet driver. "Yeah, sorry, the mood's been killed."

Nodding his head, he turned and took off running toward the valet parking lot. I needed to get away from Austin for awhile. Pulling out my phone, I sent Lark a text.

Me: Is that invite for Thanksgiving still open?

Lark: Always, dude. Can you come a few days earlier?

Me: Sounds good. I need wide open space to clear my thoughts.

Lark: You're welcome anytime. Come whenever you want.

The valet driver pulled up and parked my black BMW right in front of me. Walking to him, I handed him a tip, got in my car, and decided maybe I needed to work on moving on from Ryn.

Running my hand through my hair, I let out moan. "Time to move on, Tristan. Time to move on."

SITTING IN THE JEEP, I looked out over the hill country. "It's beautiful here."

Lark let out a chuckle. "Yeah, it is. You tired of the corporate world yet, big brother? You could come help me here."

Turning toward Lark, I smiled. "When I give up my godforsaken shit ass job, I'm heading down to the ranch."

"Ah . . . South Texas is where your heart belongs, huh?"

Closing my eyes for a brief second, I opened them and looked out over the hills again. "I'm not really sure where my heart belongs anymore."

I knew Lark was looking at me, but I kept my eyes fixed out over the countryside. "Are things over for good with Liberty?"

Laughing, I nodded my head. "Yeah. That's been over for a while now. I haven't heard from her since your wedding."

"Sierra?"

"A friend and that's all. She's going through some shit right now with her dirtbag ex and I'm not going to abandon her. Besides, she is funny as hell to hang out with."

Lark mumbled, "Fair enough."

"Before you say it, Ryn has moved on. I thought maybe there might have been something still there between us when we were at the beach house . . . but there wasn't."

Lark was silent, so I turned to look at him. He was staring straight ahead. "Are you sure about that, Tristan? What's your heart telling you?"

Dropping my head back, I laughed my ass off before looking back at Lark. "It's telling me I'm better off being single. Besides, I don't think Ryn would get into my . . . other lifestyle."

Rolling his eyes, Lark slowly shook his head. "You're not even giving her the chance to decide that for herself. Besides, from what Azurdee says, Ryn isn't as innocent as you think she is."

Looking straight ahead, I smiled as I thought about some of the moments Ryn and I shared together.

"I'm not so sure she is ready to find out I have a whole damn room in my condo in Austin for nothing but sexual fun, Lark."

"And I never thought Azurdee would screw me on my bike while people watched us . . . but she did. And she liked it."

Getting out of the Jeep, I turned to Lark. "Dude, really? I didn't need to hear that and I sure as hell didn't need the visual." Running my hands down my face, I let out a frustrated moan. "Shit. I'm never gonna get that out of my memory now."

CHAPTER
Sixteen

Ryn

ALKING INTO STARBUCKS, I LOOKED around for Sierra. She was sitting at a table talking to an older woman. The way she smiled and talked to the woman caused me to smile. I could see why Tristan would be attracted to her. I could see why any man would be attracted to Sierra. She was carefree, friendly, and funny as hell.

Sierra looked up and lifted her hand in a wave. Waving back, I pointed to the counter. Placing my order for coffee, I walked over and sat down at the table with Sierra and the older woman.

"Darling, have you always been so outspoken?" the older woman asked Sierra. Smiling, I wondered what it was Sierra had said. Glancing over to Sierra, I raised my eyebrow at her.

Grinning a Cheshire cat smile, Sierra purred, "Yes. Yes, I have."

The older woman and Sierra started laughing. My name was called out and I headed up to the counter as the older woman stood and excused herself. By the time I made it back to the table, Sierra sat back smiling at me like she didn't have a care in the world. A small tinge of jealousy raced through my body as I thought back to Tristan telling me that he and Sierra had slept together.

Sitting, I began chewing on my lip. Sierra leaned forward

and looked me in the eyes. "Tell me what's on your mind, Ryn. I can see your mind is racing with stuff."

Swallowing hard, I glanced down to my coffee before looking back up at Sierra. "I know I have no right asking this, and please set me straight if I'm overstepping my boundaries here . . ."

Placing her chin on top of her hands, Sierra said, "I feel a *but* coming on."

My hands started sweating and my heart felt like it had begun racing a hundred miles an hour. Was I sure I wanted to ask Sierra about her and Tristan? Was I ready to hear her response? Why did I even care? I gave up on guys. I was taking a break. I didn't need a man in my life.

What I did want was a friendship with Sierra and I knew this whole thing with Tristan was the reason I kept sending her calls to voicemail.

"Sierra, I'm really glad we met and I think that we could really be great friends."

"I agree, Ryn."

Blowing out a breath, I fell back in the chair. "Shit, I'm just going to come out and ask. Are you and Tristan together? What I mean is, are you dating each other?"

Sierra grinned. "No. We're friends, Ryn. That's all."

I was on a roll now and apparently my mouth moved before my head thought about it. "Friends with benefits?"

Tilting her head and giving me a look, she asked, "You mean like you and Dodge?"

Ouch. I guess I deserved that one.

"I guess I deserved that one."

Giving me a smirk, she winked. "No, Ryn. Tristan and I are not fuck buddies." Looking away for a brief second, she looked back at me. "I'm not going to lie to you and say we haven't hooked up because we have and it was fairly recently, but it meant nothing to either one of us."

Feeling the burn in my eyes, I nodded as I turned away. "I know I have no right to be jealous, Sierra, believe me I know that. I can't help it though. The idea of you and Tristan together . . ."

Sierra reached across the table and took my hand in her hand. "Ryn, please listen to what I'm about to say, okay?"

Nodding my head, I whispered, "Okay."

"I hate to see you and Tristan pushing each other away because I know how you both feel about each other. With my own husband cheating on me, I totally get where you are coming from, Ryn. You don't want to open yourself up to him hurting you again. But isn't that what love is all about? Opening our hearts up and taking that leap of faith and not having a damn clue where we are going to land."

Smiling, I agreed with Sierra. "Yes, but it is scary as hell taking that leap when you've already fallen hard once before, Sierra."

Letting out a gruff laugh, Sierra said, "Girl, don't I know. Believe me you . . . I know." Chewing on her bottom lip, I knew she wanted to say more and was conflicted about if she should or not.

Clearing her throat, Sierra said, "Um, I know this is none of my business and Tristan would be really pissed with me even saying anything, but I have to. Ryn, there is a reason Tristan got spooked last year and pushed you away, and it has nothing to do with Liberty."

Trying to keep my heart from pounding out of my chest, I slowly took a deep breath. *Tristan got spooked?* Opening my mouth to say something, I heard a familiar voice.

"Hey, Ryn, Sierra, how are you both doing?"

Glancing up, I saw Dodge standing there. Shit! Glancing back to Sierra, I had more questions for her.

Sierra looked toward Dodge and I couldn't help but notice how her eyes lit up and the smile that spread across her face seemed to light up the area around her.

Oh. My. Gosh. Sierra likes Dodge!

"Oh, hey there, Dodge. Have you always come to this Starbucks?" Sierra asked. Looking back at Dodge, he smiled and nodded his head.

"Yes ma'am."

Sierra leaned back and raised her eyebrows. "Huh. I can't believe I've never seen you here before."

"Yeah, same here."

My mouth dropped open when I saw that look move across Dodge's face. For one brief moment, he was interested in Sierra. He quickly recovered and said, "It's good seeing you both. I've got a meeting I need to get to, see y'all later."

I watched Sierra eye fuck the hell out of Dodge as he walked away. Dodge turned and gave a quick wave of his hand before walking out of Starbucks.

Sierra regained her composure, even though I'm almost positive she wiped a bit of drool from her mouth. Looking back at me, she smiled.

"Oh my gosh, you have the hots for Dodge!"

Sierra pulled her head back and gave a nervous laugh. "What?"

Pointing to her, I chuckled. "You practically undressed him as he walked out the door."

Brushing me off with her hand, she rolled her eyes. "Bitch, please. I'm in the middle of a nasty breakup. The last thing I want is another guy in my life."

Smiling until my cheeks hurt, I leaned in closer. "You know, Dodge is pretty good at making you forget things." I winked at her as she rolled her eyes.

Sierra mumbled, "Yeah right. He's done such a fabulous job with you."

Leaning back in my chair, I shook my head. "I don't count. I'm in love with Tristan. You can't stand your ex."

Jumping up and nearly knocking her chair over, Sierra pointed at me and jumped up and down while yelling out, "I knew it! I flippin' knew it! Ha! I'm so damn good at this shit!"

Grabbing her and pulling her back into her seat, I put my finger up to my lips to hush her.

"Good lord, Sierra! Keep it down." Looking around, I offered my apologies to everyone as they shook their heads in disbelief that anyone would have an outburst in their precious coffee shop.

Giggling like a schoolgirl, Sierra kept repeating. "I knew it! I so knew you were not over him."

Then her smile dropped. "Shit. That must mean, *Homerun* isn't that good with his bat."

Narrowing my eyes at her I said, "Wait. What? You mean Dodge?"

"Yeah. Huh . . . his body screams good fuck."

The table next to us started staring again. Jumping up, I

grabbed my purse, coffee, and Sierra and began walking toward the door.

Once we got outside, I started walking away from Starbucks. I was never going to be able to show my face in that place again.

"You made it so I can never set foot in there again!" I called back over my shoulder.

Laughing, Sierra came up next to me. "Nonsense, they'll get so buried in their work and forget anything that happened to them today."

Smiling, I turned to Sierra. "He's great in bed by the way."

I could see out of the corner of my eye Sierra turn and look at me. "I figured he had to be if you've been hooking up with him so long. Then there was the unfortunate incident when I had to listen to how good he was."

My mind went back to Tristan looking at the kitchen island. "Hey Sierra, can I ask you something?"

"Sure. Can't say I'll know the answer, but have at it."

"Did you tell Tristan about overhearing me and Dodge . . . um . . . you know . . . that day in the kitchen?"

I stopped walking after she remained a little too quiet. "You did tell him!"

Stopping she turned to me and held up her hands. "No! I did not tell him."

Giving her the same look my mother used to give me when she knew I was lying, I glared at her. "Sierra. You had to have told him. He knew."

Confusion swept over Sierra's face. "Wait. He talked to you about it?"

Turning my head to the side, I said, "No. When he brought me home he looked over into the kitchen and I could see it all over his face. He knew." Slowly shaking my head I whispered, "You broke the girlfriend code."

Dropping her mouth open, she snarled her upper lip. "Whoa. Whoa. Whoa. I would *never* break the girlfriend code. Well, I mean there may be situations where it calls for a time and place to break it, like if someone was about to get hurt or hurt themselves. Or if your friend had on an awful looking dress and you had to let her go out in it because . . ."

Placing my hands on my hips, I dragged in a frustrated breath. "Sierra!"

Sierra instantly stopped talking as she gave me a blank stare. "Right. What were we talking about again?"

Rolling my eyes as I tossed my hands up in the air. "Ohmygod! You telling Tristan that Dodge fucked me on the kitchen counter."

Pointing her finger at me, she said, "Hey! I didn't tell him. He saw y'all."

I sucked in a breath of air as Sierra slammed her hands over her mouth. Her eyes widened in horror before she dropped her hands and spoke barely above a whisper, "I've got to get to work. Later."

It took me all of five seconds to get my wits about me, and I was taking off after Sierra. "Oh no you don't. No, no, no! Sierra, you have to tell me the truth. Tristan saw us?"

Stopping, she dropped her head back and let out a loud moan. "Don't make me do this, Ryn. Tristan is like my best friend now and if I say anything, I'm not being a good friend."

"Well, what am I?"

Tilting her head and giving me a 'really' look she said, "A friend who has been sending my ass to voicemail for the last few weeks."

Closing my eyes for a brief second before opening them again, I grabbed her hands. "Fine, I'm sorry. I suck at the whole friend thing. I'll totally make it up to you by taking you to some overpriced fancy spa for the weekend."

Moaning, Sierra closed her eyes. "Oh that sounds like heaven."

"The whole package, massages, mani/pedis, facials, you name it and it's my treat."

Giving me a smile that screamed she had won this battle, she looked around. "Fine. But you have to swear you won't tell Tristan I told you."

Nodding my head frantically, I whispered, "I swear."

Holding up her pinky, Sierra asked, "Pinky swear? Stick a needle in your eye kind of swearing?"

"What are we, in middle school?"

Jetting her pinky out at me and raising an eyebrow she

whispered, "Swear?"

Ugh. If I didn't really like Sierra so much I'd reach back and punch her right now. I just wanted to know how Tristan saw Dodge and I together.

Twisting my pinky around Sierra's, I said, "I swear."

Looking satisfied, she opened her mouth and spilled. "Daddy and I were coming to paint for the day and we walked up to a guy who was standing on top of one of our ladders. I could already hear you and Dodge in your love fest, so I knew he was peeping in on y'all."

My face burned with embarrassment. "You need to better sound proof your damn house."

Laughing, Sierra started walking as she kept talking. I followed right next to her, waiting for her to go on with her story. "Anywho, Tristan stepped back off the ladder and it was as if he was attempting to get air in. I thought he was turned on from watching y'all and I was so pissed off until I saw the look on his face. I could tell he wasn't just a Peeping Tom. He looked devastated." Sierra stopped talking and looked at me. "His eyes were filled with regret. Kind of like when someone hurts you so badly and in that moment when they realize the mistake they've made, they regret it. *That's* how Tristan looked."

Covering my mouth with my hand, I felt sick. Tristan saw Dodge fucking me. That was probably one of the rawest moments we had been together and I had loved every minute of it. Except for when I would close my eyes and wish it was Tristan I was with.

Oh God. Tristan saw us.

"Ryn, looking in from the outside, a stranger would think that Dodge hung the moon for you and you feel the same."

Shaking my head, I felt the threat of tears. "No," I whispered. "I mean I care about him, but we were just . . ."

Looking away, I inhaled a deep breath. This is why I needed time on my own. No men, no meaningless fucking, no nothing.

Turning back to Sierra, I gave her a fake smile. "Thank you for telling me, Sierra. It helps to connect a few of the missing dots."

"Ryn, there are more missing dots. Talk to Tristan and decide once and for all if Dodge is more than what you say he is."

Nodding my head, I gave her a quick hug good-bye. "Have

a good day at work, Sierra. I'll plan that spa weekend."

Turning, I walked away as fast as I could back toward my house. I tried to make sense out of the week and a half I spent with Tristan. Was that why he was pulling back every time he attempted to get close to me? Was it because he saw Dodge and I together? What did Sierra mean when she said Tristan got spooked last Christmas? Shit! She was about to tell me when Dodge walked up. Double damn it.

Walking into my house, I looked around. I felt like I was in a cage and had no idea how to get out. My heart hurt, my head was confused and I was scared to death that Tristan would end up hurting me again if I was to let him back in.

My cell phone pinged and I pulled it out.

Dodge: Was great seeing you. Maybe we can do lunch soon?

Ugh! Why is Dodge not giving me the space I asked for? Why isn't it Tristan pursuing me like this? Maybe Sierra was wrong.

Looking back down at Dodge's message, I deleted it.

"Damn it! I hate you, Tristan! I hate you for making me fall in love with you." My mind was still racing and I had no idea how to make it stop.

Walking into my bedroom, I pulled out a suitcase and packed it up. I needed to get away for a few days.

I needed a few days away from anything that reminded me of Tristan and Dodge.

CHAPTER
Seventeen

TRISTAN

$\mathcal{S}$ ITTING AT MY DESK, I pulled in a deep frustrated breath. I stared at the report on my computer and willed myself to finish it. I worked for a semiconductor company as an engineer, and the amount of stress I had with this job was unreal. I hated my job before I was promoted, and now I hated it even more.

Scrubbing my hands down my face, I picked up my cell phone and scrolled down until I found the number I was looking for.

Me: I need something to relieve stress.

It wasn't even thirty seconds and she was texting me back.

Sierra: Sorry dude. Been there and done that. You're on your own with this one.

Laughing, I shook my head and hit call.

Glancing up through the window in my office, I could see everyone working. Rolling my eyes, I turned my chair away.

"No matter how much you sweet talk me, Williams, the answer is still no."

"Why does everything to you mean sex, Sierra?"

"Um . . . because you're a guy. Everything to a guy revolves around sex."

The knock on my office door caused me to spin around and look. Tim, my boss was standing there mouthing, *lunch?*

Shaking my head, I pointed to the monitor and mouthed, *report running*. Talking into my cellphone I said, "Not true."

"Yeah it is."

Tim gave me a head nod, and turned away. Standing up, I walked and shut my office door.

"What if I said I just wanted to go get dinner and have a couple of drinks? Would that be so bad? Besides, we already did the sex thing, Sierra. I thought we were good with that?"

"Oh we are, but when you text me saying you're stressed and need relief, what in the hell am I suppose to say to that?"

Letting out a small chuckle, I shook my head.

"Point taken. All future text messages will be better thought out. Now can we get dinner and a drink?"

Silence.

"Sierra?"

"Oh sorry. Yeah, dinner and a drink sounds good. Where?"

"I'll let you pick. Text me around six, I should be out of this hell hole by then."

Giggling, Sierra said, "Sounds good. Talk to you soon."

"Later, Sierra."

I spent the rest of the afternoon in one meeting after another. I hated this. I was a hands-on kind of guy. I loved taking shit apart and trying to figure out what was wrong with it. This sitting behind a desk shit was for the birds. Maybe I'll take a few extra days off and head down to Mom and Dad's early for Christmas.

My cell phone buzzed during the meeting. Looking down, I saw Sierra's message scrolling across my phone.

Sierra: Bess Bistro at six thirty.

Groaning, I rolled my eyes. The upper-level manager of the company I worked for glanced in my direction. Smiling, I held up my phone and he gave me a head nod. He probably thought it was a problem in the fab with one of the tools.

Hitting reply, I typed out my message.

Me: Fuck no. I am not going to that restaurant.

Sierra: You said it was my pick! I pick Bess Bistro.

Me: After our Sandra Bullock marathon the other night I know why you are picking it. No. It's a chick restaurant.

Sierra: There is no such thing as a "chick restaurant" you pussy.

Me: I hate you.

Sierra: Now now. No sweet-talking me, Mr. Williams. I'm just happy with you paying for dinner tonight. Kisses!

How in the hell did she do that? Dropping my phone back down on to the table, I tried to keep my anger in check. Damn Sierra. Looking over at my boss, he mouthed *everything okay?* Nodding my head, I gave him my fake smile, letting him know all was well.

This is why you don't have chicks for friends.

SIERRA WAS STANDING ON THE rooftop terrace looking out over the city when I walked out there. Making my way over to her, I stopped in my tracks when I heard my name being called out. Turning, I saw Dodge. I quickly began looking for Ryn. Dodge stood up and smiled and he made his way over to me as he reached out his hand to mine. "Don't panic, Tristan. She isn't with me. Ryn ended things between us a few weeks back."

My heart soared and I tried like hell not to seem happy. "I um, I'm sorry to hear that."

Dodge laughed. "No, no you aren't. What brings you here? Somehow I don't see you as a Bess Bistro kind of guy."

Chuckling, I turned and pointed to Sierra. "I left it up to her to pick."

Dodge's smile faded for one quick second. "Sierra? Are y'all? I mean are you two?"

"Fuck no! Sierra is just a friend."

"Really? Y'all seemed to be pretty close in South Padre and Ryn told me she saw . . ." Holding up his hands he said, "You know what, it's none of my business and I have no right even asking."

Looking back at Dodge, I had a brief moment of actually liking him. He seemed like a stand-up kind of guy and I appreciated him not talking shit. "Sierra and I hooked up once while we were at the beach, but it was more of a fuckfest, for lack of better words."

Dodge turned and looked at Sierra again. "She sure is beautiful, I'm not going to lie."

"Inside and out. She's going through a pretty rough time right now. Her ex-husband cheated on her and now he is being a dick about their divorce. I think the asshole is dragging it out because he is pissed she actually left him."

"Why in the hell would he cheat?" Turning, I watched closely as Dodge continued to stare at Sierra.

"Worse part was he cheated on her with her own best friend."

Looking back at me, Dodge seemed to snap out of his temporary trance. "Damn."

"That night in the club was my way of getting Sierra to relax a little. I hated Ryn saw it and thought it was something more than it was."

Dodge stared into my eyes as he narrowed his. "You hurt her really bad, Tristan. I'm not sure if you know just how bad you hurt her."

Swallowing hard, I looked away. I didn't need Ryn's fuck buddy telling me what I did to her. "Yeah, I know." Turning back, I asked, "Are you in love with her?"

He shook his head and narrowed his eyes. "I'm not sure. I know I care about her. I want to see her happy. I think if given the chance, I would make her happy." He looked down and chuckled before looking back up at me. "The problem is she loves you."

My heart dropped and it felt like the Earth wobbled for a second. "She doesn't know the real me, Dodge. I have . . . secrets."

"We all have secrets, Tristan."

"Hey, looks like you two are in a serious conversation." Sierra walked up to both of us and looked at me and then Dodge. "Dodge, we have to keep running into each other like this. It's kind of fun. Care to wager on where we will run into each other next?"

Dodge laughed. "How are you, Sierra? I didn't even see you walk up here."

Sierra looked behind Dodge. It was the first time I noticed a

116

girl sitting at the table Dodge had been sitting at. She had short brown hair and looked to be about twenty-two or so.

Sierra turned to Dodge. "New *friend* you got there, Dodge?" Staring at Sierra, Dodge shook his head. "What's that suppose to mean?"

Sierra paused for a moment before she lifted her hand loosely. "I don't know. Ryn said you were good at making women forget their problems, so I guess I just assumed she was your latest case. Unless it's your girlfriend."

Did I detect a hint of jealousy laced in Sierra's voice?

Dodge took a step toward Sierra and leaned in closer to her as he looked into her eyes. "Why, Sierra? Are you in need of forgetting?"

Sucking in a breath, Sierra took a step back as her eyes searched Dodge's face. I walked in-between them. "All right kids, no fighting. Back to your corners. Sierra, it's not nice to call Dodge a man whore, and Dodge, watch it, dude." Looking at Dodge, he glanced my way. Nodding his head, he mumbled, "I'm sorry, Sierra, I didn't mean anything by that." Dodge turned and waved to the younger girl. "That's my sister, Em."

Sierra plastered on a fake smile and tilted her head when Dodge turned back to her. Licking along the bottom of her lip, Sierra said, "No worries. Your offer does sound intriguing though, Dodge. I'll keep it in mind."

Dodge's smile dropped from his face as he took a step back. Yep, Sierra had that kind of an effect on guys. Laughing, I took Sierra by the arm and began leading her away. Calling over her shoulder, Sierra said, "It was good seeing you, Aaron."

Smirking back at Sierra, Dodge said, "Y'all too."

As we walked back down to the restaurant and up to the bar, I looked at Sierra and grinned. "Do you know how much of a cocktease you are?"

Taking a sip of her cocktail, Sierra gave me an innocent smile. "I have no idea what you're talking about, Tristan. Cock is the last thing I'm interested in; therefore, I would not be teasing it."

Taking a drink of my beer, I set it down. "I call bullshit, Sierra. Look me in the eye and tell me Dodge didn't get your panties a little moist just now."

Looking me dead square in the eye she said, "Nope," as she popped her p loudly. "Please, Ryn's already told me he has a reputation as being the go-to guy when you're wanting to forget your problems with a good screwing. No thanks. Not interested."

Turning away, I mumbled, "If you say so."

Hitting me on the shoulder she said, "I say so. Hey, did you know that Dodge almost got it on with your sister-in-law? Ryn told me all about it."

Rolling my eyes, I asked, "Why do women gossip?"

"We weren't gossiping, I asked about how Dodge and Ryn came to be and she told me."

"Oh yeah? Enlighten me."

Giving me a look that reminded me of my mother, Sierra asked, "You really want to know how the whole Dodge and Ryn thing started?"

Nodding my head, I swallowed hard and whispered, "Yes."

Raising her eyebrows, Sierra began talking. "Okay, you asked for it. Let's see, Ryn began talking to Dodge one night at the club he runs. She poured her heart out to him about you being a really big dick and pushing her away . . ." Smirking, she gave me a wink. "Well, one thing led to another and Ryn came out and asked Dodge if he would have sex with her to help her push you out of her head. He said yes and the rest is history. Ryn calls Dodge and he pretty much comes to her when she needs him to. They started out as strictly fuck buddies and it moved to something a little more."

Staring at Sierra, I attempted to find my voice. When I finally found it, I started to talk. "Do you know how much of a cold-hearted bitch you are? Why would you tell me that?"

"What? Ohmygod! Tristan, you said you wanted to know."

"I didn't think you were just going to blurt it out like that."

Dropping her mouth open, she shook her head. "What in the hell? What did you want me to do?"

"Giving me the version that doesn't rip my heart out and stomp on it would have been nice."

Sliding off the bar stool, Sierra placed her hands on her hips. "Do you know what, all you men are the same. You want me to take it easy on you when you ask how your ex . . . that's right,

Tristan, I said ex-girlfriend hooked up with her fuck buddy. There is no easy version. You fucked up, buddy. You hurt her and she did what she thought she had to do to move on. Do you think it was easy for Ryn to open her heart to you last year? To allow herself to fall head over heels in love with you, and for once in her life imagine a future with someone who would love and take care of her? Only to have you *yank* it out from under her when you call the *other* girl you're fucking on the side? What makes you men think you can play games with our hearts? What makes you think that by fucking me for one night it's going to push all the pain and hurt that my husband of six years caused me? What makes Dodge think he has a magical dick that can make any girl forget any kind of heartache? Holy fucking shit . . . it doesn't work that way. Sex is not a damn tool to be used like that." Tears formed in Sierra's eyes and my heart dropped. The last thing I wanted to do was hurt her.

"You're all the same!" Turning away, she mumbled under her breath as she headed toward the exit, "I officially hate all men."

Taking a twenty from my wallet, I put it on the bar and headed to the door. Opening it, I glanced both ways and saw Sierra walking down the street. I began jogging and caught up to her.

"Sierra, please wait. Don't leave when you're upset with me."

When she stopped walking and turned to me, my legs almost gave out. Tears were streaming down her face. Her lower lip quivered and her eyes seemed lost.

"What's going on?"

I heard someone else's voice, but I couldn't pull my eyes from Sierra.

"Tristan, what happened? Sierra, are you okay?"

Sierra turned and looked at someone as she wiped her tears away. "No, Dodge. I'm the farthest thing from okay."

"Where are you parked? Let me take you to your car, Sierra," I said as I took a step closer.

Shaking her head, she whispered, "I'm sorry. I'm okay, Tristan. It's just been a long day."

Now it was Dodge's turn to step closer to Sierra. "Will you at least let one of us walk you to your car?"

Looking between both of us, Sierra's eyes widened. "Um . . . no I'd rather be alone. Thanks though." She quickly began walking off, never once looking back.

"Tristan, what in the hell happened?"

Watching Sierra walk away, I slowly shook my head. "I'm not really sure, but I think Sierra may have just had a bit of a breakdown."

"Pesh, good going there, Tristan."

Slowly looking back at Dodge, I narrowed my eye at him. "Fuck you, asshole. At least I'm not known as the guy who is only good for a fucking. By the way, stay the hell away from Sierra."

Dodge pulled his head back and laughed. "Excuse me? Are you seriously telling me to stay away from a girl who is not even your girlfriend?"

"Yeah, I am."

Pushing past him, I began walking up Sixth Street to where my car was parked. My head was spinning right now. Seeing Sierra break down about killed me. I wasn't sure what caused Sierra to snap and that bothered me.

Running my hand through my hair, I let out a whispered, "Fuck," as I opened the door to my car and climbed in. I needed fresh air and wide open spaces. I needed the ranch. That was the only way I was going to be able to clear my head and get my game plan down on what I was going to do next with Ryn. It was decision time. I was either going to walk away from the one girl who had brought feelings alive in me that I had never experienced, or I was going to fight like hell to put my own fears aside and take a risk.

CHAPTER
Eighteen

Ryn

"S O ARE YOU GOING TO tell me what is bothering you, Sierra?"

Tipping her head up, Sierra looked at me. "Nothing is bothering me. Why do you ask?"

I looked around Nordstrom's and gestured with my hands. "We are in the middle of your favorite store, in the shoe department, and you have yet to pick up anything and say you had to have it."

Giving me a weak smile and a small shrug, Sierra walked over to a pair of silver high heel shoes. "I guess it's just the holidays are getting me down. I used to go over to my ex asshole's parents' at Christmas, and with it only being a little over two weeks away, I guess I'm starting to feel sad. It's stupid."

Placing my hand on her shoulder, I gave it a light squeeze. "It isn't stupid at all. Listen, I'm headed to Joyce and Peter's ranch, why don't you come along?"

Dropping her head and looking up at me, Sierra asked, "You mean, Tristan's parents' ranch? Um . . . does he know you're going to be there?"

"Ah . . . no?"

"Is that a fact or a question, Ryn?"

"It's a fact. Joyce called me a few weeks back and invited me. At the time, I thought I would be using this as a trip to say good-bye to them since I wasn't sure where things with Dodge were going."

Sierra asked, "So, is it a good-bye visit?"

Taking in a breath, I quickly blew it out. "No, it's not a good-bye visit. I just adore them and I don't think I could say good-bye even if I wanted to."

Picking up a leopard print boot, Sierra turned it over and let out a whistle. "Damn, that is one expensive ass boot." Lifting her hand, she waved a sales associate over. "May I try this on in a size six and a half?"

Smiling, he took the boot and excused himself to go get it.

Looking at her, I giggled. "I thought you said it was expensive?"

"It is, but if my ex thinks I'm giving him half of my savings, he has another thing coming. I'll spend it all first before I give that dick any of it."

We both started laughing as the salesman brought out the boot. "So, has this time away from all men given you the space to clear your head?"

Dropping back in the chair, I moaned in frustration. "Ugh. Why is it that you can't live with men and you can't live without them?"

"Hmm . . . that is the golden question. If you find out, please let me know."

"I do know that there could never be anything more between Dodge and I. I've already told him there would be no more . . ."

"Booty calls?"

Rolling my eyes, I glared at Sierra. "Whatever you want to call it. I think Dodge needs to move on and find someone who will love him like he deserves to be loved."

Nodding her head, Sierra moved on from the subject of Dodge. "Are you going to tell Tristan you are going to visit his parents?"

"God no! I've been there a few times since we broke up. Both times his parents invited me and I couldn't say no." Smiling, I thought about the first few days I met Joyce. She had driven me insane, but I quickly fell in love with her. "Azurdee and Lark know I've been there."

Standing up and walking over to a mirror, Sierra checked out the leopard print boots. "Why keep Tristan in the dark then?"

I didn't really know why I had wanted to keep my relationship with his parents a secret from him. "I don't know. I'm not sure how Tristan would feel about it. The first few times I went to visit them, I think he was still dating Liberty. That might have been awkward for him."

Sitting, Sierra pulled the boots off of her feet, gave the salesman a wink and purred, "I'll take them." Smiling, the salesman almost did a fist pump. I would have too, especially when I saw they were three hundred and forty dollars. His eyes lit up when Sierra asked, "Do you think they would look good with a short dress?"

"Yes ma'am. I think they'd look good on you with anything you wore."

Gag me.

"Oh . . . a man who knows how to worm his way into a girl's heart. What else do you have for me? I'm in a spending kind of mood now," Sierra said as she placed her finger in her mouth and gave him a seductive smile.

Before I knew it, we had a pile of shoes in front of us, and I swore if Sierra flirted with this guy one more time I was going to hurl. I had to admit, she had him eating out of her hand. It didn't take long after he rang up her seven hundred and ninety-two dollar bill, for him to give her his cell phone number.

Walking out of Nordstrom's, we were both loaded down with bags. Sierra tossed them all into the back of her new Audi Q7, another new purchase so her ex wouldn't get any of her money.

Starting her car, she began to back up as I asked, "Okay, I have to know. Are you going to call him?"

Chuckling, she asked, "The sales guy?"

"Yeah, I mean he was hot as hell."

"And like twenty. Call me picky, but I like a dick that has some wear and tear on it. Not one that is going to poke itself in and one minute later it's retreating and takes twelve hours to recharge."

Snapping my head over to her, I busted out laughing. "My god, do you actually hear the stuff that comes out of your mouth?"

Nodding her head, she smiled. "Tell me you don't agree with me."

"I didn't say I didn't agree, I was just wondering if you were interested is all."

"Nope. I'm done with men. I'll stick to my vibrators that do the job and I don't have to worry about it sticking itself in another woman's pussy, or playing head games with me, or wanting the money my father worked his ass off for. Yeah, vibrators all the way."

I didn't even have the words to say after that. Pulling out onto the highway, Sierra continued to talk. "Maybe I should get a T-shirt that says *vibrators over men*. I bet I'd sell a ton of those bitches."

Giggling, I agreed. My phone buzzed in my purse and I pulled it out. "Crap, I missed a call from Azurdee. I've got to introduce you to Dee sometime. The two of you would hit it off really well."

"Let's plan something then."

Smiling, I felt happy. For the first time in almost a year, my heart didn't feel broken, my head wasn't clouded with all the crap, and I had friends who I knew loved me and would be there for me.

"I'll send Dee a text back and chat about making plans for something soon."

Sierra gave me a thumbs-up and reached to turn up the radio. The drive back to my house was filled with loud music, laughing, and plans for a new year. It wasn't lost on me that neither Sierra nor I mentioned men in those plans.

PULLING UP TO JOYCE AND Peter's house, I put my car in park. My heart was racing and I wasn't sure why. I had been here before, post Tristan, but something about this trip was causing my nerves to be on edge. I almost called Tristan this morning. I wasn't sure what in the hell came over me, but I had his number pulled up and my finger hovered over it a good five minutes. I backed out and threw my bag in the car and headed to South Texas. Getting out of the car, I inhaled a deep breath.

"Oh man, clean country air." I loved it here. More than I wanted to admit. The front door to the house creaked open. Joyce and MaryLou came running out.

"Kathryn! You're here a day early!"

Giving them both a big smile, I walked up to them. Mary-Lou got to me first and gave me a big ole bear hug. Next was Joyce's turn. She pulled me in tighter and whispered in my ear, "I'm so glad you came a day early."

Pulling back some, I gave her a soft smile. "I hope you don't mind. I just love it here and thought it would be perfect for me to catch up on some work I've been pushing off."

"You know you are welcome here for as long as you want. Lark and Azurdee will be here in a few days as well. They've decided to come a few days early too."

My heart dropped and I took a step back. "Tristan?"

Giving me that motherly smile of hers, she nodded her head. "He's busy with work. They're not letting him take off over the holidays. He's very upset and insisted he would be here for Christmas, even if they fired him."

Letting out a nervous laugh, I said, "Sounds like Tristan."

"Let's get your luggage; Peter is out checking the fences. We can get some girl talk in while he is working."

Nodding my head and giving Joyce a wink, I turned and opened the backseat of my car. Reaching in, I grabbed the duffle bag I had packed and threw it over my shoulder. Reaching in again, I got my laptop case and my cowboy boots. "Wonder what Peter will be teaching me on this trip?" I asked as I rolled my eyes and shuddered to think what animal he would have me gut this time around.

Joyce, MaryLou and I talked for almost two hours before Peter walked into the kitchen. "Kathryn, why look at you. You're hair has grown longer."

Smiling, I stood. I didn't want to tell Peter I had just gotten my hair cut. It was just to my shoulders and the sides were pulled up. Pushing me back, he looked me over after he gave me a bear hug. Nodding his head, he gave me a smile like none I'd ever seen before.

"Why do I get the feeling you are planning something in your head for me?"

"Smart girl, I always knew I liked you, Kathryn. It's a shame my son is too stupid to open his eyes."

"Peter Williams!" Joyce called out. Laughing, I lifted my hand and pointed my finger at him.

"Behave."

Giving me a sly smile, Peter said, "Always."

FOUR DAYS AFTER I FIRST pulled up for my mini Joyce and Peter vacation, I found myself lost on the ranch. Peter thought it would be fun for me to take the Jeep out and go for a drive.

Get some fresh country air, Kathryn. Cause the country air on the front porch wasn't good enough he said. Even though I had my laptop all set up and I was comfy as hell. Oh no, I had to get my ass up and take a jaunt around the few thousand-acre ranch.

Stopping the Jeep, I looked around. "I'm so screwed right now."

Opening the door, I got out and began looking around. For some reason, this area of the ranch looked familiar to me. Laughing, I dropped my head back. "Oh dear God, Ryn. It's thousands of acres . . . how could this spot seem familiar?"

Turning to my right I saw a trail. Walking toward it, I pulled out my cell. Still no coverage. It was hit or miss if I had cell coverage here. I couldn't wait for Lark and Dee to show up later this evening. I loved Joyce, but something was off with her, as if she was hiding something. She kept asking me if I wanted to go into town and get facials. I finally agreed to it yesterday, thinking maybe it was Joyce who needed time away from the ranch and Peter. Smiling, I had to admit it was fun. I would have loved to have had a mother like Joyce. She was funny, said what was on her mind, yet she had a way of being gentle with you, even when she was telling you that you were flat out wrong about something.

She never brought up Tristan. Not once. On my last trip here she mentioned him a number of times. The fact that she hadn't brought him up caused me to think that maybe he had been dating someone. I asked Sierra and she said he wasn't. They saw each other once a week and I was insanely jealous of their friendship. I had to stop myself more than once from telling Sierra I didn't want her hanging out with Tristan. I knew it was selfish of me. I did however finally break down and ask her if she had maybe mentioned to Tristan I wasn't seeing Dodge anymore. All she did was smile and say, "Oh, he already knew that."

She never did elaborate on how Tristan knew this bit of information.

Making my way down the trail, I came across a hunter's cabin that Peter used for the guys who paid to hunt on his ranch. It only took a split-second for me to realize this was the same cabin Tristan and I made love in. The same cabin where he told me he was falling in love with me.

Making my way to the door, I reached down to the doorknob. I knew it would be locked. Tristan had used a master key he carried on his key ring to open the door last year.

A rush of sadness swept over my body. It was almost a year to the date when we had been here together. Closing my eyes, I tried the handle. When it turned, I let out a gasp. Pushing the door open, I stood at the threshold. I was scared to death to step into the room. Knowing the moment I did, the memory would overtake me and push away any progress I had made this week in moving on and letting Tristan go. Up until now, the visit to the ranch had been therapeutic. It was a cleansing almost. I knew in my heart I would forever love Tristan.

Taking in a deep breath, I walked into the room. My eyes landed on the bed and the memory swept into my head.

Walking over to the bed, I stared down at it. Wrapping my arms around my body, I finally let go. I dropped to the floor and began crying.

"Why? Why did you have to tell me you were falling in love with me?"

I wasn't sure how long I was on the floor. I just sat there, leaning against the bed where Tristan had changed my entire world. Dropping my head back, I realized it was late.

How long had I been in the cabin? What if I had to stay out here all night? I couldn't stay here all night. Pulling out my phone, I still had no service. Panic began to set in. Jumping up, I quickly made my way to the door and pulled it open. I was beginning to have a panic attack, knowing I was lost and night was quickly coming. I ran smack into someone and I let out a scream. Okay, that's not true. It wasn't just a scream; it was a loud blood-curdling scream. Turning, I tried to run back into the cabin.

The person grabbed me around my waist and pulled me back to them. I began trying to hit them with my fists, but my back was pulled to them. I started trying to kick, but they lifted me off the ground.

"Let go of me! I swear to God I'll kill you. Let me go!" I screamed.

"Ryn! Jesus Christ, stop fighting me!"

Oh dear God, they know my name. I started screaming out, "Help! Somebody help me!"

They started walking me toward the bed. *No! Oh God no!* Attempting to fight harder, it felt like my lungs were closing in on me. I was working hard at dragging in air.

Can't breathe . . .

They threw me onto the bed and I scrambled up it and turned around, still screaming the best I could since it felt like I was getting no air.

My eyes adjusted to the darkness of the cabin. The sun hadn't gone down yet but it was beginning to get darker.

Oh. My. God.

Tristan was standing there, breathing heavy as he stared at me. "What in the fuck are you doing here?" he shouted.

I stopped screaming and looked around. Lark was standing behind Tristan. My chest was heaving up and down, not only from my attempt at trying to get away, but from the panic attack.

I couldn't talk. Opening my mouth, I just dragged in more air.

Tristan grabbed his chin. "Motherfucker. You punched the shit out of my jaw."

Oh. Yeah me! I hadn't realized I had landed one. Serves his ass right.

Lark moved over to me. "Ryn, slow down your breathing."

Trying to do just that, I looked at Tristan. *Oh no. Tristan was here. Oh shit. Shit. Shit. Shit.*

128

Lark placed his hands on the sides of my face. "Ryn . . . look at me. Breathe in through your nose, out through your mouth."

"What in the fuck are you doing out here? Are you trying to get lost, Ryn? Do you have any fucking idea how huge this ranch is?" Moving my eyes off of Lark, I looked at Tristan. He was furious. I knew it wasn't from me getting lost. It was from me being here. Tears began to form in my eyes and I hated that I was appearing so weak in front of him.

Lark turned to Tristan. "Tristan, I don't really think yelling at her right now is a good idea. Can't you see she's scared to death?"

Right at that moment, a damn tear rolled down my cheek. Tristan just stood there, staring at me. His eyes softened a bit, but he made no attempt to come to me. I prayed like hell he would. I wanted him to hold me in his arms, not Lark. Tristan didn't move. His body was tense and his hands were balled up into fists.

I wanted to call out his name. Beg him to hold me. My heart was beating like crazy in my chest, and it wasn't from me being afraid anymore. It was from the knowledge that Tristan clearly didn't want me here.

Tristan turned and walked outside, closing the cabin door behind him. That's when I lost all control and the tears fell freely. Lark pulled me into his arms and whispered against my hair, "Shh . . . it's okay, Ryn. Please don't cry. It's all going to be okay now."

It wasn't going to be okay. Tristan didn't love me. If he had, he would have never walked away from me. Again.

Grabbing a hold of Lark's shirt, I cried like I had never cried before.

CHAPTER
Nineteen

TRISTAN

I NEEDED AIR. PUSHING BOTH my hands through my hair, I tried to get my own damn breathing under control. When I had pulled up and Dad was getting into his truck, I asked him where he was going. That's when Lark pulled up.

My father looked scared, and my father was never scared. Then he told Lark and me he had talked Ryn into taking a drive in the Jeep. At first, I was confused as hell as to why Ryn was at my family's ranch, but when he said she had been gone for over five hours, I freaked out. Lark told my dad to go back into the house and we would look for Ryn.

Luckily, it had rained earlier and her tracks were easy to follow. When we pulled up to the trail to the cabin, I froze. There was no way in hell she would remember how to get here.

Why was she here? At the ranch? At the cabin? My head was spinning and I wasn't sure if I should be feeling happy we found her or pissed that she was even here.

The cabin door opened and Ryn and Lark walked out. Ryn looked down at the ground and wouldn't even look at me. "I'm gonna take her back in the Jeep, she's really upset."

I should be the one holding her, not my brother. When I walked up to her, she wouldn't look at me. "I'll take her back in my truck, you follow us in the Jeep."

Snapping her head up, her eyes looked panicked. "No!"

Shaking her head, she began freaking out again. "No, I just want Lark to take me back."

My heart broke in two and for once in my life, I felt as if I was going to cry. "Ryn, I'm . . . I'm sorry I yelled like that. Let me take you back and . . ."

She began shaking her head as she whispered, "No. Please, I don't want to go back with you."

My knees felt like they were going to give out on me. My eyes burned with the threat of tears and my world felt destroyed. "Ryn . . ." I whispered as she looked into my eyes. I'd never seen her eyes look so sad and lost.

Lark cleared his throat. "Tristan, just let me take her back. We'll meet you at the ranch house."

Lark began walking Ryn over to the Jeep. Before she got into the Jeep, she looked over her shoulder at me. Not able to move, I watched as Lark turned the Jeep around and headed back to the house.

When I was finally able to move, I walked back to my truck. Jumping in, I headed back to the house. The closer I got, the more pissed off I was.

Why was she afraid to go back with me? Why was she even fucking here? This was my family's ranch. What game was she playing?

Pulling up behind Lark and Azurdee's SUV, I parked. I thought back to yesterday when I talked to Sierra. She *knew* Ryn was here. It was her idea for me to come early.

"You're stressed, Tristan. I think heading down to the ranch as soon as possible is what you need. Trust me."

"That little bitch." Pushing my door open, I reached in the backseat to grab my bag. Jumping out of the truck, I made my way to the front door. When I walked in, everyone was sitting in the living room. Everyone but Ryn. Looking at everyone, I asked, "Where is she?"

My mother stood up. "She's in the guest room. Resting."

Making my way to the steps, my mother called out for me. "Tristan, she's had quite a night. I think it's best we let her rest."

Letting out a laugh, I looked at my mother. "She's had quite a night? So have I, Mom. I come home for Christmas and find out the girl who walked out on me last Christmas is here hanging out with my parents."

My mother placed her hands on her hips. "I raised you better than that, Tristan Williams. Don't you dare go up there and upset that girl. I invited her here."

Azurdee walked up to me and pushed me, causing me to take a few steps back.

"You arrogant bastard. Have you forgotten how you treated her last year? She didn't run out on you. You can't run out on someone who left you first."

Lark came up and put his arm around Azurdee's waist. "Baby, let's stay out of this, okay?" Walking her back into the living room, Azurdee turned and stuck her tongue out at me.

Jerking my head back, I looked at her. Rolling my eyes, I turned my focus back on my mother. "Why, Mom? Why did you invite her here?"

"We enjoy having Kathryn here. She's fun and your father has taught her how to hunt."

My father stood. "And how to gut a hog. She's a natural."

My head was beginning to pound. Placing my fingers up to my temples, I tried to make sense of all of this. "Wait. Wait just a second. She's been here before? How many times has she been here to see y'all?"

My mother looked at my father. They exchanged a look and my mouth dropped open. "Holy shit. Mom? How many times has Ryn been here since last Christmas?"

"Counting this trip?" she asked with a slight smile.

Dropping my bag to the floor, I said, "Yes, Mom. Counting this trip."

"Three."

I took a few steps back. "You kept this from me? Why?"

"I asked them to."

Spinning around, I looked at Ryn. Her eyes were swollen and red. My eyes traveled down and I noticed her bag in her hand.

"I figured with you dating Liberty and all, it might have seemed weird to have me here." She stopped talking and sucked in a shaky breath. "It's just . . . I adore your parents and . . ."

"And you just thought you'd come and hang with them? What game were you playing at, Ryn?"

Ryn's mouth parted open slightly as I watched the tears roll down her face again. She quickly wiped them away, stood taller and cleared her throat.

"Games are your specialty, Tristan, not mine. You weren't even supposed to know I was here. Had I known you would come early, I would have left already." Turning her attention to my mother, she smiled weakly. "Thank you, Joyce, for always making me feel like I was welcomed here. I'm afraid I have to be heading out."

My mother walked past me, stopped at the bottom of the stairs and pulled Ryn into her arms. "This is my house and you are a guest in it. You march right back up and put your things away. I have you for two more days, young lady."

None of this made any sense. A part of me wanted to grab Ryn and pull her out to her car, the other part wanted me to grab her and fuck the living hell out of her.

"Joyce, thank you, but I just can't stay any longer." Ryn's voice trailed off. Her eyes caught mine. "I better get going."

Ryn leaned down and kissed my mother on the cheek before turning and walking over to my father. "Peter, thank you for the archery lesson."

"We're not done, young lady. Go put your things away."

Clearing my throat, I said, "If she wants to go, let her."

Azurdee let out a gasp. She walked up to Ryn and grabbed her arms. "Ryn, it's dark out and you're exhausted. Please don't leave."

Ryn smiled. "I have to go, Azurdee."

"No! No you don't. This is not Tristan's house." Turning to me, Azurdee looked at me with pleading eyes. "Tristan, don't do this."

Ryn quickly began walking to the door. She opened it and headed outside. Glancing over to Lark, he gave me a dirty look as he mouthed *asshole* to me.

Coming to my senses, I followed Ryn out the door. She had opened up the back door of her car and threw her bag in. She went to open the driver's side door and I stopped her. "I got the hint, Tristan. You didn't have to show me the way out."

Closing my eyes, I slowly inhaled a breath and blew it out before opening them again and capturing her eyes. "Don't go."

Her lower lip trembled. "I didn't mean to make you mad by coming here. I just really . . . love . . . your parents."

I knew Ryn had a terrible relationship with her parents and I felt like a total dick for the way I had just acted.

"Please don't go, Ryn. I'm sorry I acted like such an asshole. I was just shocked to see you here and then pulling up and Dad said you were missing for five hours. I wasn't sure if I was more scared that something happened to you or pissed off that everyone but me knew you were here."

Looking down, she sniffled. Reaching up, I wiped a tear away from her cheek. "Please don't leave, Ryn. My mother really wants you here for Christmas."

Looking at me with a confused look, Ryn said, "I was only staying for another two days."

Shaking my head, I smiled. "Mom wants you here for Christmas, please don't leave because of me."

Wiping her nose on her shirt in a very unladylike fashion, Ryn asked, "Will it make you uncomfortable? This is your home and your family."

Giving her my smile that I prayed eased her mind, I shook my head. "No, Ryn, I want you here too."

"Really?"

Nodding, I said, "Yeah. Really."

The smile that spread across her face caused something deep inside me to wake up. "I'm sorry I punched you."

Laughing, I rubbed my chin. "Damn girl, have you been taking classes or something? You got me good."

Giggling, she shook her head. "I um, guess I need to get my bag."

Jumping back, I opened the back door, grabbed her bag and led her back up the porch stairs and back into the house. My mother greeted us at the door and gave me a sweet smile. "Thank you, Tristan. Now come on, Ryn, sweetheart. You need some sleep."

I watched as the two women I loved more than the air I breathed walked up the stairs, arm in arm. Pushing my hand through my hair I walked into the living room only to find Lark and my father both staring at me. Lark started laughing. "Damn dude, I'm sure glad you snapped the hell out of it. You were really looking like a big douche there for a few minutes."

My father and Azurdee started laughing. Giving Lark the finger and telling him to go fuck off, I grabbed my bag and headed upstairs. I was exhausted and needed to get some sleep.

ROLLING OVER, I GLANCED AT the clock. It was three thirty in the morning. Lying back, I ran my hands down my face and groaned.

"Fuck, I'm so damn tired."

Sitting up, I swung my legs over and sat there for a few seconds. I hadn't been able to fall asleep since I crawled into bed at ten. Knowing Ryn was in the room next to me was driving me insane. It was also bothering me that I noticed she was limping on the same foot that she sprained her ankle. What if she hurt it when I threw her down on the bed? Or when she was trying to fight me off?

"Shit. I'm always doing the wrong thing when it comes to that girl."

Grabbing a T-shirt, I made my way downstairs. Maybe some warm milk would help me sleep better. Walking into the kitchen, I glanced over to my right and saw my father's office light on. Making my way over there, I pushed the door open. Dad was sitting behind his desk, writing in a notebook.

"Dad? What in the world are you doing up so late?"

Lifting his head, my father smiled. "Tristan, come in, come in." He motioned with his hands for me to come sit at his desk.

Heading over toward his desk, I was overcome with memories of the last time I sat in this office. Lark was sitting to the right of me. Sitting, I inhaled a deep breath through my nose.

"Do you remember the last time you sat in that chair?"

Nodding my head, I whispered, "Yes, sir, I do."

"Do you still love her, Tristan?"

Swallowing hard, I nodded my head. "I've messed up so many times with her, Dad. I'm not even sure if I got on my hands and knees and begged her, she'd come back to me."

Lifting the corner of his mouth, he said, "Never know unless you try."

Looking down, I began playing with a string that was on my sleeping pants. "Dad, what if there is something about me that I haven't been . . . truthful about with Ryn? A piece of my life that I'm not sure she would want to be a part of."

"You see, son, that's the thing, you're so worried about something that, according to you, Ryn won't want to be a part of, but I don't think that's what has you pushing her away."

"Oh really? So you're a relationship expert now, Dad?"

Chortling, he shook his head. "Nah, but I have been around the block a time or two and what I see in your eyes son is nothing but utter fear. You're so scared to give your heart to that girl that you'd rather hurt both of you with excuses and reasons why it would be better if you were apart."

Nodding my head, I whispered, "That's a big part of it. But, Dad, I don't really know how to tell you this." Pushing my hand through my hair, I whispered, "Shit."

"If she loves you, Tristan, and you love her, you'll both learn to love everything about each other. The good and the bad, son. The key is finding the right balance. This thing you're so worried about, you're not even giving her the chance to figure it out on her own."

Shaking my head, I felt the emotions coming to the surface. "Dad, I have never in my life felt this way about anyone and that scares the piss out of me. I don't want to do anything to push her away, yet that's all I ever do. It's a damn tug of war game I'm tired of playing."

Sitting back in his chair and rocking a bit, he looked at me with a serious face. "Let's just pretend that you and Ryn work things out and you finally tell that darling girl you love her."

Smiling, I said, "Okay, let's pretend."

"You tell her about this thing you're so worried about. If she asked you to pick between her and it, could you?"

"I want to say I'd pick Ryn, but it's a part of who I am, Dad."

"Then if she loves you and she knows this is part of who you are, she'll accept it. Or she'll try to anyway. You'll see that and in the end, if she can't accept it, I promise you son, love will win out every single time."

I let my father's words sink in. Never really thinking about it that way, I had a sense of hope. Leaning forward I smiled. "I don't think I'm ready for the bottle yet Dad, but I think I'm getting close."

Smiling from ear to ear, my father laughed. "This . . . this right here," pointing between us he continued to talk. "This is what makes me so proud to be your father."

"I love you, Dad."

"I love you too, Tristan. Now go get your warm milk and get some sleep."

"Yes, Sir." Standing, I turned and made my way to the door. Looking over my shoulder, I asked, "Wait, how did you know I was getting warm milk?"

Looking into my eyes he winked at me. "You used to have problems sleeping when you were about seven. Warm milk was the only thing we could give you to make you fall asleep."

Shaking my head, I let out a small laugh before leaving and going to make my warm milk.

Once I was settled back into bed and my eyes grew heavy, I decided tomorrow I was going to talk to Ryn. I was done hiding my feelings. I was going to tell her I loved her and I prayed like hell she felt the same way about me.

CHAPTER
Twenty

S TANDING, I STRETCHED MY LEGS and arms. Dropping my head back, I let the warm Texas sun beat down on me. I hardly slept last night. Lying in bed, I kept an eye on the clock. Every thirty minutes I would glance over at it. A part of me had hoped that Tristan would have snuck into the room and made love to me. Thinking about his lips on my body had the pressure growing between my legs. That hasn't happened in a few weeks. Not since I declared that I was giving up on all men.

Joyce and Azurdee laughed about something; I glanced over their way. They both had their hands in the dirt digging up something in the garden. "Do y'all want something to drink?" I asked.

Azurdee nodded her head and stuck out her tongue. "Yes! It's so hot for December. I'm fixin' to melt, I swear."

Joyce stood. "I'll get some drinks."

Holding up my hands, I gave Joyce a stern look. "No, you stay out here and do what you love doing, getting your hands dirty. I'll go in and make us a few iced teas." Giving me one of her famous motherly looks, Joyce asked, "Are you sure, Kathryn?"

"Yes. Stay out here and visit with, Dee."

"Well, if you insist, I'll take you up on that offer."

Brushing off the dirt from my knees and taking my gloves off,

138

I headed into the house. Pulling the back screen door open, I made my way to the refrigerator to get the iced tea out.

I heard a loud crash coming from Peter's office. "Peter? Peter, are you okay?"

Setting the tea down on the island, I made my way out of the kitchen and into Peter's office. The moment I walked into his office, something felt wrong. Looking around I saw his arm sticking out from behind the desk. Running over to the desk I saw Peter lying on the floor. "Oh my God."

"Tristan!" I screamed. "Lark!"

I knew both boys were in the house because I had watched a sweaty Tristan walk by and say he was going to take a shower. Lark was right behind him, giving Azurdee a look that said meet me in our room in a few minutes.

Reaching down, I tried to find a pulse on Peter's neck. "Tristan!" I screamed louder. I heard Tristan running down the stairs and into the office. I had Peter's head on my lap as Tristan fell to the floor.

"Dad! Oh my God . . . don't do this to us! Dad!"

Between my sobs, I said, "I can't find a pulse."

Lark came running in and Tristan screamed, "Call 911, Lark! Now!"

AZURDEE SAT NEXT TO ME curled up in a ball in the hospital waiting room. I had been sitting with her for at least the last hour. Glancing up, I looked at Tristan. He was leaning over with his head in his hands as they rested on his knees. Lark sat next to his mother, holding her hand. No one talked. We all sat and waited for someone to walk through the double doors to tell us about Peter.

I'd never been so scared in my life as I was watching Tristan giving his own father CPR. At the same time, my heart hurt like it had never hurt before.

Azurdee sat up and looked at me. She asked, "Do you want some coffee?"

Nodding, I stood. "I'll go get it. You stay here."

Turning, I made my way out of the waiting room to the

elevator. It felt as if I hadn't slept in a week. I couldn't even imagine how Joyce, Lark and Tristan were feeling.

The elevator opened and I slowly walked in. I felt someone come in behind me. Turning, I saw Tristan. He was standing there, staring at me. I saw the fear in his eyes and I wanted nothing more than to hold him in my arms. The door shut and Tristan hit the button for the floor that the cafeteria was on. As soon as the elevator started moving, he reached back and hit the stop button. The elevator came to a stop and I let out a small gasp.

"Tristan, why did you stop the . . ." Before I could even finish talking, he had me pined against the back of the elevator. His lips were inches from mine. My breathing picked up and my heart had all but dropped to the ground.

"I'm not letting another second go by without telling you something."

My eyes searched his face as I whispered, "Okay."

Closing his eyes, he slowly shook his head. "This isn't how I wanted to do this, Ryn."

Swallowing hard, I asked, "Do what? Tristan, are you okay?"

His eyes snapped open and they searched my face. "No, baby. I haven't been okay since last year."

Oh my. He called me baby. Oh wow, his lips are so close to mine.

"Ryn, I can't wait any longer. With my dad having a heart attack and us not knowing . . ." his voice cracked and I placed my hands on his arms.

"Tristan, he's going to be okay. I feel it in my heart."

His eyes moved up and locked with mine. The same look appeared in his eyes that was there the night he told me he was falling in love with me. "I love you, Ryn. I'll love you forever."

The air completely left my lungs as I tried to process what I just heard.

Tears built in my eyes as Tristan cupped both his hands to my face. "Please tell me I haven't lost you forever, Ryn. I don't know what I would do without you."

Opening my mouth, I fought to control the feelings rushing through my body. I was scared to death for Peter, yet at the same time, I'd never felt so alive and amazing. Then there was the guilt for feeling that way while Peter fought for his life.

Slowly shaking my head, I placed my hands over Tristan's. "Tristan, I love you too. I've never stopped loving you."

Before I could utter another word, Tristan's lips were pressed to mine. He kissed me like he was never going to be able to kiss me again. Our kiss quickly turned passionate as Tristan's hands moved all over my body.

When we finally needed air, Tristan pulled his lips back and dragged in fast shallow breaths. Leaning his forehead against mine, he said, "As soon as we find out Dad is going to be okay, I'm taking you out of here and making love to you as soon as possible."

I felt such a release from my body. It was as if everything bad vanished from one single kiss. The phone in the elevator began to ring. Tristan turned and pushed the stop button back in and the elevator began moving again.

Glancing back to me, his beautiful green eyes held my blue eyes in such a gaze, I felt as if I would combust from his stare.

"I promise to never again in my life hurt you, Ryn. I swear."

My hand ran along his chest and up behind his neck. Pulling him closer to me, I leaned up and pressed my lips to his. The elevator doors opened and I pulled back some. "I'm going to hold you to that, Williams."

Pulling me out of the elevator, Tristan walked us to the cafeteria. I wasn't sure how I should be feeling right now. I was elated. My stomach was doing all those crazy dips and spins as we walked together, Tristan holding my hand and gently brushing his thumb across my skin.

Then, I'd think of Peter and I wanted to cry. I wasn't sure how much longer my body was going to be able to hold up to all of this stress and the emotions that went along with it. From yesterday's episode to getting lost in the woods, Tristan yelling at me, Tristan asking me to stay, then Peter's heart attack. Ugh.

"Stop thinking so much, Ryn. It's all going to be okay, baby."

Smiling, I nodded my head. I knew he was right. I felt it in my heart that his father was going to be okay. Tristan held onto my hand the entire time we ordered the five coffees. Pulling out his wallet, Tristan paid for all the coffees then handed me one of the carriers. I couldn't help but smile like a silly schoolgirl. The fact that he wouldn't let go of my hand had me all kinds of giddy.

Walking back into the waiting room, Lark and Azurdee looked up. Azurdee's eyes went right to Tristan holding my hand. She smiled and looked into my eyes. Turning, she bumped Lark's shoulder and tipped her head toward Tristan and me.

Lark smiled and nodded his head. Tristan let go of my hand to get his mother's coffee and handed it to her. Her eyes were so red and swollen from crying. I sat next to her and took her hand. Smiling, she leaned over and kissed my cheek. Then she whispered, "I knew he would come around. He loves you very much."

My face blushed and I stole a peek at Tristan. He was gazing at me with such a loving expression. My heart soared and I returned the look. I never dreamed I'd be standing here with Tristan gazing upon me like I was his everything. I silently prayed this feeling would never end. This feeling of love was like nothing I'd ever imagined.

The door opened and a doctor came walking out. Everyone jumped up. Azurdee and I stood back as Joyce, Lark, and Tristan made their way up to the doctor.

"He's okay. He had a blockage in one of his main arteries that we were able to clear." We stood and listened as the doctor explained how Peter was going to have to rest and most importantly slow down. When Lark mentioned his father ran a very successful hunting ranch, the doctor said Peter was going to have to bring someone in to help manage it, most likely fulltime.

Glancing over to Tristan, I saw the conflict on his face. I knew he wanted to run this ranch, I just wasn't sure if he wanted to run it now.

Before the doctor left, he told us Peter could have one visitor at a time. Knowing his first question was going to be about the ranch, Lark brought it up. "What are we going to tell him about the ranch?"

Joyce held up her hands and said, "The ranch is the least of my worries."

"But it will be one of Dad's. You know he is going to worry about it, Mom," Lark said.

Tristan was sitting in one of the chairs. I knew his heart was being torn in two right now, and I didn't want to be one of the causes. Walking over to him, I sat down next to him.

"I don't know what to do, Ryn. I felt like for once in my life everything was falling into place and now . . ."

Reaching for his hand, I knew that we still had a lot to talk about. A lot to work through, but I knew I wanted a future with Tristan and I believed in my heart he meant what he said when he said he would never hurt me again.

"You told me once your dream was to run the ranch. Has that changed?"

Lifting his head, he whispered, "No."

My heart was breaking for Tristan. I knew he was conflicted and I needed to reassure him that he was making the right decision, not only for himself but for his family as well. I also needed to make it clear I would be there for him no matter where he was. "Tristan, I know you don't have to work. I know that if you stopped working tomorrow, you would still be set financially because of your grandparents. Quitting your job and moving here to take over the ranch should be the easiest thing you've ever done."

Taking my hand, Tristan stood and began walking down the hall. Opening a closet door, he pushed me inside and shut it. His face was filled with such angst. "Don't you see, Ryn? If I follow that dream, I lose you. The one thing I've been so worried about, pushing you away, isn't even the thing I had to worry about." Pushing his hands through his hair he yelled out, "Fuck! I can't believe this."

Reaching for his arms, I pulled them down. "Tristan, I'm going to be wherever you are. I don't care if it's in Austin, here in South Texas or in some god forsaken desert." Placing my hands on his face, I whispered, "Tristan, I promise you, I'm not going anywhere." Closing my eyes briefly before opening them again, I continued talking. "We still have a lot of talking to do and things to work out, but I just got you back, Tristan Williams. I'm not letting you go ever again."

Tristan leaned his head against mine. "Do you have any idea how much I want to fuck you right now, Ryn?"

"Hmm . . . I forgot how romantic you were."

Tristan laughed and pushed my skirt up and slipped his fingers under the sides of my panties. The moment I lifted my leg and his fingers slipped in, I let out a moan. I missed his touch so much.

Dropping my head to his chest, I began grinding against his hand. Gripping his shirt, I felt my body building up my orgasm. Oh God, this was going to be big. Tristan's expert fingers worked me up to the max. "Tristan!"

His lips pressed against mine as I came on his fingers. I could feel my insides pulsing as he slowly moved his fingers in and out of me.

"Fucking hell, Ryn. Your pussy was clamping down on my fingers like you really needed to come, baby."

Breathing into Tristan's massive chest, I nodded my head. "I needed you, Tristan. You're all I'll ever need."

Brushing his lips against mine, Tristan spoke. "I'm going to make you mine tonight, Ryn."

"I've always been yours, Tristan. Always."

CHAPTER
Twenty-One

TRISTAN

*P*ULLING UP TO THE HOUSE, Lark jumped out of the backseat of my truck and opened the passenger side door. My father pushed Lark's hand away. "Damn it. I'm perfectly fine. I don't need to be babied."

Looking over Dad's shoulder, Lark winked at me and smiled. Shaking my head, I got out of the truck and got Dad's stuff from the back seat.

"I can't believe those assholes let me out on Christmas Eve. Have the two hunters checked in, Tristan?"

Laughing, I walked up to my father. "Dad, just relax, what did the doctor say?"

Giving me a dirty look, my father replied, "He said I needed to step down and give you the ranch. I'll have you know, I'm not too happy about that. Matter of fact . . ."

Mom opened the door and came out smiling. "Peter Williams. Stop complaining right now. You know you are over the moon to know that Tristan will be moving down here fulltime."

Walking up the stairs, Dad started talking. "Tristan, you know we could hire someone and you wouldn't have to give your life in Austin up. I know how much you love it there."

"I love it here more, Dad. Stop worrying. Please just try and relax. You, Lark and I will talk shop later tomorrow. For now, you don't worry about anything."

After getting my father into the house and settled, I walked into the kitchen. My mother and Azurdee were cutting up fruit and smiled as I made my way over to them.

"Where is Ryn?" I asked. Looking over her shoulder, my mother motioned outside. Heading to the door, she cleared her throat.

"Tristan?"

Glancing back, I asked, "Yeah?"

"Thank you, for everything you are doing for your father and the ranch."

Giving my mother a smile, I winked at her and headed outside. Ryn was sitting down in a swing that had been up for years. Debating if I should tell her how old that swing was, I walked over and bent down in front of her. "Hey."

Smiling, she looked into my eyes. "Why did you tell me that your mother wanted me to stay for Christmas?"

Smiling, I gave her wink. "I wanted you to stay. Besides, Mom really did want you to stay."

"Is your dad settled?"

Letting out a chuckle, I said, "As best as he can be."

"It's been a long day."

Taking her hand in mine, I nodded my head. "Are you tired, Ryn?"

"I am but . . ."

Lifting my eyebrow, I asked, "But?"

"I want . . ."

The back door opened and mother called out. "Dinner is ready, Tristan and Ryn. Come and get it."

Ryn and I stood. Reaching for her hands, I pulled her to me as I cupped the sides of her face. Bringing my lips up against her lips I asked, "What do you want, Ryn?"

Closing her eyes, she barely spoke. "You."

Turning, I pulled her away from the house. "Tristan, where are we going? Your mom just said it was dinner time and she is gonna wonder where we went."

Walking up to a tree, I stopped. The treehouse Lark and I had built was gone. "Motherfucker, he took it down."

"Who took what down?"

Walking off into the trees, Ryn spoke. "Um ... Tristan, it's dark

146

and ..."

Coming to an abrupt halt when I saw the shop, Ryn ran into my back.

Peeking around me, she said, "Hey I didn't know that barn was back here."

"It's Lark's and mine. My father and mother stay out of it."

"You have your own barn?" Ryn asked as she laughed.

Dropping her hand as I fished my keys out of my pocket, I glanced over at her. "It's not a barn, it's a shop. You'll see why they aren't allowed in there in a second."

Walking in, the lights automatically came on and Ryn let out a gasp.

Two sports cars sat parked in the middle of the shop. Smiling, I looked over at my baby. Blue Thunder. Blue Thunder was my cobalt-blue nineteen sixty-eight Camaro that Lark and I had spent almost two years restoring.

"Wow. Look at those cars."

Smiling, I nodded my head and looked at Lark's nineteen-seventy Chevy Nova SS. Both cars had the same paint theme, cobalt blue with white racing strips down the middle of the entire car.

I watched as Ryn walked up to my Camaro. "What a beautiful car." Turning she smiled. "Is this why you won't let your parents in here? Afraid they might take the toys out for a spin?"

Throwing my head back, I laughed. "Not these toys, baby." Motioning to the back of the shop, Ryn turned and looked.

"What's behind the doors?"

"Lark and I had two bedrooms put in when we had the shop built. With as much time as we spent visiting our parents, we had wanted a place to get away. Maybe bring back dates if we were lucky."

Raising an eyebrow, Ryn gave me a wicked smile. "Why didn't we visit this bedroom last year? It would have made it a lot easier."

My smile faded briefly before I grabbed her hand and began walking toward the back. Unlocking my door, I pushed it open.

My room was a little different from Lark's. His pretty much had a bed and a bathroom in there. Mine had a bed, another bathroom . . . and a few of my *other* toys.

Walking into the room, the motion lights in the room turned on. Nothing had been touched since the last time I walked in this room. Turning, I watched as Ryn took in the room. Walking over to the small chest that was on the left side of the king-size bed, Ryn ran her hand over the ornate design. "What's in here?"

My heart was racing and I'd never in my life been so terrified. What would Ryn think when she opened the drawers and saw the sex toys? Would she change her mind about us? Closing my eyes and saying a silent prayer, I opened them and whispered, "Only one way to find out."

Ryn's fingers ran up and down the three-drawer chest. Stopping on the second drawer down, she slowly began to open it. I held my breath as she opened the drawer. I couldn't pull my eyes away from her face.

Glancing back at me, Ryn lifted her mouth into a smile. Looking back into the drawer, Ryn reached in and took out the flogger. Ryn ran the leather tails across her other hand.

"What is this?"

Not being able to move, I barely said, "A flogger."

Her eyes lit up. "Sex toys?"

Slowly nodding my head, I managed to speak. "Yes."

Narrowing her eyes at me and chewing on her lower lip she asked, "Is this something new you are into or—"

I swallowed hard. "No. I wanted to share this side of me with you, but I wasn't sure how you would feel about it."

Smiling bigger she said, "This explains why you're so good in bed with . . . other things."

I couldn't help but smile. If she only knew the different ways I could make her feel good.

"Can we use this . . . on me . . . now?"

My heart dropped to my stomach and something new washed over my body. The fact that Ryn wanted to even entertain the idea of using the flogger filled my body with hope and eased my tension a bit.

Damn, I love this girl.

The idea that my love for Ryn was growing faster had me a bit freaked out, but I wasn't going to let it push her away from me. Giving her a smile I knew would have her panties off in less than thirty seconds, I began to walk over to her.

Placing my hand on the side of her face, I leaned over and sucked her lower lip into my mouth then bit down on it. Ryn let out a moan that went straight to my dick. Pulling back, I looked into her eyes. "Baby, I'd love to use that on you, but we would have to work you into it. There's something else I want to do to you first though."

Ryn's eyes lit up with desire. Ever since I gave her the orgasm a few days ago in the closet, I'd been dying to bury my cock deep inside of her. My plan to take her that night failed when Ryn passed out in my arms from exhaustion. I didn't have the heart to wake her up.

Licking her lips, the words barely made it out of her mouth. "What do you want to do to me?"

"The first time I laid eyes on you I fantasized about having your tits up against my Camaro while I fucked you from behind."

"Oh. God," Ryn whimpered out.

Running my thumb along her soft skin I asked, "Ryn, would you rather our first time be slower, I'm dying to make love to you as well. But my cock is so hard and all he wants is to fuck you hard and fast."

Her chest began to heave up and down as she began panting. Placing her hands on my chest, Ryn looked into my eyes. "I'll take sex against your car please." My heart was beating crazy wild as I let Ryn's words soak in.

Smiling, I moved my hands and had her undressed in no time. I stood back and looked at her beautiful body. "Fuck, Ryn. I've never seen a woman with such an amazing body."

Ryn's cheeks flushed as she stood there in a nervous stance. Lifting my shirt over my head, I threw it onto the floor and then unbuttoned my pants. I wanted Ryn's mouth around my cock, but I knew I had to wait.

Unbuttoning my pants, I pushed them to the ground. Ryn let out a soft moan as she placed her hand over my hard dick. She quickly pushed my briefs down and grabbed my dick in her hand and began moving up and down my shaft, pulling out a low deep moan from my lips.

"I've missed you so damn much, Ryn."

Smiling, she whispered, "I've missed you too."

Not wanting to wait another minute, I reached down, picked her up and carried her back out into the shop and to my Camaro. I'd been dreaming of this moment since I first laid eyes on Ryn. Never mind the fact that I wanted her so bad my dick was throbbing, but having her on my baby.

Fan-fucking-tastic.

CHAPTER
Twenty-Two

*M*Y HEART WAS PRACTICALLY BEATING out of my chest as Tristan carried me over to his Camaro. I wasn't sure what I was more excited about. Finally being with Tristan again, Tristan taking me up against his classic car, or the fact that he had a chest full of sex toys.

Closing my eyes, I felt the heat move across my face. I couldn't believe how horny I was and how the thought of Tristan doing naughty things to me ramped that feeling up about a thousand times.

Then a thought occurred to me. How many women had he fucked against his Camaro? How many women had he brought back to this shop and had his naughty way with them?

Tristan slowly slid me down his body; his hard dick was pressed up against me and I let out a soft moan. No, it was more of a whimper. I wanted him so much. But I knew I wasn't going to be able to push the nagging questions from my mind.

"Tristan?"

His lips traveled along my neck, causing the most amazing tingling sensation to erupt across my entire body.

"Yeah, baby?"

"I don't want to ruin this moment, but I have to ask you something and I'm not even really sure why it's so important to me." Shaking my head, I looked into his eyes.

"No, that's not true. I do know why it's so important. This is our first time together again and I want it to be—" Looking away, I whispered, "Special."

Grabbing my face with his hands, he pulled my face back to his. "Baby, I'll take you to the bed and make love to you, if that's what you want. I just want to be buried inside you and stay there all night."

Tears threatened to spill from my eyes. "No. No, I want to do this. It's just . . . well . . . I mean I have no right to ask . . ."

"Jesus, Ryn. Ask me for Christ's sake, cause you're freaking me out."

Swallowing hard, I forced myself to look into his eyes. "Have you ever had another girl . . . you know . . . on your car? Am I the first?"

The smile that spread across his face was my answer and I couldn't help but smile back in return. He leaned in and brushed his lips across mine. "Baby, I've never even let a girl touch my Camaro before."

Smiling, I leaned against the hood of his muscle car and watched as every one of his muscles seemed to flex. Glancing down, I licked my lips at the small amount of pre cum on the tip of his dick. I wanted to wrap my mouth around him and listen while he called out my name as he came.

Sliding my hand between my legs, I felt incredibly brazen. Tristan had always brought out another side of me when we were intimate. Slipping my fingers inside me, I dropped my head back and moaned when I felt how wet I was.

Tristan grabbed my hand and pulled it away. His eyes were on fire. His breathing was labored and I knew he was more than ready, just like I was.

"Do you want me to come before I even begin fucking you, Ryn?"

Smiling, I bit down on my lower lip. "I want to come so bad, Tristan. I want to remember how you took me to heaven."

Dropping down, Tristan had me lying on the hood, my legs over his shoulders, and his mouth on me faster than I even knew what was happening. Letting out a gasp, I grabbed on to his hair and began moving my hips to the rhythm of his tongue.

Feels. So. Amazing.

No one I had ever been with made me feel like Tristan did. Not even Dodge. Tristan had a way of making my body feel like it was coming to life. I could feel my orgasm building and a part of me wanted this to last longer. The feel of his tongue and mouth moving against me was incredible.

"Tristan . . . I don't want to . . . come yet!"

Pulling his mouth away, I instantly missed the feeling. I thrashed my head back and forth as I felt him blowing hot air on me. "Jesus," I whispered.

Slipping his fingers in, he let out a low rumble. "Fucking hell. You're pussy is so ready for my cock, Ryn."

"OhMyGod!" I cried out. Tristan talking dirty was one of my favorite things.

"More. I need more, Tristan. I changed my mind! I want to come. Now!"

Hearing him chuckle, I looked at him as he licked his lips. I watched him bury his face between my legs as he moved his fingers slowly in and out of my body. Watching him work me with his mouth and tongue was more than I could take.

I put my head back and Tristan pulled away. "Watch me, Ryn. I want you to watch as I make you come."

Lifting my head up, I did what he said. I could feel the tingling beginning as it built up. I hadn't been this worked up in over a year.

Then it happened. Tristan did something with his fingers as he sucked on my clit and winked at me. He fucking winked at me and my world fell apart. I began calling out his name as I watched him suck and lick like he couldn't get enough.

I'd never had an orgasm hit me so hard. Closing my eyes, I continued to call out his name as I saw stars exploding.

Coming down from the most amazing orgasm ever, I realized I was in Tristan's arms. Opening my eyes, I looked into his beautiful green eyes. "You're so good at that."

Laughing, Tristan pressed his lips to mine. I could taste myself on this tongue and I loved every second of it. I wanted more. I needed more.

"Ryn, I'm going to fuck you hard and fast, baby. I don't think I could do it slow, even if I wanted to."

Nodding my head, I whispered, "Hard and fast is good."

Standing, he set me down. "I want your tits against the car, baby."

Turning, I laid flat against the cold hood of Tristan's car. My nipples hardened more as I sucked in a breath of air.

Tristan's hand ran over my ass as he said, "So fucking beautiful. I'm going to train that ass for my cock, Ryn. Would you like that?"

Looking over my shoulder at him, my mouth dropped open slightly. I was stunned at the rush of wetness between my legs as Tristan spoke to me.

"Tristan."

Pushing his finger gently against my ass, I let out a moan. "Answer me, Ryn. Would you like that?"

Closing my eyes tightly in an attempt to regain some sort of a normal thinking level, 1whimpered and pushed my ass against him as I looked at him. "Yes. Yes, Tristan I would like that."

He closed his eyes and it was as if relief washed over his face. That thought alone, of Tristan taking my ass, almost had me screaming out another orgasm. I'd always wanted a guy to be more daring in the bedroom. That was one thing I had loved about Tristan. He had more sex positions then a sex coach would have and I had loved trying them with him.

Opening his eyes, I watched Tristan grab his dick tightly as he began stroking himself.

Hottest thing ever.

"You like that, Ryn?"

Nodding my head, I replied, "Yes. A lot."

"I need to get a condom, baby, I left it in the room."

Pushing up, I yelled out, "No!"

Tristan didn't move. He stood there in a state of shock. "What do you mean no? Have you changed your mind?"

I watched as he kept his hand on his dick. "I mean, I've never been with anyone where they didn't use a condom. I want . . . I want to feel you, Tristan. I don't want anything between us."

His eyes widened in surprise. "Birth control?"

Nodding my head, I said, "Yes. I'm on the pill. Have you ever?"

"Never, Ryn. I've never had sex with anyone without a condom, and I was tested not long ago and I'm clean."

Looking down, I said, "I was tested after I broke things off with . . . um . . . Dodge and I'm clean too. If you're not comfortable with it we—" Tristan slammed his lips to mine and kissed the living shit out of me. Our tongues twisted against each other as my hands went to his hair and pulled on it hard.

Pulling away, Tristan growled, "Turn around, baby."

Turning quickly, I took my position again against the cold hood. Tristan used his foot to spread my legs wider. If I hadn't known any better, I would have thought I just got done running a marathon with how heavy my breathing was.

Tristan slipped his fingers inside me and began priming my body for him. "I'm not going to last one minute with no condom on and you laying on my car."

"Tristan! Hurry! I want you in me now."

Tristan pressed his tip at my entrance, barely pushing it in. Moaning, I pushed back to gain more of him. "So bossy. I like it, Ryn."

"Fuck me, Tristan! Please!"

Grabbing my hips, Tristan pushed in fast and hard. So hard I felt his balls hit up against me. *Yes! Yes this is what I have been missing.*

"Fucking yes! Oh God, Tristan."

He wasn't kidding when he said he was going to fuck me hard and fast. My body was hitting up against the cold hood and the sensation of rubbing against the car and Tristan slamming into me had me screaming out in an orgasm.

"So fucking beautiful. Shit!" Tristan called out. Feeling his hand slid up my back, he grabbed my hair and pulled back gently.

"Yes!" I screamed out as another orgasm ripped through my body. I could feel Tristan's dick swelling as I came hard. Griping my hip harder, he pulled almost all the way out and pushed back in deeper.

"Motherfucker. Ryn, baby I'm going to come. Ahh . . . *fuck!*"

I could feel his warm cum spilling into my body as he called out my name. I'd never felt anything so intense. The feel of Tristan, bare inside me, had my stomach diving and my heart racing.

I never wanted this to end. I wanted this always. Forever.

I WASN'T EVEN SURE WHEN Tristan had picked me up and carried back into the bedroom. Laying me gently on the bed, Tristan kissed me softly on the lips. "That was amazing, Ryn."

Smiling, I nodded my head. "Yeah it was. I've missed you so much, Tristan."

"I've missed you too, baby."

Stretching, I let my body feel the aftereffects of my orgasms. I felt like I was in heaven.

Closing my eyes, I let out a contented moan. Tristan laid next to me and pulled me into his body. "Ryn, being with you and not wearing a condom made it all the more amazing."

Smiling, I nodded my head. "Mmm . . . it did, didn't it?"

Tristan kissed me lightly on my shoulder as he moved his hand up and down my side. My eyes opened when I remembered the flogger. Turning, I smiled as I felt the blush hit my cheeks.

Tristan chuckled. "What is that naughty mind of yours thinking about?"

"The flogger. Will you use it on me?"

His smile faded for a brief second before it was replaced with a naughty smile. "Yes, but we have to start out slow since you've never had one used on you before."

"I need you to know something though, Ryn. I would never hurt you. I'll never push you into doing something you are not one-hundred percent in agreement with."

Smiling, I placed my hand on the side of his face. "I know you wouldn't."

Wiggling his eyebrows up and down he asked, "Do you want me to introduce you to the flogger now?"

Bam. There it was. Instant mass flooding between my legs as the idea of Tristan doing anything naughty to me perked up my libido. Placing my finger into my mouth, I nodded my head.

Tristan's eyes lit up with a desire I'd never seen before. "You're so damn sexy, Ryn. You turn me on like you would not believe."

Tristan got up and walked over to the chair where I had set the flogger down. Picking it up, he began moving it over his hand as he walked toward me. My eyes scanned his perfect body as I chewed nervously on my bottom lip.

"Do you trust me, Ryn?"

"Always."

Tristan nodded his head. He reached into the drawer I had pulled the flogger out of and held up some restraints. Four to be exact. Setting the flogger down, he moved to the bottom of the bed. It was then I noticed the bed frame was a sturdy iron frame. Tristan ran his hand along my leg down to my ankle and pulled it to him. Attaching the restraint onto the main bedpost, he attached the other part around my ankle.

Watching his every move, he walked over to the other side of the bed and repeated the process. My legs were spread open and I felt a blush move across my cheeks as he stood there and stared at me.

"Your pussy is perfect, Ryn."

Closing my eyes, I let out a moan. "Oh God. When you talk dirty to me, it turns me on even more."

"Open your eyes, Ryn."

Snapping my eyes open, I felt my hand moving down my body. Slipping my fingers across my clit, I jumped. "That turns me on, baby. I like getting you horny. Push your fingers inside you, Ryn, and finger fuck yourself."

Sucking in a deep breath, I pushed two fingers inside of me and moaned. Tristan's mouth parted open and his breathing increased. I loved knowing that pleasuring myself was turning him on so much.

"Jesus, that's fucking hot," Tristan barely whispered. His desire fueled me on as I moved faster and began moaning.

"I'm so close. Oh God!" I yelled out as I closed my eyes. Right before I came, my hand was pulled away, leaving me yelling out, "No!"

Opening my eyes, Tristan was holding my hand. "Not yet."

"What do you mean not yet? Yes! Yes . . . I mean . . . I think now is the perfect time."

Winking, Tristan pulled my hand over my head and quickly restrained my hand. Crawling over me he restrained the other hand. Then he placed himself over me, his legs on either side of my body. I watched as his dick began coming up again. I lifted my hips in an attempt to feel him against me.

Tristan took the flogger and began moving it over my body lightly. I instantly relaxed and let out a long soft moan. The feeling of the flogger moving over my skin was amazing. It didn't tickle, yet it did. Tristan moved it lightly over my breasts and I let out a moan. "Feels so good."

Tristan positioned himself to where the tip of his dick was positioned right at my entrance. "Yes. Tristan, please."

Barely pushing in and out he teased me with the flogger as he lightly brushed it back and forth over my sensitive clit and lips. The feeling was amazing.

"Does that feel good, Ryn?"

Frantically nodding my head, I panted out, "Yes! More, Tristan! More!"

Pushing in further, he kept running the flogger over my body. "Damn, Ryn. We are going to have so much fun training you to use the flogger."

My eyes caught Tristan's and something happened. He stopped moving as he stared at me. Pulling the flogger away from my body he dropped it on the floor beside the bed. I was in a trance with the way his eyes were holding mine. He turned and took both ankles from the restraints and then my arms.

Tristan pushed all the way inside of me as I lifted my body to accommodate his fullness. Leaning forward, he placed his hands on the side of my face as he slowly moved in and out of me.

"Ryn, this also feels amazing. More than amazing, baby. This feels so right."

"It does. It's magical, Tristan."

Tristan hadn't made love to me like this before except for one other time. The time he told me he was falling in love with me and then pushed me away. As he continued to make beautiful love to me, I fought to keep the tears at bay. Fear was slowly beginning to build. What if he got spooked again? I couldn't bear the thought of him pushing me away again.

Tristan began hitting the spot that had my orgasm building. Wrapping my legs around him, I moved along with him as I whispered his name against his lips.

I could feel Tristan's body shudder as he kissed me hard.

Moaning into my mouth, Tristan poured himself into my body.

I held on to him as he stayed buried inside of me. Not sure if I should move or not, I kept my legs around him as my hands held onto his upper arms.

Tristan pulled back some as I dropped my legs. His eyes were filled with something I'd never seen before.

Placing his hand on the side of my face, I leaned into it. "I love you, Ryn."

A small sob escaped between my lips as I lost the battle to keep my tears at bay. They slowly spilled out and onto my cheeks. Sucking in a breath, I managed to speak. "I love you too, Tristan."

Instead of him pulling out and moving away from me, he kissed away my tears before turning to my lips and softly kissing me. It was a tender kiss, one filled with love. It was if I could feel it pouring from his body into mine.

Tristan may have a naughty side to him, one that I was eager to learn more about, but this side of Tristan was the one I knew he had saved only for me.

Moving his lips to my neck, he kept placing soft kisses until he reached below my ear.

"I'm going to love you forever, Ryn."

"Tristan, I love you."

Smiling against my lips he said, "We missed dinner."

CHAPTER
Twenty-Three

TRISTAN

*F*EELING RYN IN MY ARMS as we fell asleep was the best feeling in the world. No, the best feeling in the world was hearing her tell me she loved me.

Closing my eyes, I thought about my father. Tomorrow I was going to have to ask him more questions about this bottle of his. It seemed to be working for my parents, and Lark.

Ryn let out a sweet little sound and I smiled. I had missed sleeping next to her. Missed her quirky ways. Like how she did a funny little dance every morning in the mirror to get herself ready for the day. Or how she had to wear her socks inside out because she couldn't stand the edging on the inside.

As I let my body slowly relax, I began to plan out how and when I would introduce Ryn to my playroom back in Austin. Hoping that she would be just as eager to play in there as she was to play this evening.

Sleep finally took over and I dreamed of walking along the beach with Ryn as we tossed a bottle into the ocean.

WALKING INTO THE KITCHEN, I ran my hand through my wet hair. Four sets of eyes looked at me and stared.

Stopping, I looked at my parents, Lark and then over to Azurdee, who wore a smile as big as the Grand Canyon.

"What? Why the hell are y'all looking at me with goofy-ass smiles on your face?" Pointing to Azurdee I said, "You're the worst of them all."

She began jumping up and down clapping her hands. "Oh my gosh! Oh my gosh!"

Shaking my head, I held up my hand to Azurdee. She reminded me so much of Sierra. They were both peppy. Sometimes peppy was not good when it was so early in the morning.

"Put it in a box and store that shit away, Azurdee. Too much. Too early."

Azurdee and my mother laughed. Pouring myself a cup of coffee, I turned around and leaned against the counter. Lark was staring at me. Raising my coffee mug to him I said, "Morning, bro."

Winking he said, "Late night, bro?"

My lips stopped at the rim of my coffee cup.

"Maybe."

Lark let out a chuckle. Looking away, I turned to my dad. "Hey, Dad. If you have a few extra minutes today, I'd like to talk to you."

"About what?" Lark and Azurdee both said at once.

Glancing over at them, I asked, "What in the hell is wrong with you two?"

"Whatcha need to talk to Dad about, Tristan?" Azurdee asked.

"Um . . . ranch stuff."

Raising an eyebrow, Lark asked, "That it?"

"Yeah, why? What does it matter to you what I need to talk to him about?"

My mother chortled and lightly hit Lark on the arm. "Leave your brother be, Michael. You're teaching sweet Azurdee bad habits." Smirking at Lark, he raised his middle finger up at me. Michael was my brother's first name and only my mother and father called him that. Dad would sometimes call him Lark.

Azurdee laughed and wrapped her arms around Lark. I was about to say something when Ryn walked into the kitchen and I watched the whole thing play over as they did pretty much the same thing to her. She got the stares and then the goofy smiles.

"So, what did you do last night, Ryn?" Azurdee asked.

Ryn began looking around at everyone. We had snuck back into the house around five am and crawled into her bed in the guest room and slept until six.

"Um . . . Tristan showed me his Camaro."

"I bet he did," Lark said under his breath.

"Michael, stop."

Ryn walked further into the kitchen and kissed my mother on the cheek. "Good morning, Joyce."

Smiling like a fool, my mother held Ryn back and gave her a once over before letting her go. "Good morning, sweetheart. Oh the glow on your face is beautiful."

Ryn blushed and looked my way. Giving her a wink, she blushed even more. I couldn't wait to see that shade of red on other parts of her body. Feeling my dick jump in my pants, I tried to focus on something else.

Placing her hand over her cheek, Ryn whispered, "A glow?"

Nodding her head, my mother handed Ryn a coffee cup. Taking it from my mother, Ryn poured herself a cup of coffee and leaned against the counter next to me. I could feel the pull of attraction between us. If I hadn't just made love to her in the shower, I'd be pulling her back into the bedroom.

Azurdee motioned toward us with her hand. "So?"

Lifting her shoulders loosely, Ryn asked, "So . . . what?"

Rolling her eyes and placing her hands on her hip, Azurdee blew out a frustrated breath. "Holding hands in the hospital, sneaking away for the evening. Are y'all back together or not?"

Turning, Ryn and I looked at each other and smiled. Nodding my head and not even caring that my parents were in the room, I said, "We are very much indeed back together."

Azurdee let out a small scream as my mother walked over to me and wrapped me in a warm embrace. She moved her mouth close to my ear and said, "It's about time, Tristan."

Pulling back and giving her a warm smile, I agreed. "Yes ma'am it is."

Azurdee was hugging Ryn as Lark reached his hand out for mine and pulled me into a hug. Pulling back slightly, he said, "The Camaro?"

Nodding my head, I whispered, "Hell yes. On the hood."

Lark raised an eyebrow and mumbled, "I claim the shop

tonight."

Throwing my head back, I laughed. "It's yours."

Lark pulled Azurdee into a hug as she let out a giggle. Reaching for Ryn's hand, I pulled her closer to me. She nuzzled into my side and I couldn't believe how perfect this moment felt. "I'm stealing Ryn for the day, Mom."

Smiling she asked, "Oh, are you heading into town?"

Glancing over to Ryn, she smiled. "Nope. We are picking out a spot on the ranch to build a house."

The dish my mother had been drying off slipped from her hands and fell to the floor. I was shocked it hadn't broken into pieces.

Placing her hand over her mouth, I saw the tears forming in her eyes. "What did you say?"

Grinning, I repeated what I had said. "Ryn and I talked last night and we are going to pick out a spot for a building location. If it's okay with you and Dad, I'd like to keep it within a half-mile or so of here. Probably on the other side of the shop Lark and I built."

Ryn squeezed my hand when I mentioned the shop.

My mom turned and looked at Ryn. "Ryn, darling. What about your business?"

Holding her closer to me, Ryn gave my mother the sweetest smile and my heart about burst open. "I can work from any-where, Joyce. I'll keep my office in Austin. I have three wonder-ful managers that don't need me there all the time checking on them. They work better when I'm not in the office anyway. I spend ninety percent of my time working from home. I'll just have to make a trip to Austin once a month for meetings that I can't attend on Skype." Turning and looking at me, Ryn's ex-pression changed. Her eyes were filled with happiness and love. I'd never felt so happy in my entire life. "Besides, my place is here, with Tristan."

Leaning over, I pressed my lips to hers. Before I knew it, I was setting my coffee down and wrapping my arms around her and kissing her like I'd never see her again. My father cleared his throat and I broke our kiss. Pulling back enough to look into her eyes I whispered, "I'm sorry I broke your heart, but I swear I'll spend the rest of my life putting it back together."

One single tear fell from her eye as she pressed her lips to mine and whispered against them, "Tristan."

RYN AND I HAD BEEN driving over a two-mile radius as we checked out possible building locations. When I asked Ryn what she was thinking about for our house, she smiled and said, "I don't know. This is all so crazy! I have a million ideas floating in my head."

"What are you thinking you want to do with your house in Austin?" I asked.

"I'm not sure I want to sell my house in, Austin. It's in such a great area and I think I could rent it out for over two thousand a month. I have some money saved up in my savings, so I guess we'll have to come up with a budget we are both comfortable with. This is a huge step, Tristan, and we just got back together so I'm trying to process it all."

Nodding my head, I took her hand. "I know, baby. I don't want you to give up anything. I realize this is huge, I mean, I basically asked you to move in with me, in the middle of South Texas. And oh yeah, we have to build a house. I'm doing one hell of a good job scaring you away."

Laughing, she punched me lightly in the stomach. "You could never scare me away. I finally feel like I'm home and I never want to leave."

Placing my hand on the side of her face, I gave her smile. "Ryn, you know you don't have to worry about money, baby. I can afford to build the house no problem."

Nodding her head, she barely said, "I know."

She looked a million miles away and I wanted to know what was making her pull back. Ryn knew I had money, a lot of money, but she never asked me how I came into it. My parents were well off, but both sets of my grandparents were very well off. Lark and I both received a good chunk of money from them when they passed away. After we each bought expensive-ass condos in down town Austin, we treated ourselves to the shop and our toy cars. The rest we have invested in real estate and other ventures.

"Talk to me, Ryn."

Pursing her lips, she looked away. Placing my finger on her chin, I turned her face back to me and pulled her lip out from her teeth. Leaning in, I gently kissed her. "Please don't pull away, baby."

Smiling weakly, she began talking. "I know you have money, Tristan. I know Lark has money. Azurdee mentioned once y'all getting some from your grandparents but I never questioned or asked anything else, it wasn't my business. This is such a big step and I'd be lying if I said I wasn't scared. You pushed me away once when things got to serious, what if—"

"I'm not going anywhere, Ryn. I swear to you. I know what life was like without you and I don't ever want to go there again. Ever."

Smiling, she nodded her head. "Okay. I believe you. If we do this though, build a house and move in together, I want to feel like I've contributed to it. I don't want you to have to foot the bill for everything just because you can. I don't want you to think I'm going to take advantage of that."

Placing my hands on the sides of her face, I tilted her head back, exposing her neck to me. Running my tongue along her neck, Ryn let out a moan. "You taste so damn good, Ryn."

"Don't change the subject, Tristan."

Laughing, I placed a gentle kiss on her neck. "How about I let you decorate the entire inside?"

"All of it?"

Hmm . . . that got her attention. "Yep. All of it. It's your blank canvas to do what you want."

Giving me an incredulous stare, she raised an eyebrow up at me. "I can pay for decorating the inside of the house?"

Letting out a chuckle, I said, "Well, since you're in charge of the inside it's only fair you can pay for decorating the inside of the house."

The smile that moved across her face caused my knees to wobble. "How does this happen? How do we go from pushing each other way to building a house and moving in together?"

Pulling my head back, I said, "You forgot the part where we are having great sex."

Making a face she slowly nodded her head as she pointed

to me. "That's what it is. The sex. You won me over with your high-performance dick."

Laughing, I said, "Hell yeah, I did!"

Ryn gave me a small push and caused me to lose my balance. Grabbing her, I pulled her to me. The look in her eyes told me she was thinking the same thing I was. We wanted each other.

"Are you cold, baby?"

Looking at me funny, Ryn shook her head. "No, it's seventy-two degrees outside."

Moving my hands to the bottom of her T-shirt, I quickly lifted it over her head and tossed it to the ground.

"What are you doing?"

"I'm going to take you now, Ryn. Take off your clothes but not your bra and panties."

I watched as Ryn's mouth slowly parted open. I was pretty sure I heard a whimper come from her lips as she stared at me. "You want me naked? Here? Now?"

Giving her a sexy grin, I said, "I want your clothes off, except your panties and bra, yes. Here. Now."

Ryn's eyes sparkled with excitement as she began to unbutton her jeans. "Keep your boots on, baby."

Ryn reached for my arm as she removed her boot from her foot and then her leg from the left side of her jeans. Slipping her boot back on her left foot, she repeated the process with her right side.

After she had removed her jeans, Ryn stood before me in nothing but her bra, panties and cowboy boots.

"Fucking hell. You're body drives me crazy."

Pulling my shirt over my head, I tossed it on top of Ryn's clothes. Unbuttoning my jeans, I pulled them down just enough to let my hard cock out. Grabbing it with my hands, I started sliding my hand up and down.

"Tristan," Ryn whispered as she pushed her legs together. I knew from her reaction last night she liked seeing me play with myself.

"Take off your bra, Ryn."

Moving as fast as she could, Ryn reached behind her and unclasped her bra, handing it to me with a girlish grin.

Reaching down, I took the bra from her hand. "Walk over to the ranch Jeep and put your hands on the hood."

Raising her eyebrows, she gave me a slight smile. I watched her turn and shake that fine ass as she walked toward the Jeep. Turning, she looked over her shoulder and slid her finger into her mouth and smiled bigger.

Following her, I kept stroking my hard as a rock dick. Fuck I wanted to take her in the ass so damn bad.

Soon. Very soon I would start training that ass for my cock. Moaning, I watched her rest her hands on the hood. My heartbeat had sped up and I couldn't help but notice how excited I got every time I thought about having sex with Ryn. I had never been like this with any other girl. It has always been about sex. Sure I wanted to pleasure them, and I always made sure they came at least once, but with Ryn it was so much more. I wanted to touch and feel every inch of her body. I wanted to feel her come hard on my tongue, fingers, and cock.

Running my hand down the middle of her back, Ryn moaned.

Grinning, I asked, "Do you want me, baby?"

"Yes. Tristan, I want you so much I can't take it."

"Tell me what you can't take."

"The wait! The need to come is incredible. It's pulsing."

Leaning over, I kissed her back. "Tell me what's pulsing."

"Oh God, Tristan. Don't make me say it."

Smacking her ass with my hand, Ryn jumped and let out a small scream. "Say it, Ryn."

"My pussy! My pussy is pulsing."

Rubbing my hand along her ass, Ryn let out a deep rumbled moan. "Tell me what you want, baby. I want to hear you tell me you want my cock buried in your pussy."

Looking over her shoulder, Ryn's breathing had increased. She was turned on and I knew if I stuck my fingers into her, she would be soaking wet. My dick was painfully hard as I continued to slide my hand up and down.

"Does it turn you on to hear me talk like that, Tristan?"

Smiling, I said, "Yes."

Giving me a sexy grin, Ryn purred, "I want you to bury your cock deep inside my pussy, Tristan. I'm so wet and I need you to fuck me. I want you balls deep inside me."

Holy fucking shit. My girl knew how to talk dirty. Dropping my dick, I grabbed her arms and pulled them behind her back. Tying them up with her bra, I pushed her legs open.

"I want to taste how wet you are, Ryn."

"Oh God, Tristan. I've never. I'm so close. Oh God!"

I loved how responsive Ryn was to me. Dropping down, I placed both my hands on her ass. Her thong panties were made of lace and I knew in one pull they would fall apart in my hands. Thinking Ryn would think this was hotter, I moved her panties out of the way and pushed my fingers inside of her. My eyes about rolled in the back of my head as I felt how wet she was. Getting my fingers good and covered with her sweetness, I pulled my fingers out. Slowly moving up I pushed my index finger against her ass and slowly pushed in. Ryn let out a long moan as she stood there with her hands tied behind her back.

"Ohmygod!" she called out. "Tristan! Oh God!"

Smiling, I moved my finger in and out of her ass as she fell apart.

Beautiful. Fucking beautiful.

Standing, I slowly leaned her against the Jeep as I grabbed onto her tied hands.

"Ryn, if I hurt you, you have to tell me."

Nodding her head, she frantically panted out. "Yes. Yes. I'll tell you."

Pushing her ass against me, she mumbled, "Again! Tristan, do it again."

This girl was killing me. With each time we were together, I grew more hopeful that Ryn would love my playroom.

"Please, Tristan, I'm so horny. Please!"

Reaching between her legs, I pushed my fingers in deep and began working her up. Pulling out she let out a frustrated sigh, but moaned when I pushed my index finger into her ass again. "Yes!" she yelled out as I placed my dick at the entrance to her pussy. I couldn't wait to fuck her. Feel her cunt pulsing and covering my cock with her sweetness.

As I pulled back on her hands, I pushed my dick into her, balls deep like she asked for. Ryn let out a scream.

"Baby, are you okay?"

"Give me a second. I just need to adjust to you like this. It's . . . so . . . deep. So, deep!"

Smiling, I pulled back on her bra some. "Go. Tristan, move!"

Pulling out slowly, I pushed back in as I followed the same pattern with my finger in her ass. I knew Ryn had three different sensations going on at once. The feel of my finger in her ass, my cock in her pussy, and the pain of me pulling her arms back as I fucked her.

"Oh God. What's happening?"

"Talk to me, Ryn."

Slowing down some, she shook her head. "Feels so good. Tristan, don't stop. Harder! Give it to me harder."

"Fuck yeah, baby. That's it."

It didn't take long for Ryn and I to both fall apart. I quickly untied her bra and began massaging her arms. It took a few minutes for our breathing to get under control.

Ryn smiled and wrapped her arms around my neck and kissed my nose. "I have to say. I like this side of you . . . a lot."

Closing my eyes, I pulled her to me. I knew just because she liked rough fucking wasn't going to mean she would be into everything. The flogger was fun, but what would she think when I showed her everything else?

I decided in that moment, I needed to entertain the thought of possibly giving up my other lifestyle if Ryn would not be into it. I was falling more and more in love with her as the seconds ticked off the clock.

I would not lose her again.

CHAPTER
Twenty-Four

Ryn

WO WEEKS HAD PASSED SINCE Tristan and I had come back from his parents' ranch. Things had been blissfully wonderful between us. We were beginning to settle into a routine of being together again. Tristan's stress level was up though as he prepared to head back home and permanently take over the ranch. Peter had hired on two guys Tristan had known since high school to come and help with the ranch until Tristan could get everything back in Austin squared away. He was keeping his downtown condo that I had yet to go to. I had always thought it was strange he never brought me there, but hadn't really given it too much thought.

Tristan's house went up for sale yesterday morning and this afternoon he was meeting with his realtor to look at an offer. Round Rock was a very sought out area of Austin and Tristan didn't think he would have a problem selling his house. It had been completely remodeled. My favorite part of his house was his backyard. It was amazing. The stone patio pretty much took up most of the yard with a giant fire pit in the middle that was surrounded by built-in stone benches. More than once we had made love on those benches.

Smiling, I let the memories of Tristan and I together in the house flood my memory. Closing my eyes, I could almost feel Tristan's lips on my body.

"Jesus, Ryn. Don't break out into an orgasm right here in the middle of Starbucks."

Smiling at the familiar voice, I opened my eyes and gave Sierra a playful look. "Hello to you too, Sierra."

Tilting her head, she stared at me. Then she narrowed her left eye at me. Taking a step back she moved her eyes up and down my body. Just as she was about to say something, Dodge walked through the door.

"Hey, Ryn!" Sierra's whole posture changed and I couldn't help but notice the slight flush move across her cheeks as she looked at Dodge.

Turning, Dodge saw Sierra. "Hey Sierra, how are you doing?"

Sucking her lower lip into her mouth, Sierra gave Dodge a nod and then said, "Hey, how's it going?"

Dodge turned back to me and smiled. Then he did almost the same thing Sierra had done not even two minutes ago. Narrowing his eyes at me, he looked me up and down before his baby blues were looking into my eyes. "Holy shit. It's all over your face."

Sierra sucked in a breath and before I could say anything, she pushed Dodge out of the way. "Oh, no you don't. I noticed it first, so back off, boy toy."

Dodge glared at Sierra. "I don't think so, short stack. I noticed the moment I walked in."

"I call bullshit," Sierra said as she threw her hands onto her hips. Glancing over Sierra's shoulder, I smiled. My body came alive the moment Tristan walked through the door. Tristan walked in and immediately came to my side. Walking by Dodge and Sierra arguing, he pointed at them and said, "What are Bonnie and Clyde arguing about?"

Chucking, I said, "I have no clue. The bigger question here is, how has Sierra not been banned from this Starbucks?"

Tristan laughed then whispered in my ear, "I think the manager wants in her pants."

Giggling, I playfully hit Tristan. The smell of his cologne caused my stomach to clench with desire.

"Listen, dickhead, you think you saw what you saw, but really you didn't see anything at all because you're probably still hung up on her. Being hung up on her, you *thought* you saw something there, but you didn't. You didn't see anything."

Dodge pulled his head back and stared at Sierra. "What in the fuck do you smoke every morning?"

"Language kids."

Tristan and I both looked over to an older woman who I had seen Sierra talking to a number of times.

Taking Sierra by the arm, Dodge pulled her out of the Starbucks. Smiling at the older woman, I grabbed Tristan's arm as we followed Dodge and Sierra out of Starbucks. "Did you know Sierra had the hots for Dodge?"

Laughing, Tristan said, "Oh, yeah. I saw those eyes light up the first time she ever laid eyes on the man whore."

"Tristan!" I said as I glared at him.

Lifting his hands in surrender, Tristan laughed. "Sorry, I know he is a friend."

Dodge had pulled Sierra away from the door. "Listen, why don't you get your coffee and head on out of here? Go to work and do whatever it is you do." Looking at Sierra dressed in her scrubs, Dodge laughed. "What do you do? You a secretary to some hot doctor who you screw at night before he goes home to his sad, lonely wife?"

"Oh shit," Tristan said.

Sierra stared at Dodge. I was waiting for her to pop off with a comeback, but she didn't say a word. I knew his words stung her to the core. Sierra's ex was a doctor who had cheated on her with her best friend, who happened to work in his office as his office manager. Dodge's smirk faded as his eyes searched Sierra's stricken face. You could see the hurt laced in her features.

Turning, Sierra began to walk away. I saw the tear moving down her cheek and I quickly made my way over to her.

Dodge called out, "Wait! Sierra, I didn't mean to—"

Looking at Dodge, I said, "Stop. Just stop talking."

Tristan came walking up and asked if Sierra was okay. Nodding her head, she was barely able to talk. "I'm gonna head to work. I'll give y'all a call later. Let's do dinner so I can hear all about how y'all got back together again."

Looking over my shoulder to Dodge, Sierra shouted, "Because I knew first she was back with him, you stupid asshole!"

Turning, Sierra made her way over to her car that was parked across the street. Tristan and I stood there and watched as Sierra got in her car and pulled out, headed to St. David's Hospital.

Spinning on my heels, I glared at Dodge. "Why would you say something so awful?"

Tristan placed his hand around my waist. "Ryn, Dodge didn't know."

Looking away, I attempted to calm down. Dodge looked between Tristan and me. "What don't I know?"

"Sierra's husband—"

"Soon to be ex-husband," I interjected.

Nodding his head, Tristan continued, "Her soon to be ex-husband cheated on her. Sierra came home early one night from work. It was their six-year anniversary and she wanted to surprise him. He's a doctor and they hardly ever got to spend time together. Sierra walked into their bedroom and he was fucking her best friend, who happens to also work for him as his office manager."

Dodge's mouth fell open. "What?"

"Yeah, dude; couldn't you pick a better scenario? Do you not remember me telling you her husband cheated on her?" Tristan asked as sarcasm fell from his lips. I knew it was going to take Tristan some time to get used to the fact that I still wanted to be friends with Dodge. We had talked about it a few nights ago when Dodge sent a text asking how my New Year had gone.

Dodge jerked back like someone had just hit him with a fire poker. "I didn't . . . I mean I had forgotten . . . how in the hell would I have known that her best friend worked for her ex and was the one who fucked him? I don't know anything about Sierra besides the fact that she is spit and fire. I see her in Starbucks at least three times a week and every single time she pops off with some smartass remark."

Rolling my eyes, I looked at Dodge. "Can't you see she likes you, Dodge?"

Dodge snapped his head over to me. "What?" Then he started laughing. To the point where he pretended he had tears and held his stomach like it was all too much.

Tristan gave Dodge a nudge. "Knock it off, your ass would be lucky to have someone like Sierra."

Dodge stopped laughing and looked at Tristan and then

173

me. "Um . . . yeah. No thanks, dude. I think I'll pass."

Shaking my head, I looked at Tristan as he brought me into his arms. I knew it was his way of showing Dodge that he had no chance of being with me ever again. "Congratulations by the way. I could see it on your face, Ryn, when I walked into Starbucks. You look really happy."

Reaching for Tristan's hand, they shook hands as Dodge gave Tristan a nod. "Listen, I've got to get to work and with my little argument with Princess Smartass, I'm going to be late for a meeting. Y'all should stop by the club sometime."

Tristan half smiled. "Yeah, maybe we will before we leave for South Texas."

My body went stiff. I hadn't been planning on telling anyone just yet that I'd be moving to South Texas.

Dodge turned my way. "What? You're moving, Ryn?"

Trying to smile the best I could, I said, "Yeah. I'll um, tell you all about it over coffee."

Tristan's grip on my waist tightened. A clear indication he was still uneasy about my friendship with Dodge. I knew Dodge was not going to take the news of me leaving Austin very well.

"Wait a second here, Ryn. You just got back with him and now you're going to follow him to South Texas?" My body tensed at Dodge's response. I knew it wasn't very long ago Dodge wanted something more from our relationship, but he also knew how much I loved Tristan. I wasn't prepared for a showdown right now with Dodge over my moving to South Texas. Especially with Tristan standing right next to me.

Tristan dropped his arm from my waist and took a step closer to Dodge. Knowing Tristan was pissed, I stood between the two of them; I put my hand on Tristan's chest to stop him. "Tristan, let me take care of this please."

"This is insane, Ryn. He can't just tell you he's sorry, and you decide you're giving everything up to follow him there. Jesus, Ryn. Don't be so stupid. What, is he that great of a fuck?"

Tristan moved me out of the way so fast, I didn't have time to stop him from doing what I knew was coming next.

Tristan punched Dodge square in the mouth. Grabbing him by the shirt, he yelled, "You apologize to her right now, asshole!"

Dodge pushed Tristan back and was about to raise his fist to hit Tristan when I jumped between them. The moment Dodge's fist hit my face, I swore I saw stars.

Yelling out my name, Tristan grabbed me before I hit the ground.

"You motherfucker! You hit her!"

Everything was blurry in my left eye and I instantly had a headache. I'd never been punched before. Okay that was a lie. Once in fifth grade, I called my best friend Mindy a fat cow and she hauled back and punched me right in the nose. It was safe to say, I'd rather take Mindy's punch over a guy's punch any day.

"Ryn, baby, are you okay?"

Slowly nodding my head, I barely forced out the word, "Yes," as I attempted to focus my left eye. The throbbing pain quickly moved up through my head and into an instant headache.

"I swear to God if she didn't look like she was going to pass out I'd kick the living shit out of you," Tristan told Dodge. There was a tightness in Tristan's eyes and his face was red. The pulsing vein in his neck indicated he was upset.

Glancing up to Dodge, he looked like he was going to be sick. "Ryn, I didn't mean to hit you. You stepped in between us and I couldn't stop in time."

Trying to smile, I said, "It's okay. It was stupid of me to get in between two grown men who were acting like stupid high school boys."

My eyes, or rather, eye, traveled to each guy. Tristan was still glaring at Dodge, but at least he was not threatening to kill him, and Dodge looked like someone had just taken away his favorite . . . um . . . what did Dodge like to do? I thought about it for a few seconds as Tristan held me in his arms in front of my favorite Starbucks. I was pretty sure after today, I was banned for life from my favorite Starbucks.

"Do you have any hobbies, Dodge?"

Rubbing the back of his neck, Dodge started mumbling. "Oh God. Oh shit. She's got brain damage. I swear I didn't hit her that hard. Shit! Ah shit."

"She doesn't have brain damage you ass," Tristan said.

Dodge pointed to me. "She is talking nonsense."

Holding up my hand, I said, "No. I was trying to think of how to describe your face and it looked like someone had taken away your favorite thing. But then I didn't know what your favorite thing was. So that's why I asked, do you have any hobbies?"

Tristan and Dodge both stared at me. "Holy fuck, you did give her brain damage," Tristan said.

Closing my eyes, I let out a heavy breath. "Tristan? Will you please take me home?"

Dodge reached out and took my hand. "I swear I didn't mean—"

Giving Dodge a weak smile, I said, "I know. We'll talk soon."

As Tristan walked me back to my house, he kept saying how the next time he saw Dodge he was going to beat his ass into the ground. I stopped trying to argue with him about it. He was pissed that Dodge said what he said to me, and he was even more pissed that Dodge ended up almost knocking my lights out.

As Tristan laid me down on my bed, I tried to figure out what I was going to do about the whole Dodge and Tristan thing. I needed to talk to Dodge. Alone. I should have done it the moment I came back. Even though I had been clear with Dodge that there would never be a future with the two of us, I should have told him how serious things were with Tristan and I. Closing my eyes, I knew the reason I put off telling Dodge I was back with Tristan was because he was going to be hurt.

Tristan placed a bag of frozen carrots onto my eye. Letting out a gasp, I jumped as Tristan winced. "I'm sorry, baby. I hate that you got hurt because of me."

Looking at Tristan, I noticed how his eyes appeared wet from the tears he was holding back. "I didn't get hurt because of you."

"Yeah, you did. I let my temper get the better of me. It's just, I'm tense around Dodge anyway because of your past relationship and him saying that. It just pissed me off. I'll be glad when you are away from him."

Sitting up, I pushed the bag of carrots off of my eye. "Excuse me?"

Tristan stared at me. "What?"

"You'll be glad when I'm away from him? Dodge is a friend of mine. I don't plan on giving up my friendship with him. Would you give up your friendship with Sierra? You didn't hear me getting upset when you talked to her on the phone last night and made plans to go over to her house to fix her garage door."

Tristan laughed. "That's different, Ryn."

Feeling the anger begin to boil in my blood, I inhaled a deep breath. "How is that different? It's the same, Tristan. What if I don't want you hanging around your college sweetheart who you just happened to have fucked after you ran into each other at the . . ."

Tristan stood up, clearly agitated.

"Wait, I only fucked Sierra one time and it meant nothing. It was a fuck that is all. No emotion."

Swallowing hard, I asked, "Isn't that how all your fucks are, Tristan? No emotions."

Pushing his hand through his hair, he nodded his head. "That's not fair, Ryn. I've never treated you like that."

Laughing, I threw the bag of carrots at him. "The moment you called Liberty on the phone, you treated me that way, asshole."

Tristan looked stunned. "Wait. What in the hell is going on here, Ryn? Why are you bringing up Sierra? She's just a friend I met a few months ago."

I was pretty sure my heart stopped beating. "What did you say?"

Tristan looked at me confused. "I said she's just a friend I met a few months ago."

"You lied?"

Tristan looked baffled until it hit him. Closing his eyes he shook his head, "No wait let me explain, Ryn, Sierra and I meet on the side of her house—"

"When you were watching Dodge fuck me?"

A grave expression rolled across Tristan's face. He hesitated before speaking. "She told you?"

Dropping my head back, I laughed. "Oh my God. You were playing me? What did you two come up with some plan to make me jealous and beg for you back?"

Tristan looked away, "No . . . not really."

"Oh my God! I thought she was my friend. I thought . . ." Turning away from Tristan, I tried to pull my anger back in. Not bothering to look back at Tristan, I asked, "So you only met Sierra that day. Then you finger fucked her in a club and what?" Spinning back around, I walked over to Tristan and pushed him. "Took her back to your house and fucked her?"

Tristan grabbed my arms to keep me from hitting him. "Stop this, Ryn. We weren't together. You can't get upset with me when you were fucking Dodge!"

His words stung for some reason. I instantly knew he was right. Why I had brought it all up was beyond me. I was upset he and Sierra had played me, but I knew the reason why. Tristan was trying to get me back. It was wrong, but I got the reason behind it.

Taking a few steps back, I stared at Tristan. His eyes filled with something I'd never seen before. Fear.

"I'll leave you alone tonight, Ryn."

Turning, Tristan headed to the front door. I was instantly brought back to the day at the beach when he walked away from me.

"Tristan. Please don't go. *Please!*"

Turning, he gave me the saddest look. "Ryn, I don't want to fight with you. I especially don't want to fight about Sierra. If my friendship with her bothers you, I'll walk away and let the two of you just be friends. As far as Dodge goes, I trust you and trust your judgment. Right now, I'm tired, Ryn and I don't feel like doing this."

Fearing he was going to walk away, I ran over to him and threw myself into his body. Tristan wrapped his arms around me and held me tight.

"I love you. Please don't leave. Please don't leave me," I cried as Tristan ran his hand down the back of my head gently.

"Shh . . . baby, I'm not going anywhere."

I couldn't stop my sobbing. "I'm sorry. I don't know what came over me and why I was bringing all that up. I know you have a lot on your plate right now, Tristan. You've quit your job, you're selling your house." Burying my head in Tristan's chest, I wanted to beg him to make love to me.

"My eye and head hurts," I whimpered as I grabbed onto his shirt and held onto him, as if I was afraid he would walk away.

Moving his lips to the top of my head, Tristan whispered,

"Let's go lay down, Ryn."

Letting Tristan lead me to my bedroom, the throbbing in my head moved to between my legs. Lying down on the bed, I snuggled into his body. His breathing immediately began lulling me to sleep.

Whispering against his chest, I asked, "Will you make love to me, Tristan?"

"Baby, you never have to ask me to make love to you."

Tristan moved quickly to undress himself and then me. He hovered over my body as he looked into my eyes. Slowly pushing into my body, he brushed his lips against mine. "I love you, Ryn. I'll always love you."

Tristan spent the rest of the morning making love to me until we both were overcome with exhaustion and sleep won us over.

CHAPTER
Twenty-Five

TRISTAN

$\mathcal{W}$ ALKING UP TO RYN'S HOUSE, I breathed in a deep breath as I pushed my hand through my wavy brown hair. We were going out for dinner, some dancing, and then I was planning on taking her back to my condo. Tonight I was going to show her the side of me I had been holding back. I prayed like hell she wouldn't turn and walk away. My playroom wasn't set up nearly like other's I had been in. I'd walked into a few and turned my ass around and walked right back out. I wasn't into the dominant and submissive thing at all.

I didn't get into all the BDSM shit that my buddy, Nick, from college did. I did however like to play hard. You were either into it or not into it. Nick took it serious though and was hard-core. Had the whole girl calling him sir and all that shit. All it took was that night we had spent with Michelle and Ash, and Nick was hooked for life. He spent over a year with Ash as she molded him to how she wanted him.

Opening the door before I could knock, Ryn stood there dressed in a beautiful teal blue cocktail dress. My eyes wandered over her body until they finally made their way to her black high heel shoes. Letting out a moan, I adjusted my instantly hard dick.

"Fucking hell, Ryn. You look amazing, baby."

Giving me a smile that caused a zip of energy to rush through my entire body, Ryn said, "Thank you. You look pretty handsome yourself."

Looking down at my clothes, I tried to wonder what she thought was different. I was dressed in jeans, cowboy boots, a blue button down shirt, and a cowboy hat. Glancing back at her, she had her finger in her mouth and I knew she was undressing me with her eyes.

"We can skip dinner and dancing if you want."

Letting out a sexy giggle, she shook her head. "No, this is your last night before you leave. I want it to be special. I have a feeling we are going to be in for an adventure tonight."

Giving her a quick wink, I finally stepped in through the door and took her in my arms. "You have no idea, baby. No idea at all."

"I just need to grab my wrap and purse then we can leave." Turning, she began walking through her house. The way her ass moved in that dress I knew I was going to have a hard time keeping my hands off of her. I couldn't help but notice she slightly limped on her left foot still.

Looking around, I noticed Ryn had begun packing. My heart soared at the idea of Ryn and I being together. I hated that my father had a heart attack, but in a sense, it finally woke me up to how miserable I was in my life. It felt like the last year I had been on autopilot, nothing to really look forward to each day.

Things were different now. I was going to be back home, running my family's hunting ranch and doing what I loved to do, and Ryn would be with me.

Smiling, I shook my head. What a difference a year makes. I still had the feeling deep in my gut that scared the shit out of me about Ryn and I. We certainly had been on full throttle since getting back together and a part of me wondered if it was just the excitement of finally having her back.

Then there was the playroom. Putting my fingers up to my temples, I began massaging them.

"Do you have a headache, Tristan? We can stay here and order take out if you want."

Giving her a smile, I shook my head, "It's just stress from everything that's going on. All the moving and getting things settled. Once we eat, I'll be fine. You ready?"

Ryn tilted her head and gave me a look like she didn't believe me. "I promise you, Ryn."

Walking up to me, she reached up on her toes and gently kissed my lips. "Sometimes I have to pinch myself."

Raising an eyebrow, I asked, "Why?"

Her eyes lit up and her face turned serious. "I've never in my life been this happy. I loved what we had before, but now it feels—"

"Special? Magical?"

Nodding her head and dabbing a tear from the corner of her eye she kissed me again. "Tell me," she whispered against my lips.

Ryn had gotten into the habit of asking me to tell her I loved her. If I could tell her every second of the day, I would.

"I love you, baby."

Smiling, she laced her fingers through my hair and pulled my mouth closer to hers. The kiss was passionate from the get go. Our tongues danced around each other as Ryn moaned into my mouth. I was two seconds away from lifting her dress, pulling off her panties and fucking her.

Pulling back and panting to catch her breath, Ryn spoke. "We . . . better . . . get going."

"Yeah, we better." Taking her hand, we made our way out to the car. My nerves began acting up again and I tried like hell to push them down. If I let it show how scared shitless I was, Ryn would pick up on it. "So, have you told your office yet about the move?"

Ryn rolled her eyes and mumbled under her breath. "I'd rather not talk about the office right now."

Pulling my head back in shock, I nodded. "Okay. No shop talk."

Swinging her legs into the car, Ryn simply replied with, "Thanks."

Whatever had been bothering Ryn, she quickly pushed it aside on the drive to the restaurant. She began talking about how excited she was to start the process of finding a builder.

"I've been meaning to tell you what Dad said. His best friend from high school is a builder. I should say, was a builder. His company built the house Lark and I grew up in. His son has taken over the business and they'd love to talk to us about building our house."

Ryn turned to me and smiled. "I love that idea. That adds a whole other sentimental element to the whole process."

Nodding, I agreed. "I think you're right, it does."

Pulling in front of The Driskill, I waited for the valet to come and give me a claim ticket. "Are you staying the evening with us, sir?"

"No, dining at the Driskill Grill."

Smiling, he gave me a polite handshake. "Enjoy your meal with your wife, sir."

Stunned into silence, I couldn't move. "What?"

The young kid looked at me like I was crazy. "Um, excuse me, sir?"

Glancing over toward Ryn, I watched as she smiled and had every single guys attention as she walked toward the entrance. Shaking her head, she laughed at something an older gentleman said to her.

Turning back to the valet, I had no idea what possessed me, but I answered him back with, "She's not my wife. Girlfriend. She's um . . . my girlfriend."

Grinning he said, "Wife or girlfriend, enjoy your evening, sir."

Walking toward Ryn, I was unsure why this kid's comment had thrown me for a loop. Placing my hand on the small of Ryn's back, I guided her into the hotel and made our way to the restaurant.

I had never been to this restaurant, but Lark had brought Azurdee. Walking into it, I was not disappointed.

"Oh, it's breathtaking. So romantic," Ryn whispered as we walked in. Glancing around the restaurant, all of the tables had white linens on them; the chairs were covered in velvet fabric and there were so many glittery lights everywhere it felt like I was about to go into a damn spasm.

The hostess gave us a warm smile as she said, "Follow me to your table. We have you set back in the corner, Mr. Williams, for a bit more privacy, per your request."

Pulling the chair out for Ryn, she quickly gave me a seductive grin.

Our waiter approached as Ryn was about to sit. Stepping in front of me, he cut me off and began helping Ryn with her wrap. The way his hand lingered on her arm pissed me off.

Pushing her chair in, he gave her a smile. "May I start the beautiful lady out with a glass of our house red wine?"

Ryn gave the waiter a polite smile. "I'm going to stick with water for right now, but thank you."

Finally pulling his eyes off of Ryn, the little fucker looked at me. He couldn't have been more than twenty-one years old. Giving me a smirk he asked, "Sir, a drink?"

Prick.

"Do you have Nolet's Gin?" I asked.

"Yes, sir we do."

"Gin and tonic. Heavy on the gin."

Giving me a quick nod of his head he turned on his heels and headed to the bar.

Ryn started giggling as I snapped my head back to her. "That fucking bastard. He's flirting with you."

"Stop, Tristan, he's not. He's just a nice young man who is being kind."

Sitting back in my chair, I glared over at him. "He knows what he is doing. He is trying to make a play for my girl. Probably doesn't even know how to handle his peter."

"Tristan!"

Shrugging my shoulders, I gave Ryn a wink. "Maybe we should hook him up with Sierra."

Covering her mouth she shook her head as she laughed. "You are so bad. Leave poor Sierra be."

"Have you talked to her since the whole thing with Dodge happened?" I asked as our prick waiter came back over and set our drinks down.

"Have you had a chance to look at this evening's menu? May I start you out with a starter?"

Clearing my throat so he would look at me and not down at Ryn's breasts, I began talking. "We'll take an order of bacon-wrapped Sea Robin."

"Excellent choice. The young lady will enjoy the succulent taste the fish leaves on her pallet."

Dropping my mouth open as Ryn choked on her water, I shot the guy daggers. "Just go put the order in, dude."

Ryn busted out laughing as soon as the waiter walked away.

"Holy shit! Can you believe that motherfucker?"

"Tristan, keep your voice down."

"That little bastard is two seconds away from tasting my fist on his pallet."

Chuckling again, Ryn reached across the table and took my hand. "Stop. You know I only have eyes for you. And as far as Sierra goes, no. She sent me a text and said she had been working a lot of overtime and would call when she could."

Frowning, I glanced at the menu.

Returning back with our starter the little bastard turned and looked at Ryn. Again. "Are we ready to order?"

Ryn's eyes snapped over to mine. "Tristan, will you order for us?"

Smiling, I looked at the little fucker. "We'll both have the aged filet mignon, medium well. Roasted potatoes for the sides."

Writing it down, he gave me a polite nod, asked if we need anything else and headed to the kitchen.

Ryn and I mostly talked about the move back down to the ranch. I was headed down before Ryn. She needed to stay back for a bit to take care of her business and get her place packed up and rented out.

"I'm thinking I only want to bring a few pieces of furniture with me. Mostly everything I bought when I first bought my place is junk."

"Baby, we can bring anything down you want."

Giving me a sexy ass grin, Ryn leaned across the table. "I'm thinking this is a new chapter to our lives. One we are starting together. I want everything to be about us. I think picking out our furniture together will kind of be fun."

Rolling my eyes, I laughed. "Somehow your idea of fun and mine are way different."

Laughing, Ryn looked up at the waiter. Setting the dessert we ordered in the middle of the table, he turned and walked off.

"Huh. Dickhead must have found someone better to flirt with."

Dropping her mouth open, Ryn said, "Hey! You just intimidated him with daggers you've been shooting at him with your eyes since we sat down."

Taking Ryn's hand in mine, I smiled. "You ready to go

dancing?"

Nodding her head she whispered, "Very ready. Where are we going?"

Pulling out some money and tossing it down on the table, I stood. I knew how much Dodge's friendship meant to Ryn. I had gone to Dodge's club the day after we got in the fight at Starbucks. After a long chat, we both came to terms with things and I knew this would make things easier for all of us. "Let's forget dessert and head to Dodge's club."

Smiling she stood up. "Really?"

"Yeah, let's go have some fun, baby."

Wrapping my arm around Ryn's waist, we made our way out of the restaurant. Taking one last look at our waiter, I gave him my best go to hell look as we passed by.

WALKING INTO RED 7, I had my arm draped over Ryn's shoulders. The loud music was not helping the dull pulsing in my temples. As the seconds ticked off the clock, I knew I was that much closer to showing Ryn my playroom.

Pushing the sick feeling from my gut, I placed my lips to her ear. "You look beautiful this evening."

Turning, Ryn smiled. "You've mentioned that already."

Grinning, I yelled, "I think I'd rather fight off the waiter. The moment you walked in here about fifty guys started eye fucking you."

Laughing, Ryn playfully hit me in the stomach. "Stop it! Let's find Dodge, say hi and then get our dance on before my ankle gives out in these heels."

Nodding my head, I turned Ryn toward the bar. Walking up to the bar, I shouted to the red-haired bartender. She had more piercings on her face than I'd ever seen. "Dodge around?"

Nodding she yelled, "He's in his office. He expecting you?"

Shouting back I said, "Yes."

Motioning with her head the bartender said, "Head on back then, handsome."

Feeling Ryn grip my arm harder, I let out a chuckle. Looks like we both had a bit of a jealous streak.

Pulling me from the bar, Ryn headed to the side of the bar and to the hallway that led back to Dodge's office.

Quickly knocking once, Ryn opened the door and we walked into Dodge's office. "Ohmygod! So sorry!" Ryn shouted as she quickly shut the door and turned to look at me. Her hand went up to her mouth and she began laughing.

"Holy shit. There is a guy in Dodge's office and he was . . . um . . . busy!"

"Is he fucking someone in there?"

"Ah . . ." Ryn's face was bright red. "It's not Dodge. It's a guy with brown hair."

Pulling my face back, I looked at Ryn confused. "This is Dodge's office, right?"

Ryn turned and looked at the door. "Yeah, but the sign that said Dodge Walker General Manager is gone."

Now my curiosity was getting the better of me. Reaching for the door, I went to open it.

Ryn grabbed my arm and pulled back. "Tristan, no! There is a couple having sex."

"In Dodge's office, Ryn? Where is Dodge?"

Confusion spread across Ryn's face. "Maybe he's not working tonight."

The sound of the bass in the music in the club was penetrating the walls. For some reason the beat had my dick jumping. Opening the door, I pushed it open.

Yep. There was for sure a couple in here fucking. The guy was sitting in the chair and a blonde-haired girl with blue streaks throughout was riding the hell out of the guy.

"Yes! Yes, your cock fills my pussy to the max, Dodge."

Smiling, I shook my head. Dodge must have dyed his hair brown and that's why Ryn thought it was a strange couple. "Fuck me harder, Chase. Come on, baby."

Turning, I looked at Ryn standing outside the office door with a look of horror on her face. She kept motioning with her hands for me to come back out. Smiling, I shook my head.

Time for me to have a little fun.

Slowly making my way over to the chair, I wiped the smile from my face. Dodge's back was to me and the blonde had her eyes closed as she kept repeating how great Dodge's dick was.

Taking in a deep breath, I put my game face on. "Why? Why would you do this to us?" I shouted.

The blonde kept riding Dodge as she opened her eyes. Dodge attempted to turn his chair but the blonde was riding him hard as she just looked at me smiling. "Who . . . are . . . you?"

Looking at Dodge who now placed his hands on her hips to get her to stop moving. "Chase, stop."

Looking back at the blonde, I said as I pointed to myself, "Who am I? Who. Am. I? Who the hell are you?"

Smiling, she purred back, "I asked first, handsome."

Pointing to Dodge I said, "I'm his partner. We just got married last week."

Dodge, the blonde, *and* Ryn all said, "What?"

Turning, I glanced over my shoulder to Ryn who was now laughing.

Walking up to Dodge, I smacked the shit out of the back of his head. "How could you? How long have you been unfaithful to me?"

The blonde sitting on Dodge's lap jumped off of him, causing Dodge to quickly cover his now limp dick.

"What in the fuck are you doing?" Dodge asked as he stood.

"Just be honest with me, Dodge. If you wanted to try something new, I would have been all for it."

"Really? Cause I've never had two guys at once. I heard two dicks at once are amazing."

Dodge and I both turned and looked at the blonde who was just standing there smiling.

Dodge quickly pulled his pants up and grabbed his shirt. "Chase, can you please get dressed and get back to work?"

Nodding her head she smiled. "Sure, boss."

Looking back at Ryn, she had her back to the office and all I could see was her shoulders bouncing up and down. I loved that Ryn had a good sense of humor.

"Listen here, handsome dude . . ."

"It's Tristan, my name is Tristan."

Muttering something under her breath, the blonde continued, "Listen, I had no idea that Dodge was taken. Had I known, I would have never have made a move. But you should probably know, Tristan. I think Dodge is into girls, too. Like a lot. A whole lot."

Turning, she walked away as Dodge was attempting to find his voice. "Chase! Chase, he's only kidding! We are not together. That is his girlfriend, Ryn."

The blonde stopped and looked at Ryn. Grinning she said, "Are y'all down for a foursome?"

"No!" Me, Dodge, and Ryn all shouted at once.

Giving Dodge and me a disappointed look, the blonde turned and walked away.

I busted out laughing as Ryn walked up and sat down in one of the chairs, laughing her ass off. "Oh my gosh! You should have seen your face, Dodge. It was priceless."

Lifting her hand in a high five motion, I slapped it.

"You're a real asshole, do you know that? Do you know how long it took me to get into that girl's pants, you prick?"

Making a disgusted sound, Ryn mumbled, "Nice. Real nice."

Dodge pulled his shirt over his head and grunted in frustration. "Fuck! What in the hell do you two want anyway?"

Pulling my head back, I knew Dodge couldn't have been that frustrated by losing out on a fuck that clearly meant nothing to him. Something must have been up.

"What's with the hair, Dodge?" Ryn asked. Pushing his hand through his hair, Dodge shrugged half-heartedly.

"Put it back to my natural color."

Ryn looked shocked. "You're not a blond?"

Dodge glanced over to Ryn for one quick second before he picked up some papers off of his desk and threw them into a box on the floor. "No, Ryn. I'm not."

Looking around for the first time, I saw all the boxes. "Wait, what's going on? Why all the boxes?"

Dodge stopped grabbing shit and throwing it into the box and sat in his chair. "I'm no longer the general manager here. Tonight is my last night managing the club."

Ryn stood up quickly. "What? Why? Dodge, you love your job!"

Rubbing the back of his neck, Dodge let out a frustrated moan. "Fuck! This is bullshit. My life just went to the shits."

Sitting down next to Ryn, we exchanged looks. This could not be good.

CHAPTER
Twenty Six

I HAD NEVER SEEN DODGE so upset and stressed before. I reached for Tristan's hand as we sat there and listed to Dodge rambling on about his father, the club being his life, and having to go back to a job he hated.

"Wait, I thought your dad was a lawyer?" I asked.

Dodge closed his eyes and nodded his head. "He is."

"Okay, so you said you have to go back to a job you hated. What did you do for your father?"

Dodge looked away. It was almost as if he didn't want to acknowledge what he used to do for his dad.

"I was a lawyer, Ryn. I worked for my dad for a year before I couldn't take it anymore. It was bad enough my father pushed me hard in high school and college, working for him was worse."

My mouth dropped open. As Tristan asked, "You . . . were a lawyer?"

Dodge glared at Tristan. "Yeah, I was. Don't act too surprised."

Holding up his hands Tristan said, "Hey, not judging dude, that just threw me for a loop."

Looking at Tristan and giving him a smile, I wanted to say I was thrown too. But I didn't. I did however have a million questions. Dodge was a lawyer. "What did your dad do that made you hate it so much, Dodge?"

"First off, he made me a partner, almost immediately, which didn't sit too well with the other established lawyers. Nothing like walking into a party and having everyone moan because the party pooper just showed up."

"Damn, that would suck," Tristan said.

Pinching his lips together, Dodge agreed. "It did. Then he stuck me with the stupidest cases. Shit that a first year law student could win. It was frustrating." Dodge dropped his head back against the headrest of his chair. "I don't know what to do."

Tristan leaned forward and put his elbows on Dodge's desk. "Don't go work for him. Why are you letting him have the upper hand, Dodge? I mean, unless daddy is sending you a shit load of money every month, the last time I checked you were a grown man. Don't let your old man run your life."

Dodge's eyes filled with sadness and for some reason my heart broke for him. I knew Dodge well enough to know he wasn't just rolling over and letting his dad walk all over him. I also knew what it was like to have parents who tried to control your entire life.

"I don't have a choice," Dodge whispered in the saddest voice I'd ever heard.

"Why?" I asked.

Looking away before I could see the tears forming in his eyes, he tried to talk but his voice cracked. Clearing his throat, Dodge began talking.

"My mother was thrilled when I told her I wanted to be a lawyer. She was a lawyer herself, but she was also a CPA. She loved her job and wanted me to love mine as well. I breezed through high school and graduated early, making my mother proud and my father ecstatic he had something to brag about to his partners at the law firm. I knew right away I wanted to do business law. My father specializes in family law." Shaking his head and laughing, he looked away. "Really my father specialized in everything. I don't think I've ever seen him lose a case. Any case."

Looking back at Tristan and me, Dodge continued talking as he messed with a piece of paper on this desk. "When my father showed he had no faith in me being a real-time lawyer,

I told him I was leaving. If he couldn't give me the cases I deserved and the experience I needed to be a good lawyer then I'd go manage a damn club. He laughed and told me I'd never make it without him. I got pissed and walked out of his office, never looking back. Two days later, I changed my hair color to dirty-blond and was general manager of Red 7. My mother was heartbroken and my father was just downright pissed off that his son would walk away from one of the biggest law firms in Austin and be a bartender."

"Oh Dodge, you're more than that."

Nodding he said, "I know, Ryn. He doesn't though and he convinced my mother I was doing it just to piss him off. I told him it would take hell freezing over before I would ever return to law. As much as I missed it, I wouldn't go back just to be spiteful." Letting out a gruff laugh, Dodge's face fell into his hands. "Hell has frozen over and I'm walking right in the middle of it."

Dragging his hands down his face, when someone knocked on his door, he turned and looked at a young girl standing there. "Hey, are you okay? Chase is out here saying some serious shit right now."

Giving her a weak smile he nodded, "Yeah, she's just pissed our . . . time. . . . got interrupted." Dodge looked at Tristan and gave him a dirty look, eliciting a laugh from Tristan.

"Did you need any help?" the girl asked. I could see it in her eyes. She had a thing for Dodge. I wondered how many of his employees he actually fucked. If I were to guess, I'd say Chase, the blonde from earlier, was his first.

"We're good. Will you please shut the door on your way out?"

The girl's face dropped as she nodded her head. Turning to Tristan and I, she gave us a weak smile. Poor thing. She had it bad for Dodge. In the ten months or so we had been together, I'd seen my fair share of girls giving Dodge that same look. He on the other hand, was oblivious to all of it.

Tristan cleared his throat. "Okay, so I'm still confused as to what your dad has over you to make you go back to work for him."

Tears filled Dodge's eyes and I sucked in a breath of air. Looking away from us, he quickly wiped his tears away. "It's a long story. The short version is my mother has lung cancer and I'm only doing it for her. I'll fill y'all in on all of it sometime."

My eyes filled with tears. "Dodge, I'm so sorry this is happening to you. Your poor mother, I wish there was something we could do."

Pushing his hand through his hair again, a clear sign he was stressed, Dodge chuckled. "There is nothing anyone can do, Ryn. I'm not going to let my mother down. I love her too much. If going back and working for my prick father will make my mother happy and hopefully help her fight this, then that's what I'm going to do."

"Damn, Dodge, I'm really sorry to hear about your mother. Please let Ryn and I know if there is anything we can do. Anything."

Smiling, Dodge stood and held his hand out for Tristan. "I appreciate that, Tristan. More than you know."

Looking back at me, Dodge gave me wink. "Enough of this downer bullshit. Let's go get you two a drink."

The rest of the evening at Red 7 was spent visiting with Dodge, dancing, and having a great time.

Sitting at the bar, Tristan leaned over and spoke in my ear. "Are you ready to head to my condo, baby?"

My heart dropped. I'd never been to Tristan's condo. I had always figured he didn't want to seem like he was bragging, so he just never brought me there. We always went to his house, which was now officially sold. Giving him a smile, I slipped off the chair. Giving Dodge a wave goodbye, he smiled.

"Y'all be safe! Talk to you soon," Dodge shouted from behind the bar.

Ten minutes later we were pulling into the underground parking for Tristan's condo unit. My mind was brought back to Azurdee telling me how her and Lark had sex out in public on his motorcycle. It had been the hottest thing she had ever done.

"Why don't you have a condo at the Austonian like Lark?" I asked as I watched Tristan pull into a reserved parking spot.

Giving me a wicked smile he said, "Because that bastard took the best unit in the building. He beat me to it, so I had to one up him. I love living at The Milago, though. It's a better fit for me."

"Oh," I whispered. I'd been to Lark's condo. I could not imagine anyone one-upping that thing. It had three hundred and sixty degree views. Solid windows all around.

Jumping out of his car, Tristan walked around to open my door. Dragging in a deep breath, I couldn't shake the fluttery feelings in my stomach. I knew I was picking up Tristan's vibes and I had no idea what he was nervous about. The only thing I could think of was he was having second thoughts about me moving down to South Texas. Closing my eyes, I said a quick prayer that was not the case. I didn't think my heart could take it if he was telling me he changed his mind.

Taking my hand, we walked to the elevator. "So, how long have you had this condo?" I asked.

Pushing the button, Tristan looked my way. "About three years I'd say. I bought it when they were still building it. I had it designed exactly how I wanted. There are a lot of . . . custom things added to this unit."

"Oh, that's nice," I said nervously. "And you're keeping it? Not selling it?"

He looked at me with a serious face. "No, I figured we'd want a place to stay when we come to Austin to visit or for your work." His face dropped a little as he added, "If you don't like it though or it makes you feel uncomfortable, I can sell it."

Pulling my head back in surprise, I wanted to ask him why his condo would make me uncomfortable. "No, Tristan I'm sure I'm going to love it."

The elevators opened and Tristan motioned for me to get it. He paused for a few brief seconds before he finally stepped into the elevator. Running a card in front of a reader, he hit the top button that read, penthouse.

Oh. Shit. I'm beginning to think the Williams boys have plenty of play money.

"Ryn, I'm about to show you another side of me. I'm scared to death, baby, that you're going to run away from me."

Looking into Tristan's eyes, I swallowed hard.

Oh holy shit.

CHAPTER
Twenty-Seven

THE COLOR IN RYN'S FACE disappeared. I don't think she meant to whisper *oh holy shit* out loud, but she did. I was beginning to sweat and my stomach was in knots. I had no idea how Ryn was going to react to what I was about to show her. A part of me didn't want to show her. I'd just sell the condo and we would buy something new. I could live with handcuffs and a flogger.

The elevator opened and the smell of leather hit me in the face. No. No, I knew I wouldn't be happy living a lie. I wasn't going to hide this part of who I was. Maybe Ryn wouldn't be upset. After all, I wasn't into hardcore BDSM at all. I had a few suspension things in my room, the x-cross with the shackles. I guess those things might come across as scary. If Ryn doesn't turn and walk away, I will be able to quickly explain to her. If she's anything like Liberty, she'll quickly turn away and tell me my days of needing sexual pleasure like that are over. Liberty thought I had found love with her, and that I could leave all this behind because I would be satisfied with just her.

Would it take just meeting the right girl to walk away from this?

If Ryn asked me to give up this side of me, would I? I had already said I would entertain the thought. Ryn meant the world to me and I knew deep in my heart I would do whatever it took to make her happy.

Ryn stepped off the elevator and I followed. It opened right up into the massive open floor plan. "Oh my gosh." Turning back and looking at me she smiled. "Tristan, why were you not living here? It's amazing!"

Smiling, I watched as she made her way into the main living area of the condo. She ran her hand along the back of the leather sectional as she looked out the massive wall of windows. The entire condo was lined with windows. No walls at all except in the interior of the condo. The living room had a sectional, a large chair and bookcase that held a seventy-two-inch television and state of the art music center.

Ryn made her way toward the kitchen. "Tristan, this kitchen is beautiful." Looking over her shoulder, she wiggled her eyebrows as she purred, "Marble countertops. I've always wanted to have sex on marble countertops."

Raising an eyebrow, I whispered, "I can make that want come true."

Spinning her body around she began walking backward as she giggled. "Really? I wonder what other wants you could grant me?"

"No telling," I said as I adjusted my dick in my pants that were growing too small by the second.

"Are these commercial grade appliances? What in the world do you need with a six-burner stovetop?"

Shrugging my shoulder, I leaned against the counter. "I don't know. Might have a party here or something."

Dropping her mouth open, she asked, "You've never had a party here?"

Feeling my hands start to sweat, I wiped them on my pants. I didn't want to tell Ryn the only people who had ever been here were Lark and women I brought here to fuck. The last thought caused me to feel sick. How would Ryn feel knowing I had brought women here just to fuck them?

Shaking my head, I cleared my throat. "No. Never had any parties here."

"Huh, that's a shame. It would be perfect."

"Yeah, I guess so," I mumbled as I pushed off the counter. "There's more to see."

Giving me a huge grin, she walked toward me. "Like . . . bedrooms?"

My heart froze before it began pounding. "Um . . . yeah."

Motioning with her hand, Ryn said, "Lead the way then."

Turning and heading down a hall, I began rubbing the back of my neck. The closer we got to the playroom, the more anxious I became. Looking over my shoulder, Ryn wrinkled her brow.

"Tristan, if you're tired or not feeling well, we can go back to my house or just go crash in your room."

Straining a smile, I shook my head. "No, baby. Let's finish the tour."

"O-okay, if you're sure."

I pushed open the door to the first guest room. It was decorated in a very simple style that my mom had come up with. The colors were taupe and green.

"Wow, did you decorate this room?"

Letting out a small chuckle, I shook my head. "Hell no. My mom decorated most of this place. Except two rooms. I did those."

Giving me a sweet grin, Ryn scrounged her nose up. "Well, she did an awesome job. I'm going to have to recruit her help for our place."

"She'd really love that, Ryn."

We continued to make our way around the condo. Showing Ryn the media room, she again mentioned how she couldn't believe I hadn't had a party here. "Stadium seating for eight plus all the bean bags on the floor. Makes me want to jump in one right now."

My smile faded as I thought back to Michelle being here one night after I first moved in. She had wanted to see my playroom and be the first to try it out. Try it out we did. Then we moved into here. We had watched porn on the large screen and fucked each other senseless in one of the beanbags. Making a decision to throw all the beanbag chairs away the first chance I got and buy new ones, I led Ryn out of that room.

Another guest room, my office, and the game room were next on the tour. As we walked into each room, Ryn complimented the decorating and repeated how amazing and wonderful the condo was. "There is so much room, it's unbelievable.

No wonder you needed the top floor."

Giving her a wide grin, I said, "It's two floors baby."

Dropping her mouth open, her eyes widened. "You for sure one-upped Lark."

Tossing my head back, I laughed.

We rounded the corner and came into the den. It faced the west side of the building and the views from this room alone are what sold me on the place. I'd sat in this room plenty of times and watched the sunsets.

"Oh my, Tristan. I can't imagine what this view looks like during the day."

Taking her hand in mine, I pulled her over to the piano. "I have a surprise for you."

Biting on her lip, she gave me the sexiest damn look I'd ever seen. "Are we going to have sex on your piano?"

Stopping, I looked into her eyes. "Is that a want?"

Nodding her head she whispered, "Oh, yes."

Sitting down at the piano, I let out a chuckle. "Then we will add that to the list."

"You play the piano? That is the sexiest thing ever."

Cracking my knuckles, I placed my fingers onto the keys. "Be prepared to be swept off your feet, Ryn."

Placing her chin on the back of her hand she smiled. I started playing chopsticks and Ryn busted out laughing. "Oh wow. Why, Mr. Williams, you are a man of many talents."

Giving her a wink, I whispered, "Baby, you have no idea."

Ryn's lips parted slightly as my dick jumped in my pants. Adjusting myself, I stood. "Two more rooms to show you."

Taking Ryn's hand, we headed to the spiral stairs that led upstairs. As we walked up to the door that led to my bedroom, I inhaled a deep breath. Ryn giggled next to me. "Why, Tristan, are you nervous about showing me your bedroom?"

Reaching for the door, I turned and pushed it open. I had never had anyone in my room. Not even Liberty when I brought her here. She never even thought to question why we always used the bedroom downstairs next to my office. Although by most standards, that room was a master bedroom. It was large with an en suite bathroom.

Pushing all thoughts of Liberty from my head, I walked into

the bedroom. Ryn let out a gasp as she walked in. The four-poster wood bed was across the room against the wall of windows. The walls were painted a neutral beige. The bedspread was a light blue that I had picked out with my mother. The decorations on the walls were paintings I had found while in Italy two summers ago.

Ryn walked around the room taking it all in. "Tristan, this room is breathtaking. You decorated this?"

Nodding my head, I smiled. "Yep. Wait until you see the bathroom."

Spinning around, Ryn headed straight for a door. Opening it she let out a small yelp. "Holy mother of God. This is the biggest closet I've ever seen! I may have just had a mini orgasm walking into here."

I sat on the bed and listened to Ryn in the closet going on and on. "I think this is as big as my master bedroom!"

"You want to stay in the closet, baby, or do you want to see the bathroom?"

Skipping out into the room, Ryn flew into my arms. We fell backward onto the bed and Ryn started grinding against my semi-hard dick. "I'm feeling a little horny."

Grabbing her ass, I pulled her body close to me so she could feel my hard dick. "Mmm, baby you have no idea how happy that makes me."

Slapping her ass, I moved her off of me and stood up. "Come on, let's look at the bathroom and then one more room."

Ryn fell onto her back. "Ugh, Tristan, I'm kind of over the house tour for right now."

Reaching for her hand, I pulled her into a standing position. "Come on, let me show you my shower. I'm thinking you need a good fucking up against the wall in there."

"Oh God," Ryn whispered as she followed me into the bathroom. Grinning, I shook my head. My girl loved being fucked in the shower.

As we stepped into the bathroom, Ryn let out a moan. Running her hands over the cool marble, she made her way over to the walk-in shower. Stepping into the travertine shower, you had to turn around a corner to get into the actual shower.

"Oh. My. God. How many shower heads are in here?" Ryn

called out. Walking out of the shower, she made her way over to the bathtub. Staring into the tub, Ryn let out a soft whimper. "This house is amazing! There are so many places I want you to fuck me, I don't know where to begin."

Glancing over her shoulder at me, I felt my face drain.

This was it.

This was the very moment I had dreaded since the first time Ryn smiled her beautiful smile at me.

Swallowing hard, I rubbed my hand on the back of my neck. "I know where to start. We have the last room."

The look that washed over Ryn's face confused me. I wasn't sure how to read her at all. Her face was blank. Emotionless.

Walking up to Ryn, I placed my hands on her face. "I want you to know I love you. I love you so very much, baby, and no matter what, I will do whatever makes you feel comfortable."

Leaning her head into my hand, Ryn closed her eyes. I knew she could feel my tension. She could see on my face I was scared.

"I love you too, Tristan. I'll love you no matter what."

Taking her hand and turning on my heels, I walked her out of the bathroom, through my bedroom and to the room across the hall. Taking my keys out of my pocket, I unlocked the door and pushed it open. I watched Ryn's face as she took a step inside the playroom.

Her eyes widened in surprise as they wandered around the room.

She was speechless. I wasn't sure if that was a good sign or not. Ryn walked into the room more as she looked around. She moved ultra-slow as her eyes took it all in.

Finally, she turned to me. The slack expression in her eyes had my heart pounding against my chest.

"Ryn, talk to me."

CHAPTER
Twenty-Eight

I KNEW TRISTAN WAS NERVOUS about something regarding his condo, but when he opened the door and I walked into the room, never did I imagine I'd be walking into a sex room.

My eyes wandered all over the room. The first thing I noticed was the king-size iron four-post bed sitting in front of a floor-to-ceiling mirror. There were handcuffs attached to each side and I thought back to the night in the shop when Tristan had cuffed my hands and feet. Looking at the bottom of the bed, there were more cuffs. Moving my eyes to the right, there was an array of different items hung up. I recognized the flogger immediately. There were different floggers, about six in all. The riding whip caught my attention next, along with the blue velvet eye mask.

Oh. My. God.

Moving along, I noticed a chair that looked like a chaise lounge. Hmm . . . that looked to be fun. A beanbag-like chair like what was in the media room was next to the chaise-looking chair. Sucking in a breath of air at the next chair, I bit down on my lip. It looked to be made of plastic and had places for a person to put their feet. I'd be safe to guess it was for when you were riding someone.

Interesting.

Looking back, on the other side of the bed there was a

chest of drawers, this one was bigger than the one Tristan had in the bedroom at his shop. My mind was racing with what could be in there. Turning more, I noticed a sex swing hanging from the ceiling. *That* could be fun.

Placing my hand on my stomach, I felt sick as a thought occurred to me. How many woman had Tristan brought into this room and fucked? My mind raced as I tried to accept the fact that he had been with a number of women before me.

One more turn and my heart stopped. Attached to the wall was a giant wooden St. Andrew's Cross with cuffs attached at each end. Next to the cross was a plain wood table. I didn't even want think what that was used for.

How long had Tristan been into this? Why was he into this? How much was he into this?

A million questions flooded my mind at once as I turned and looked into Tristan's eyes. The only way for me to get the answers was to talk to him.

I couldn't move though. I was almost afraid to find out the answers to the questions. I hadn't ever really played with sex toys before. The most I'd ever done was that night with Tristan and playing with my own vibrator.

Tristan sucked in a shaky breath. Fear was laced in his eyes and a shiver moved across the back of my neck.

"Ryn, talk to me."

Closing my eyes, I attempted to push away the confusing thoughts I had. "How much are you into this? Do you do all the . . . hardcore stuff?"

Shaking his head, he said, "No. I'm not into all that. I don't do role playing, I'm not into the dominant and submissive thing, although I do like to be in control sometimes."

Looking around again, I quickly turned back to Tristan. "What are you into?"

"Fucking. Fucking hard and fast. Sometimes being a little . . . rough, and then the need for a safe word would be needed."

Safe word.

"How long have you been doing this?"

Swallowing hard, he said, "Since I was twenty-three."

"Oh. How did you come upon it?"

Looking away from me for a brief second, I knew he was

conflicted in telling me, but I wanted to know. "My college buddy, Nick, and I were out one night. Midnight Rodeo."

"The club we ran into each other at?"

Shaking his head he mumbled, "Yes."

"We met two older women there. They came on to us, asked us back to their place and we went. I spent most of the evening in her playroom while she introduced me to a world that intrigued me. I've never gotten into the heavy stuff, but I like sex, Ryn. I enjoy fucking. One half of the club, the side you were on and I got pissed and made you leave, it is filled with mostly BDSM folks. It's basically a pick-up spot."

Placing my hands to my mouth, I asked, "Is that why you were there that night? You were looking for someone to bring back here?"

With a pained expression, he looked into my eyes. I could see the regret on his face as he began to speak. "You were the first girl I've ever seriously dated. I started having strange feelings for you that I'd never had for anyone before in my life. That's when I met Liberty and started seeing her as well. I gave up the club scene as soon as I began dating you and then the whole mess last year and well . . . you know."

Nodding my head, I wrapped my arms around my body in an attempt to warm up. Cold shivers ran across my body as I tried to determine if I needed to hear all of this. It was Tristan's past . . . wasn't it?

Clearing his throat, Tristan kept talking. "Things with Liberty were a joke, it was a show and I tried to make it work, but my heart belonged to someone else. So I did what I've always done, I ran away from my feelings. I realized that I was escaping my reality with sex. Mindless, hard fucking sex. So that's what I did. I used sex as a means to forget."

Tears filled my eyes and I didn't want Tristan to see. Turning, I faced the bed. "How many women have you been with?"

"Ryn . . ."

"Please, Tristan."

"A lot."

"More than ten?" I asked as I squeezed my arms tightly around me.

"Yes," Tristan whispered.

"Fifty?"

"No! Not that many, no."

Spinning around I asked, "How many?"

Looking away he answered. "Twenty, maybe twenty-five at the most. Sometimes I was with the same girl more than once. It was a lot worse after college and when I got this place."

Okay. So at least he hasn't fucked all of Austin.

"Ryn, I need you to know that I would never push you into anything you didn't want to do. I would never hurt you; I swear to God, I would never hurt you. I love you and I've . . . I've never—"

I had no idea what Tristan was going to say to me and I could hear my heart pounding in my ears. Capturing his eyes with mine, I asked, "You've never what?"

"I've never had anyone I've cared about share this part of my life and I think that's been a part of my fear with you. I love you so much and this is such a part of who I am and if you didn't . . . if you didn't . . . if you wanted to leave I'd understand . . . but—" Swallowing hard, I attempted to control the emotions swirling around in my head. I was standing in the middle of Tristan's playroom and he was professing his fear to me. His fear of losing me.

Tristan's voice faded away as I walked up to him. "Stop. I see it in your eyes, the fear. Please stop. I'm not leaving you, Tristan. I won't lie and say this didn't take me somewhat off guard, but I'm also very interested. There are a number of things in this room that caught my attention." Smiling, I wiggled my eyebrows up and down. The smile that spread across Tristan's face caused my heart to stop beating for a moment.

"Yeah?"

Nodding, I slipped my hand around his neck and pulled him down to my lips. "Yeah. I really want to see what we can do in that sex swing."

Laughing, Tristan pulled his head back. His face growing serious he placed his hand on the side of my face. "Everything is new. I didn't want you to ever be in here and have any fears or doubts. I had it all changed out over three weeks ago."

Lifting my brow, I asked, "Everything?"

"Yes, Everything except for the bedframe itself." My heart

dropped in my stomach at the idea of trying out all of Tristan's toys. The sex swing really peaked my interest. Knowing Tristan cared enough about me to not only be willing to walk away from this, but taking my feelings into consideration, had me wanting him more than ever.

"Tristan?"

"Yeah, baby?"

"I want you to fuck me. Hard and fast."

Tristan licked his lips before slamming them to mine. My hands wrapped around his neck as I moaned into his mouth. I could feel his hard dick pressing against my stomach. This lifestyle was a part of Tristan. I wasn't sure where this road was going to lead me, but I knew if I was with the man I loved, I was on the right road.

Tristan picked me up and carried me over to the bed. "Tristan? One more thing before we get started."

"What's that, baby?"

"We're going to need a safe word."

Giving me a smile that would have dropped me to my knees had I been standing, Tristan began unbuttoning his shirt as he kicked his boots off. Dropping his shirt from his beautiful body, I let my eyes graze all over him. "What word did you have in mind?"

Narrowing my eyes as I thought, I finally smiled. "Mickey."

Tristan looked at me like I was crazy. "Mickey? As in Mickey Mouse?"

Nodding my head I said, "Yeah. Mickey."

"Mickey?"

Giggling, I said, "Yes, Tristan. Mickey!"

"Okay, but after tonight you may never look at Mickey Mouse the same."

Laughing, I fell back onto the bed and got ready for the night of my life.

"GET ON YOUR KNEES, RYN. I'm taking you from behind, baby."

Moving quickly, I did as he said. The feel of the satin sheets on my body was sensual. Tristan positioned himself from behind me as he placed his fingers inside me and began priming me for his dick. Pulling his fingers out, he pushed a finger into my ass, pulling a long deep moan from my throat. It felt like heaven and I couldn't wait to explore more with that.

Pushing into me hard and fast, Tristan gave me exactly what I asked for. A good, hard and fast fucking. The moment my orgasm started coming down, Tristan pulled out of me and lifted me off the bed. Carrying me over to the sex swing, he put me into it. Restraining my arms and then legs, I felt exposed to him like never before. Dropping down he buried his face between my legs. Pulling onto the restraints, I moaned with delight, the need to touch him, fueling on my buildup.

"Jesus!" I screamed out. Tristan kept building up my orgasm and then pulling back. "I need to come, Tristan. Please!" I begged. Grabbing onto the swing, he positioned himself and pushed into me. The feel of his dick filling my body would always make my body quiver with desire.

"Yes, finally."

Tristan began fucking me again, and the orgasm didn't take long at all. My body was beginning to feel the effects of all the sex, the unbelievable orgasms, and the energy it took to keep up with Tristan.

Moving me to the St. Andrew's Cross, he told me to hold onto the shackles. He didn't cuff me and I was thankful. Lifting me up, he said, "Hold yourself up, Ryn."

Swallowing hard, I was unsure if I had the strength. "I want to take your pussy with my mouth again."

I had the strength.

Lifting myself up, I held on while Tristan held me up by my ass. He sucked and licked me to two more mind-blowing orgasms and then brought me down and onto his hard, thick dick. Once he was full in, I dropped my head back and let out a moan.

"I'm gonna fuck you until I come. Don't come, Ryn."

Snapping my head forward, my breathing heavy, I asked, "What? How do I not make myself come?"

Pulling his dick out, he pushed so hard into me I slammed into the back of the cross.

"Don't. Come."

Tristan began to thrust, in and out, faster and harder as my arms began to shake from trying to hold myself up. The buildup started in my toes.

Oh shit! Oh no. I'm going to come.

"Tristan, please!" I begged as I fought to keep my orgasm at bay.

"Don't come, Ryn. I'm not done with you."

Biting onto my lower lip hard, I began to taste the blood. I wasn't sure how much longer I could hold it off.

Tristan pulled out and slammed back into me as he let out a moan. "Fuuck yes, baby come now. Ryn, come."

And like that, I came. Hard. The most mind-blowing orgasm I'd ever had. I was pretty sure I blacked out for a few seconds.

My breathing had never been so labored. My body so spent. Tristan had given every single inch of my body attention with both his hands and his tongue. I didn't realize I could have so many orgasms.

Now we were on something that I knew I was going to love. The chair was curved in a way that you could have sex in any position. I was for sure going to look into yoga first thing tomorrow.

Tristan had me lay on my side as he straddled the chair. Lifting my leg he put it against his chest as I felt the pull of muscles I hadn't used in a long time. Looking at me, Tristan let out a low growl from the back of his throat.

"Your pussy looks so good, Ryn. You're mine. You'll only ever be mine."

Panting, I answered, "Yes!"

I needed him. I needed to feel him filling my body. I was beginning to feel desperate. I liked this side of me that was emerging. I liked it *very* much.

"Tristan, please."

Giving me a sexy grin he teased my entrance with his dick. "Tell me what you want, Ryn."

"You!" I called out as I tried to push him into me. Pulling back he shook his head. "I want to hear the words from your lips, baby."

My mind was beginning to fog over. I was exhausted, yet at the same time, I wanted more.

"You, inside me."

Leaning over he gentle took my breast in his hand and began rolling my nipple between his fingers. Letting out a scream, it almost felt like I was about to come.

"Give it to me, Tristan."

Sliding into me just enough to give me hope, he pulled out. "Give you what, baby?"

Lifting my head, I looked straight into his eyes. I felt like a crazed person. If I didn't have his dick filling me soon, it felt as if I might explode. "Your cock, filling my pussy, Tristan."

"Fuck yes!" Tristan said as he thrust into me so hard I screamed and he stopped moving. "Talk to me, Ryn."

I began moving to get friction. I was on the edge, so close to an orgasm and I felt like I would go insane if I didn't come soon.

"Feels . . . so . . . good. Harder, Tristan, I'm so close."

"Don't come yet, Ryn."

Snapping my eyes open, I looked at him. "What?"

Not again.

Grabbing my hips he began moving faster. "Don't. Come."

Thrashing my head back and forth, I gasped for air. "I can't . . . stop myself, Tristan!"

Pulling almost all the way out, Tristan slammed back into me. Screaming out in pleasure, I felt my orgasm building. "Tristan!" I called out.

"Jesus Christ, Ryn! You're so amazing, baby." Leaning over, he fondled my breasts as he continued to build my orgasm. My leg stretched up his chest and allowed me to see him moving in and out of my body. *Oh God. Oh God. Oh God.* I'd never seen anything so incredibly hot in my entire life. Tristan pounded over and over into my body as I somehow held my orgasm back.

"Tristan, I need to come. Please!" I begged.

"Fuck, Ryn, baby. I'm going to come. Come with me!"

His words were my undoing. I fell apart. My entire world shattered as my body was swept up in my orgasm. I could feel the heat of Tristan's cum spilling into my body, which threw me into another round of convulsions. My body was trembling as Tristan pulled out and moved my legs. Pulling me to him, we slid down into the chair as I barely had energy to wrap my legs around him.

Our heartbeats were pounding against each other and with each breath our bodies felt closer. Tristan had his arms wrapped around me tightly as he gently brushed his fingertips up and down my back.

Finding my voice, I whispered, "Tell me."

"I love you so much. Ryn, I'll love you forever."

Something moved inside of me. It was as if a switch turned on and I would never be able to go back and turn it off. I was lost to this man. In this moment, I was forever his. My heart, my soul, my body—

His.

CHAPTER
Twenty-Nine

TRISTAN

*H*OLDING RYN IN MY ARMS, I had the most amazing feeling wash over me. It was as if everything I had worried about was gone. Ryn and I had been in my playroom almost all night. I could see it in her eyes she was enjoying herself and not doing this just to please me. Although, I'm sure that is how she started out feeling. She would try this to please me, to try and fit into this part of my world. It didn't take us long to discover another side to our relationship.

Sex with Ryn had always been amazing. This was just the cherry on top.

Lifting Ryn up, I carried her out of the playroom and into my bedroom. Pulling the comforter and sheet back, I gently set her down, crawled into bed next to her and pulled her into my body. Inhaling a deep breath, I let her scent invade my body. I never wanted to forget this night.

"Tristan?" Ryn's voice sounded sleepy.

Kissing the back of her head, I asked, "Yeah, baby?"

"I think it's safe to say you have for sure one-upped Lark's condo. Big time."

Smiling, I pulled her closer to me. "Go to sleep, baby."

"I love you, Tristan."

"I love you too, Ryn."

Taking in a deep breath, she whispered, "I'm going to miss

you after tomorrow."

Leaning my forehead against the back of her head, I fought back the urge to beg her to come with me tomorrow. "I know. I'm going to miss you too, but you'll be down soon. No longer than two weeks right?"

Ryn yawned as she mumbled, "Right. Two weeks max."

STEPPING UP TO THE BAR, I yelled for the bartender whose back was to me. Holding up her finger to motion one second, I glanced over to the entrance. I had been back home three days now and my old high school buddy, Chris, invited me out for a beer. I couldn't turn him down because I was actually hoping to hire him on to help with the ranch. Dad used to have cattle on our ranch, but ended up taking them off to solely focus on outfitting; I was interested in putting them back on. Lark and I had always thought it was a mistake. I was now looking into getting them back. I had talked to my father about it last night and he shocked the hell out of me by agreeing that it was a good move for the ranch.

"What can I do ya?"

Turning back to the bar I was about to talk when piercing green eyes looked into mine. "Angela?"

Lifting her mouth into a smile, Angela tilted her head. "Why if it isn't Tristan Williams. I heard you were headed back to town."

Smiling, I gave her a nod.

"Hey, I'm sorry about your daddy. I'm glad he's okay though."

"Thanks. Yeah, he is doing really good. Trying to keep him relaxed is kind of hard to do though.

Chuckling she said, "Oh man, I bet. Hey, I heard through the grapevine that you have yourself a classic car. I'd love to take a peek at it. You know my daddy used to restore old cars. Remember?"

Giving her a look, I nodded my head. "Oh, I remember."

Her face flushed as she looked away and then back at me. Angela and I had been each other's firsts. I took her virginity and she took mine. In the back of one of her daddy's nineteen fifty-five Chevys. I was pretty sure her daddy knew I had been fucking his daughter. Not only did we have fun in that car, but we snuck into his shop one night and had sex in every single car in there. I was scared shitless we were gonna get caught. "Would you mind if I came by some time and took a few pictures for Daddy? I know he would love to see what you got your hands on."

"Nah, I don't mind at all. Stop on by anytime and I'll take you down there. I'm at the ranch most days now."

Smiling she nodded her head quickly. "Perfect. I'll stop by in the next few days."

"I'll be there." Angela lifted her head and her smile faded some as she nodded and said, "Chris, how are you?"

Looking back behind me, I saw Chris. Jumping up, I reached out my hand to him. "Damn it's been a long time, Williams."

Smiling, I nodded my head. "It sure has hell has been."

"What do you boys want?" Angela shouted.

After giving her our drink orders, we sat at the bar and talked for a bit. When Angela placed my beer down, she slid a piece of paper my way. Picking it up, I frowned.

"Let me guess, her phone number right?"

Glancing over to Angela and back to Chris, I nodded my head. "Yeah, that's insane. She isn't married yet?"

Chris threw his head back and lost it laughing. I chuckled even though I didn't know why we were laughing. "Dude, she is married but if she thought you would fuck her, she'd be all over that."

Rolling my eyes, I dropped the number back onto the bar. Chris looked at it. "You're not interested?"

"No. My girlfriend is actually going to be here next week. We're building a place on the ranch."

Placing his hand on my shoulder he gave me a gently push and squeeze. "Holy hell, there were two girls out there to tame the Williams brothers. Who would have thought?"

Pushing his hand away, I laughed. "Listen, I want to talk business. I want to offer you a job."

Pulling his head back in surprise he asked, "A job?"

Taking a sip of my beer I nodded my head. "I need a vet."

Raising an eyebrow, he smiled. "You need a vet, for what

reason?"

"I'm bringing cattle onto the ranch and a few exotic animals to add to the hunting. I know my dad's done great with just white tail and hogs, but I really want to expand it. I need a vet to check on the new animals when we bring them in and you're also one hell of a fence mender."

After Chris stared at me for a few seconds he chuckled. Then his face tightened and he narrowed his eyes. "Wait. You're serious, Tristan?"

Nodding my head, I took another sip. "Yes, Chris. I'm serious. How has your vet clinic been doing?"

"Very well, I'm not sure I want to walk away from my practice. I've finally built up some clients."

"I'm not asking you to. I'm asking you to help me on the ranch when I need helping out. Some days it might be just a quick peek at an animal and others it might be a day full of work."

Chris rubbed his chin with his hand. "Your dad has a vet he has used for years."

"Not anymore. He is retiring and I've already talked with Dad and told him my vision. The things I want to see happen with the ranch and he agrees. It's time for a change."

Chris nodded his head while he thought about it. Taking another drink of my beer, I noticed two girls staring at us. Looking back at Chris, I wondered why he hadn't settled down with anyone yet. Neither one of us ever had problems picking up girls. Chris had gotten most of his mother's traits. She was part Hispanic and always said Chris's brown eyes and hair came from her daddy's side of the family. Chris's father had blond hair and blue eyes.

Nodding his head, he held up his beer. "It will be a change working on cattle compared to my normal cats, dogs, and rodents, but I think I'm up for the challenge."

Smiling, I held out my hand. "Perfect. I have a feeling this is going to be a hell of a lot of fun."

Shaking his head and laughing, Chris put his beer up to his lips and smiled. "I agree, dude. I agree."

SLAMMING THE HOOD OF THE Jeep, I let out a string of curse words. Chris sat in the passenger seat and laughed.

"Jesus, Tristan. What in the hell is wrong with you?"

Cursing under my breath, I climbed into the driver's seat and started the Jeep. Finally it started. "I'm just frustrated. Ryn was supposed to be here already. We're going on a month now and I don't understand what is taking so damn long."

Chris hit my arm and I glanced over at him. "Tristan, listen to yourself. From what all you filled me in on, this girl is uprooting her entire life to be with you. That's a big gamble considering how things ended with y'all the first time around. She has a business, a house to get ready to rent out; and you want her to just up and leave it all to be by your side. You even said last week she had a ton of shit on her plate with you up and leaving her to deal with it all. Cut her some slack."

Rubbing my hands down my face, I let out a frustrated groan. "I know. I know. Fuck. It's just I finally got her back and I feel like I've lost her again."

Chris laughed. "So this is what love is like? No thank you. I'd rather just keep it open to the random date which, if I'm lucky, ends with me getting lucky."

Turning to look at Chris, Sierra popped into my head. "You know, you would get along great with our friend, Sierra. She is spit and fire, but she's a good fuck."

As soon as it came out of my mouth I wanted to punch myself in the face. I had never once thought of Sierra like that. That day we were together was something we had shared together and I had no right talking about it like I just did.

Chris's eyes widened in surprise. "Did you just say this Sierra girl was your and Ryn's friend, but you've fucked her?" Shaking his head he finally looked back at me and said, "Please tell me you didn't cheat on Ryn."

"No! Fuck no. Ah shit. I didn't even mean for that to come out. Ryn and I weren't together and Sierra and I are like best friends. It was one time, she needed it. Her husband of six years left her and she was sexually frustrated and well . . . it was a onetime thing for both of us and it meant nothing. We were both lonely and feeling frustrated and I'm glad we did it. Took the awkwardness away from our friendship."

Lifting his eyebrows he mumbled, "I bet it did."

Letting out a breath of air, I started driving. "Doesn't matter, it didn't mean anything to either one of us and Ryn knows about it."

"Wow. I'm impressed. You're really in love with this girl, aren't you?"

My lips moved up into a grin. I was still getting used to this amazing feeling of love. Never in my wildest imagination did I think I'd be talking to one of my best friends about this. "Yeah, I love her more than anything. I'd never do anything to jeopardize my relationship with her. Ever."

I could see Chris nodding from the corner of my eye. "Just stay away from Angela. That girl has got her sights on you."

Rolling my eyes I simply said, "Yeah. I know." My mind drifted back to last week when she stopped by to take a look at the classic cars.

STEPPING INTO THE SHOP, THE lights turned on and Angela let out a whistle as she made her way over to my Camaro. She knew better than to put her hands on it so she just walked around it slowly, taking it all in. "You did all this?"

Laughing, I shook my head. "Pretty much everything but the paint job."

Smiling she looked up at me. "Impressive. Can I take a few pictures for Daddy?"

Gesturing with my hand I said, "Have at it. Take as many pictures as you want. I'll be right back."

Walking into the bedroom, I took a look around. I was going to surprise Ryn and put a playroom in our house we were having built. Since I'd have a house now down here, I decided to change this bedroom into a business office. I didn't need the bedroom anymore, so why not make use of the spot. I planned on putting a desk in here for Lark as well. I had a feeling he was going to want to keep his hand in the ranch and nothing would make Dad and me happier. I knew he was busy getting his own place up and running, so I would talk to him about it the next time he was down here.

Looking down at the bed, I couldn't help but smile as I thought back to the night I was in here with Ryn. Adjusting my growing dick, I dropped my head back and moaned. I just wanted her here with me.

"It's about time we picked up where we left off."

Spinning around, I took a step back. "Holy fucking shit! Angela, what in the hell are you doing?"

Angela stood before me completely naked. She must have followed me into the bedroom and just stripped out of her clothes. They were piled at her feet as she moved her hands up and down her body. "I've been trying to be patient, Tristan. But I want that dick buried deep in my pussy."

Turning, I said, "Get dressed, Angela, it's not going to happen. I need you to get dressed and to leave. Now."

"Ahh, come on now, cowboy. Tell me you weren't adjusting that big thick dick because you were thinking of me?"

Blowing out a frustrated breath, I quickly made my way over to Angela. She smiled and bit down on her lip. Walking up to her, she whispered, "Yes, I knew you wanted me, Tristan."

Reaching down, I scoped up her clothes and pushed them into her. Taking her by the arm, I led her out of the room and through the shop.

"Tristan! What are you doing? I thought you brought me here to fuck me."

Walking toward the door I let out a gruff laugh. "I don't know what in the hell gave you that impression, Angela. I've never once led you on. Besides, I have a girlfriend whom I love very much and will be here any day. She is who I want to bury my dick in. No one else."

Stopping by the front door, I turned away from her. "Please get dressed and leave."

Hearing her huff and puff while she got dressed, I waited before I turned around. The door to the shop opened and quickly slammed shut. Slowly turning around, I let out the breath I had been holding. My hands pushed through my hair and I closed my eyes.

"Ryn, baby, I need you here."

PULLING UP TO THE HOUSE, Chris and I got out of the Jeep. "Can you come in for a few minutes? I want to talk to you about the party I want to throw for Ryn."

Giving me a smile, Chris slapped my back. "Sure. You know I'm down for any kind of party."

As we headed into the house, I pulled out my phone. I hadn't heard from Ryn in over five hours. She had told me she would be in a meeting today and wasn't sure how long it would last. It was nearing five and I figured I'd be hearing from her soon.

Stepping into the house I inhaled a deep breath. "Son-of-a-bitch, that smells good," I said making my way to the kitchen. Mom and Dad were both in the kitchen cooking. I couldn't help but smile looking at my dad in an apron that said, "I'm the cook's sidekick." As much as my father loved to work, having the heart attack changed him in so many ways. He gave up control of the ranch easier than we would have ever dreamed. The first few weeks it was a hard adjustment for him, but now he was happier than I had seen him in years. He and Mom were planning on taking a cruise in March, and my mother was beyond thrilled.

Looking at Chris, he was smiling with a wide grin. "What's cooking, Mr. and Mrs. Williams?"

Mom turned and gave Chris a big smile. "Christopher! It's so wonderful to see you and don't you dare call me, Mrs. Williams. Tristan said you would be here today. Come, come. I remember how much you loved tasting my homemade sauce."

I hadn't seen Chris move that fast in a long time. Before I knew it, he was making homemade pasta and I was cutting everything up for a salad. I couldn't remember the last time I stood in my mother's kitchen and had so much fun. The only thing missing was Ryn, Lark, and Azurdee.

After helping my mother, Chris and I walked out onto the back porch and sat. It was a beautiful evening for it being February. The temperatures were in the mid-sixties and the sky was clear and filled with stars.

"So, you have everything planned and taken care of?"

Nodding my head I said, "Yep. The only thing I really need to do is get a band lined up. Ryn loves to dance and I think having someone there instead of a DJ would be better."

"I agree. Let me ask around. One of my patient's dad's is in a band."

My beer stopped at my lips and I turned to look at Chris. Tilting my head I asked, "Did you just say one of your patient's dad's? Wouldn't that be the owner of the animal? You call them mom and dad?"

Chris looked at me like I had grown two heads. "Of course I do. Some of these people only have their pets. They are their kids. I'm even thinking of starting a boarding business. Doggy daycare along with boarding of both dogs and cats."

Chris's face beamed with excitement and I was honestly happy for him that he had found his passion. But doggy daycare? I was *not* letting that shit go.

"Doggy. Daycare? What in the hell is that?"

"You've never heard of doggy daycare? What is wrong with you? You need a dog, dude."

Laughing, I shook my head and said, "Um, no I don't. Again though, what is doggy daycare?"

Leaning back, Chris took a swig of beer. "It's what it sounds like. People drop their dogs off for the day while they go to work. It's daycare for dogs."

I sat there stunned. Did people really love their dogs that much? Why didn't they just keep them in the back yard? Or in a crate? "People pay for that? Seriously?"

Chuckling, Chris nodded his head. "Yep."

Leaning back in my chair, I said, "Wow. I've got nothing. Jesus, the day I pay to put a dog in doggy daycare is the day someone better take me to an open field and shoot me."

My phone went off and I saw it was Ryn letting me know she was done for the day. I quickly responded back to her text.

Chris laughed as he finished off his beer. "So, back to the party. You think she'll be surprised and not expecting what you're going to do?"

Grinning, I said, "Yeah, she's not gonna expect a surprise party at all."

"I agree. Do you think you should tell her though, you know at least give her a heads up?"

Shaking my head, I said, "I don't know, I really wanted it to be a surprise."

Standing up, Chris slapped me on the back. "Okay, well I hope you know what you're doing."

Smiling, I nodded my head. Ryn hated any attention on her. When I had asked Azurdee about throwing Ryn a surprise welcome party to introduce her to all my parents' friends and friends of mine, she told me I needed to give Ryn a heads up. I was hell bent on surprising her though. I wanted to show her how happy I was she was picking up her life and moving here to be with me. Who doesn't love a surprise party? I started having second thoughts. The last thing I wanted to do was start our new life and have her be upset with me.

Standing with Chris I was doubting my decision on the whole surprise aspect of this party. "Yeah, maybe I should talk to Ryn first about this."

CHAPTER
Thirty

*M*Y HANDS BEGAN SHAKING THE moment I pulled up to the house. I wasn't sure why—new life, new home, new adventures? There was still a very small part of me that was scared to death Tristan would get spooked again, but it was slowly fading away as the days passed.

I had dinner with Dodge, Azurdee, and Lark last night. Azurdee and Lark filled me in on everything happening in their world. I was so happy for them both. They had gone through so much and to come out in the end so head over heels in love was just heartwarming.

Closing my eyes, I thought back to my phone conversation with my mother.

"WHAT DO YOU MEAN YOU'RE moving to South Texas? Do you mean south Austin?"

Rolling my eyes I said, "No, Mom, I mean I'm moving to be with Tristan on his family's ranch. His father had a heart attack and Tristan is now going to run his family's ranch. It's something he has been dreaming of doing for a while now."

"And tell me why, Kathryn, we paid good money for you to get a college degree so you could go be a farmer's wife?"

Wife?

Pushing that thought from my mind, I took in a sharp breath and blew it out. "Mom, it's a ranch. Not a farm. I still have my business that is growing more and more. I've just landed a huge company that is really going to change things for me."

"The only thing that needs changing is your way of thinking. Home is where you need to be."

INHALING A DEEP BREATH IN, I shook my hands a few times and got ready to start my new life. Opening the door, I stepped out and smiled when I looked at Peter and Joyce's house.

Home. This was now my home.

My heart filled with hope. Hope for a future that was going to be more amazing than I had ever dreamed.

Tristan didn't think I was heading back until next week. I had moved up a few business meetings that I had to be present for and got those out of the way yesterday. It had been one hell of a day yesterday, but it was worth it. Knowing I would be in Tristan's arms four days earlier than we thought had my libido jumping with excitement.

Reaching into the back seat of my car, I pulled out my day bag and decided to leave my other stuff for later. I had my back seat and trunk full of stuff. I must have mailed twenty-five huge boxes over the last two weeks down here of just business stuff.

Walking up to the house, I pulled my phone out and sent Tristan a text.

Me: Done for the day. I miss you.

Not even a minute later he responded.

Tristan: Phone sex?

Laughing, I slipped it back into my pocket and headed into the house. I set my bag down on the chair in the foyer as I heard Joyce and Peter talking. Walking into the kitchen, I had my finger over my mouth. Joyce's eyes lit up as she made her way over to me.

"Oh my darling, Kathryn!" Pulling back she looked my body up and down, just like you would picture your mother doing as she made sure you were in one piece. "He has no idea you are coming. Let me tell you something, that boy has been grumpy. It's safe to say he missed you."

Walking up with his arms extended, Peter gave me the sweetest smile. "He missed you a lot, sweetheart."

Kissing Joyce on the cheek and then Peter, I looked around the kitchen as I took in the smells through my nose. "You made my favorite!"

Joyce gave me a wink, "Of course I did. Now the boys are on the back porch. Go put that son of mine out of misery and let him know you are here."

Glancing to the back door, I asked, "Boys?"

Peter went to the stove and started the pot of water for what I was guessing was for the pile of homemade pasta sitting on a plate. "Chris is with him."

"Oh right, Tristan has been talking a lot about Chris. I'm glad I get to meet him." Looking at them both bustling about I asked, "Did you um . . . need any help in here?"

Turning and looking at me, the both wore shocked expressions. "Kathryn, go see Tristan, sweetheart."

Smiling, I gave them a polite nod and headed to the back door, anxious to see Tristan. Pulling it open, I walked through the screened in back porch and to the back deck. My stomach dropped when I heard Tristan's voice. It filled my body with warmth instantly.

Standing up, Tristan turned to Chris. "Yeah, maybe I should talk to Ryn first about this."

Peaking my curiosity and giving me a good excuse to make myself known, I pushed open the door and asked, "Talk to me about what?"

Tristan turned and looked as did his friend, Chris. I couldn't help but notice the smile that spread across Chris's face. Looking at Tristan he seemed confused at first, but then he gave me that grin that had changed my entire life less than two years ago. It was dark, but I swore I saw his green eyes light up.

"Ryn, you're . . . baby, you're here."

I quickly moved to him and he had me wrapped in his arms in seconds. My heart slammed against my chest. I don't think I would ever be able to explain to Tristan how his response in seeing me just erased any doubts and fears I had about our relationship.

I heard it in his voice. I saw it in the expression he wore on his face. I felt it in the way he was holding me. This man loved me and needed me as much as I loved and needed him.

Pulling back, he cupped my face within in his hands. "You're here."

Grinning like fool, I could only whisper, "Yes."

Tristan pressed his lips to mine as he kissed me. I was still very aware of his friend Chris standing there. When Tristan pulled away, my eyes went to Chris.

Tristan stepped back and looked at Chris who was standing there with a smile on his face. "Sorry, Chris." Glancing back to me, Tristan wrapped his arm around me. "This is my Ryn."

My Ryn.

Walking up to me, Chris held out his hand. Shaking his hand quickly, I began to talk. "Tristan has been talking a lot about you. Y'all were good friends in high school, right?"

"Yes, we were. It's a pleasure finally getting to meet you, Ryn. I'm not sure how you did it, but you managed to tame the wild child."

Looking into each other's eyes everything seemed to have fallen into place in that very moment. Tristan leaned in and said, "Best surprise ever."

Placing my hand on his bicep, I needed control. My knees wobbled and I was sure everything was spinning while I stood perfectly still. "I hope so."

Tristan and I were caught in a trance, neither of us pulling away. I felt as if I could see my entire future within in his eyes.

Clearing his throat, Chris clapped his hands, causing us to break free from the hold. "Well, this was fun, but I think I'll head out."

"You don't have to leave on my account," I said as I took a step back from Tristan. I needed to create space between us before the heat grew more.

Tristan chuckled as he pushed Chris toward the door. "Yeah, he does."

Laughing, I playfully hit Tristan on the shoulder. "Stop that."

Walking into the kitchen Joyce let out a happy yelp. "Dinner is ready. Chris, please say you'll join us?"

Holding up his hands, he shook his head. "No, no, Joyce, I don't want to impose on family time."

Tristan pulled my seat out for me as he said, "Sure you do. You want to talk about your doggy daycare set up?"

Chris glared at Tristan. "You don't know how lucky you are there are women in the room right now."

Peter laughed, "Shit, that's never stopped me from speaking my mind and it sure as hell has never stopped my sons."

"Peter Williams. Christopher, sit down, I want to hear all about this."

Smiling, I nodded my head. "Oh, me too! I've always wanted a dog."

Tristan dropped into his seat. "No. No dogs in a brand new house. Nope, I'm putting my foot down right now before this even comes up again."

Patting Tristan on the leg, I calmly said, "Okay, okay. Don't get all upset about it. No dogs."

Glancing over to Chris, I mouthed, for now.

Chuckling, he sat.

Joyce set a giant bowl of homemade pasta on the table and another of homemade sauce. My mouth watered. I loved to cook but I never did. Cooking for just me was a pain. I always ended up making way too much and throwing it away or giving it to the single guy who lived next door. The last time I brought food over, he came out and asked me if I just wanted to come in and have sex. When I said no, his face dropped. Then he said, "I take it I won't be getting any leftovers from now on." Smiling, I informed him he would indeed not be getting any more.

Joyce started asking Chris about the vet clinic. Then the conversation moved to the doggy daycare. "Christopher, where are you going to find time? With the vet clinic keeping you so busy and now you helping out Tristan with the animals here, how will you be able to do all three?"

Giving Joyce the sweetest smile he nodded his head. "Well, I would probably have to hire some employees for the boarding side. It wouldn't just be doggy daycare." Looking toward Tristan, Chris shot him a dirty look while Tristan laughed.

Taking Tristan's hand in mine, I gave it a light squeeze. "I think it's a great idea, Chris. I'd even be interested in volunteering part-time for you."

Tristan's head snapped up. "What?"

"Yeah, I love animals and I think it would be fun. It would for sure be a way for me to meet people. Of course, I'd only be able to help out a few hours a week."

Chris sat up straighter. "Really, Ryn? Are you serious?"

Giving him a wide grin, I said, "Yes! I'm totally serious. I run my own company, so I make my own hours. If you'd have me, I'd love to help you get things set up."

Chris's eyes lit up and Tristan squeezed my hand. When I looked at Tristan, his smile was soft and gentle. Giving me a quick wink, I knew he was just as excited for Chris but he was having more fun giving him a hard time.

I sat back and listened to Chris talking to Peter and Joyce. Peter was full of wonderful pieces of advice on where to start. Of course with Chris opening his own Vet clinic, he had a good sense on where to begin. It was then I took a really good look at him.

Dark hair. Dark deep chocolate eyes. His skin looked like he had been touched with a kiss of sun. I wondered if that was part of his heritage or if he hit the tanning beds. His smile was warm and friendly. You could for sure tell he grew up on a ranch or farm. He had muscles but nothing too extreme.

Leaning over to Tristan, I whispered, "Don't you think Chris and Sierra would make a cute couple?"

Tristan chuckled. "I was thinking the same damn thing earlier, I kid you not."

"Too bad she doesn't live down here."

Tristan brought me in closer to him and kissed my forehead. "I'm so glad you're here, Ryn. I've been feeling so lost without you."

My heart began to beat faster. Hearing those words from Tristan had me all kinds of gushy on the inside.

I've been feeling so lost without you.

Looking up at him, I smiled and whispered, "I love you."

Placing his finger on my chin, he brought my lips closer. "Oh, Ryn, baby, I love you."

Tristan Williams had officially taken hold of my heart . . .

forever.

TRISTAN HAD PULLED UP TO the local honky tonk and parked behind another truck. "You sure you feel like going danc-ing?"

"Yeah. I'm positive. Hey, Tristan, there's something I've been meaning to ask you and I keep forgetting. The night I walked up on you and Chris talking, you had mentioned something about talking to me first about something. I forgot about it that night because the incredible hot sex down at the shop pushed it from my mind. I just remembered it."

Tristan's face dropped. For one brief second, I felt uneasy. *Shit.*

Pushing the fear aside, I waved my hand as if to blow it off. "You know what, never mind. Let's go have some fun." Grab-bing my arm Tristan stopped me from moving.

"Um . . . well . . . I probably should have told you this but . . . well . . . um . . ."

Now I was really worried. And to top it off, Tristan was fidget-ing. His eyes were looking everywhere but at me. "Tristan, you're starting to worry me."

Biting down on his lip, I wasn't sure if I should be worried, or utterly turned on. My eyes zeroed in on his teeth grasping his lip and I let out a soft moan.

"Ah shit, I'm just gonna say it."

Still staring at his lip that he had just been biting on, I fanta-sized about having his mouth between my legs. His lips moving in such a way that he pulled out one incredible orgasm after another.

I wanted him. I didn't even care that we were sitting in a parking lot. The need to have him inside me was so incredible, I was fighting the urge to strip out of my panties and tell him to fuck me senseless.

"Ryn, I organized a party for you. A surprise party. I know, I know you hate surprises. Azurdee told me, but I thought this would be fun and a great way to introduce you to all of Dad and Mom's friends, as well as mine. I should have given you a warning. Baby, are you mad?"

His lips were moving, but I wasn't paying attention to anything he said. Something about Azurdee having a surprise party.

I reached over and began unbuttoning his pants.

"Um . . . what are you going to do?"

Snapping my eyes up to his, I gave him a sexy smile. Unzipping his pants, I let out a groan when I saw his dick. Leaning down I took him in my mouth as his hips jumped.

"Holy shit! Fucking A, Ryn, I should have told you sooner."

It didn't take long before his dick was hard and ready. Crawling on top of him, I pushed my panties to the side and slowly sank down on him as I dropped my head back and let out a hiss.

"Yes, you feel so good, Tristan. I needed this so badly."

Grabbing my hips, Tristan began kissing my neck. "Baby, people might see."

Lifting up slowly, I felt the heavenly feel of his dick sliding out of me. Dropping down quickly, we both moaned.

"Fuck, yeah. Ride me, Ryn. Ride me hard."

Repeating the process over and over, I felt my build up. I was going to come hard and I was torn. I wanted to make this last longer and at the same time, I wanted to feel him explode around me while I fell apart.

"Faster, Ryn. Come on baby, fuck me."

Doing as he asked, I began going faster. "Tristan, oh God, baby I'm so close."

"Goddamn it, Ryn. Fucking hottest thing every. I should have told you about your surprise party the first night you were home."

Surprise party? I slowed down to let what he had just said in. *What surprise party?*

"Baby, no. Faster. Fucking hell, Ryn. Pound that shit down on me."

I organized a party for you.

His words from earlier were starting to sink in.

All of Dad and Mom's friends, as well as mine.

Oh. My. God. Holy hell.

I quickly stopped moving and began looking around. It was two in the afternoon and anyone could see if they were walking by.

"Ohmygod."

"Hell yes, baby. I know it's hot as hell, but baby I'm so close. Move, Ryn. Baby I need you to move."

Slamming my hands onto his chest, Tristan cried out. "Hell yes!"

Hitting him again, he groaned and bucked his hips. "That's it, baby. Fuck me, Ryn."

Then I began hitting him with my fists. He finally grabbed them and said, "Jesus, what is wrong with you?"

"You. You did not."

Tilting his head as he wondered what in the hell I was talking about, he looked up and then looked back at me. "Am I supposed to know what you are asking me?"

"Tristan! You planned a surprise party? And you didn't tell me!"

"Um . . . isn't that what I just said a few minutes ago? I thought you were all into it and that's what got you turned on."

Dropping my mouth open, I lifted off of him. I instantly missed him filling my body. I quickly dropped back into my seat and began looking around.

"I can't believe I did that. Anyone could have seen us and I just went to town on you like a horny slut."

Tristan laughed. "Yeah, ya did. It was awesome, but why did we stop?"

Looking at him, I shook my head. "First off, I was turned on by you biting down on your lip. It was the sexiest damn thing ever."

Lifting an eyebrow, Tristan smiled. "Really?"

Smacking him, I said, "Really. I tuned out what you were saying, you ass! All I could think about was you being inside me. Then it all hit me."

Dropping my head back, I let out a small scream. "Why would you let me fuck you in broad daylight in your truck, knowing all of your parents' friends were in there?"

"So you *are* mad about the surprise party?"

Widening my eyes in surprise that he even asked, I shut them quickly to gain some control over my emotions. "Tristan! I'm not only mad about the surprise party, but you let me fuck you in the parking lot of said surprise party! What were you thinking?"

"I was thinking that I told you about it and the next thing I knew, my dick was in your mouth. What in the hell, Ryn, you're sending me mixed signals here!"

We sat there and stared at each other before I finally brought my hand up to my mouth and busted out laughing. It didn't take long for Tristan to start laughing.

Dropping his head back, he tried to take in breaths. Finally getting our laughter under control, Tristan let out a long sigh. "Oh shit. I'm sorry, Ryn. I should have said something about the party. I wanted you to be surprised."

Taking his hand in mine, I brought it up to my lips and kissed the back of it. "I'm not upset about the party. I know where your heart is, Tristan." Looking around I peeked back over to him. "Do you think anyone saw us?"

Tristan looked around. "Nah, I'm sure everyone is pretty much here and already inside. We should probably go in though." Lifting his hips, he began zipping up his pants as I adjusted my panties and dress.

Tristan got out of the truck and made his way over to my door. Opening it, he took my hand and helped me down. As we walked to the entrance, Tristan leaned down and said, "We will finish that fuck session in my truck tonight."

Smiling, I nodded my head and said, "Yes, we will."

The second we walked through the door, everyone yelled surprise and I was faced with an onslaught of people that I had no idea who they were. A giant sign hung up that said *Welcome Kathryn.* I knew that was Joyce's doing. The only two people I knew at this surprise party besides Tristan and his parents were Chris and MaryLou, Joyce's friend.

The evening was spent being introduced to a plethora of people, drinking more drinks than I cared to count, and being in such a frenzied state of wanting Tristan, I could hardly think straight. The more I drank, the more I thought about what we were doing before walking into the party.

Making my way over to my man, I reached up on my tippy toes and said, "I want to finish what I started. And I want to go back to the shop and start training my ass for you."

The drink in Tristan's hand slipped out and crashed to the floor. Turning, he looked at his father who had been talking to I think Billy Saddler. Yep. That was his name. Owned one of the banks in town.

"Dad, Ryn's not feeling well. I'm taking her home. Bye."

Peter didn't even have time to respond when Tristan reached down and picked me up. As he carried me out everyone began letting out whistles and catcalls. Waving, I yelled, "Bye y'all! It was nice meeting everyone!"

Pushing the door open, Tristan started jogging to his truck.

Opening the door and putting me in the truck, Tristan asked, "Honesty means everything, Ryn. How drunk are you?"

Giving him a come hither look, I purred back to him, "I'm tipsy but I'm nowhere near drunk."

"Good, you're about to have an evening you'll never forget."

CHAPTER
Thirty-One

TRISTAN

KNOCKING ON THE DOOR TO my father's office, I tried to push my nerves away. I had wanted to talk to him for a few weeks now, but something always got in the way of it. Not anymore. I actually had to schedule it on my calendar to talk to my own father.

"Come on in, Tristan."

Opening the door, the smell of the leather hit me first. Smiling, I shut the door and made my way over to one of the leather chairs that sat in front of his desk.

He was reading through something and about to sign it. "I'll have to send some of this paperwork over to you, Tristan. I just don't seem to have interest in any of it anymore."

Nodding my head, I said, "Yeah, of course, Dad. Send me whatever you want me to handle and you know I'll take care of it."

Looking up, he gave me a smile. It had been four months since his heart attack. Ryn and I were more than half way through with the building of our house. I couldn't wait to get in there. Living with my parents was not something either one of us wanted to do. After two weeks of sleeping in my parents' house, Ryn and I decided to just sleep in the shop's bedroom. Of course, my parents knew why and never said a word about it. Even with our room upstairs, it still felt weird making love to Ryn with Mom and Dad downstairs. The one thing that pushed our decision was the night I went down to the kitchen and almost threw up after listening to my mother and father in the passions of having sex.

No thank you.

I watched as my dad signed the paperwork and set it to the side. Leaning back, he gave me that all knowing look of his. I wondered how long we were going to sit there and stare at each other before one of us began talking.

Reaching into his drawer, he pulled out the bottle. Setting it on the desk he slid it over to me.

"Your journey of love with Ryn has so far been a bouncy one, has it not?"

Glancing at the bottle, I nodded. "Yes, sir. It has."

"This journey called love, it's a crazy ride, Tristan. Like I told you and your brother before, love is a road we travel down. The road isn't always a smooth paved road. There are times we feel so lost on that road that we want to take a detour, find an easy way out. That never works though, I think you've discovered as much."

Nodding my head, I whispered, "Yes, sir, I have."

"I look at you and Kathryn together, Tristan, and do you want to know what I see?"

Gazing into my father's eyes, I asked, "What do you see?"

"A young couple madly in love. It's almost as if the air around them is charged with the energy from that love. You can't help but feel it any time they step into a room. It's a powerful thing, love. It has the power to make you so incredibly happy you can't even think straight, and the capability of completely destroying another person to the point of no return." Nodding his head, he looked down. "When I told you the story of the journey of love, I left out something important."

"What was that, Dad?"

Lifting his eyes, I couldn't help but notice the tears forming. "Once you start the journey, there is no going back. Love takes a hold of your heart, Tristan, and it grips it like a vice. *Hard and strong.* But that vice can be broken easily. The journey is meant to be a lifetime, but not everyone gets to experience such a love."

Swallowing hard, I looked away.

"Are you willing to fight for it, son? Not just a month from now, or a year from now, but twenty years down the road, will you be willing to fight for your love with everything you got?"

Tears formed in my eyes as I thought about how badly I had hurt Ryn. Going to talk my voice cracked. Closing my eyes, I cleared my throat, "I'm willing, Dad, with everything in my heart and soul. I'd die first before I ever hurt her."

Smiling, he slowly gave me a nod. "Then you know what to do."

Reaching out for the bottle, I pulled it into my hand. I was ready to commit the rest of my life to Ryn. I was ready to pour my heart and soul out to her. Standing, I looked at my father.

"I know the idea is to not read the letters."

Dad nodded his head and lifted the corner of his mouth into a smirk.

"I'd like to change that tradition."

Letting out a chortle, he said, "Somehow son, I knew you would."

"I'd like for Ryn and I both to write a letter to each other. Then exchange the letters and read them together before tossing it into the ocean. I'm not very good with expressing my love to Ryn. I'm not romantic in the least bit and with this . . . I just think it's important to share with each other what is in our hearts."

"I think that is a beautiful new tradition, Tristan."

Turning on my heels, I headed back to the door. Before opening it, I looked over my shoulder. "You and Mom read your letters to each other, didn't you?"

Lifting an eyebrow, he said, "There is not a damn thing I can keep from that woman. Not a damn thing."

Letting out a chuckle, I opened the door and left my father's office. Gripping the bottle in my hand, I headed to the barn. I sat on the hay and started planning my future with, Ryn. The more I saw, the happier I was.

Our bottle would surely hit calm seas and rough seas. But it would last though the strongest hurricane. This I felt in the very being of my soul.

WALKING THROUGH THE HOUSE, RYN carried a notebook while she took notes on things that I saw needed to be finished still.

"Looks like we are more than halfway done," Ryn said with hope in her voice.

Looking toward the ceiling, I nodded in agreement. "Yeah, I'd say we were for sure over halfway done. The only problem I can see are the cabinets. The custom cabinet maker is running a few weeks behind."

Ryn scrunched up her nose and said, "Crap, I forgot about that. Who picked those stupid cabinets anyway?"

Spinning around on my heels, I looked at her. "I believe it was you."

Giggling, she took a few steps back. "What? I have no idea what you are talking about. None."

Reaching her in record time, I pulled her into my arms. All the stress of taking over my family's ranch and building this house had my nerves shot. I wanted to spend some time with Ryn away from it all. "I need a couple days out of here, Ryn. What do you say we head to the beach?"

Raising her eyebrows, her eyes lit up. "That, sounds like heaven. Would your folks mind?"

"Nah, I bet we could even talk Lark and Azurdee into coming down too."

Ryn did a little hop. "Yes! Oh that would be amazing, Tristan. I haven't seen Azurdee since I left Austin."

Kissing the tip of her nose, I grinned like a crazy fool in love. "I'll take care of it all. I'll call Lark tonight."

Dropping her head back, Ryn let out a moan "Oh man. A few days alone, no parents, no barking dogs."

Laughing, I pulled her into my arms. "You, my dear, volunteered to help at the puppy doggy care place. I knew you weren't going to be able to do a couple hours a week."

Jetting out her lower lip and giving me her best pout, she said, "I can't help it if I love the dogs. If *someone* let me get a dog of my own, I wouldn't have to go there so much."

"Oh no, you are not guiltin' me into that bullshit. Forget it. No. Dog."

Giving me a slight push, I took a few steps back. "Fine, but no sex for you tonight."

Dropping my mouth open, I watched as she walked away. "What? How is that fair in any way?"

Waving her hand as if dismissing me, she put a little extra humph into her hip swing as she continued to walk away from me.

Letting out a laugh, I followed her out of the house and to my truck. Getting in, she looked my way.

"Would it be okay if we spent at least one day and night alone together at the beach? Then we can invite Lark and Azurdee?"

Letting out a deep growl, I wiggled my eyebrows up and down. "Hell yeah, we can have a day or two alone. Leave it up to me, baby. I'll take care of all the plans. I promise it will be a trip neither one of us will forget."

Smiling, she settled into the seat. "I can't wait to see Azurdee and Lark. I have to admit, I miss home."

A plan began to formulate in my head. I was going to make this trip one Ryn would never forget.

CHAPTER
Thirty-Two

$\mathcal{W}$ ALKING OUT ONTO THE BACK deck, I let the ocean breeze hit me in the face. It had seemed like forever ago when Tristan and I were here last. Lark and Azurdee would be here in two days. Tristan said he had a surprise for me and I couldn't wait to see what it was.

Shivers raced down my body as I felt Tristan's arms wrap around my body. Dropping my head back against him, I tilted my head, giving him better access. His lips began to lightly graze across my skin.

"I love you, Ryn."

Feeling the warmth of his love spread through my body, I spoke barely above a whisper, "I love you too, Tristan."

My eyes were closed as I felt the breeze blow a few brown curls that hung down from my pulled up hair.

"I have a journey I want to go on with you, baby."

Keeping my eyes closed, a low moan formed at the base of my throat. "I like the sound of that."

Hot breath hit my neck, causing a throbbing sensation between my legs. Instantly wet, I began having that familiar draw that I couldn't resist.

"It's a life long journey of love."

My eyes snapped opened as I dropped my head forward and I saw the bottle sitting on the railing. My heart slammed against the wall of my chest as my stomach dropped.

The bottle.

Turning around, I looked up into Tristan's eyes. "The bottle?"

Placing his hand on the side of my face, he gently brushed his thumb across my face. "Azurdee?"

Nodding my head, I felt a tear roll down my cheek. "Tristan . . ." I couldn't even begin to form the words in my brain to express how I felt. I didn't need the bottle to confirm Tristan's commitment to me. Matter of fact, I had forgotten all about it until I opened my eyes and saw it. But knowing the meaning behind it, I'd never in my life felt the way I was feeling this very moment.

"I told my father I wanted to do something different with the tradition. Before, each person wrote their letter and put it in the bottle. I want us to write our letters, but I want to exchange them before we put them into the bottle."

"You want to read each other's letter?"

His other hand moved up to my face as he held my face firmly in his hands. "I wish I was more romantic and swept you off your feet more, Ryn. There are so many things I feel in my heart that I want more than anything to express to you. I know by writing it down, I'll express it better. My hopes and dreams for our future, but my fears from the past as well. I want to share everything with you."

A small sob escaped through my lips as I placed my hands over Tristan's. "Tristan," I whispered as he pressed his lips to mine. The kiss was slow, soft, and utterly romantic. *How can he even say he doesn't sweep me off my feet?*

Pulling away, he whispered against my lips. "Okay, I know what I want to say." Dropping his hands, he quickly grabbed the bottle and made his way around the pool and into the house. I stood there stunned. I began to look around as if a joke was being played on me. Rushing into the house, I called out his name. "Tristan?"

"In the office, baby."

Making my way into the office, Tristan was behind the desk with a piece of paper and pen in his hand. Looking up he said, "I can't talk, the words are flowing. You need to find a spot to write."

Pulling my head back, I said, "Um . . . okay . . . well I'll just go to the kitchen table I guess?"

Pushing a few pages of paper in my direction, he nodded his head. Trying not to laugh, I took the paper and headed to the kitchen.

Sitting down at the table I stared at the paper.

Nothing.

Picking up the paper, I headed outside and sat on the deck overlooking the ocean.

Nothing.

Oh shit. Here Tristan was pouring his heart to me in words and I sat here with not a single thing written down.

Closing my eyes, I took in a deep breath and slowly blew it out. I thought back to the first time I'd ever seen Tristan. The first time he kissed me, made love to me, looked at me like I was his everything, and the first time he told me he loved me.

Opening my eyes, I looked out over the ocean and smiled. Picking up my pen, I began writing.

Dear Tristan,

I sat here for what seemed like forever, trying to put into words how I feel about you, our hopes, dreams, and desires of what our future will be.

I stared at the paper and nothing would come out. Then it hit me. Life is a journey, much like the journey of love that we will embark on ourselves.

I look at my parents, and your parents, and even Lark and Azurdee. I see people who are madly in love. I also see human beings who will make mistakes and have regrets along their journey. I think what is important though is that they have each other during all of it. The good times and the bad times. They are each other's strengths.

That is what I want our journey to be. A journey filled with lessons, mistakes, triumphs, good times, bad times, and most of all . . . a journey filled with love.

I'll never be able to put into words how much I love you. I can show you though. I promise to show you every single day what your love does to me.

My hopes and desires for our journey are simple. A future filled with love and a lot of laughter. The smile on your face when I tell you we are expecting a child, the sound of our baby crying, the feel of your body next to mine every night as we fall asleep, and the touch of your hand when we walk along the beach in our later years.

I love you, Tristan. I promise to love you forever. I promise to never go to sleep when we are fighting, and I promise to always be your strength.

Love,

Kathryn

I WASN'T SURE HOW LONG I had been sitting on the deck before I felt him behind me. Turning, I looked up and saw Tristan gazing down at me. "I wrote like six letters."

Laughing, I pulled my knees up into my chest as I watched him sit across from me. "You wrote six letters? Damn. I only wrote one."

Giving me a smirk, he shook his head. "No, I started writing at least six times, each time I tore it up."

"Did you finish one?"

Peeking at me through his beautiful long eyelashes, he winked. "Yes, I did."

"Can I read it?"

Lifting his eyebrow, he said, "Maybe we should draw straws."

Giggling, I stood up. "Do we have straws?"

Glancing back toward the house, Tristan said, "If we do I have no idea where they would be."

"Rock, paper, scissors?"

Tristan jumped. "Yes! I love that game."

Tristan and I prepared our fists. "Ready?" I asked.

Tristan nodded his head as he adjusted his body and got ready to play. "Ready."

"One, two, three, show!"

I had rock, Tristan had paper. Doing a fist pump he shouted, "Yes!"

Rolling my eyes, I started counting. "One, two, three, show!"

I had scissors and Tristan had paper. "Fuck! I fucking hate paper."

Giggling, I said, "You won the first round with paper. How can you say you hate paper?"

"Just count, Ryn!"

Snarling my lip up at him, I said, "Gesh, man oh man. You really want to go first."

Looking at me with a frustrated look, he whispered, "Count."

"Fine! One, two, three . . . show!"

I had rock and Tristan had scissors. I started jumping and yelling out, "I won! I won! Woohoo I won!"

Tristan glared at me. "Really, Ryn? What are you, five?"

My mouth gaped open and I couldn't help but smile at the pathetic face he was making. "Oh. My. Gosh. You sore loser you. I didn't say that when you were all fist pumping your freaking paper win."

Dropping back into the seat, Tristan crossed his arms and pouted. Oh dear lord. If that wasn't the sexiest thing I'd ever seen. This man . . . the one who has a room filled with sex toys . . . is pouting because he lost at rock, paper, scissors. I was so going to swallow tonight when I gave him a blowjob.

"Okay, since I won, I get to pick." Handing him my letter, he looked up at me and smiled the most beautiful smile I'd ever seen on his face. It took my breath away.

"Really?"

Nodding my head, I spoke above a whisper, "Yes. I want you to read it."

Sitting, I tucked my legs into my body and rested my chin on my knees as I watched Tristan read my letter. Tears began to form in his eyes as he continued to read. Once he finished reading, he slowly looked up at me.

Standing, he pulled a folded piece of paper from his back pocket and handed it to me. He sat back down as I unfolded the paper, never once taking my eyes off of him.

Looking down, I sucked in a breath of air as read the first line.

My dearest Kathryn,

I promise to always be your strength.

I promise to hold you in my arms when you are sad, angry, and happy, but most of all, when you are scared.

I promise to kiss you at least ten times a day.

I promise to be the best husband and father I can be.

I promise to make mistakes. With every mistake comes greater knowledge.

I promise to never hurt you. Ever.

I promise you that I will protect you with every fiber of my being.

I promise to love you . . . only you . . . forever.

I promise all these things because you are my

entire world. My everything I've ever dreamed of and feared. My love for you once scared me, now it is the driving force behind wanting to make every single one of your dreams come true. Which leads me to my last promise.

I promise to make all your dreams come true.
Forever and always yours,
Tristan

CHAPTER
Thirty-Three

TRISTAN

 WAS PRETTY SURE I was about to pass out. My heart had stopped beating the moment I handed Ryn my letter. I wasn't any good at this kind of stuff. I knew what I wanted to say to her, I just couldn't get it out.

Finally she looked up at me. Tears were streaming down her face.

Shit. Is that good? Maybe it's bad? Her letter had been amazing and brought me to tears. *What if mine sucked so bad . . . it forced her to cry?*

The next thing I knew, Ryn was up and in my arms. "I love you. I've never in my life loved anyone like I love you."

Wrapping my arms around her, I smiled into her hair. "And you never will."

"Tristan, make love to me. Please."

Lifting her up, I carried her back into the house. I had brought all our bags to the master bedroom downstairs since I had invited a few of our friends to join us this weekend.

Setting her on the bed, I stood up and slowly got undressed while Ryn watched my every move. Moving over her body, I gently kissed her lips, pulling her lower lip between my teeth and giving it a gentle pull. Ryn whimpered with need underneath me.

Slowly lifting her up, I pulled her shirt over her head and

tossed it onto the floor. Reaching behind her, I unclasped her bra and slowly pulled it off of her.

"Lay back, Ryn."

Falling back onto the pillow, Ryn began squirming. Reaching my hands for her shorts, I unsnapped the button and slowly began pulling the zipper down.

Closing her eyes tightly as she lifted her hips. In one fast movement, I had her shorts and panties off. She lay gloriously naked on the bed.

"So damn beautiful," I whispered as I crawled over her. Kissing her lips gently, I moved my lips down to her neck. Placing soft kissing along her collarbone, I moved down her chest. Each nipple was placed in my mouth as my tongue rolled over it before my teeth gently bit down. Arching her back, Ryn let out a whimper, "Ahh . . . Tristan . . . please!"

Using my tongue, I trailed a path to her navel. Dipping my tongue in, Ryn begged me for more.

Kissing the inside of her leg, I pushed her legs open. "Jesus, Ryn. You're perfect everywhere, baby."

Gripping the sheets, Ryn's hips jerked up as my tongue made a slow swipe up her lips to her clit.

"Ohmygod!"

Smiling, I began teasing her clit with my tongue. Ryn's hands were in my hair, pulling and then pushing me into her more.

"Please."

Pulling back, I spread her lips open and before I dipped my tongue inside, I looked up at her. She was looking at me, her eyes filled with lust. Her chest rising and falling with desire. "Your pussy is so wet, Ryn."

Dropping her head back, she hissed, "Fuuuck."

Smiling, I pushed my tongue into her. Licking and tasting her want for me. Slowly pushing two fingers into her ass, she jumped. I had been working her ass slowly and I couldn't wait to fuck her there. My dick throbbed at the idea as I moved my fingers in and out of her ass while my tongue fucked her.

"Tristan!"

I felt her orgasm hit as she squeezed onto my fingers, pushing another finger in, I spread her open more as she screamed out and fell apart again.

"Stop, I can't . . . I can't . . ."

Pulling my fingers out, I licked up her pussy to her clit and flicked it a few more times. Ryn squirmed as she yelled out. Her body was so responsive, I loved it.

Moving up between her legs, I positioned myself at her entrance. Slowly pushing in, Ryn and I both let out a long deep moan. Placing my lips to her ear, I whispered, "You feel so good."

Wrapping her legs around me, we slowly began moving. It was a perfect rhythm. Kissing along her neck, my lips found hers. Our tongues moved against each other as if they were in a slow dance. Cupping her face within my hands, I kissed her harder. Faster. The passion was heating up as I pumped in and out of her faster.

Pulling back, I looked into her eyes. "I love you," I whispered as I pushed deep inside her and came.

A tear slowly moved down her cheek as she whispered back, "Forever, Tristan. Forever."

RYN CAME RUNNING DOWN THE stairs. She had been up there making sure the bedrooms had everything that would be needed. She only thought Lark, Azurdee, and Chris were coming. I had extended an invite to Sierra, but she said she couldn't make it. With her not coming, I went ahead and invited Dodge. Ryn would be over the moon to see him.

"They're here! I just saw a car pull up."

Smiling, I wiped my hands on the hand towel next to me. I was making homemade pizza sauce for the individual pizzas I was putting together. Ryn had asked why I was making so much food. I had turned and looked at the island and all the food I had ordered. A cheese and fruit tray, a vegetable tray, some funky pinwheel sandwich shit the girl at HEB said everyone would love, chips, pretzels, Cheetos . . . there was a lot of food.

The door flew up and Ryn screamed, "Ohmygod! Sierra!"

My mouth fell open as I quickly came out of the kitchen. "Oh fuck," I whispered. "What in the hell is she doing here? She said no!"

Walking into the house, Sierra gave Ryn a big hug. "I told

Tristan I didn't think I would be able to make it. I couldn't get anyone to cover my shift, but turns out someone needed to switch."

Shit. Shit. Shit. Okay, this could still work. Her house was two doors down from here. I'll just tell her she needs to stay there. If she asks why, I'll make up something.

As they made their way toward the kitchen, I gave Sierra a smile. "Hey, you made it after all."

Grinning, she walked up and kissed me on the cheek. "I did. I hope you didn't give my room away." Ryn and Sierra laughed. "Because my winter Texans are still in my house."

Fuck me.

Ryn looked at me and frowned. She must have seen the look on my face when Sierra said her house was being rented out.

Giving her a wink and smile, I asked, "Hey, did you want some wine? We've got beer or soda. Pick your flavor."

"Oh man, I think I'll stick with just water this weekend."

The doorbell rang and Ryn ran over and threw it open. Letting out another scream, she yelled, "Ohmygod! Dodge."

Sierra's head snapped over and looked at me. Looking at her, I whispered, "You said you couldn't make it!"

Turning back toward where Ryn was with Dodge, Sierra mumbled, "I think I'll take that glass of wine *and* the beer."

Laughing, I turned and headed into the kitchen, opening the refrigerator, I pulled out three beers. One for Sierra, one for Dodge for when he saw Sierra, and one for me, to prepare for Ryn asking me why I would invite Dodge and Sierra together.

Walking back to Sierra, I handed her the beer. Dodge walked up and shook my hand and gave me a quick hug with a slap on the back. "Good to see you, Tristan."

Handing the beer to him, I replied, "Great to see you, too."

Dodge turned and looked at Sierra who was staring at him. "Why are you staring at me?"

Reaching over I closed poor Sierra's gaped open mouth. She shook her head and said, "Your hair. You look so good . . . I mean . . . it looks so good . . . better. It looks better b-brown."

I attempted not to laugh as Sierra fumbled around her words. Dodge smiled, "Thanks, Sierra. It's naturally brown."

Not being able to take her eyes from him she said, "Huh."

Finally she looked away and to the front door when Azurdee and Lark walked in.

Azurdee screamed, Ryn screamed, Lark rolled his eyes and made a beeline straight to the kitchen. Passing Dodge, he gave him a head pop and a quick hello.

We all sat around the island bar and talked, ate, drank, and then ate some more. Azurdee, Ryn, and Sierra were going on and on about some new fashion show. We eventually moved into the living room. I couldn't help but notice how Dodge kept sneaking a peek at Sierra. She of course wanted to look, but refused to. I knew this because I knew Sierra. It was killing her not to look at Dodge.

The doorbell rang and I quickly stood up. Shit. Oh motherfucker. I had forgotten about Chris. Pushing my hand through my hair, I looked at Sierra and then Dodge.

"Who's that?" Ryn asked.

Giving her a wink, I didn't answer as I turned and headed to the door. I had originally asked Chris, thinking Sierra would be here, thinking they might hook up for the weekend. I knew Chris would be attracted to Sierra instantly. Sierra on the other hand was up in the air. She could either be in the mood for a hook up or not want anything to do with Chris. Then when Sierra couldn't make it, I invited Dodge, thinking Chris and Dodge would get along okay. They both ate, slept, and breathed the Dallas Cowboys and the Texas Rangers.

Opening the door, I smiled. *This ought to be interesting.* "Hey, Tristan, sorry I'm late. I got a late start."

Behind me I heard Ryn. "Chris! Oh my gosh this so great!" Taking Chris's bag, I motioned for him to head in. He was familiar with the house since he had come with us to the coast every summer since sixth grade.

Walking in, Dodge stood and introduced himself. Okay, so far so good. Lark jumped up and gave Chris a hug as he said, "Jesus H. Christ. It's been awhile."

Azurdee gave Chris a hug. When Chris turned to Sierra, he paused for a brief second. I was pretty sure no one saw it. Sierra's eyes lit up, even though she tried to play it cool. One peek at Dodge and it didn't appear he noticed anything.

Slapping Chris on the back, I asked, "You hungry?"

"Yes, man I'm starved."

Chris and I headed into the kitchen to grab him some pizza. Standing in the kitchen talking to him, I couldn't help but notice Sierra kept looking in here.

Everyone started getting tired around one in the morning. After saying good night to everyone, Ryn and I headed to our room.

As we laid in bed, Ryn started chuckling. Looking over at her I asked, "What's so funny?"

Turning on her side, she rested her head in her hand. "Sierra, Dodge, and Chris. This should be an interesting few days."

Letting out a laugh, I nodded my head. "Interesting is one word you could use."

Pulling her onto me, I rolled onto my back. "You tired?"

Giving me that sexy smile of hers, she nodded and pouted. "I am. As much as I'd love to make love, my body is longing for sleep."

Rolling over and placing her back onto the bed, I kissed her softly. "Sleep good, baby."

Pulling her into my side, we both quickly fell asleep.

THE LAST TWO DAYS HAD been a blast as we all just hung out and relaxed. Ryn seemed to really be enjoying herself. I decided we were going to have to do this more often. Sierra and Chris hit it off, just like I thought they would. They were currently sitting next to each other talking about the damn dog boarding business. *What is it with girls and dogs?*

Walking out onto the deck where everyone was, I carried a bottle of champagne and five glasses. Setting the champagne down onto the table, I looked around at everyone. Ryn was smiling and laughing as Lark told a story about a time he was in the Marines. This was the perfect time.

Walking up to Ryn, she looked up at me. She was breathtaking. The most beautiful woman I had every laid my eyes on.

Reaching into my pocket, I pulled out the ring box as I got down on one knee. Ryn's eyes instantly began watering.

Azurdee and Sierra both let out gasps and placed their hands over their mouths.

Smiling, I took Ryn's hand in mine as I looked into her eyes.

"Ryn, when I close my eyes and picture my life, I picture you standing looking out over the ocean and my hands on your pregnant stomach."

Tears rolled down, Ryn's face and I fought like hell to keep my composure in front of everyone. Swallowing hard, I kept talking.

"When I'm holding you, Ryn, I'm holding my entire world. I'm nothing without you, baby. You're the best part of who I am."

Ryn began crying harder as I took the princess cut diamond out of the box and held it up. "Ryn, will you marry me?"

Her hand was shaking as she nodded her head frantically. "Yes. Yes, I'll marry you."

Dropping to her knees, Ryn wrapped her arms around me as everyone began standing up and saying their congratulations. I'd been nervous as hell to ask Ryn to marry me in front of our friends. Seeing the happiness in her eyes would be something I would never forget. I wasn't sure how long Ryn and I held each other before we stood. Lark was the first to hug Ryn.

Azurdee and Ryn both started crying again when they hugged. Sierra came walking up and gave me a hug and whispered, "It's about time."

Dodge and Chris both shook my hand and gave Ryn a kiss on the cheek.

Clapping his hands together, Lark said, "This calls for a celebration."

Smiling, I looked at Ryn. She walked up to me and kissed me gently on the lips. "You want to go out, baby, and celebrate?"

"As long as I'm with you, I don't care where we are."

Looking around I said, "All right, let's party."

CHAPTER
Thirty-Four

G LANCING DOWN AGAIN, I LOOKED at the ring on my finger. Smiling, I looked at Tristan. He hadn't let go of me since we walked into the dance club. He either had my hand in his or had his arm around my waist.

Looking up, I noticed Dodge staring out to the dance floor. Following his gaze, I saw Chris and Sierra dancing. "Freak Me" was playing and Chris and Sierra were for sure getting their freak on. I wouldn't be surprised if Chris ended up in Sierra's bed tonight.

I knew Sierra secretly wished for Dodge to make some kind of move, but he ended up dancing with some red head almost as soon as we walked into the club. I saw the hurt move across Sierra's face. But as soon as I saw it, it was gone and her attention was turned to the man who had been making a move for the last two days.

"You want to dance, baby?"

Giving Tristan a smile, I nodded and let him lead me to the dance floor. The beat of the song moved through my body as Tristan took me into his arms. Tristan was an amazing dancer. He pulled me closer and began moving his hands over my body as I melted into his body. The last few days had been amazing. I never wanted this time to end.

"Tell me what you are thinking right now," Tristan said in my ear.

"I'm thinking about life after this weekend."

Giving me a smile that melted my heart, Tristan placed his lips back to my ear. "Slow. Life is going to be slow. I want to enjoy every single second with you. Every night I want to lie in the back of my truck and look up at the clear sky full of stars. Every morning I want to wake up with you in my arms as we listen to the world come alive."

Moving my lips along his jaw, I said, "Hmm . . . cowboy take me home and make love to me."

"Gladly."

Walking back over to the bar, Tristan told Lark and Azurdee we were heading back to the house. Lark gave Tristan a thumbs-up as Azurdee stood and gave me a kiss on the cheek and then Tristan.

The rest of the evening was spent with Tristan making slow passionate love to me as he whispered in my ear how much he desired me.

This night would forever be the most romantic night of my life.

STANDING AT THE WATER'S EDGE, Tristan held the bottle in his hand. We had put both our letters into the bottle and Tristan had sealed it the same day we wrote them. We had both agreed to throw the bottle into the ocean at sunrise. This was our last day at the beach and the first official full day as an engaged couple.

The sun was beginning to rise as Tristan and I stood in front of each other. "Are we supposed to say something?" I asked.

Tristan looked out over the water. "Um . . . like what?"

Giggling, I said, "Maybe we just kiss and then give it a toss."

"I like that plan."

Taking a step forward, Tristan began screaming out, "Ouch! Shit! Oh, what the hell?"

I jumped back and looked at him. "What's wrong? Tristan. What's wrong?"

Tristan was jumping around on one foot as he kept screaming

out. "Fuuck! Get it off. Get. It. Off!"

Trying to see what was wrong, I bent over. "Stay still, stop jumping around!" I yelled out.

Then I saw what was wrong. In that moment I felt something hit my foot and I screamed bloody murder. "Crab. Holy shit you have a crab on your toe."

I began jumping as I tried to look around. The sun was rising and I was able to see around my feet.

"Why are you jumping? It's on my foot!"

Tristan began trying to shake the crab off of his foot as I busted out laughing.

"Ryn! It's not funny. Get it off."

Tristan started hitting the crab with our bottle. "Stop! Our bottle. Are you insane? You'll bust our bottle!"

"It hurts. Ryn, grab it. Get it off!"

Taking a step back, I looked at the giant crab gripping onto Tristan's toe. There was no way I was touching that thing. "Hit it with the bottle. Just hit it with the bottle!"

Tristan held up the bottle and was about to swing when the crab let go and scurried off.

Jumping up and down, I began yelling out. "Yay! He let go!"

Tristan dropped to the ground as I continued to celebrate. Looking at me, he wore a frustrated expression. "Um . . . I'm in pain here, Ryn."

Flopping down in front of him, I grabbed his face and planted a kiss on his lips. Pulling back, I spoke against his lips. "You saved our bottle. My hero."

Smiling, he pushed me back and put most of his weight on me as he kissed me. The waves came in and barely washed up around us as our tongues found the perfect rhythm.

"Get a room!" someone said as I saw three sets of running shoes pass us by. Looking up Tristan yelled, "Hey! We are newly engaged! Give us a break."

The jogger must have turned and faced back to us as he shouted, "All the more reason to get a room!"

Laughing, Tristan shook his head as I chuckled. "Are you ready, baby?"

Smiling, I said, "I've never been more ready."

Tristan stood and then helped me up. Looking out over the

water, he asked, "Do you want to throw it or me?"

"No, you throw it. I won't be able to throw it that far and I don't want it washing back up."

Tristan raised his arm and was about to throw it when I yelled, "Wait!"

"What?"

"Maybe you should go out a little further and then throw it."

Tristan furrowed his brow and then looked out over the water. He probed the water as the expression on his face turned serious. "You want me . . . to go out into the water . . . where the crab is?"

Attempting to hold back my laughter, I nodded my head. "Uh huh. Yeah, just walk waist deep in . . . and toss it."

Lifting his chin and perking up his shoulders, Tristan nodded his head. "I've got this."

Slapping his back a few times I said, "Of course you do, baby."

"Yeah." Taking a step into the water, Tristan paused. Glancing over his shoulder at me, he gave me a weary smile. Using my hands, I prompted him on in a shooing manner.

"Go on. You've got this."

Slowly making his way into the water, he walked until he was waist deep. "Perfect! Baby, throw it as hard as you can."

Tristan screamed and jumped. And when I say screamed, he girly screamed. Reaching back with his arm he threw that bottle as hard and as far as he could. I smiled as I watched it soar through the air.

Jumping, I let out a victory call.

The next thing I knew Tristan was running out of the water as fast as he could. "Fucking crab! I'm never gonna be able to swim in the ocean again."

Stomping off toward the house, I turned and watched as the sun's rays danced across the ocean waves. I'd never felt so happy and so at peace. This was it. The start of our new life together. Looking down at my beautiful ring, I let the one lone tear fall.

There was no doubting it. Our love was undeniable.

IT HAD BEEN THREE WEEKS since Tristan had asked me to marry him. I had called my mother and told her the news that I was getting married. The call lasted ten minutes and eight of those were her telling me how I was making another mistake in my life. Why I even bothered, I'll never know.

Pulling up to the house, my stomach did all kinds of crazy flip-flops. Tristan had busted his ass when we came back from the beach and our house was now finished. We had done the walk-through a few days ago, closed on it yesterday afternoon, then came back and made love in almost every room of the house. There was one room Tristan kept locked the entire time. I knew what the room was, but it was kind of funny watching Tristan squirm around it when his mother or father would ask why that door was locked and why they couldn't see it.

Stepping out of my car, I walked up to the front door. Smiling, I pushed the door open and stepped into the giant foyer. Looking up, I was in awe of the giant chandelier hanging from the ceiling. Some of the fixtures we used in the house were from one of Tristan's grandparents' houses. They fit in perfect with our house and it made it that much more special for Tristan. He was close to both sets of grandparents, so it made me so happy when I suggested it and he thought it was a great idea.

Heading into the living room, I did a little hop and clapped my hands. All of the furniture had been delivered earlier and set up. I hadn't been there to see it because I was helping Chris out today at the vet clinic.

Making my way through the living room, I walked through the formal dining room and into the kitchen. This was my dream kitchen with stone countertops, high-end appliances, and a trash compactor. I had no idea why I was so excited for that damn thing. Tristan laughed his ass off when I got giddy in the store while picking it out. The rest of the first floor was my office, a guest bedroom and the master suite, which was amazing. The bedroom was huge with a separate section for sitting. The fireplace would be so romantic and I couldn't wait to make love in front of it. The bathroom was like stepping into a spa. Last night while taking a shower in there, Tristan had walked in with hand-cuffs that had suctions on the end. At first there was no way I was gonna use them. I didn't trust them. Soon I was lost in Tristan fucking the hell out of me while my hands were above my head in the handcuffs. He had held most of my weight the entire time.

Biting on my lip, I smiled as the memory washed over my body. Letting out a deep breath, I pushed my building desire down.

Heading up the staircase, I walked onto the second-floor landing. Three bedrooms were on this floor, each with their own bathroom. It was important for Tristan to have each room have its own private bath. I agreed. For guests it would be nice, but some day when we had kids there would be no fighting over a bathroom to share. Rounding the corner, I climbed more stairs that led to the third floor. Giggling, I thought back to Lark bitching Tristan out. *"You just always have to one-up me, don't you? Two stories wasn't enough, you went for three!"*

Walking up, I looked at the two doors that were across from each other. Each room was huge. To the left was Tristan's home office. To the right, the playroom that I had yet to see. Walking toward Tristan's office, I heard him on the phone. We had planned on spending today moving all of our stuff from the shop into the house, but Tristan was sidetracked and Chris called begging for me to run his front desk for him. The receptionist had slipped and fallen, spraining her ankle. I knew how much pain she was in, so it wasn't a hard choice to go and help out.

Standing in the doorway to Tristan's office, I leaned against the door jamb. Tristan looked up and smiled. Then he pulled his head back in wonder. I was wearing a long raincoat and it was over eighty degrees outside. Pushing off the jamb, I slowly opened my coat and dropped it to the floor.

Tristan's mouth dropped open as his eyes perused over my body as he took it all in. I was wearing a red corset and thigh-high stockings that were attached with a red garter belt. My high heel red fuck-me shoes rounded it all out.

Swallowing hard, Tristan said, "An angel dressed in red."

Placing my finger in my mouth, I slowly sucked on it as I pulled my finger out and buried it between my cleavage. I loved how the corset lifted and pushed out my breasts.

"What? Oh, no, James I'm not talking to you. I was . . . distracted."

Giving him my sexiest grin, I walked to him and placed my foot on one of the chairs. I was sans panties as I moved my fingers between my legs as I began to rub on my clit, letting out a small moan.

"Um . . . ahh . . . the fall hunts . . . yeah . . . we're looking . . . I mean booking them now."

I had slipped the balls out of my jacket pocket and had them in my other hand that was behind my back. Moving my hand out, I placed two small round silver balls on his desk. Tristan's eyes widened in surprise as he stared at the Ben Wa balls on his desk.

Removing my fingers from my pussy, I slowly put them into my mouth. I had been building myself up to do that for months. Placing my hands on his desk and dropping my foot back to the floor, I whispered, "Oh yes, Mr. Williams, I've been doing my homework."

"James, I don't mean to cut you off but I've got a situation that needs, hammering out."

Lifting my eyebrows, I grinned.

Hanging up his phone, Tristan stood. "Is this your way at trying to get into the playroom, baby?"

Sitting on the chair, I placed a leg over each armrest. Spreading myself open for him to see.

"Jesus," he whispered. Moving around his desk, Tristan said, "Stay just like that, Ryn. Don't move."

My breathing picked up and I licked my lips in anticipation of what was going to happen next.

Grabbing the balls he slipped them into his pocket. Oh God. I was both excited and terrified of the balls.

Tristan walked up, pushed the chair back and dropped to his knees. "Don't move and don't touch me, Ryn or I'll stop."

Whimpering, I closed my eyes. I was so horny I could practically feel my juices flowing out of me. Tristan slipped his fingers inside me and let out a long moan.

"You're so damn wet, Ryn. Baby, are you horny?"

Nodding my head, I said, "Yes."

His lips moved to my inner thigh and my body shuddered. "Are you wanting to play, Ryn?"

Frantically nodding my head, I moaned as his fingers slowly moved in and out. Pulling his fingers out, I didn't have time to express my disappointment in the loss before his mouth was over me, licking and sucking me into an orgasm.

When I finally came down from my high, Tristan kissed me. The taste of myself on his tongue took some getting used to, but I thought it was the hottest thing ever having Tristan kiss me after oral sex.

Lifting me from the chair, he carried me across the hall. "We only had one night in my playroom in Austin, so we not only have to break in our new playroom, we have some serious making up to do." I had gone back to Austin a few times for work, but Tristan was never free to go back with me.

Smiling, I buried my face into his neck as Tristan unlocked the door and opened it. Shutting the door, he locked it before turning and carrying me over to the bed. This was the first time I got to look at the playroom. It was set up almost like the one in Austin, but a few things were different.

Setting me down on the bed, I drew in a breath and slowly released it when I felt the satin sheets. Running my hand along it I smiled when I saw they were blue. My favorite color. Then I noticed the color of the walls. They were a silver-blue, similar to the color I had picked out for the house.

My heart swelled with love knowing that Tristan had been paying attention to all the little details.

Reaching into his pocket he took the two silver balls out and set them down on the bed. Then he quickly got undressed. "I'm keeping you dressed in that outfit, Ryn. It's fucking sexy as hell."

The feeling of excitement just intensified a hundred times. I loved pleasing Tristan, in any way.

Picking up the balls he held them up and gave me a drop-dead sexy smile. "Do you know what they are, Ryn?"

Nodding my head, I whispered, "Yes."

"Tell me what you want me to do with them."

Sucking in a deep breath, I blew it out slowly. "Put them inside me and then fuck me, Tristan."

His smile lit up even more. "Yes, baby."

Tristin slipped his fingers inside me as he primed me. Sliding the balls into me, I gasped at how cold they were. "So fucking wet, it's perfect."

Once both balls were in, Tristan began finger fucking me. "More! I want more!" I begged as I grabbed the satin sheets within in my hands.

Tristan moved over my body and slid his dick inside of me. "Ohmygod!" I yelled out. The feeling was exquisite. Unlike anything I'd ever experienced before. My mind was spinning out of control as I let the feeling of the balls and Tristan's dick move inside me.

"Oh hell, Ryn, fuck this feels amazing, baby."

"Can't . . . Tristan . . . amazing . . ." The buildup was beginning and I felt my whole body preparing for it. Holy hell, this was going to be big.

"Yes, Tristan, right there!" I screamed out. The way he was fucking me had the balls hitting the spot that would take me to heaven.

Tristan pulled out and pushed in and that was it. He had moved in such a way that it hit the spot. The balls were being forced by his dick and hitting the exact spot that I needed them to hit. My orgasm raced through my body, causing me to scream out. I'd never in my life felt my pussy contracting with my orgasm like it was. Tristan continued to fuck me as my orgasm continued to go on, and on, and on.

"Can't . . . take . . . anymore!" I yelled out.

"Fucking hell, your pussy is squeezing down on my cock, Ryn. Baby I'm going to come."

Tristan's words threw me into another orgasm; I began yelling out incoherently. I felt him stilling inside my body as I slowly felt myself grounded again. "Baby, I need you to stand."

Opening my eyes, I stood up. Glancing back at the bed, the balls were laying on the bed. "How did they come out?" I asked as Tristan brought me over to the St. Andrew's Cross.

"Your orgasm pushed them out."

"Oh," was all I could manage.

Lifting my hands, I watched as Tristan attached the handcuffs. When he dropped down to cuff my ankles, I closed my eyes in anticipation of what was to come.

Standing he gave me a smile. "What's our word, Ryn?"

Licking my lips, I said, "Mickey."

"Mickey. Don't take on more than you can handle, Ryn. Do you understand me?"

My breathing was labored and I couldn't wait for what was next. "Yes."

Tristan walked his beautiful naked ass over to where all the riding crops and floggers where hung up. Reaching for a riding crop, he turned and made his way back over to me.

"Say it, Ryn."

"Mickey! Damn it, Tristan."

Reaching his fingers between my legs, he let out a hiss. "So fucking wet."

Crying out, I begged him, "Please!"

His fingers quickly slid into me as he began his assault. "You like that, Ryn?"

"Yes, harder. More. Tristan, I want more."

I couldn't believe how wanton I sounded. Closing my eyes tightly, I begged him for more. When my eyes opened, I looked across the room to the bed. I saw a mirror hung up behind the bed. "Is that . . . is that the mirror from South Padres?"

Tristan's eyes met mine. The look of seduction that crossed over his face caused me to let out a moan. "It is. I thought that was the perfect place for it. This way when you ride me hard and fast, you can watch yourself in the mirror." Grinning, I looked into Tristan's eyes. They were filled with love and passion.

"I want more," I said in the most seductive voice I could muster up.

"Hell yeah, Ryn. That's it, baby."

Removing his fingers, he hit me with the riding crop on my lips. Jerking, I let out a scream. The pain mixed with the sense of pleasure was unlike anything I'd ever experienced before. I loved it and found myself wanting more.

Placing his fingers back inside me he began moving them in and out again. Just as I would feel the build of my orgasm, he pulled out and hit me with riding crop again.

I wanted more. It felt as if my body physically needed more. I ached with desire.

"Harder!"

Tristan hesitated. "Tristan, please."

Hitting me slightly harder with the riding crop, I cried out as I felt my orgasm building.

"Ryn . . ."

Looking into Tristan's concern-filled eyes, I attempted to show him how desperately I wanted this. "More, I want more. Please."

His fingers impaled me again, working me up into a frenzy. "I'm so close. Oh God, Tristan."

Pulling his fingers out, he hit the riding crop on me again, throwing me into an orgasm. His fingers sliding in me caused me to scream out again as it felt like another wave hit me.

Before long, I was hanging limp from the cross. Tristan took me down and carried me back over to the bed, where he gently laid me down. Looking at him, I saw his dick was hard again.

Looking into my eyes he asked, "Enough?"

Shaking my head, I whispered, "More."

CHAPTER
Thirty-Five

TRISTAN

$\mathcal{M}$ Y EYES WIDENED IN SHOCK when Ryn whispered more. In my wildest dreams I'd never imagined the love of my life in our playroom, enjoying it more than I could have asked. I knew she was curious and she wanted to try everything; I had pushed her with the riding crop, hitting her not nearly as hard as I've hit other women, but this was my Ryn. My girl. I never wanted to do anything to cause her pain.

"Roll over, Ryn; it's time to train that ass of yours a little more."

Ryn's eyes lit up as I moved off the bed and made my way over to the drawers. A part of me wanted to keep pushing her to the brink, the other part wanted to hold back. The second I saw her eyes light up at the mention of training her ass, I knew she wanted it as much as I did. Pulling out a butt plug, I grabbed the lube and headed back to Ryn.

Running my hand over her ass, I whispered, "On your hands and knees, baby."

Moving quickly, I watched as her arms shook. Fear hit me like a brick wall. I've pushed her too far. "Ryn, do you want to stop?"

Looking over her shoulder, she shook her head. "No! Please don't stop."

Seeing the desire in her eyes, I began to put lube onto my fingers. I rubbed it over her puckered hole then slowly slid my fingers in, getting her ready for the butt plug. I didn't want to hurt her. Ever.

Leaning over I kissed her back. "What's the safe word, Ryn?" She panted out, "Mickey."

Rubbing her ass with my other hand I smiled. "Yes, baby."

Sliding another finger into her ass, Ryn moaned. Getting her good and ready, I slid the butt plug in. "Ohmygod!" Ryn cried.

"I'm going to fuck you from behind while I play with your ass."

Dropping her head she whimpered. "Fuck . . . feels . . . so good."

Pushing my dick into her, I began pumping. Playing just a little with the butt plug.

Ryn cried out in pleasure. The thought of taking her ass as I pushed a vibrator in and out of her pussy about pushed me over the edge.

Smiling, I gave her what she asked for. Fucking her harder, I began moving the butt plug in and out. Ryn started yelling out incoherently and it didn't take long until I felt her pussy sucking my cock in with her orgasm.

Pulling the butt plug and my dick out of her, she collapsed onto the bed. Her breathing erratic as she moaned over and over, "That was amazing. Ohmygod . . . so amazing."

"Are you done, baby?" I asked as my eyes moved over her sweat-sheened, worn out body.

Rolling over, she looked at me as her chest heaved up and down. "I want more, Tristan. I want you to come while you're buried deep inside of my pussy."

Holy fucking shit. Nothing was hotter than Ryn talking dirty to me.

"Tell me what you want, Ryn," I whispered against her neck as I watched goose bumps ignite across her body.

"Spreader bar."

Letting out a moan, I moved off of her and got the spreader bar. My heart was racing at the idea of using the bar on Ryn for the first time.

Grabbing it, I walked back over to the bed. After getting Ryn in the bar, I looked down at her glistening wet pussy.

"You're mine, Ryn."

"Always, Tristan."

Taking my cock in my hand, I slowly stuck it into her wet, hot pussy. I knew I would not last long; I was so fucking turned on. Pushing into her balls deep, I sucked in a breath of air.

"Is it too much, Ryn?"

Thrashing her head back and forth, she whimpered, "So deep. So wonderfully deep."

My eyes practically rolled into the back of my head. Ryn was so open for me and with each push in, I let out a moan. *So fucking deep.*

I began moving in and out, slow at first but listening to Ryn calling out how good it felt. Her body began to shake and she lifted her head and looked right at me as she screamed out in pleasure. Two seconds later, I was deep inside her as my cum poured into her body.

Pulling out of her, I quickly got her out of the spreader bar. Lying next to her, I pulled her body to me. I knew she had to be exhausted.

Her breathing finally settled into a rhythm that was calming. "You could keep going, couldn't you?" Ryn asked.

"If you wanted me to, yes."

Turning over she faced me as we lay on our sides and stared into each other's eyes. Placing her hand on the side of my face, she gently moved her thumb against my skin.

"Thank you," Ryn whispered as she reached out and kissed my lips gently.

"For what?"

"Giving me the chance to be a part of this side of you."

My eyes drifted down to her lips and then back up to her beautiful blue eyes. Her light-brown hair was laid out across the satin-covered pillow. "I was so afraid, Ryn. First I was afraid of my intense feelings for you, then of what you would do when you found out about all of this. I would have walked away from it all had you asked me to."

Smiling, she shook her head. "I'd never ask you to change who you were. I'm glad you didn't stay scared though."

Chuckling, I whispered, "Me too, baby. Me too."

Turning back around, Ryn snuggled into my side. A feeling of happiness and peace moved across my body as I held in my arms the woman I loved more than life itself.

Drifting off to sleep, I dreamed of Ryn walking along the beach holding a bucket in one hand, while the other hand held onto a curly brown-haired little girl.

Three years later.

WALKING ALONG THE BEACH, I laughed as I watched Lark run after his daughter, Akayla, as she yelled out, "Daddy, get me!" She would be turning three in the fall and she was the light in the center of Lark's world, besides Azurdee of course.

Reaching down for her, he lifted her up and began tickling her stomach. Glancing over my shoulder, I saw two of the most beautiful women I'd ever lay my eyes on. Stopping, I waited for Ryn and our one-year-old daughter, Eden, to catch up. Eden had just started walking and was loving the fact that she could jump in the water and make it splash. One big jump by Eden caused water to splash up in her face and eyes. Letting out a scream and then a cry, I quickly ran up to her and scooped her up.

"Shh, it's just salt water baby. It will stop burning, Daddy promises."

Burying her face into my neck, Eden cried and my heart stopped. I couldn't stand to hear her cry or know she was hurt.

Ryn gave me that look as she walked up to me. "You wonder why she's a Daddy's girl?"

Giving Ryn a smile, I held onto my baby girl. Besides Ryn, I never in my life imagined I could love another person as much as I loved Eden. She was my life.

Grabbing Ryn's hand, we started walking again. Once Eden recovered from the salt water in the eye incident she was back on the ground. "Where is Azurdee?" I asked as I kept an eye on my daughter.

"Back at the house. She needed a few minutes to rest."

Laughing, I shook my head. "I can't believe her and Lark will have a little boy in two months."

"I know. Azurdee said she told Lark he was going to have to

get his balls snipped after this one."

Making a face, I pulled my head back and said, "Ouch. I'm sure the big tough Marine didn't take that so well."

Ryn giggled as a seagull landed and Eden got down and was ready to make her move, until Mickey came running by barking, scaring the bird.

Rolling my eyes, I yelled at the two-month-old golden retriever. "Mickey, no! Bad girl."

Eden ran up to Mickey laughing as they chased each around on the sand. "Bad. Goggy," Eden said in between laughs.

Scraping my hands down my face, I cursed under my breath. "Why did I let you talk me into that damn dog?"

Hitting me on the arm, Ryn laughed. "You love that dog, admit it."

Stopping, I stared at Ryn. She turned and faced me, hands on her hips as if she was daring me to debate with her on whether or not I liked the dog. "You named the damn thing your safe word, Ryn."

Giving me an evil little laugh, Ryn scrunched her nose up and said, "What? It's a cute name." Grabbing her, I picked her up and spun her around. As I set her down, our eyes met. Letting out a gasp, she stepped back.

"I felt him! I felt him move." Looking down at Ryn's barely swollen, pregnant stomach, I placed my hands over it.

"Eden! Your baby brother is moving," I yelled out for Eden. Not having a clue as to what I was saying, Eden ran over and placed her hands on Ryn's stomach.

"Ohh!" she said as she jumped up and started yelling for Mickey.

Ryn laughed as I stood up. "You felt him, huh?"

Nodding her head, I watched the tears build in her eyes. Reaching up, I wiped away the tear that was rolling down her face.

"It's undeniable," I whispered.

"What is?" she asked barely above a whisper.

"My love for you, Kathryn Williams."

Giving me a smile that would forever be my undoing, she nodded her head. "I will love you forever, Tristan."

Pulling her into my arms, I watched as our daughter ran

around with Mickey, Akayla, and Lark. Closing my eyes, I was filled with an enormous amount of love.

"Forever, Ryn."

The end.

Coming Soon

JUNE 2015

UNFORGETTABLE *Love*

S ITTING IN MY OFFICE, I looked out the wall of windows to the state capital. I'd been back to work for my father's law firm for a couple of months now and he was keeping me busy as hell. Letting out a frustrated breath, I went back to looking over the case notes for a trial I was helping another lawyer in the firm work on.

The knock on my door startled me as I quickly looked up. "Come in."

Renee, my secretary, stood in the doorway wearing the same fake smile she had the day I met her. "Mr. Walker, I mean, Aaron, your father will be down to speak with you in a few minutes." It took two weeks to train her to call me Aaron and not Mr. Walker. Mr. Walker was my father, not me.

Frowning, I pushed my hand through my hair as she stared at me. "Thanks, Renee. Just leave the door open."

She nodded slightly and headed back to her desk. I couldn't read Renee. Some days she acted as if she hated me, other days it was like she wanted to pounce on me. One of the other lawyers informed me she was good at one thing, blowjobs.

I wasn't gonna go there. Ever.

Looking back down at the notes, I began reading the depositions. Two minutes later I heard my father's voice booming throughout the office.

"Renee, is my son in?"

"Yes, sir."

Standing up, I held my breath and waited for what was to come.

Strolling into my office like he owned the world, my father wore a smile that screamed he was the most confident man in the building. I swear the only reason he won so many cases was because he scared the hell out of the jury.

Gesturing with his hand for me to sit back down, my father shut the door. "Sit, Aaron. I want to discuss a case with you."

Doing as he asked, I sat down in my chair and leaned back with a confident smile of my own. I was probably the only man in this building who was not afraid of my father.

"What kind of case?"

Taking in a deep breath, he blew it out slowly as he took in my office. "You like the office?"

Rolling my eyes, I cleared my throat. "I do. Thank you for asking. Again."

Raising his mouth in a half smile, he asked, "Have I already asked that?"

Giving a halfhearted smile in return, I said, "Three times, sir."

Picking at a piece of imaginary lint, he looked at me. "It's a divorce case. The lawyer I originally assigned to the case is a jackass and I'm pretty sure he is afraid of the judge. The asshole husband is turning out to be a bigger dick than I thought. He cheated, wife caught him, but he is pleading he was neglected by the wife and searched out companionship. Now he claims she was cheating on him. I want this fucker taken down. I like the girl. She's a hard worker and you know how much I dislike cheaters."

Attempting to calm my heart that was now pounding in my chest, I leaned forward. "And you want me take over this case?"

Narrowing his eyes at me, he asked, "Do you not feel like you can handle it, Aaron?"

Sitting up straighter, I let out a gruff laugh. No fucking way I'm turning down this case. "I'm more than up for the challenge. You want the husband taken down—I'll take him down. That's a promise." I was shocked my father was putting so much confidence in me. He clearly wanted the husband to lose this case, so by him bringing me onto the case it showed he thought I could win this. My heart was beating so loud I was sure he heard it.

The smile that spread across my father's face told me he was pleased with my answer. Standing up, he smoothed out his suit. "I knew I could count on you, Aaron. Show me you can win this one, and the next case you fight will be alongside me."

Pressing my lips together, I kept from showing my father what he said pleased the hell out of me. Nodding, I stood up, reached for his hand and said, "Sounds good."

"Now that you're ready, your client is waiting in conference room six. I just spoke with her and told her I was assigning a new lawyer. This girl is sweet and innocent. I want her taken care of, Aaron."

My eyes widened in horror. Holy shit. He just pushed this onto my plate and he wants me to meet the client right now? "She's here? Now? I haven't even looked at her case."

Winking and turning away from me, he said, "She's here, right now. Head on over and introduce yourself. The file is in the conference room. Take it home tonight and look it over. Meanwhile, I want her getting to know her new lawyer as soon as possible."

Turning, he headed to the door. Before opening it, he glanced back at me. "Make me proud, Aaron."

The air left my lungs as he opened the door and shut it. Collapsing back down in my chair, I dragged in deep breaths.

Make me proud, Aaron.

This is it. This is the case I've been waiting for to prove to my father I had what it took to be a good lawyer. Grabbing a notepad and pen, I made my way to conference room six.

Quickly walking by Renee's, desk she called out, "Do you need me for your meeting, Mr. . . . um . . . Aaron?" Giving Renee a wink, I shook my head.

Standing outside the door to the conference room, I took a few seconds to get my thoughts straight. The first thing I had to do was win over the client. I needed to make sure she knew I was on her side. For all I knew she was a fifty-year-old bored housewife with a husband trying to find his lost youth.

Fuck. Why didn't I ask Dad what her name was?

Taking in a deep breath, I smelled a familiar perfume. My body instantly warmed. *Where did I know that perfume?*

Reaching for the door, I plastered on the smile I knew caused panties to melt no matter what their age was. Turning the knob, I pushed the door open and walked into the room. Sitting at the end of the long conference table was . . . Sierra?

What in the hell is she doing here?

Holy hell. Please, God, tell me this is not happening. I'm so fucked.

Slowly standing up, Sierra stared at me with that cute little thing she did with her mouth when she was at a loss for words. Which wasn't often. Slowly wetting her lips, she went to talk, but nothing came out.

Moaning internally at the action, I stared at her lips. Damn how I wanted those lips wrapped around my cock.

No. Wait. Stop. You're her lawyer. Shit. I'm Sierra's lawyer.

The last time I saw Sierra was at the coast. Our mutual friends got engaged and invited a few of us to spend a few days with them.

"Sierra, it's um—" Clearing my throat, I motioned for her to sit down. Staring at me for a few more seconds, Sierra slowly sat down as a look of pure shock and confusion swept over her face.

Shutting the door, I moved to the table and took a seat about three seats down from her. Just being near Sierra had my body aching with desire.

"W-what are you doing here, Dodge?"

I wasn't about to let my rocky relationship with Sierra, or the fact that I wanted nothing more than to fuck her senseless, ruin my chance at showing my father what I could do on this case.

Smiling, I adjusted my suddenly too tight tie. "It's, ah, it's Aaron, not Dodge." Sierra's eyes lit up and I wanted desperately to find out why my real name caused her to look like she just had a mini fantasy.

Swallowing hard, Sierra shook her head as if clearing her thoughts. "Okay, Aaron. Why are you here? I'm about to have a meeting with my new lawyer, so you're gonna have—"

Suddenly her eyes widened. I was pretty sure Tristan and Ryn had let Sierra know I was working for my father's law firm again.

Here goes nothing. "I'm here, Mrs. Jackson, because I'm your new lawyer."

Darrin—Thank you for always standing by me and supporting me. It means the world to me. Your love amazes me every day.

Lauren—It's undeniable . . . you are your mother's daughter. Never change for anyone! I love you so very much.

Kristin Mayer—AKA "K-Dawg" Since you are currently sitting on the sofa across from me writing during our girls weekend, I'll just give you my thanks to you now. Just in case I forget though, thank you for being such an amazing friend. Thank you for your support, your help, your listening ear and your ever infectious laughter. Love ya girl!

Nikola Sievert—Thank you for always making time to read my books. And for being the last eyes on each one! It means the world to me!

Danielle Sanchez—Thank you for everything you do for me. You're the best publicist an author could ask for. I truly appreciate everything you do for me!

Vilma Gonzalez, Anna Easter, Molly McAdams, and Danielle Sanchez—"The lunch crew"—I am so thankful for you girls. I love you each dearly. I look forward to our lunches and you have no idea what they mean to me. #Legend

Nichole Strauss—Thank you for your amazing editing skills! I appreciate all that you do for me.

Laura Hansen—Thank you so very much for beta reading for me and for all of your input with this book. You'll never know how much I appreciate it. You're the best! Love you girl!

To my Chasers group—Thank you for your support and for making me laugh each and every day. Y'all are truly the best group out there!

The Wranglers—Y'all know who you are. All I can say is thank you for all you do. My cup runneth over for you ladies.

To all my readers—You never cease to amaze me with your support and love. Thank you for allowing me to travel down this road with you! Love you to the moon and back.

CPSIA information can be obtained
at www.ICGtesting.com
Printed in the USA
BVHW01s1836160118
505414BV00011B/281/P